Maybe while he was visiting the US he should think of himself as a cop. Then again, maybe not. That would be going a bit too Hollywood.

JAMAICA PLAIN

JAMAICA PLAIN

A RESURRECTION MAN NOVEL

COLIN CAMPBELL

First Edition
First Printing, 2013

Cover design: Kevin R. Brown
Cover illustration: Steven McAfee
Explosion: iStockphoto.com/Lisa Anderson
City street: iStockphoto.com/Denis Jr. Tangney

Midnight Ink, an imprint of Llewellyn Worldwide Ltd.

Library of Congress Cataloging-in-Publication Data
Campbell, Colin, 1955–
Jamaica plain : a resurrection man novel / Colin Campbell.—1st ed.
p. cm. — (Resurrection man ; #1)
ISBN 978-0-7387-3583-2
1. Police—England—Yorkshire—Fiction. 2. British—Massachusetts—Boston—Fiction. 3. Mystery fiction. I. Title.
PR6103.A48J36 2013
823'.92—dc23

2012039077

Midnight Ink
Llewellyn Worldwide Ltd.
2143 Wooddale Drive
Woodbury, MN 55125-2989

www.midnightinkbooks.com

Printed in the United States of America

For my dad

...enough said

PART ONE

That's the job. Shit rolls downhill.
Cops live in the valley.
—Jim Grant

ONE

THE FIRST THING Jim Grant did when he landed in Boston was buy a map. The second thing was get laid. The third was almost get himself killed interviewing a prisoner who was into something far bigger than what the detective came to interview him about.

Detective. That sounded good, but Grant knew it was only a temporary assignment while his inspector cleaned up the mess he'd left behind in Yorkshire. He was still just a plain old constable: PC 367 Grant. Maybe while he was visiting the US he should think of himself as a cop. Then again, maybe not. That would be going a bit too Hollywood.

First things first. If he were going to find his way around Boston, he'd need a map. Ignoring the other passengers collecting their wheeled cases from the luggage carousel, Grant hefted the battered leather holdall in one hand and went in search of the concession stands. That was his first mistake. Three thousand miles from home, and trouble still managed to find him straightaway.

LOGAN INTERNATIONAL was bigger than Manchester Airport, but the basics were the same. Wide open spaces, big windows looking out onto the runways, and dozens of preformed waiting-room chairs in rows of four with a low table in between, all connected so if one person sat down, all four seats bounced. Grant had lost count of how many cups of coffee he'd spilled because some heavyweight couldn't lower himself into his seat.

The place smelled of plastic and canned air.

There were fewer seats in the arrivals lounge than in departures. Fewer people wanted to sit down after spending a long flight cramped in a seat with no legroom and someone in front leaning back so that what little room you did have was crushed against your knees. At least that was Grant's experience of international travel. At six feet four he'd have troubling stretching out in first class. West Yorkshire Police hadn't paid for first class. Prisoner extradition might have warranted the expense. Getting your bad egg out of the way meant the cheapest seat available and forget the legroom.

Logan had one other thing in common with Manchester. Airports attracted criminals like flies around shit. For some reason, Grant was the embodiment of human flypaper. He wasn't looking, but his eyes couldn't help roving. It was a reflex action. Any room he entered, the first thing he'd do was scan the crowd, quickly followed by a check of the exits and any mirrors that could be used for extra viewing. He never sat anywhere he couldn't see behind him. He never stood anywhere he couldn't get out of fast if trouble started.

This wasn't trouble. It was two kids dipping pockets and doing it very well.

Distraction was the main technique for most crimes apart from blatant armed robbery. Thieves didn't want to get caught, so it was better if nobody saw what they were stealing. Burglars usually broke in at night. Thieves usually stole when nobody was looking. Only complete idiots or hardened criminals stuck a gun in your face and demanded your money. The victims would remember you for the rest of their lives. Some might even shoot you. If nobody saw you take their wallet, then who was going to be a witness in court? Nobody.

Movement and noise were the best distractions. An airport arrivals lounge had plenty of both. Everyone was in a rush. Suitcases were being wheeled around. Visitors were looking for their relatives. Airport transfer drivers were milling around with name cards written in thick black letters. People were buying coffee, magazines, and maps.

Grant was paying for the Boston street map at Hudson News when he spotted the teenage tag team. Their target was an attractive woman in a business suit he'd seen at the luggage carousels. Tidy figure. Tight trousers. Nice arse. He focused on that for a while, but his peripheral vision saw the hunters circling. Part of his brain wanted to chat with the businesswoman. Part of him wanted to arrest the pickpockets. The rest of him remembered his inspector giving a stern warning before setting off.

Keep out of trouble. Don't get involved. You're off-duty.

That wasn't strictly true. This was a holiday assignment, yes. Interview the prisoner. Eliminate him from the inquiry. Release him and come home. He'd been sent on it to keep him out of the way while Discipline and Complaints investigated the mess at Snake Pass. But he'd be on-duty during the interview, and technically you were on-duty while traveling to and from work for the purposes of injury-on-duty claims. Have an accident on the way to work and it was classed as an injury on-duty. So if he spotted a crime on his way to work…

Keep out of trouble. Don't get involved.

That part went against the grain. If there was one thing Jim Grant found hard to do, it was ignore a crime right in front of his face. Bad guys did bad things. It was up to the good guys to stop them. Grant was one of the good guys. Always had been. Keeping out of trouble should be easy with a pair of teenagers. Maybe thirteen or fourteen. It just required a bit of tact.

He paid for the map and watched.

THE TEENAGE BOY WAS very good. The girl was even better. What they had going for them was how innocent they both looked. Butter wouldn't melt in their mouths, you'd think. Grant watched them hanging around outside the magazine stand. They appeared to be waiting for their parents—only they weren't watching for someone joining them, they were scouring the shoppers for easy marks.

The businesswoman wheeled her suitcase into the shop, an expensive shoulder bag hanging open around her back. The boy nodded. The girl split off and held position ten feet away. The dance began.

The woman bought a pack of breath mints and an orange juice. The boy stayed a few feet behind her. The girl kept station ten feet away. When the woman left the shop, the boy followed. The girl never let the distance alter—ten feet—until the boy nodded again. The girl moved in front and bumped into the woman. The boy's hand was so fast Grant hardly saw it. In and out of the bag in a flash. He broke left and the girl apologized, going right. A quick half-circle and they crossed paths. A dull brown shape was switched, and now it was the girl, all cute and innocent, with the stolen goods. The woman didn't even know she'd been targeted.

Don't get involved.

Not an option. Grant moved quick, before the boy and girl separated too far. Without being obvious, he grabbed the boy's arm and guided him towards the girl. He identified himself as police and told the girl to follow them. She did. Fear shone in her eyes. Caught in the act. It was the look every kid he'd ever arrested had the first time. He didn't squeeze. There was no need. The threesome gathered by a water fountain against the wall.

"Okay, kids. I haven't got time for this. Hand it over."

The girl's eyes darted at the boy and then over his shoulder. The boy had no resistance. The girl gave Grant the wallet. He kept half an eye on the teenagers and the other half on the businesswoman. She had stopped to take a drink of orange juice and drop the mints in her bag. Grant towered over the teenagers.

"Now beat it. You won't be so lucky next time."

Without waiting for an answer, he set off across the concourse. The woman was on her second swig of juice when he held the wallet out. "I think you dropped this."

Her first reaction was to look him in the eyes. A hard, straight look that sized him up in an instant. Big guy in worn jeans and a faded orange windcheater. Then she reverted to victim mode. She swung the shoulder bag round front and rummaged inside. Grant handed the wallet over. Gratitude feathered a smile across her lips. A twinkle in her eyes. "What sharp little eyes you've got."

"Not so little."

"No, you aren't, are you?"

This was interesting. Grant was about to explore the possibilities when he saw the teenagers over the woman's shoulder. The fear in the girl's eyes had multiplied tenfold. The angry man herding them away didn't look like their father.

Keep out of trouble.

That didn't look like an option now either. The man was big in a lumpy fat man sort of way. There was bulk and muscle, but he was out of shape. That didn't matter when it came to intimidating kids. The kids looked plenty intimidated. The girl looked terrified.

"Excuse me."

Grant dodged around the woman and set off after Fagin. The man looked angry they'd missed picking the latest pocket or two. The grip he exerted on the boy was harder than Grant's had been. He didn't need to grip the girl. She'd go wherever the boy went. Loyalty. An admirable quality. Grant was glad he'd let them go. He wasn't glad he'd steered them into this spot of bother.

Fagin took the pair round the corner into an alcove between the left luggage office and the restrooms. As soon as he was out of sight, he slapped the boy round the back of the head. Bad move.

Grant heard the slap before he came around the corner. Heard the boy's muted cry and the girl's whimper. He switched the hold-all into his right hand, freeing up his stronger left. He was a lefty. Conflict was unavoidable, and his instincts took over. Calmness settled over him. It was his combat preparation, a technique that had served him well in the army and worked just fine as a frontline cop. Most people tensed up in the line of fire. Grant did the opposite. He relaxed. His muscles became loose. His mind smoothed out any wrinkles. Nothing obstructed the flow of action. Nothing deflected his point of focus.

His point of focus now was a fat man picking on a couple of kids.

Grant came around the corner like a force of nature. He swung the holdall and let go. It sailed out and upwards, catching Fagin by surprise. Fagin instinctively turned and caught it in both arms. That left no hands free and Grant with two. He only needed one. The strong left hand grabbed Fagin by the shoulder and pushed him backwards. The right hand stayed loose just in case. Momentum and the heavy bag propelled Fagin towards the restrooms. Grant guided him through the door into the gents'.

The door swung shut behind them.

"What the fuck?"

Fagin found his tongue and rediscovered some of his bravado. He held the holdall across his chest like a shield, flexing his shoulders and giving his head a little nudge forwards like a boxer ducking and diving. He wasn't any boxer. Tension etched itself on his face. Surprise factor had won the first round.

"Fuck you think you're doin'?"

Grant surged forward and shoved the holdall hard. The bag was heavy. The left hand was heavier. Height and weight and muscle were all in Grant's favor. The blow transferred through the bag and thumped Fagin in the chest like a sledgehammer. He stumbled backwards and came up against the washbasins. Grant stood in front of him and slightly off-center to avoid being kicked in the gonads.

"I know just what I'm doing."

He stepped to the side and raised one leg slightly. He stamped on the outside edge of Fagin's left leg below the knee, and the overweight bully collapsed like a broken twig.

"And that's my bag you've got there."

He snatched the holdall left-handed and swung it in a short underarm arc. The weight of it multiplied on the back swing. It grew even more on the follow-through. Grant leaned into the swing, staying relaxed but with his feet apart for a solid base, and brought the bag forward hard and fast. It caught Fagin under the chin and snapped his head back against the built-in marble-topped washbasins.

He flopped like a boned fish. No spine. All wet.

Three men using the basins down the row quickly collected their bags and dashed out of the restroom. The hot-air hand dryer one of them had been using kept working for a few seconds. An automatic faucet dribbled cold water. The door flip-flapped shut like the swing doors of a Western saloon. The water stopped. The hand dryer switched itself off. Hot metal ticked as it cooled.

Grant nudged Fagin awake with his foot, then dragged him into a sitting position by the collar. He instinctively reached for the handcuffs on his hip before realizing he was plainclothes. No protective equipment. No handcuffs. Off-duty.

He stood up and to one side. The most dangerous beast is a cornered animal. A fighting arc didn't just mean a swinging fist. A well-aimed kick could bring down even the strongest man. Grant kept out of kicking range even though Fagin didn't look like he had a good kick left in him. He switched the bag to his right hand, freeing up his left.

"That's theft. Now why do you want to take stuff that don't belong to you?"

"I don't take stuff that's not mine."

Grant dropped the holdall onto Fagin's outstretched legs and knelt down on it fast and heavy, pinning the fat man and bringing Grant's face right into Fagin's personal space. Grant's strong left hand came up, and Fagin flinched. Grant didn't hit him. He grabbed his nose between thumb and forefinger and twisted. Blood and snot oozed like a squeezed tube of toothpaste.

"No, you don't, do you? You get kids to take it for you."

Fagin moaned in pain. Grant twisted harder.

"They your kids?"

"No."

The word came out all mashed but just about intelligible.

"Whose?"

Fagin tried to speak and flapped a hand towards his nose. Grant let go.

"City orphanage."

"Wrong. They're my kids now. See what happens if you touch them again."

He didn't finish. Instead he stood up and washed his hands. The hand dryer was still hot. He dried his hands. There wasn't even a hint of post-action adrenaline shakes—another benefit of Grant's relaxation technique. He picked the bag up and went to the door.

"You're lucky I'm on vacation. That's what you call a holiday over here, isn't it?"

He pushed the swing door and reentered the world of noise and movement. *Keep out of trouble. Don't get involved.* One out of two wasn't so bad. He wasn't surprised that the kids had gone. What did surprise him was who had stayed.

"You're not that small at all, are you?"

The businesswoman smirked. Grant smiled. He looked down at her from a great height and flexed the muscles of his neck. Bones cracked like firecrackers. He lowered his voice. "You know what I could do with right now?"

"I think I do. Welcome to Boston."

TWO

Terri Avellone stood in front of the lace curtains and unbuttoned her jacket. Her room at the Airport Hilton was way above Grant's West Yorkshire Police expenses chit. Bright daylight outside turned her into a silhouette. The jacket looked expensive, and it slid off her shoulders like silk off smooth skin. She tossed it expertly onto the chair next to the window. It landed neatly folded over the armrest. The white blouse she wore was thin and sheer. With the light behind her Grant could see right through it, the delicate shoulders forming a perfect frame for her slender waist and full breasts. He reckoned that was exactly the view she wanted to give.

He glanced around to take in his surroundings. It was like no hotel room he'd ever been in. Deep pile carpet and hidden lighting supported the neutral colors and plush furnishings. The writing desk was leather-topped and wide as an aircraft carrier.

The bed was bigger than HMS *Ark Royal.*

Grant dropped the holdall next to the built-in wardrobe and unzipped his windcheater. He stopped. She was staring at him with the same hard straight look she'd employed in the arrivals lounge. There was a twist of a smile on her lips. She seemed to like what she saw. Grant sniffed twice. He pulled the neck of his T-shirt away from his body and sniffed again.

"Long flight."

She nodded. "Longer than mine, I'm sure."

He hadn't asked where she'd flown in from. He hadn't asked her anything at all. The bathroom door was open in the far corner. Ceiling lights and wall mirrors made it look like a honey-coated grotto of infinite possibilities. Grant nodded towards the door.

"That's the other thing I could do with."

"Be my guest."

"I *am* your guest."

Avellone unbuttoned her blouse, slowly. Top button. Pause. Second button. Another pause. Third and fourth. Then she stopped. The smirk was partially hidden by the darkness of her silhouette. "Don't forget to wash behind your ears."

He smiled back at her. This was a woman who knew just what she wanted and wasn't afraid to ask for it. She also shared his dry sense of humor. Boston was shaping up to be the perfect holiday assignment. He shrugged out of the windcheater and threw it on the bed. The crumpled heap wasn't as neat as Avellone's jacket toss. He didn't mind. It was time for a shower.

STINGING WATER hit his face and shoulders. Hot and steamy. The shower cubicle was bigger than most hotel rooms he'd stayed in. There was a corner bath that could fit three and a pair of washbasins with a full-width mirror. There was a toilet and more towels than you could use in a week. Baths didn't interest him. For Grant it was always the shower.

The glass-walled cubicle stood floor to ceiling in a fully tiled angle of the bathroom. The Hilton obviously catered to tall guests. The showerhead was high on the back wall. The glass door sealed the spray in. It steamed up immediately. Grant soaped himself from a dispenser on the wall. He felt cleaner already. He closed his eyes and let the spray spark him back to life. He sensed the door open and close rather than heard it. He kept his voice conversational. "You need to get clean too?"

Hissing spray filtered her voice to a whisper. "No. I need to get dirty."

He felt her breasts brush across his back. They were firm and smooth and tipped with hard nipples. They felt like fingernails scraping across his skin. Then they were gone. He waited. Five seconds. Ten. Her breasts brushed him again, twice, then pushed against the muscles banding his spine. He felt them flatten against him, followed by the rest of her body. Her stomach pressed against his buttocks and she moved it gently side to side. The smooth, soft plane of her abdomen felt good. The small, hard mound below it felt better. She pressed that against him briefly. Water and soap lubricated the friction until it wasn't really friction at all. It was just soft and gentle pleasure.

One hand snaked around his stomach.

Despite his relaxation technique, there was no escaping the effect that single hand had on him. His buttocks tensed, prompting her to rub herself against them even harder. She flexed her legs, lowering and rising, adding a new direction to the gentle movement.

Her other hand snaked around his stomach.

Something below the waist twitched into life. Electricity sparked goose bumps across his chest and abdomen. The hairs on his forearms stood on end. He took a deep breath but stood still. This was her show. Her breasts were flattened against his back. Her stomach swirled in tiny movements that shifted her breasts as well. The twitch grew firmer.

One hand slid up Grant's stomach towards his chest. The palm caressed the muscles in small, slow circles. She crabbed the hand and used her fingernails instead. The light touch sparked more goose pimples, and she used her thumb and forefinger to tweak his nipple. Nobody has ever been able to explain why men have nipples, but right now Grant was glad they did. He could feel Avellone's nipples harden against him. Something else grew hard as well.

Her other hand caressed his stomach for a few seconds more, then slid down and to one side. It bypassed what she really wanted to touch and stroked his inner thigh instead. The result was electrifying. She teased him by sliding her hand up to the top, brushing his manhood before moving back down. Three more accidental touches. She was moaning quietly behind him.

Then she took the weight of him and cupped it in her hand.

This was where a porn movie would record gratuitous dialog—moans and verbal encouragement and talk that would provoke laughter instead of arousal. Terri Avellone didn't say anything. She kissed his back, flicking her tongue across the taught muscles. She continued to gyrate against him. Her hands continued to diversify, one caressing his chest, the other kneading his manhood. It grew too big for her hand. Slowly she flexed her knees. Her entire body slid down him. She kissed his spine, one vertebrae at a time. Her breasts were pushed aside by his buttocks as they moved below his waist. She stopped, and he heard a throaty chuckle. He glanced over his shoulder and saw her looking at the base of his spine. She smiled up at him.

"What's this?"

The tattoo had faded over the years but was still clearly visible now that the soap lather had rinsed off. A large red circle with a white line through it, replicating an English road sign. There was black lettering below it with an arrow pointing down.

NO ENTRY

He smiled at a private memory. The smile held a hint of sadness. "Old war wound."

"Well, at least we agree on one thing."

"Only one?"

"No."

She leaned close again. Her top hand moved from his chest to his stomach. Her other hand simply squeezed and stroked. What she was holding wasn't a dead weight any more. It had a life of its own and didn't need holding up. Her voice became low and suggestive. "Cleanliness is next to godliness."

He turned to face her, his body still protecting her from the spray that had cleansed him. The soap was all gone. Water ran down his body like rivulets of sweat. Her hair was plastered to her head. Her body was gleaming. For the first time he saw what a magnificent woman she was. Tiny waist. Firm breasts. Taught muscles across everything. Strong thighs that were keeping her balanced now. He laid a hand on her shoulder and caressed the slender neck. "Don't talk with your mouth full."

She didn't. Her head rocked forward, and he almost exploded. Her hands caressed his buttocks. Her breasts caressed his thighs. It was his turn in the shower. He'd already decided it would be her turn once he took her to bed.

Her turn took longer than his. There was no rushing. They had plenty of time. He explored everything that she had explored in the shower and more. The stolen wallet was forgotten. The kids from the city orphanage were history. The bullying fat man was no longer important. This was R and R of the finest quality.

Afterwards they lay in each other's arms, spent, quiet, and contented. Traffic noise was barely audible through the double glazing. The overnight flight began to take its toll. The soft pillows and comfortable mattress sucked him down. He drifted towards sleep half covered by the top sheet and still draped in a towel that was big enough to wrap around him twice. As his eyes grew heavy, he felt a familiar stirring in the back of his mind. He wasn't sure if it was the strange surroundings or the lace curtains, but even before he was fully asleep he knew what was coming next.

The lace curtains were threadbare and grey. If they bore any resemblance to the life of young James Grant, twelve going on thirteen, it was that they appeared to shift aimlessly in the unseen draft. Grant had been drifting aimlessly through life ever since he'd been sent to boarding school at an age too early to remember. The curtains were long and heavy, blurring the view from the tall arched window on the half-landing. The staircase doubled back on itself as it climbed to the upper dormitories. The carpet was threadbare too. Moor Grange School for Boys wasn't an expensive boarding school.

The curtains wafted open occasionally, revealing the sunlit beauty of life on the outside. Grant's "road to Damascus" moment came in a much darker place. His first step on the journey from boy to man, or maybe it was his second. The slap and the cry and the bullying voices coming from the communal toilets.

"Give us yer pocket money."

The bully was a fat lump of lard, a year ahead of Grant and three years ahead of the smaller boy he was picking on. He might have been a fat lump of lard, but fat carried weight when it was added to a slap across the face. The boy whimpered and dropped to his knees.

"Come on. I saw yer mum give it to yer."

Another slap. This time from the bully's accomplice, another juggernaut but with a smaller head. Bully Number Two appeared to consider himself the strong, silent type because he didn't speak, leaving that to his more verbose friend.

The boy cowered away from any further blows to the head. "It's all I've got."

"And it's all I want you to give us."

Number One clicked his fingers, and Number Two dragged the boy up by the scruff of the neck and stuck his face into the nearest sink. He put the plug in and turned the cold tap on full, holding the boy underwater until he came up coughing and spluttering. Water splashed across the tiled floor.

"All right. All right." Number One clicked his fingers again, and Number Two released the captive.

Grant closed the door behind him as he stepped into the toilets. "That's very good. Can you get him to roll over and beg?"

The two piggy-eyed sixth-formers turned towards the intruder. They weren't used to being opposed. They weren't afraid of throwing their weight around, not when it was two against one and not when the one was a skinny preteen whose voice hadn't even broken yet. Number One was still the spokesman. "Mind yer own business unless you want a dunkin' as well."

Grant looked at the two bullies and weighed his options. Weighing was an appropriate term because the sixth-formers outweighed him by four to one. They were taller and broader and fatter than the skinny featherweight. Grant hadn't had his teenage growth spurt yet. He wasn't strong, but he was determined, and he was fast. He reckoned that and his ability to size up situations would stand him in good stead. Speed and a wet floor would be his allies today. "Why don't you let him be, and I'll let you keep your teeth?"

The bullies squared off against their impudent foe. The boy scurried backwards out of the firing line. Number One recognized the intruder. "Jimmy Grant, isn't it? You still putting out for Mr. Reid at bed check?"

Grant felt his cheeks flush but kept quiet. Number One did not. "He make you squeal like a pig, did he?"

Grant didn't know how these two had seen *Deliverance*. Probably the same way Grant and the other underage kids had. Sneaked in the back doors of the cinema on its latest rerelease. The implication was plain, though. "He didn't make me do anything."

Grant remembered the late-night bed check and his reaction to it. The first true step on his journey from boy to man. Not everyone had been so lucky. Number One wasn't giving up on a rich vein. "You probably weren't young enough for him."

Grant found his voice. "He probably likes chubby arse cheeks like yours."

This time it was Number One whose cheeks flushed. With anger. "If you're after a stomping, you've chosen the right place."

He took a step forward and his accomplice backed him up, standing shoulder to shoulder with the overweight bully, forming an impenetrable barrier across the tiled floor. A sly look crossed

Number One's face, and he tilted his head. "Oh, I forgot. You didn't choose to come here, did you? Your dad sent you when you killed your mother."

This time the heat running up Grant's neck wasn't a blush. It was barely restrained anger. He tried to bite his tongue but couldn't help responding. "She died in childbirth. It was nothing to do with me."

"Dying in childbirth is everything to do with you."

That shut Grant up. Because it was true. If his mother hadn't given birth to him, she wouldn't have died. If she hadn't died, then his father wouldn't have resented him so much—a vicious circle that he was unable to escape. Being a naval commander, his father could have had Grant brought up on the bases where he served, but instead he packed his son off to boarding school at the earliest opportunity. Whatever else Grant would do with his life, he vowed never to join the navy.

Number One threw a final barb before he lost his teeth. "No wonder your old man wants nothing to do with you."

The heat became a rush of blood. Red mist descended and removed all restraint from Grant's psyche. He reached for the towel hanging behind the door and dangled the end in the water that was puddling the floor. The bullies saw it but weren't afraid. A wet towel wasn't going to protect this young upstart. They took a step towards Grant. Grant planted his feet and turned sideways. He flicked the towel in a vicious whip that cracked like a gunshot as it stung Number One's cheek.

"You little fucker."

The bullies lunged forward in unison—just what Grant had hoped for. Their feet slipped from under them, and they went down heavy. Number Two cracked his skull on the tiled floor, blood leaking from his ears, and didn't move again. Number One slithered like a beached whale. Grant stung him with three more whip cracks that brought red wheals across his face and neck. He tried to control the anger, but it was off the leash. He wrapped the towel around the fallen bully's neck and grabbed the other end. Tightening the noose, he pulled backwards, and the bully was forced to get up. Before the big lug could regain his balance, Grant jerked his knee up into the unprotected groin, doubling him over. The forward momentum was all he required. Grant grabbed the sixth-former's head and smashed it against the porcelain sink, breaking his nose.

The boy in the corner screamed for Grant to stop, but Grant was out of control. Any restraint or calming techniques he might learn later were nowhere in evidence in the toilets of Moor Grange School for Boys. He slammed the head against the sink again and again. Blood and teeth splashed the tiled floor. Grant was still pulping the fat bully's face when his own feet slipped and he fell backwards, out of the dream.

He jerked awake three hours later. It was mid-afternoon. Lace curtains diffused the January sunshine, but it was still bright enough to hurt his eyes. The rectangle of light had crawled across the floor and confirmed the passage of time. He rolled onto his back and stretched. Bones in his back and neck cracked. He flexed his muscles until the travel aches diminished, then turned to his left.

Terri Avellone had gone.

The used condom and its matchbook packaging were in the bin.

So be it. He hated goodbyes and false promises. A clean break was a good break. He swung his legs out of bed and went into the bathroom.

Twenty minutes later he was fresh and clean and ready for action. Faded jeans and a crumpled T-shirt. Black K-Swiss tennis shoes. He shrugged into the faded orange windcheater and took out the map. Time to get back to work. Time to find out where he was going. Grant squinted at the topography in a shaft of sunlight, unaware that his latest "road to Damascus" moment would come in a much darker place: Jamaica Plain.

THREE

"YEAH?"

The desk sergeant was chiseled out of stone. The one-word response came after three minutes of silence as he ignored the man standing with a battered leather holdall in one hand.

The Jamaica Plain police station was at 3345 Washington Street. Intersection of Green and Washington. The District E-13 station house was a modern red brick building and, like most police stations, it was plain and functional. Nothing fancy. All business. Apart from the clock tower that housed the staircase to the second floor. Grant had taken the T from the airport, and the subway journey on top of the long flight made the desk sergeant's attitude even more annoying.

Keep out of trouble.

Grant waited patiently, not one of his strengths, and took his inspector's words to heart. Over the years he'd arrived at new posts many times, both in the army and in the police. There was always a macho pissing contest that went on during the opening salvos. He was prepared to weather the storm. *This is a holiday assignment.* He kept telling himself that. It almost worked.

"DC Grant."

"He doesn't work here."

So it was going to be like that. He pointed a finger at his own chest. "DC Grant. From England."

The sergeant stopped writing in the ledger on the counter and looked over the glasses on his nose. Grant detected a hint of the old country in the tilt of his head—a touch of Irish brogue in the voice. "You expect that's going to open any doors?"

There was no winning this guy over. So be it. "I've got a piece of shamrock up my arse if that'll help."

"It won't. And that kind of attitude will get your pretty little ass kicked all sides up—shamrock or not."

Radio traffic crackled in the background. A door slammed upstairs. Muted voices and the scrape of chairs came from offices beyond the reception desk. There was a smell of coffee and cracked leather that was at odds with the newness of the building. This was a frontline police station. Real cops needed to create an atmosphere of mutual support. They also needed to protect themselves from outsiders until they proved they weren't out to hang the police or free the criminals. Grant respected that, but he wasn't going to roll over and beg. "At least you've got one less face than the clocks outside."

"Your meaning?"

"I mean one clock says half four. The other says quarter past five. All you say is 'fuck you,' whichever face you show."

"That'd be 'fuck you, Englishman.'"

"Fuck you, English copper."

"Cop."

"Don't like the English, huh?"

"Not a bit."

"Me neither. I'm a Yorkshireman, born and bred. Fuck the English."

The sergeant put his pen down and stood back from the desk. He considered the visitor for a few seconds, and then the chiseled features softened. Didn't exactly break into a smile, but Grant would take whatever he could get. The pissing contest was over. A leathery thumb jerked towards a door beside the counter. "You here for Sullivan?"

"Yes."

"Second floor, rear. Detectives. You want Kincaid."

The thumb disappeared under the counter, and an electronic buzz unlocked the door. Grant picked up his bag and yanked the door open. "Much obliged."

"Have a nice day."

There was only a hint of sarcasm in the voice.

THE STAIRCASE circled the clock tower and came out on a split corridor with signs on the wall. A short corridor went straight ahead with only one door at the end. A longer corridor to the right had several doors on either side and two at the end. The sign said the detectives' office was straight ahead—at the rear of the station.

The corridor was carpeted but not deep-piled. Back in Bradford the police stations had linoleum floors until a few years ago. Some interior designer had decided it was better for morale to have soft furnishings and carpets. All that meant was the mess cops made was harder to clean up. It looked like the Boston Police Department had gone down the carpet route.

He didn't knock, but he didn't barge in either. He simply opened the door and stood on the threshold for a moment while he got his bearings. The office was big and square, with two windows facing Green Street and two overlooking the parking lane behind the station. There were no blast curtains, just vertical blinds drawn back to let the light in.

Detective bureaus were the same the world over. The CID office at Ecclesfield Police Station back home was the same as the MP Investigation Unit in the army and the BPD detectives' office at E-13. Open-plan office. Desks grouped into blocks of three or four facing each other, depending on the size of the office. Grey metal filing cabinets (green in the army) and a stationary cupboard. Some had their own radio storage and battery chargers, unlike West Yorkshire where the radios were signed out from the help desk downstairs.

Most detective squads had an excess of takeaway food cartons and disposable coffee cups, but Grant had never seen one with this many pizza boxes. There must have been seven or eight on the middle set of desks, some open and empty, some with partly eaten pizza, some closed. None of the three detectives working at separate desks was eating. Grant looked at the pizzas and, since he didn't know which detective was Kincaid, he addressed the room. "If I'd known there was a party, I'd have brought some beers."

The detectives stopped working. Three heads turned towards the intruder. Nobody spoke. A heavyset detective with dark hair dusted with grey pushed his chair back from the desk. That was the only sound. Grant half expected a tumbleweed to come rolling across the office on a breath of wind. "Diet sodas then?"

The heavyset detective stood up, leaving his jacket hanging over the back of the chair. His shirtsleeves were rolled up to his elbows, the sign of paperwork getting on his nerves. The forearms were solid, indicating that the spreading waistline didn't mean a lack of strength. He was tall, just a couple of inches shorter than Grant but broader. His face was set in a frown of interrupted concentration. "With that accent, you must be the guy from England."

"You don't like the English either?"

"I don't give a fuck. Criminals is what I don't like." He focused on Grant. "Idiots just take up time."

Grant let the words sink in, then looked at the pizza boxes again. The pizzas were cold. No steam or wavering heat lines. The cheese toppings looked congealed. Each box had an evidence label beside it waiting to be attached once the box was packaged or bagged. Grant smiled. This was just like being back in Bradford. "Pizza robbery?"

The big guy came around his desk and stood in front of Grant. He jerked a thumb at the evidence labels.

"Last night. Two kids over in Roxbury ordered eight pizzas on the phone for apartment thirty-five. Delivery guy turns up and is robbed at knifepoint. Pizzas. Money. Wallet. Cops arrive at the apartment block; no apartment thirty-five. Find the insulated delivery boxes on the top floor. K-9 unit tracks the smell of pizza to an apartment on the second floor. Pizza sauce smeared on the door. Whaddaya know? Buncha kids eating pizza."

Grant consulted the district map in his head. "Thought Roxbury was B-2."

"Across the border. Pizza was from E-13. Just my luck."

"Want my shamrock?"

"That's four-leafed clover, not shamrock." He waved a finger at Grant. "And don't let O'Rourke hear you say anything like that."

"The desk sergeant?"

The big guy nodded.

"What's all this 'Fuck the English, I'm a Yorkshireman' shit?"

"He mentioned that, huh?"

"In a rare moment of cooperation."

"God's own county, Yorkshire. A breed apart."

"Just like Texas, then?"

Grant smiled. "Only without the Alamo."

"O'Rourke give you a hard time?"

"Moderate to hard."

"He's the station's shit deflector."

Kincaid indicated a battered cash register on a separate desk. "Us? We're a fast-food deflector squad. Last night again—McDonald's just up the road from here. Local guy tries to steal the cash register through the take-out window while the staff are watching. Drops it outside and gets chased off. Runs the wrong way. Straight towards the station house."

Grant put his bag on a spare seat. "Local boys rule. Thought you had serious criminals in Boston."

The big guy fixed Grant with a serious glare. "Oh, we got a few. Most of our low-rent crooks are imported. Even got one from Yorkshire."

Grant smiled. "Freddy Sullivan?"

"Dickweed of the lowest order."

Grant nodded. "That he is. Got a dick like a weedy shallot, I heard." He held out a hand. "Jim Grant."

The big guy shook it in a firm, dry fist. "Sam Kincaid."

The room was suddenly a friendlier place. Grant thought this holiday task should be quick and easy, and then he could enjoy the sights. He was about to ask about interview facilities when Kincaid threw a spanner in the works.

"You won't be talking to Sullivan today, though."

Grant felt a shadow enter the room despite the sunshine through the windows. "How come?"

"He's with the doctor. Started foaming at the mouth half an hour ago."

FOUR

GRANT SHIFTED HIS BAG to the floor and sat down. A siren started up outside as a patrol car sped off to some unseen emergency. A young detective at the far desk stood up and waggled an empty mug towards the others. "Coffee, anybody?"

Kincaid glanced at Tyson Miller and then back at Grant. "One good thing about mentoring: endless coffee. You?"

A brief thought flashed through Grant's mind. Being training officer to Jamie Hope and covering the probationary constable's back at Snake Pass. The right decision but not Grant's finest hour. There had been the coffee-making benefits, though.

"Thanks. Milk and sugar?"

Miller nodded. "You betcha."

Enthusiasm oozed out of Miller's pores like sweat. Grant remembered being like that. He remembered Jamie Hope. Eager to please. Fast to learn. A good combination. He liked Miller already. He wasn't sure about Kincaid yet. Grant spoke firmly. "Sullivan's pulling a flanker. You know that, right?"

Kincaid threw Grant a quizzical look. "Don't know about a flanker, but he's shining us on, sure."

"What's he after?"

"My guess: release or hospital. He's only here for you. Got picked up on a routine traffic stop. System showed him wanted in the UK. Probably figures if he's sick, we'll bail him rather than pay the medical."

"Things that tight?"

"Modern policing—budgets always tight. Cut back on overtime, can't get vehicles back from the shop in less than two weeks, detectives dealing with pizza thieves to free up uniforms. Yeah, things are tight."

"I'll save you some money, then. Let me talk to him."

"No can do. Doc gets to see him first. Hospital or detention. Then he has to rule if Sullivan's fit for interview. By then he'll be on rest period. Rules we live and die by."

Grant huffed a laugh that had nothing to do with humor. Some things didn't change no matter where you served—army, police, or Boston. They were all slaves to the rulebook. Miller came over from the coffee machine that every CID office had in the corner. Back at Ecclesfield Police Station, it had been a kettle and a refrigerator. At E-13 it was a percolator and filter jug. Miller set a mug on the desk.

"There you go, Officer Grant."

"Jim. I was never an officer."

Miller seemed pleased to be on first-name terms. Grant wondered what the young detective had been told about him. Kincaid sat on the edge of the desk, avoiding the mug of coffee. "You made sergeant, though, didn't you? Army, wasn't it?"

Grant looked at the detective but didn't answer.

Kincaid gave him a you-know-how-it-is shrug. "I checked you out."

Grant studied Kincaid but already knew what to say. He'd said it many times before. Sooner or later it was a subject that always cropped up.

"Not for long."

"Eight years. Long enough."

"No. Sergeant. Not for long."

Kincaid shrugged again as if that wasn't important. "Eight years. What was your field?"

"If you checked me out, then you know already."

"Restricted access. They wouldn't say."

"There you go, then."

Kincaid leaned forward and rested his elbows on his knee. He lowered his voice but kept the tone friendly. "Look. If I'm stuck with you, it helps to know what I'm stuck with. Fair enough?"

Grant could understand that. He leaned back in his chair and stretched his legs. "Fair enough. I was a typist."

"And that's restricted?"

"Important stuff I typed."

It was what he always said. Tension in the office turned up a notch, but Grant relaxed. He stayed loose. The best way to keep a secret was to convince yourself that it never happened. Grant had told this story so many times he almost believed it himself. The secret was safe with him.

Miller took a swig of his coffee. The young detective was obviously growing comfortable with the visitor from across the pond because he smiled when he spoke. "Snake Pass isn't restricted, though. That was some serious ass you kicked."

Grant considered him. "You can't make an omelette without breaking some eggs."

Kincaid slid off the desk and stood but didn't move away. "Yeah, well. We're walking on eggs in JP. Don't want any breaking."

Grant shifted in his chair and sat up straight. He laced his fingers together, turned his hands palm outwards, and flexed. The knuckles cracked. He flexed his neck. Bones cracked there too. He rubbed his chin, then smiled up at Kincaid. "When you're up to your neck in shit, don't make waves."

"Exactly."

Grant shrugged his shoulders and held his hands out palms upwards. "This is a holiday assignment."

"Vacation."

"*Vacation assignment* doesn't roll off the tongue."

Kincaid didn't look amused. Grant poured oil on troubled water. "They sent me to interview Sullivan, then bin him off. The crime's a nonstarter. Insufficient evidence. They just want his explanation for the report before they file it."

Kincaid lowered his voice again, but this time the tone wasn't friendly. "They sent you here because of the shit you pulled at Snake Pass. Wouldn't spend that kind of money on a no-mark shit heel like Sullivan. You're trouble they wanted out of the way. We don't need any more trouble here than we've got already. Do your job and go home."

"So let me see him."

"Tomorrow. See the sights. He'll be ready in the morning."

Grant got to his feet. "You a doctor now as well? What about the foaming at the mouth?"

Kincaid stood his ground. "I know more than the doctor. He'll be ready in the morning."

The two big guys glared at each other like bulls preparing to charge. The pissing contest was suddenly back full force. Kincaid was staking out his territory. Grant was the intruder. He could understand that. He respected Kincaid's position but wasn't going down without letting the detective know he knew what was going on too.

"Prison soap. Happens a lot, does it?"

"Not a lot. But when they get desperate, anything goes."

"Why's he so desperate?"

"Ask him tomorrow. Miller will drop you at your hotel."

Miller grabbed the car keys from the desk and shrugged into his jacket. The smile was ear to ear. He came around the desk and held out a hand. "Tyson Miller."

Grant shook it. "I know."

Miller looked confused.

Grant pointed at the name badge pinned to Miller's jacket. Enthusiasm became embarrassment, but the young detective smiled through it. He waved towards the door and took the lead. Grant picked up his bag and followed, part of his mind wondering what Freddy Sullivan was afraid of that made him so desperate to get out of jail. Another part of his mind was thinking something else.

Snake Pass isn't restricted, though. That was some serious ass you kicked.

Snake Pass might not have been restricted, but the official report only covered the numbers. One building demolished. Three vehicles burnt out. Eight dead, including six bad guys and two innocent bystanders, one of them an off-duty cop. All because Grant wanted a quiet drink after being dismissed from duty early. That and the fact that his words always came back to haunt him. The words this time were his warning to probationary constable Jamie Hope about not getting involved when you were off-duty.

"Case in point: young copper I knew goes for a Chinese down at Mean Wood junction. Pubs are shutting. Lot of drunks ordering a takeaway. Trouble brews. A fight ensues. Young copper whips out his warrant card and orders them all to cease and desist. What do you think happened?"

Hope tried to keep the hero worship off his face. Having a legend of the West Yorkshire Police as your training officer was like manna from heaven for a young probationary constable. He answered with a question. "They didn't cease and desist?"

"They did not. He got the shit kicked out of him and spent three days in hospital. The riot he provoked wrecked the Chinese and two shops either side of it and put everybody on double shifts for a week. Point is: drunks fighting each other are par for the course. Serves 'em right if they've got sore heads and a few bruises the following morning. It's no big deal."

Three hours later his words proved to be almost prophetic. Only it wasn't a few drunks fighting each other, it was a bunch of Ukrainian drug manufacturers and the Dominguez cartel fighting a turf war in the Yorkshire hills. Blood, snot, and the last big snowfall of winter made it a long, dark night.

You can't make an omelette without breaking some eggs.

That might well be true, but Grant hadn't started the omelette. He couldn't deny breaking a few eggs, but it was the Ukrainians that broke the first one when they slapped the waitress across the face. Grant had been pulling out of the car park at Woodlands Truck Stop and Diner when that had happened. The slap had triggered one of Grant's reflex actions—protecting the weak. Only now he had developed a calm-in-the-face-of-danger technique that had served him well in the army and was a godsend in the police. He turned the engine off and got out of the car. Crossing the car park, he stepped out of the cold night air and into hot water, because this turned out to be more than a boarding-school bully picking on an easy target.

The snow got heavier. Snake Pass was closed to traffic. And the opposition grew in numbers as the true nature of the house behind the truck stop emerged. But the body count didn't begin until a wet-behind-the-ears probationer decided to join Grant for an after-shift drink. That had triggered one of Grant's other character traits—always back your colleagues, no matter what the cost. The cost that night had been very high.

FIVE

Miller dropped Grant outside the reception lobby, then left. The Seaverns Hotel wasn't the Airport Hilton, but it was clean and tidy and better than some places Grant had rested his head. It was a three-story building with an extension around back for the dining room. Grant made a mental note to convert floor descriptions into US terms. Back in England, the floor you entered for reception was the ground floor. In America it was the first floor. That would make Grant's top-floor room the second floor back home but the third floor here. Important difference when scoping out a location.

Grant always scoped out his location.

He unpacked the holdall and stowed his clothes, more jeans and T-shirts and a couple of sweat tops. He placed a long velvet case under the folded T-shirts, then showered and changed and ended up looking exactly the same as before: faded blue jeans, dark T-shirt, orange windcheater, black K-Swiss tennis shoes. Sensible, practical, and comfortable. He was off-duty and out of division and ready to eat.

Grant ended up at Flanagan's Bar at the bottom of Jamaica Plain's Centre Street, which was basically Main Street USA. Mostly single-story flat-roofed businesses with hardware stores and laundromats, a CVS Pharmacy, and a handful of restaurants and bars. He was still reeling from the Santa Fe chicken salad he'd eaten at the Purple Cactus—more specifically, the size of the salad. He reckoned you could have grazed a herd for a week just off that one plate.

Flanagan's was a traditional pub with dark woodwork, dirty red-brick walls, and a green sign with gold letters that were picked out by a row of brass light fittings. Music and laughter came from inside and polluted the street. It sounded like Grant's kind of place.

That was his first mistake.

The second was not being careful who he spoke to once he got inside.

The main room was long and narrow and not as full as the noise outside suggested. There were tables and booths along the left-hand wall. The wall was stripped-back red brick with sepia photos of the old country and the Boston seafront back in the days of sail. A traditional bar ran the length of the room on the right. Glass shelves with mirrored backing carried every possible variation of whiskey and rye, not inverted with delivery optics like the UK but stood on the shelf, ready to be poured if selected.

Most of the booths were occupied. The ones that were empty were halfway along. Not in the corner for good viewing potential and too far in to allow a quick exit if trouble started. Booths weren't good tactical options. They penned you in with your legs under the table and your back against the seat behind you. Grant dismissed them and looked at the bar instead.

There were more spaces along the bar than the noise indicated. Several barstools and plenty of room in between. Men stood in irregular groups along the bar. A couple of women mixed in, but there were no all-female gatherings. This wasn't that kind of bar. There was a door to the restrooms at the far end with a red neon fire exit sign above it. Good. Grant chose a space about two-thirds along the bar, ignored the vacant barstool, and rested one foot on the brass rail along the bottom. The mirror gave a good view behind him. Standing instead of sitting gave him fast access to the fire exit. Now he could drink in peace.

Two bartenders worked the crowd. A young lad with a beaming smile reminded Grant of Tom Cruise in that film about a cocktail waiter. He didn't pull any fancy moves with the bottles or try party tricks with the glasses, though. It wasn't that kind of bar either. The older bartender looked hard as nails and was probably the owner. His smile, when it showed, looked more genuine. It was earned, not given freely. Grant waited for a gap in the serving, then held a hand out to get his attention. The older guy came over. "What can I getcha, fella?"

"Pint, please. Nearest thing you've got to Tetley's."

"Yorkshire ale. A bit out of your neighborhood, aren't you?"

"Just visiting."

"Well, you're in luck. We cater for all tastes in here. Can't get you draught, but we do carry some bottled."

"Tetley's?"

"The very same."

"You're a saint."

"That's what I keep telling the boss. He don't pay me more, though."

The bartender selected a bottle of Tetley's from the display below the mirror and expertly flipped the lid. He poured it at an angle to achieve the perfect head. Grant was impressed.

"Figured you for the owner."

"Don't let Mr. Delaney hear you say that. Concrete shoes aren't out of fashion just yet."

Grant laughed. The bartender smiled. A rare honor, Grant reckoned, for a first-time customer. He paid for the beer. "How come it's called Flanagan's, then?"

"Same reason McDonald's is called McDonald's."

"You make burgers?"

"No, and neither does the fella that owns McDonald's. I'm the public face."

"You Flanagan?"

"At your service."

"I'm honored. You don't exactly welcome the English round here."

"Being a cop is more of a problem."

"You can tell, huh?"

"Comes off you like a bad smell. Don't try going undercover."

"Not me. Straight ahead and open is my way. Good job I'm on vacation."

Flanagan indicated a large glass jar half filled with banknotes and coins next to the hand pumps. There was a slit cut into the screw lid. A piece of card with black lettering was taped across the front.

WIDOWS AND ORPHANS OF THE CONFLICT

"All donations gratefully received. That'd settle folks' nerves."

Grant looked at the jar and then back at Flanagan. It appeared that pissing contests came in all shapes and sizes. He smiled to take the sting out of his words.

"The famous gun-running jar. I wondered if you people still had those."

Flanagan kept a straight face.

"It's for the widows and orphans. Says so there, look."

He pointed out the words on the jar. Grant didn't look. He was watching the two big guys in the mirror who'd slipped into the booth behind him. They'd been watching Grant ever since they came in five minutes ago. He looked Flanagan in the eye, gauging how far to push this. "It says beef on McDonald's burgers. Don't make it so."

There was a moment's silence when this could have gone either way. The jars had been an open secret for years. Donations for the conflict, even though the official conflict was over. The IRA was history; politics had taken over. It was just the splinter groups that still caused trouble, but Northern Ireland was mainly a peaceful place now. Flanagan broke into a warm smile. Pissing contest over. "And it says Flanagan's on the wall outside."

Grant nodded. "As far as I'm concerned, it says Flanagan's in here too."

"Enjoy your drink, and go with God."

"Not sure God would want me, but I'll enjoy this for sure."

Flanagan moved along the bar to serve a group near the front door. Grant kept an eye on the pair behind him through the mirror. There had been no exchange of glances with the bartender. It didn't look as if they had anything to do with the bar. That left two possibilities. Either they were scoping out a target for a robbery or they didn't like the English. Maybe a third option. They didn't like the police. Flanagan had already made it plain that Grant's status was common knowledge. That didn't surprise Grant. It was in the way he carried himself. The way he looked at people. He didn't need a uniform.

The long flight and extended day began to catch up with him. He decided that one beer was enough and finished it in twenty minutes. Flanagan didn't wave him farewell. He was busy with other customers. A big guy on the barstool next to him gave Grant a withering look. Either the donation-jar speech had been overheard or his Englishness was counting against him. Grant didn't care. What he cared about was what the two guys in the booth did next.

He walked slowly to the restrooms at the rear, keeping half an eye on the booth. One of the guys shuffled out of the seat and began to follow him. The other got up and went towards the front door. They weren't going to fall for the sneak-out-the-back-door routine. They were going to cover both doors.

SIX

GRANT WENT THROUGH THE DOOR into the rear corridor. It swung shut behind him. The corridor was poorly lit by two wall lights, one on either side. The fire exit door was at the far end. The gents' restroom was on the left and the ladies' on the right. He quickly shoved the door to the gents, then ducked into the ladies' opposite, the smell of piss and disinfectant reminding him of Moor Grange School for Boys. He didn't plan on having this confrontation amid the white tiles and washbasins, though.

Timing was everything. Grant heard the door from the bar open again, followed immediately by the gents' door. He was moving before it even slammed shut. Back into the corridor and turn left. Fast. Into the bar and close the door behind him to stop it swinging. He walked straight through the bar and out the front door. The guy who'd followed him would take a few seconds to check the restroom and then go out the fire exit. Grant had just reduced the opposition by half.

The other half was waiting on the right under the brass light fittings that lit the Flanagan's Bar sign. It gave Grant a good look at his face in case an ID was needed later. He didn't think it would be. Grant came out fast but not running and turned left, back up Centre Street. The big guy had last seen him going through the rear door and wasn't ready.

Grant crossed the road. He stayed in plain sight, walking up the middle of the sidewalk and close to the curb. The streetlamps were bright. He passed the first Dunkin' Donuts and scouted ahead. The CVS Pharmacy was still open. The main entrance was at the far end as he approached. The exit door was nearest to him. He glanced in a darkened shop window to his right and saw a hulking figure cross the road to follow him. Just one. Good. He hadn't waited for his partner. He didn't have time. There was no doubt this was enemy action, though. They weren't after his autograph.

The CVS Pharmacy. Grant hoped it didn't have automatic doors and cash-register barriers. He swept past the exit door and went in the main entrance. It wasn't automatic. He was through in a split second and already heading for the exit before the salesgirl knew what was happening. He saw the big fella speed up towards the pharmacy, eyes glued on the main door. Not seeing the exit until it was too late.

Grant came out of the door like a thunderclap just as the guy sped past. Weight and momentum doubled the impact. Grant brought a knee up into the guy's wedding tackle and dropped him like a deadweight. He bunched his left fist around the guy's collar and dragged him into the deliveries alley. It was all over in five seconds. Even as he was kneeling on the moaning figure's chest, a voice played loud and clear in Grant's head.

Keep out of trouble. Don't get involved. You're off-duty.

If he'd paid attention to that voice back at Snake Pass, he wouldn't be here now. If he'd been the kind of guy to sit back and do nothing, he wouldn't have joined the army and he wouldn't be a cop. His inspector was an okay boss, but the West Yorkshire Police was ruled by statistics and target figures. Edicts handed down from on high. It had nothing to do with right and wrong anymore, merely accountability. Grant couldn't play that game. Accountability for Grant was catching the bad guys and putting them in prison.

Sometimes accountability was under his knee.

He slapped the shadowy face awake and leaned forward. "You know, if you're going to rob a fella, you really need to get in shape."

The man's eyes were cloudy with pain. Grant didn't wait for a response. "And pay attention to the little things. Target acquisition. Surprise attack. Pick on somebody a bit smaller. Don't split your forces."

Grant slapped him again for emphasis. "Means stick together."

The man shifted under Grant's knee, so Grant leaned in again. The extra weight made him groan, but he didn't speak. Grant kept an eye on the mouth of the alley. Nobody came rushing past. Nobody had called the police. The other half of the attacking force was lost and confused. Grant kept his tone conversational. "That's assuming you're after my wallet. If it's an anti-English thing, I'm a Yorkshireman. Different breed. If it's a cop thing, you're lucky I'm on vacation."

There was another possibility, but he didn't voice it. Could these two have been trying to rough him up to stop him interviewing Freddy Sullivan tomorrow? If so, what the fuck was Freddy mixed up in? Grant took five dollars out of his wallet and tucked it under the scuffed collar. "Get something for the swelling. Pharmacy's next door."

He stood up and backwards, out of the wounded tiger's kicking arc. There were no post-action shakes. There was no adrenaline rush. There never was. It was a bonus of Grant's calm approach. He glanced down at his fallen adversary, then out of the alley. The street was quiet. Just to be on the safe side, he went out of the other end of the alley and skirted the rear of the shops. Jamaica Pond was a dark presence in the distance to his left. Grant knew it was there but couldn't see it through the network of back streets that filled the space between the hotel and the lake. The family homes of the better-off. Jamaica Plain. The face of Middle America. Peaceful America.

THE SIRENS AND THE FLAMES and the fighting didn't start until he was back at the Seaverns Hotel and had nothing to do with him—or so he thought. Tomorrow he'd get the interview out of the way, then chill out for a couple of days before heading home. He was looking forward to a more peaceful day. As he climbed into bed and blocked out the sirens, he didn't know it would prove to be anything but. He'd bought the map. He'd gotten laid. Now it was time for the third part of his Boston trifecta.

SEVEN

THE DESK SERGEANT didn't need to ignore Grant for effect this time. O'Rourke had his hands full with the throng of bodies milling around the reception counter. He was talking to a miniature Chinese man who could barely see over the desktop. A second officer was talking to an agitated woman. Everyone else was waiting their turn and didn't seem happy about it. The place was a madhouse.

The smell of smoke was even stronger in here than outside, obviously brought in on the clothes of Jamaica Plain's citizens. Grant didn't think that would carry much weight with O'Rourke. He'd seen at least three marked units parked along the street with smashed windscreens or replacement wheels, the originals presumably slashed during the disturbance. If BPD policy was anything like West Yorkshire Police, they wouldn't classify it as a riot until it was no longer newsworthy.

Grant's orange windcheater caught O'Rourke's eye.

Surprisingly, the grizzled desk sergeant jerked a thumb towards the side door, then pressed the button under the counter. The door lock buzzed open and the foreigner from across the pond took a step towards acceptance. He went through with a nod of thanks, then climbed the stairs in the clock tower. When he pushed the door marked Detectives open, the activity was no less frenetic but slightly more controlled. Telephones rang. People talked. Detectives took reports from disgruntled members of the public who had been filtered through from downstairs.

Miller was taking a report from a Hispanic with singed eyebrows.

Kincaid was talking on the phone.

This was not a good day to be interviewing a no-mark prisoner held as a courtesy for a foreign force. Grant already felt the futility of this entire visit. It was an exercise in cover-your-ass. Normally they would have simply asked the detaining force, the BPD, to perform a brief interview and fax a copy to Ecclesfield. Then the crime could be written off as undetected and Sullivan released. Cheap and easy. The only reason for this expensive variation was to protect the service by hiding the key figure in the Snake Pass debacle.

Police Constable Jim Grant.

Grant didn't like running and hiding. He preferred to face things head-on. He hadn't done anything wrong. It had been other people's mistake for underestimating him. The good guys won. The bad guys lost, big-time. That was a good scenario in Grant's book. Now this. It felt less like a holiday assignment and more like a slap on the wrist.

Well, if cover-your-ass was all they wanted, that's all they were going to get. He wanted this interview over and done with so he could go home and face the music. He wasn't the one who would come out of it looking bad.

Kincaid stopped talking and hung up the phone. The orange windcheater caught his attention, and he nodded towards the corridor. Grant got the message. There would be more privacy in the hallway than in the office today. He dropped the empty soda can he'd bought across the road in the bin and went outside. Kincaid burst through the door and kept on walking along the corridor and round the corner.

Grant felt his hackles rise but controlled his temper.

He found Kincaid drinking from a paper cup at the water cooler just beyond the stairwell door. The second corridor was longer, with more offices along the left and more windows along the right. The windows overlooked the front of the station. The damaged patrol cars were parked directly below. That put things in perspective, but Grant was still annoyed at being blanked by the senior detective. "What's up? Somebody burn the barbecue?"

Kincaid stopped with the cup halfway to his mouth. "Don't push your luck."

Grant indicated the damaged cars through the window. "Anybody hurt?"

Meaning officers, not citizens. Kincaid understood. It was the first thing any cop asked after the shit hit the fan. Check on your colleagues first. There was no less concern for the victims, but if the cops got injured, they couldn't prevent it happening to anyone else. Grant's first sergeant had told him, after graduating from driving school, that driving fast with blue lights and sirens was okay, but you still had to drive safely because you couldn't help who you were speeding to help if you ploughed your car into a tree. Same principle here. Kincaid's demeanor softened. "Two. Minor injuries. Band-aid, then back on duty."

"Good."

"The only fucking thing that is."

"That's the job. Shit rolls downhill. Cops live in the valley."

"Is that some quaint English folk saying? 'Cause if it is, I'm not surprised every fucker left to discover America."

"That'd be Columbus. He wasn't English."

"Whatever. Probably had a bit of Irish in him. Thick Mick thought he'd discovered India. Should have sent the rest of Ireland to Delhi."

"Yeah. But where would the Boston Mafia be without the Irish?"

"You've been watching too many movies. Every fucking cop show, there are shootouts like it's the OK Corral. Me? Never drawn my weapon in fifteen years. Boston Mafia? I've shit 'em."

Despite having just finished a soda, Grant filled a paper cup from the cooler. "If that's the case, how come Whitey Bulger was number two on the FBI's most wanted?"

"Frank was number two? Who was number one?"

"Bin Laden. With all your OK Corrals, look how long it took you to catch either one of them."

"Fuck you. With all your Peelers, you haven't caught Jack the Ripper yet."

Grant laughed. "Touché."

He held his cup up and Kincaid tapped it with his. They both took a drink of cold, clear water. Kincaid calmed down a notch. "JP's got vehicle B&Es going through the roof, here and West Roxbury. The mayor's vowed to reduce crime, so we've got to get the figures down. Best way to do that is catch the little bastards or cook the figures. Trying to put together intelligence on the two we think it is, and what happens? Half the Irish population decides to square off and ruin my fucking day."

"Welcome to happy valley."

"Fuckin' shit-wankin' motherfuckers."

The corridor fell silent. Grant waited a few seconds. "Feel better?"

"Much. What can I do for you today?"

"You know what. Cells are going to be heaving. Custody sergeant might need a bit of a nudge to let me use an interview room. I think you're pretty good with the nudge."

Kincaid finished his water and screwed the paper cup into a ball. With the expression on his face, he looked just like Robert Shaw in *Jaws*. Grant was no Richard Dreyfuss, but not to be outdone he crushed his cup too. "We're not going to be showing off war wounds now, are we?"

"Thought you were a typist."

"Even war zones need typists. Got a nasty paper cut once."

"Don't show me. I might faint."

They threw their paper cups into the waste bin together. A dead heat. Pissing contest for today was a draw. Honors even. Kincaid headed back along the corridor to the stairs. "I'd better come down with you. O'Rourke's a pussy compared to Rooney."

Grant followed. Out of the frying pan, into the fire.

IF THE FRONT OFFICE WAS BUSY, then the custody area was bedlam. This wasn't helped by the fact that JP's prisoner facility was only intended for overnight detainees and minor infringements. Public disturbance was only a minor infringement until you multiplied it by ten. Throw in damage, arson, and assault, and it got busy real quick.

Grant felt right at home. Apart from the village cop shop, all police stations were basically the same. The differences were merely cosmetic. They all had a public front counter. They all had a report-writing room for uniform patrol. Most had a CID/detectives office, and all had admin offices that trumped all of the above. When it came to the cell area, the differences were even more similar. British police, military police, American police—it was only the color scheme and the accents that changed. Everything else remained the same.

Cells for the miscreants, the number depending on the size of the station. Livescan machine for fingerprinting the miscreants; ink and paper in the less affluent forces. Charge desk and booking-in counter, the same counter in most cell areas. And one man in charge of it all. The custody sergeant, or whatever they called him here in the Boston Police Department.

What they called him here was Sergeant Rooney. "Get dem feckers out da way. Move along, people. This ain't a Saint Patrick's Day parade."

There wasn't a hint of American in the accent. Grant could feel another Bunker Hill moment coming. He might as well be trying to interview a prisoner in Northern Ireland—or southern Ireland at a pinch. The feckers Rooney was referring to were two prisoners being given back their property in a plastic bag. They'd just signed the custody record and were trying to tear open the seal. A single uniform cop countersigned the receipt. It was tough luck if the prisoners wanted to check their property first. Grant didn't think Rooney was the patient type.

"Feck off, the lot of yer. Out the door before I decide to keep yer for court."

The prisoners gave up on the bags and were hustled towards a heavy door to the backyard. It slammed shut behind them, and two more were free. The conveyer belt wheeled out another one who had just been fingerprinted and photographed.

Kincaid handed his firearm to a detention officer behind the counter, who secured it in a network of small, square lockers and gave Kincaid a numbered tag. The big detective waved a hand at Grant in a give-it-to-me gesture. Grant shook his head and held his hands out, palms upwards. Kincaid looked surprised. "No sidearm?"

"I hate guns. Back home we use kind words and CS spray."

"CS spray?"

"Like aerosol mace."

"English cops are unarmed?"

"I've got a side-handled baton and a stab vest back home."

"But no guns?"

Grant shook his head. "Frontline bobbies don't carry firearms. If we turn up at something where there's guns, we call for backup and they deploy an armed response vehicle. They carry the guns."

"But you're firearms trained, right? Being in the army and all."

"I was a typist. Had no use for guns."

Sergeant Rooney overheard the exchange and came over. "Feckin' Jesus. No wonder we tanned the English at Bunker Hill."

Grant ignored the jibe.

Rooney did not. "You must be our English guest. Hard to miss you in that gay cavalier orange."

"That's the idea. Not the gay part."

"Not sure about that. A man that don't like guns in a country that loves 'em."

"Crooks shoot at cops because they know you're going to shoot at them. Best way to avoid getting shot is hold your arms out and wear an orange jacket."

Rooney glanced at Kincaid like he'd got shit on his shoe. "Must be the training page that got torn out—by the last man tried to tackle an armed robber with a kind word and his dick in his hand."

"Dick in his hand would make him a wanker. Maybe that's why he got shot."

"A philosophizing Yorkshireman. I've seen everything now."

Kincaid leaned against the counter and jerked a thumb at Grant. Rooney leaned on the opposite side like two conspirators plotting an explosives night. Guy Fawkes in the modern age.

"This Yorkshireman's ready to clear you some space."

"Sullivan? That foaming little shit."

"Exactly. Quick interview and kick him out. You can charge him with soap theft if you want."

Rooney waved a hand around the room with a frown that bordered on comical. "You seen it around here? Not a chance of an interview room until tonight at the earliest. Maybe even tomorrow."

Grant was losing patience. He knew it was busy. He'd done busy in the past and knew what it was like. The difference was that he'd always look for ways to help get it less busy, not put obstacles in the way. This whole Anglo-Irish debate was wearing pretty thin. They were all cops together in his book. Not as if he was a firefighter—he could understand the rivalry there. "What about the one out in reception?"

Kincaid and Rooney turned to him as if an unwanted child had spoken. Grant felt as welcome as a fart in the bath. The bubbles settled. Rooney found his voice first. "That interview room is for witnesses and visitors only."

"I am a visitor."

"Sullivan is a prisoner. Prisoners can't go out to an insecure interview room."

"He's getting released as soon as I've finished."

"But not before. Until then he's a prisoner and cannot be interviewed in an insecure room."

Grant noticed that the Oirish had left Rooney's delivery. He reckoned it had been laid on thick for the Englishman. For a veteran sergeant he was beginning to sound like a jobsworth to Grant. "Look. You want him gone. I want him interviewed. Win-win situation."

"Not if he absconds during the interview and I'm stuck with his bag of shit."

"Give him his shit back first."

"Can't do that while he's still a prisoner."

"Release him first then."

"You can't interview him unless he is in custody."

"Fuck me. No wonder the Irish left Ireland. Who could live with a philosophy like that?"

"Be careful now, lad."

"Go fuck yourself with a sporran."

Kincaid stepped back, out of the firing line. Rooney beetled his brows. "How about tossing your caber—right out the feckin' door."

"Do Irish toss the caber? Thought that was Scottish."

"Sporrans or cabers. You're gone or dead meat."

This pissing contest was getting out of hand. Kincaid poured oil on troubled water. He stepped back in and lightened the tone. "Come on, girls. We don't want this to end up as handbags at dawn. Maybe some creative bookkeeping is called for here. What do you say?"

What Rooney said was, "Okay." Leading to him to nearly being right. In forty-five minutes Grant was almost dead meat.

EIGHT

FREDDY SULLIVAN was a low-life piece of shit whom Grant had been chasing all his service without much success. He burgled houses big and small. He screwed shops and supermarkets. He dealt drugs and dabbled in prostitution. He had a sheet as long as your arm but absolutely zero criminal convictions. How on earth the little fuck had persuaded America to let him and his brother immigrate was a mystery.

The last time Grant had spoken to Sullivan had been over the garden fence of a house on Ravenscliffe Avenue in Bradford. There had been insufficient grounds for an arrest but plenty of reason to exchange harsh words, most of them from Grant. That had been five years ago. Sullivan didn't look happy to see his hometown cop now. "I'm stuck in this shit 'cause of you. Fuck me."

Kincaid had gone back upstairs, but Sergeant Rooney listened with undisguised disdain. The custody sergeant was processing another prisoner further down the counter, handing a bag of personal possessions to an Irishman with a black eye and a torn shirt. Grant's tone was friendly even if his words weren't.

"You're in this shit because you're a burgling bastard with no redeeming qualities whatsoever, but today's your lucky day. And I'm your get-out-of-jail card. So don't try my patience."

Sullivan looked skittish. The Bradford burglar's eyes flicked around the custody area. He had developed a nervous twitch that Grant didn't remember from his days on Ecclesfield's most-wanted list. That list might not be as high profile as Whitey Bulger making number two on the FBI's most wanted, but back in Bradford it was big enough.

Grant didn't like burglars. He didn't like thieves. He didn't like anyone who took what wasn't theirs from people who barely had enough to make ends meet as it was. Robbing banks was one thing. Stealing from little old ladies something else. He didn't like Sullivan but wanted to make this as simple as possible. The smoother this went, the sooner he'd be on a plane home.

"Let me make this easy for you. Try receiving instead of transmitting for a change. First, there'll be no charges against you. Second, you answer all my questions in the negative and you'll be walking out of here in half an hour."

Sergeant Rooney coughed loudly and shook his head. He held one finger up.

Grant amended his speech. "One hour. So let's keep things simple."

Sullivan twitched. The Irish prisoner with the black eye took his property bag and glanced at the nervous Englishman. Rooney barked an order and the prisoner tucked the bag under one arm and left. Grant tilted his head to one side. "Okay?"

Sullivan nodded, which wasn't much different than his twitch, so Grant pressed for an answer. The skinny wretch spoke in a whisper. "Okay."

Grant waved a hand at the sergeant. "We're good to go. That way, is it?"

Sergeant Rooney pointed at the door into the station and pressed the release button. The lock buzzed and Grant pushed the door open. He gestured for Sullivan to go through, then followed, carrying a sheaf of papers and a pair of audiotapes. The door slammed shut behind them.

A short walk down two internal corridors and they were at the door he'd gone through twice already, in the opposite direction. There was a lock-release button on the wall next to it. He pressed it and led the way into the reception area. It was still busy. He navigated through the crowd to a room at the far end marked Interview 1. He used the key he'd been given and opened the door. Sullivan threw nervous glances at the faces around him, then went inside.

Grant followed and closed the door.

Outside, a figure wearing a grey sweatshirt with the hood up looked through the glass of the front doors, then signaled to someone around the corner. There were just twenty-five minutes to go.

The interview room was cramped and square and completely functional. There was a solid metal table pushed against the far wall, with two heavy chairs on either side. A twin tape-recording deck sat on the table with the tape caddies open and empty. A wired glass window with vertical shades let in morning sunshine from Washington Street. Apart from that, the room was empty.

Grant indicated for Sullivan to sit on the far side of the table, then pulled out a chair nearest the tape deck. He waited for Sullivan to sit down, then sat himself. He shuffled the papers into a neat square and began unwrapping the cellophane from the twin pack of tapes. "Right, Freddy. Here's how it goes."

He looked for a waste bin for the cellophane. There wasn't one.

"This is a formal interview just so we can say it's been done, but the objective is this. There's no evidence. No witnesses. You deny everything. Interview over. You go home. I write the crime off. Undetected."

It went against the grain. Grant put a brave face on it, but this was the opposite of everything he stood for. Bad guys did bad things. It was up to the good guys to stop them. Grant was one of the good guys. Always had been. This didn't feel like being a good guy.

Sullivan looked like he was giving serious consideration to Grant's words. The concentration on his face was nothing new. Grant remembered it from the days before the Sullivan family emigrated, a great day for Ravenscliffe. If someone asked Sullivan whether the sky was up or down, he would still spend a long time making his mind up. "I say that—then I'm out of here?"

"Gone baby gone."

Sullivan smiled. "Filmed that around here."

Grant stopped loading the tapes. "What?"

"*Gone Baby Gone*. They filmed that in JP."

"The missing kid film?"

"Yeah. Set in Boston. Some of it in Jamaica Plain."

"You get a part in it? Walk-on? Background?"

"Naw. They didn't want my face getting seen."

"Then what the fuck's it got to do with anything?"

Sullivan looked embarrassed and Grant suddenly felt ashamed, like he'd kicked a puppy or something. The smile went out of Sullivan's voice. "Just saying, is all."

Then he brightened. "My brother was an extra. Crossed the street in one scene."

"How come he crossed the pond with you? You twins or something?"

"You know we ain't. He's my kid brother. We go everywhere together."

"Oh yeah? What's Sean doing these days?"

"He stamps car number plates."

"In prison? That's what they do over here, isn't it? Like sewing mailbags."

"Naw. At Delaney's over in West Roxbury. He don't do prison. He's the good brother."

That last part came out soft, almost soulful. Grant finished loading the tapes and snapped the caddies shut but didn't start recording. Instead he took the record of interview sheet and filled in the names at the top. They weren't the official West Yorkshire forms, but they'd do. This wasn't going to court anyway. He filled in the spaces marked, location, date, name of interviewee, and interviewing officer. He left the time blank.

"Okay, Freddy. You ready?"

Sullivan nodded. The look of concentration was back on his face. He looked like a man with the weight of the world on his shoulders. Like a man with a serious decision to make, and it wasn't coming easy.

Grant leaned over and pressed the Record button. He waited for the tapes to spool past the leader before he began the official preamble. "This interview is being tape recorded. The date is…"

He stated the date.

"And the time is…"

He stated the time and wrote it down on the form.

"I am PC three-six-seven Grant of the West Yorkshire Police and I am interviewing—will you state your name and date of birth for the tape, please?"

Sullivan gave his name but stumbled over his date of birth. He had to repeat it twice before he got it right.

"Thank you. We are in an interview room at District E-13 in Boston, USA. Can you please confirm that there is no one else present?"

"What?"

"That there's nobody else in the room."

"There's nobody else in the room."

"Thank you. Right, Freddy, I am investigating a report of burglary at Patel's Grocery Store, Ravenscliffe Avenue, Bradford, between the times of…"

He stated the time and date of the burglary, then went on to describe how CCTV footage showed a white male approach the front of the shop at night, kick open the front door, then steal money from the cash register and cigarettes from the display. A witness saw this male leave the premises and walk behind the shops, out of sight. The description of this person matched that of Sullivan, leading to him being circulated on suspicion of burglary.

"I thought you said there weren't no witnesses."

"The witness was unable to make a positive identification through personal knowledge or photographic records."

"Oh, right. Yeah."

This was more information than Grant would normally give out at the beginning of an interview. Best practice was to simply state what offense he was investigating, then ask open questions about the suspect's movements at a specific time and date. Get them to commit to a story before producing evidence to prove it was a lie. Even small lies could undermine the best defense. Get them caught in a lie early on, and it made it easier for the bigger lies later on.

This was the opposite of that.

This was laying it all out to get a quick denial.

Only Sullivan didn't deny it.

Grant was taken aback for a moment. The confession had been blurted out in one short sentence, and it blew Grant's strategy right out of the water. Under normal circumstances the suspect admitting the offense was exactly what you wanted. It was the whole purpose of an interview. Box them into a corner until they confessed everything, then get details that only the thief would know so they couldn't say they made it up later.

These weren't normal circumstances.

Ten seconds ticked by.

Fifteen.

Then Grant spoke firmly into the speaker. "Interview terminated at"—he stated the time and wrote it on the form—"for the interviewee to take legal advice."

He snapped the recorder off. "What the fuck do you mean, 'I did it'?"

"I did Patel's."

"All this 'it's a fair cop, guv' bullshit only happens in the movies. What the fuck are you playing at?"

Sullivan wasn't afraid of Grant. Never had been. But there was fear in his eyes now. Nerves twitched in his left eye. He drummed the fingers of his right hand on the table. He was sweating. "I can't stay here. You got to take me back."

"Take you back where?"

"Extricate me. Back to Ravo."

"They aren't going to pay to extradite you for a corner shop burglary."

"They paid for you to come over here for a corner shop burglary."

Grant ignored that and leaned forward, elbows on the table. "You've never admitted your name and address before. What you confessing to burglary for all of a sudden?"

Sullivan glanced at the window, then at the door. He looked like a junky on a comedown seeing spiders on the walls. He began to bite his nails. There weren't any nails left to bite, so he nibbled his fingertips. Grant sat upright and pushed his chair back from the table. It scraped across the carpet. "What's going on?"

Sullivan stopped nibbling. He stared at the table and shook his head slowly. "This shit ain't my fault."

Grant looked blank and kept quiet.

"I was just the importer." Sullivan was almost crying. "This long in the nick. They ain't gonna believe I said nowt. I'm dead."

"Slow down, Freddy. What you talkin' about?"

"Extricate me. Get me out of here. But promise me." He was practically wringing his hands. "Officer Grant. Promise you'll protect my brother. He's nowt to do with this."

Grant leaned back in his chair to give Sullivan some space. He didn't want to crowd him. Keeping his voice conversational, almost friendly, he tried to take the sting out of the situation while still getting an important piece of information.

"What you been smuggling, Freddy? Dope again?"

It was Sullivan's turn to look blank. His lips moved, but no words came out. Grant was about to probe with gentle questions when a loud bang on the window snapped his head around.

The wired glass splintered. A large hand, fingers splayed, was silhouetted black against the daylight. It was the size of a baseball glove. A giant's hand. Slivers of glass from the inside dusted the carpet but the window held. Sullivan's eyes were bulging out of his head in panic. Grant was halfway to his feet and turning towards the window when the door opened.

The distraction was complete.

Neither of them noticed until the door slammed shut. The nasty black object bounced across the carpet and under the table. Sullivan screamed and stood up so fast he flipped the table forward. Grant recognized the grenade a split second before it exploded, then the world was full of light and pain.

NINE

I WAS A TYPIST.

The words echoed through Grant's brain.

I HATE GUNS.

The follow-up words boomed just as loud.

AND I'M NOT THAT STRUCK ON BOMBS EITHER.

In his mind's eye he saw legs clad in desert camouflage combat pants. Dusty boots laced up beneath canvas anklets. Blancoed webbing belt and straps with dull, tarnished brass fittings. Sand and stones and debris choked his lungs.

I WAS A TYPIST.

The camouflage pants became faded blue jeans and the boots transformed into dusty black K-Swiss tennis shoes. The sand and stones and debris remained the same. It choked his lungs, and he coughed himself awake. He could barely open his eyes. His ears were ringing like Quasimodo in the bell tower. He coughed harder and cleared some of the obstruction from his throat, but his mouth was dry and claggy. He tried to spit but couldn't create any moisture.

Pain filled his world.

He kept still. First thing to do was take stock, but since everything hurt it was difficult to know where to start. Visual examination. After a traumatic experience, your physical senses could lie. Amputees often felt like they still had their limbs. Fingers and toes were notoriously fickle about transmitting data to the brain. It was all just pain. How many toes were left was impossible to gauge until you counted them. There was something heavy lying on top of him.

His eyes. He blinked them clear, but they stung with dust and scratches. They worked, though. He ignored the pain and did a quick circuit of the room without moving his head. Grant was lying in an awkward twisted position against the back wall with the table upside down across his lower body. The pain down there was worrying, but he argued that he had to be alive to feel pain. That was the first positive.

The second was that he still seemed to have both hands.

Sullivan was missing at least one. It was curled on the floor in the middle of the room. Red stringy blood vessels and white shards of bone protruded from the severed wrist. Grant wondered where the rest of him was and how badly he was injured. Then he glanced up and stopped wondering. A squashed eyeball stared down at him from the ceiling with a swatch of flesh and one ear.

Grant concentrated on his own situation. He had two hands, both eyes, and his head moved without snapping his neck. The table felt like a dead weight across his chest and legs, but at least his senses were reporting that he had legs—he hoped. The solid metal table was hard to move. He pushed with his arms, but shock had robbed him of his strength.

The window had blown out into the street, and Grant became aware of sirens rushing from the outside world. Air horns indicated the fire department was on its way. The ringing in his ears toned down a notch. Somebody knocked on the door.

"You gotta be kiddin'. Come in."

His voice was harsh and rasping. There were situations where gallows humor helped save the day and situations where silence was the only answer. This was one of those situations—the interview room demolished, Freddy Sullivan blasted apart, and pain wracking Grant's body. He couldn't believe somebody was knocking on the door. Then he realized it wasn't a knock on the door. It was someone outside trying to knock their way through the door.

The door shook but didn't budge. Dust was dislodged from the door frame and the ceiling with each kick, but the door wouldn't open. Faces looked in through the hole where the window used to be. Voices called into the room, but Grant couldn't make out the words. His ears were still out of focus. He glanced at the base of the door and saw why it was blocked.

The biggest part of Freddy Sullivan lay amid a pile of bricks and plasterboard and a twisted metal chair. His torso, or most of it minus one shoulder, was laid on its side like he was resting. The door banged again and thumped the corpse. Grant felt anger ball up in his throat. The indignity of Freddy being abused even after death was too much for him. He shouted for whoever was kicking the door to stop, mustered enough strength to push the table off his legs, then crawled over to the door.

He paused. Words should be spoken, but now wasn't the time. He took a deep breath through his nose—his mouth was still too dry—and gently rolled Sullivan onto his back. He tried to take his orange windcheater off to cover him but couldn't flex his shoulders enough. Instead he scrabbled the bricks aside, then slid backwards on his ass.

"Come in."

Not joking. Deadly serious.

The door opened six inches, then caught on the chippings. It closed and then was forced open wider. Twelve inches. Two feet. On the third attempt it opened all the way, and Sam Kincaid barged a shoulder into the room.

"Christ almighty."

The big detective took in the scene with one glance. He ignored the corpse and went straight into first-aid mode. He crouched beside Grant and began checking him for major cuts and fractures. It was chaos outside. The reception area had been full of milling bodies. Shock had turned them into a panicking mob. Grant could hear O'Rourke yelling orders. Other cops responded by herding the crowd into the street for triage.

Sirens grew closer. Ambulances racing to the scene. The air horns were deafening, but Grant didn't think the firefighters would be needed. As far as Sullivan was concerned, the paramedics wouldn't be needed either. Grant noticed Kincaid glancing around the room, his eyes noting everything and appearing to tick them off one thing at a time. Good police practice. This was a crime scene. As soon as the fire department and paramedics got in here, there'd be no evidence left.

First priority was always to preserve life or put out the fire. There was no fire, but they'd still have to check and maybe damp the room down. Preserving life would mean treating Grant. Kincaid was making a mental note of what the scene looked like for later use. Grant had already done the same with his initial scan.

The sirens stopped. The air horns too. The emergency services had arrived. Heavy boots crunched into the room, and the new arrivals began to prioritize. Make sure the building was safe. Treat the patient. Grant was the patient, but he was impatient. Being injured wasn't an option.

THE AMBULANCE WAS BIG and square and roomy. It made the ones he was used to in Bradford seem like pedal cars in comparison. By some miracle Grant was the only injury. Everyone else—the crowd in the reception area and the pedestrians outside—were simply shocked, not injured. The other ambulances had been released after triaging the crowd. Strapped to a backboard, Grant was carried and loaded into the last one.

Kincaid stood over him so they could talk without Grant trying to crane his neck. He argued with the paramedic that his neck had been okay when he was moving the mutilated torso, so why wasn't it okay now? It didn't wash. Procedures were set in stone. In a country where you could sue the microwave manufacturer for not stating you *couldn't* dry your poodle in it, litigation-proofing was almost as important as saving lives.

It was half an hour before Grant could give his first account, the one that would be in any file created about the bombing of the police station. The one that would set the tone for the forthcoming investigation.

He told Kincaid about the interview and the unexpected confession. He detailed the conversation after the tapes were turned off. He described the slap on the window for distraction and the grenade through the door. Sullivan jerking upright and flipping the table that had saved Grant's life. The retelling of it brought a sense of calm. Grant began to feel more like his old self. Survivor guilt transferred into giddiness. Gallows humor resurfaced when Kincaid mentioned the hole in the police station wall. Grant smiled. "I suppose the police are looking into it."

Kincaid scratched his chin. Grant finished with the traditional follow-up. "If it had blown out the toilets, the police wouldn't have anything to go on."

Kincaid wasn't going with the flow. "Yeah, well, we don't have anything to go on yet. So stop fucking about."

"Sorry."

"Look. You know how this goes. Best time to get at your memory is as soon as you can talk. Deep memory trawls up little details anything from twenty-four hours to a week later. We need a statement as soon as you can."

"Get me out of this, and I'll write one now."

Kincaid shook his head. A WCVB news helicopter hovered, trying to get one last shot of the breaking story. The noise was deafening, so he closed the back door. It didn't help much. He raised his voice.

"Can't. Once they've checked you out at the hospital, I'll drop some statement forms off. Oh"—he jerked a thumb at the helicopter noise—"and don't talk to the press."

Grant would have shaken his head if it hadn't been strapped tight. "Me and the press—not on good terms."

"Snake Pass?"

"Among other things."

"They're not going to make you a police spokesman, then?"

"It's spokesperson in the UK now."

"Here too. But fuck 'em, I say."

"D'you still have manholes in the US?"

"Only the ones we shit out of."

“So long as you don’t say fuck them too.”

Kincaid laughed. It was a deep, booming sound that rivaled the helicopter. It gave Grant hope for the future. A laugh like that meant Kincaid was a man’s man. At a time like this, men’s men were what you needed. Call it sexist, but Grant was a man’s man too. The door opened, and throbbing helicopter noise filled the ambulance. It slowly died away as the chopper gained height, then flew off.

Miller stood on the step and looked inside, concern etched on his face. Grant could only see him if he depressed his eyes. Miller’s concern touched him. He was a good kid—would no doubt make a good cop.

Kincaid climbed out the back. “Miller will ride with you. In case you give a dying declaration.”

“Here’s a declaration.” Kincaid waited for the parting shot, but Grant was being serious. “Sullivan said to look after his brother. You know where he is?”

“We’re working on it. Get well soon.”

Miller climbed in. Kincaid stepped back and shut the door. He slapped the side of the ambulance, and it set off for the hospital.

TEN

They wanted to cut Grant's clothes off. Massachusetts General may have been the third oldest hospital in America and the largest in New England, but they didn't have enough staff for Grant to let them cut his clothes off. Boston Medical almost became *Boston Legal* until the nurse examining him realized Grant could take his clothes off himself.

The nurse wasn't amused.

The pain wasn't funny either.

The nurse smiled. "You're going to look awful stupid if your arm drops off trying to get out of that orange jacket."

"It's my favorite."

"Which is your favorite arm? The other one?"

"My favorite nurse was the other one."

"There is no other one."

"Any other one. Give me a hand here, will you?"

The nurse pursed her lips and folded her arms. She tapped one shoe as if keeping beat with an unheard song. It was a soft and sensible shoe. It didn't tap at all, but the effect was the same. Don't mess with me, the pose said. Grant stopped struggling with his jacket and looked her square in the eye. It was his turn to smile. “Please?”

The shoe stopped tapping, but the arms remained stubbornly folded. Despite the smell of antiseptic and voided bowels, a flowery scent wafted off her like roses in the summer. She was short and wiry and looked like she could wrestle alligators. All muscle and determination. The smile didn’t work on her. Not straightaway.

“You’re that cop from England, aren’t you?”

Grant looked blank. He wondered what Miller had said before he left. There wasn’t going to be any dying declaration, and they’d needed him back at E-13. The nurse raised an eyebrow. “It’s all over the news. You can’t hide in that orange signpost.”

“I’m not trying to hide.”

“Maybe you should try ducking then.”

She stepped forward and helped Grant slip his arms out of the sleeves. He tugged the T-shirt out of his jeans, and she pulled it off over his head. She was about to throw them into a grey plastic bag marked MGH, but he took them from her and folded them up. Military training stretched to more than self-defense and typing. If he’d ever known his mother he might have blamed her, but keeping his clothes tidy was an army trait.

The nurse began tapping her shoe again.

Grant paused in mid-fold. “Don’t tell me you’re Irish too. Hated the English from birth?”

The shoe stopped. “Third-generation English. From York.”

“A Yorkshire lass. Hallelujah. D’you know the secret?”

She looked nonplussed. “What secret?”

“For making Yorkshire puddings. The one thing you can’t get supersized in America. A decent Yorkshire pudding.”

"Well, don't hold your breath. Hospital food is functional. Not big enough to feed you, not good enough for you to want to stay."

"I don't want to stay."

"We'll see after I've examined you. Drop your pants."

"But nurse, I hardly know you."

"You're not going to get to know me either." She produced a hospital gown and dropped it on the bed. "Put this on and lie down."

"I hope you warm your hands before you ask me to cough." He thought that got through her defenses because there was a hint of a blush. It took a lot to make a nurse blush. He turned away from her and dropped his jeans. The laugh was deep and throaty, and he glanced over his shoulder. The nurse was looking at the No Entry sign above his back passage.

"No confusing your sexual leanings."

"Like an orange jacket in a gunfight."

"Right. Well, let's see what's wrong with the rest of you."

It was like waiting to see the school nurse at Moor Grange. Grant shrugged the hospital gown on and prepared to be abused.

There were no broken bones and no internal injuries. That was the conclusion after four hours of poking and prodding and examinations by all manner of electronic devices. The ER was busy and quiet in waves. From his place inside the curtained cubicle he could hear emergencies rolling in, followed by periods of relative inactivity—just like any hospital in any major city. It was only the scale that separated the MGH from the BRI. Bradford Royal Infirmary performed the same function in Yorkshire but with a smaller population and restricted budget.

Americans even supersized their hospitals.

The voided bowels and antiseptic smells gave way to perfume and hot food. When the nurse came to check on him, it was the perfume. When she fed him, it was the food. No Yorkshire puddings. There was a brief spell when he could smell gunshot residue, like a freshly struck match or the aftermath of a fireworks display. Some kid shot over on Parker Street. A second victim had been taken to Brigham and Women's Hospital but died on arrival. Grant picked that up by listening to the attending officer. He picked up a lot by simply listening. It was a cop's most important tool.

The x-rays and scans confirmed what he already knew about his own injuries. The rest was simply scratches and sore eyes. The nurse cleaned and dressed the cuts. She rinsed his eyes with some kind of solution that stung at first, then produced blessed relief. His ears had stopped ringing hours ago, but his hearing was muted slightly. She told him that would ease by tomorrow.

The main concern was the bang on the head and his initial disorientation. He hadn't told the doctor about the combat trousers and boots but had to admit to feeling woozy when he'd come round immediately after the explosion. The fact that he'd lost consciousness, even briefly, was the deciding factor. Grant was going to have to stay overnight for observation.

That was the hospital's plan. Grant's plan was completely different.

"THEY'LL COME TAKE YOU to a ward after dinner."

Grant didn't speak. It wasn't because his mouth was full of whatever the orderly had just served him, but because he didn't want to give a heads-up that he wouldn't be here when the porter came to pick him up.

The curtain swished shut.

Grant counted to ten. He swung his legs off the examination bed and put the food tray on the mattress. The grey plastic bag was on a shelf under the bed. His back, legs, and arms ached, but he managed to struggle into his jeans and T-shirt. Tying his shoes was too hard so he just slipped them on. He carried the orange jacket over one arm. No point causing more pain than he had to.

He waited for the next pulse of activity and raised voices. A car-crash victim was rushed past on a gurney, with all the staff that entailed. The gurney and the nurses went one way. Grant stepped out of his cubicle and went the other. Along the corridor, turn right, and he was away from the examination area. It looked like it was always busy out here. The pulses of action and peace in the ER smoothed into constant activity front of house.

Without the orange windcheater, Grant didn't stand out. He was just another body amid a shifting sea of bodies. He waited until a group of student doctors went out into the reception area and tagged along.

He was almost to the front door when a voice stopped him in his tracks. "I don't suppose you've signed yourself out, have you?"

Grant turned around slowly. Terri Avellone had a twinkle in her eye, tempered with concern on her face. She nodded towards the reception desk. "They're going to be very unhappy when they've lost you."

"I'm not lost. Just misplaced."

He saw the plastic name badge with a fancy chemical-firm logo. "I didn't know you worked here."

"Just visiting. Business."

He pointed at the front doors. "Just leaving. Business."

She handed Grant an embossed business card with the name of a pharmaceutical company he couldn't pronounce. Terri Avellone was identified as its chief representative. There was a contact number across the bottom. He slipped the card into his pocket. "Sales?"

"Product placement."

"A bit late for selling your wares, isn't it?"

"The guys I have to see work shifts. So I work late sometimes." The concern transferred to her eyes but the smirk was still there. "You're not easy to forget."

"Well, you know what they say. A good man is hard to find."

"No. A hard man is good to find."

He tilted his head as he looked at her. "You are a very naughty girl."

"I need spanking."

"Very naughty."

She waved a hand towards the reception desk. The staff looked busy and harassed. Beyond them the ER continued its trench warfare.

"Professional courtesy—sign yourself out, then I'll give you a ride."

Grant walked over to the reception desk, gave his details, and told the woman he was leaving. She was even less impressed than the nurse who'd examined him. Using as few words as possible, she shoved a clipboard at him across the counter. "Next of kin details, then sign. Against medical advice."

"Next of kin?"

"Preferably in Boston, so they can get your body."

"I don't have anyone in Boston."

"You must know somebody."

Grant paused for a moment, then smiled. He scribbled on the form and signed it, then went out for his ride.

ELEVEN

Terri Avellone gave Grant the ride of his life after a bit of small talk. She explained about supplying and importing drugs to hospitals. He explained about the explosive interview with the prisoner from the UK.

"How is he?"

"Apart from the fact that his arse is two miles away from his elbow and they're playing hunt the thimble for the rest of him?"

"Did you just make that up?"

"No. *The Long Good Friday.* Bob Hoskins. But the quote fits."

"I'm sorry. The news didn't say."

Out of sympathy for his condition, Avellone did most of the riding. Everything ached. Everything was sore and bruised. Almost everything. Sex was God's greatest invention, as far as Grant was concerned. It helped take your mind off the problems of life. It helped revitalize you after long international flights. And it relieved pain by focusing your attention on something else. It was the equivalent of stamping on your toe to divert your attention from a broken finger.

Avellone diverted Grant's attention. Big-time.

THE SHOWER WASN'T AN option today. She helped him undress and put his jeans and T-shirt in a laundry bag outside the door. The orange jacket she dusted off and hung on a coat hanger. If this was a game of doctors and nurses, then she was the nurse and this was bath time.

She spread a towel on the bed and had him lie on his stomach. There was a small bowl under the sink. She filled it with hot water and set it beside the bed with a bar of scented soap and a sponge. The sponge was hers. Grant didn't ask where she kept it. The matchbook condom pack was open on the bedside table.

She soaped his back and shoulders. Most of the shrapnel cuts were on his front. Gentle hands, lubricated by scented foam, worked the band of muscles all the way from his shoulder blades to his No Entry sign. They were hard and tight, giving him core strength that meant if he planted himself firmly nobody was going to throw him over.

Her hands cleaned the sign, teased his buttocks, then slid beneath him to clean something else. He groaned with pain as much as pleasure. She was kneeling astride him and he could feel the flesh of her thighs clamped tight around him. He could only imagine what she was wearing. He'd bet it involved a smile.

She slapped his ass. "Turn over."

"You didn't wash behind my ears."

She slapped him harder. "Turn over."

He turned over, rolling onto his back while remaining in position between her thighs. She had stripped down to her stockings and bra and tight black knickers. The stockings were so sheer they felt like velvet skin. The bra was so small her breasts almost spilled over the top. She wet the sponge, worked some soap into it, then leaned forward to wash his chest. Her breasts jiggled enticingly. He couldn't take his eyes off them.

Her stomach was hard and flat. She had plenty of core strength of her own. The muscles in her stomach and lower back kept her upright while she leaned into the job. She was gentler this time. His face was scratched and bruised, but his chest bore only a few signs of the explosion. His stomach and legs were also predominantly free of cuts, although ugly purple bruises showed in places like ink blots. The table had not only saved his life, but it had protected the bulk of him from serious injury.

Her hands slid down his stomach.

She pushed herself back down his legs to allow more room.

Grant closed his eyes. Everything else was sensory overload. He felt her thighs tense as she leaned forward. He felt her breath on his abdomen, warm and inviting. Then something hot and wet enveloped him in that private place, and he forgot the pain. Her tongue worked even though her mouth was full. Her teeth bit gently. She teased and stopped. Teased and stopped. Then he felt her lean over, and he opened his eyes. She flicked the matchbook open and unwrapped a condom.

"Here's a party trick. Don't try this at home, children."

She flicked her tongue out to moisten her lips, and he waited. He didn't know it was possible to put a condom on with no hands. Five minutes later he'd forgotten even that. Some things you had to learn several times before they took root.

"CAN YOU DROP ME at JP station?" He finished brushing his teeth and waited for a reply.

"Sure. No problem."

He rinsed and spat and felt completely rejuvenated. They should give out sex on the national health plan. Americans should be able to get it as part of their health insurance. He noticed the plastic name band on his wrist and remembered what had got him here. Water under the bridge. Now it was time to catch the bastard who'd tried to kill him, even if he had only been collateral damage.

Grant wasn't in a forgiving mood.

He put his toothbrush away and dried his mouth. He didn't spray himself with deodorant. He could still smell Terri Avellone all over him. That was better. A stray thought crossed his mind. Avellone worked for a pharmaceutical company, selling and importing drugs for the hospitals.

This shit ain't my fault. I was just the importer.

Knowing Sullivan, drugs were the most likely commodities he'd be trading in. It was time to start digging. Grant was only a visiting officer with no jurisdiction in the US. The Anglo-Irish thing wouldn't help. Finesse would be needed if he was going to persuade Kincaid to let him tag along. Finesse and a little mild distraction. A look at the station CCTV seemed like a good starting point.

TWELVE

THE CCTV RECORDING was a problem. Kincaid wasn't trained in using the Multiplex system, but Miller was. That meant all three of them sitting in the small back room while they scanned and dissected the view from several cameras around the station until they narrowed it down to one. The problem was that the camera in reception was blank at the time of the bombing.

Grant was standing behind Miller, pressed against the back wall. "Shit. What button did you press?"

Grant was no more technical than Kincaid. Both were hands-on cops, in-the-trenches and get-your-hands-dirty kind of police. Miller was happy to be mixing with such legends of law enforcement. Kincaid had years of service and local history in his favor. Grant was rapidly becoming a media star. Snake Pass had made the national news in America because of the drug baron connection, and the JP explosion had seen his orange jacket front and center on the WCVB news.

Miller tapped a couple of buttons, then pressed Rewind. "It's not the recording."

The blank screen broke up with static. It was the only indication that the image was going backwards. A timer counted down in minutes and seconds. Past the time of the explosion. Still blank.

Then the reception sprang into focus, and Miller pressed Play.

The image was in black and white. The reception desk across the back of the frame and the crowd milling around in the foreground. The interview room door was barely visible on the extreme right of the screen. The front doors weren't shown—they were somewhere behind the camera.

A hand came up fast, and the camera went black.

Grant was about to speak, but Miller was in his element. He was glad of the opportunity to shine. His fingers danced across the controls. Feathering rewind, then play, then slow motion. The reception desk came back on, then slowed down. Sergeant O'Rourke shouted in silence. The other cop spoke patiently to a dark-haired woman. The hand came up slowly. Miller froze the picture.

"There you go." He couldn't keep the pride out of this voice.

Kincaid leaned in for a closer look. "Bastard."

Grant squinted at the screen. "Sly fucking bastard."

The hand was formed into a fist and the fist held a can of spray paint. One burst of the spray and the camera went dead. There was no sign of the artist entering the reception. He was invisible until the single hand came into view.

Grant leaned against the wall. "Camera's pointing the wrong way."

Miller hit Rewind, then paused the image showing the reception desk. "Not really. In-house cameras are for staff protection—assaults and threats at the counter. They aren't for security like burglary CCTV. Cameras point outwards for that, covering points of entry. So, really, they're pointing the right way for what they're supposed to record."

Kincaid patted Miller on the back. It was as much praise as he'd ever received from the veteran detective. He almost blushed. He hoped that Grant was similarly impressed. He was disappointed when the Englishman simply turned and left the room. Kincaid followed. Miller stood up and shouted after them. "What's up? Where you going?"

Grant shouted back. "Where cameras fail, you can't beat the real thing."

Miller tumbled out of the room and raced to catch up.

Kincaid called over his shoulder to his protégé. "Basic rule of crime scenes. Photograph everything, but get down and dirty."

Miller fell in step with the older men. He understood. CCTV might capture the suspect in the act but, failing that, physical evidence was at the scene, not on film. He felt like he was learning every day. He was smiling as he followed the two big men down the stairs.

Grant checked the waste bin in the corner. Sometimes the simplest thing was the obvious mistake. Not this time. He hadn't expected the spray can to be dumped at the scene of the crime, but it was worth a shot. He glanced at Kincaid, but the senior detective was already ahead of him. Kincaid nodded at Miller. "Get uniforms to check every bin for half a mile. All directions."

Miller looked like he wanted to stay where the action was. Grant liked him even more. The young detective did as he was told and went to see the patrol sergeant for manpower. Grant concentrated on the camera. It was high up on the front wall above and to the left of the doors. It was angled down so that its wide-angle lens covered most of the reception.

The lens was black. Paint covered the entire front face of the camera and speckled the wall on either side of it. One quick burst. A direct hit. Some collateral damage—the speckled wall—no reason to touch the camera. No point having it fingerprinted. He glanced at the interview-room door. Kincaid was already looking at it.

The door was half off its hinges because of Kincaid's shoulder charge when he'd been trying to get in. The fire department had barged it open even further. Even so, the door and frame near the lock mechanism was shrouded in fingerprint powder. Nothing but smudges and partials. Grant would be surprised if anybody got identified off them, and even then there were plenty of reasons their prints might be there.

The front door was the same. Grant was pleased to see the BPD were taking care of the fine details. It was the least he expected from the oldest police force in America. The outside and inside surfaces had been powdered; even more smudges and partials. Trouble with fingerprinting a front door was how many people used it during a day, let alone a week. Fingerprints would stay on a surface until they were cleaned off. Someone else using the door would overlay the original print. Multiply that by a hundred, and you didn't have a snowflake in hell's chance of getting an identity. But you had to try. A snowflake in hell's chance was better than no chance. For certain, if you didn't try, you'd lose. Trying gave you options.

Kincaid joined Grant at the front doors. They both looked outside through the dirty glass. Grant focused on Yessenia's Market across the intersection. He was searching for cameras but could only see one. It was on the front wall angled down towards the shop door, facing away from the police station. Kincaid saw where he was looking.

"We checked it. Ruggiero's as well. Nothing obvious. Seized the tapes just in case. Whoever it was came from somewhere. If he passed the market—who knows?"

Grant cocked his head to look round the corner. "The guy with the big hand slapped the window hard."

Kincaid shook his head. "Nothing to print. Blast took it out in pieces."

"No doubt everyone in here's been interviewed?"

"Everyone that stayed. Twice. Nobody saw anything."

"O'Rourke?"

"Same. And the desk cop helping him. They were so busy, Bin Laden could have come in, shit on their heads, and they wouldn't have noticed."

"Or Whitey Bulger?"

"No. Him they'd recognize."

Grant looked towards the front desk. The counter was high and wide and ran the width of the reception. There was a hinged flap and a door to one side. Staff working the desk would be facing the right way, but, like Kincaid said, they'd be heads-down and working hard.

Something glinted in the light from the fluorescents, high up on the far wall. Grant squinted to see what it was, then felt his pulse begin to race. Excitement at discovering fresh evidence had the opposite effect on him than approaching battle. The calmness that descended on him in action worked differently when his mind was the prime mover.

He smiled and tapped Kincaid on the shoulder.

Kincaid smiled too. He raised his voice to a sonic boom. "Miller."

The young detective popped his head out of the patrol sergeant's office. Kincaid pointed at the internal office camera, and Miller blushed to the roots of his hair. Separate camera. Different system. It had only been added three weeks ago, and it pointed towards the front of the office, with the main doors in the background.

The Multiplex room was crowded again. Three men and a sophisticated box of tricks for splitting the images from all the station's cameras, including the one that had recently been added but was not linked to the system yet. Miller had to input it manually. He was still blushing at not having noticed the camera earlier. Grant laid a hand on his shoulder. "Don't worry. I've got your back. Won't tell a soul."

The wide-angle view filled the screen. Office staff worked at their desks. The desk sergeant and his assistant had their backs to the camera. They were busy dealing with the crowded reception beyond the front counter. Miller found the correct time and slowed the tape down. Everyone began to move like they were wading through treacle.

A big guy walked along the sidewalk past the front doors, in the direction of the interview room. At the same time, the front door opened and a shorter figure came into the reception. He wore a baseball cap pulled down over his eyes and a hood pulled up over the cap. In one movement he turned around, sprayed the camera, then walked to the interview-room door.

Grant felt a chill crawl up his spine. He remembered what had been happening inside the room.

Officer Grant. Promise you'll protect my brother. He's nowt to do with this.

Grant leaned back in his chair to give Sullivan some space. He didn't want to crowd him. Keeping his voice conversational, almost friendly, he tried to take the sting out of the situation while still getting an important piece of information.

What you been smuggling, Freddy? Dope again?

Then there had been the slap against the window. He watched the monitor. The hooded figure put the spray can in one pocket and took a round black object out of the other. He listened at the interview-room door. He appeared to hear something inside. His hand came up. He pulled the pin and released the trigger mechanism. The trigger arm flew off. He opened the door immediately and tossed the grenade inside.

Grant gritted his teeth at the memory.

A loud bang on the window snapped his head round. The wired glass splintered. A large hand, fingers splayed, was silhouetted black against the daylight. The door opened. Neither of them noticed until it slammed shut. The nasty black object bounced across the carpet and under the table. Sullivan screamed and stood up so fast he flipped the table forward. Grant recognized the grenade a split second before it exploded, then the world was full of light and pain.

"Replay that bit."

Miller paused the tape, rewound it, then pressed Play. The hooded figure listened at the door. Pulled the pin. Released the trigger, then threw the grenade into the room. He dashed out of the front door just before the explosion shook the camera. Panic and shock flashed on everyone's face. Grant leaned closer to the monitor. "Can you zoom in?"

"Sure." Miller did the finger dance on the controls, and a segment of the image was centered and enlarged. The section with the front doors and the interview room. With the enlarged image came enlarged grain. The picture was fuzzy, blurred.

"Replay."

Miller pressed Play.

Grant was focusing on the figure's hands. Pull the pin. Release the trigger arm. Toss the grenade. One, two, three. Almost simultaneously. Grant nodded and let out a sigh. "Amateur. Not ex-military or mercenary."

Kincaid agreed. "Too quick. No pause to let the fuse count down. Probably saved your life."

Miller looked confused. Grant explained. "Ten-second fuse. You drop a grenade in a gun emplacement, you don't want them having time to toss it back out. Count to five, then throw it. Boom. No time to react."

Kincaid elaborated. "No time for Sullivan to flip the table in panic."

"Boom."

They fell silent. It was easy to be flippant with the cushion of time. It was more difficult so soon after the event. Freddy Sullivan had been blown to pieces. Even if they didn't like him, he was still flesh and blood. Miller broke the silence. "We'd better search the reception again. He didn't pick up the trigger arm."

Another pat on the back from Kincaid. A smile from Grant. He was liking this kid more every time he met him. Miller continued. "And he wasn't wearing gloves."

Kincaid stepped back to clear the door. "Go to it."

Miller stepped into the corridor and headed for the stairs. Kincaid leaned against the Multiplex console and examined Grant's face. "Drop a grenade in a gun emplacement? Thought you were a typist."

"I was. You read my statement, didn't you?"

"I did."

"There you go, then."

A crackle of radio static filled the small room. Kincaid took the radio out of his inside pocket. The jacket resumed its normal shape. The static became words. Grant heard a call sign he didn't recognize. Kincaid did. Ignoring radio protocol, he spoke in plain English. Grant was beginning to like the big detective too. Kincaid pressed the Transmit button. "Go ahead. What you got?"

"Better get over to West Roxbury. They found your boy."

"Who?"

"Sullivan's brother."

"Give me the address. I'll be right over."

The dispatcher gave him the address but didn't stop with that. "Better bring the artillery. Boy's dug in deeper than a tick in a dog's ass."

Kincaid acknowledged. He glanced at the English cop but didn't speak. They both knew that Grant would be riding along. Grant wasn't sure he liked the idea of that. He hated guns.

THIRTEEN

The address in West Roxbury was an apartment above Parkway Auto Repair on VFW Parkway, just across the tracks from Home Depot. It wasn't Sean Sullivan's registered address, but his boss let him stay there as a favor to the boy whose brother was connected to people the boss didn't want to mess with. The number plate–pressing plant was out back behind the Mobil gas station. It had proved to be a handy arrangement until the world descended on the apartment like Armageddon.

The world included BPD uniform and detectives, an army of SWAT officers, the police helicopter, and a squadron of news choppers providing eye-in-the-sky views for twenty-four-hour news channels. The media circus was only just deploying by the time Kincaid and Grant pulled into the dusty triangular turn-in for the road opposite. The single-lane blacktop led to the sports fields beside the railroad tracks. The road was now choked with squad cars, a mobile forward command center, and the SWAT truck. Grant thought it looked like they were about to assault Iwo Jima. "Jesus. What'd he do, shoot the president?"

"Don't even joke about that."

Kincaid looked deadly serious. Grant lowered his voice to a stage whisper. "What—they got feds behind every tree now?"

"Not the feds. And not the trees. Every blade of grass. Anyone even farts a threat at the president, and they'll be in your life like straw through horse shit."

"And horse shit rolls downhill. I get it."

"No, you don't. Since 9/11, you check out a bomb-making book or stray into the wrong website, and they'll flop you lower than whale shit."

"Okay. I get the picture. What I'm saying is, Sean Sullivan ain't no terrorist. He's a scared kid whose brother just got splattered on the ceiling of an official building. Maybe he's not too sure which side the BPD is on."

"That's stupid."

"I know the Sullivans. Stupid's a family tradition."

A helicopter swooped low overhead, the thumping blades drowning out any conversation. Higher up, two more choppers circled, trying to beat each other to the money shot, the best angle on the ramshackle auto shop and its dusty parking lot. A uniform cop ran across the road beneath the railroad bridge on the right to string yellow crime-scene tape and stop any civilian traffic. A hundred yards to the left, another cop did the same.

Grant felt a shiver run down his spine, but it wasn't anticipation of forthcoming action. It was the street sign on the meridian between the twin lanes of the VFW. The full name was Veterans of Foreign Wars Parkway. He had to remind himself that he'd only been a typist. Some days he was harder to convince.

The helicopter drifted west along the unmade road to the sports fields. There were two baseball diamonds and a football pitch with secondary markings for soccer and three tennis courts. The hedgerow was neatly shaped into a WRHS sign from the sky. The camera crew no doubt wanted an angled shot of the armed siege with the more innocent pastime of American sports in the foreground, not to mention the army of cops camped across the twin-lane VFW from the target premises.

Grant concentrated on the target premises.

The Mobil gas station was set back from the road, its gravel and tarmac forecourt dusty and unkempt. The auto repair building was part of the same facility and took up the bulk of the single-story structure—single-story apart from the slope-roofed addition somebody had plonked on top like a bowler hat on a cowboy. The living accommodation looked small and square and functional, with an angled roof and gable ends facing the sides of the garage. There was a dormer window in the front slope of the roof.

Grant quartered the building in his mind, a traditional approach back in West Yorkshire. He wasn't sure what approach the weapon-heavy police presence would adopt in Boston, but he wasn't hopeful. He allocated the separate faces of the building four different colors. Red for the front. Black for the rear. Yellow, left, and green, right. He couldn't see the rear, but he could map out the yellow and green faces by walking ten paces either side of the triangular turn-in. Nothing extraordinary. Couple of windows on the right. A window and wide double doors on the left. The main entrance to the workshops. The front had the payment window and a small grocery tagged on for passing trade. Three fuel pumps under a wide, flat awning with *MOBIL* in big letters.

It was a nightmare of open ground, with explosive consequences for the frontal assault that the SWAT guys were planning. Grant shook his head. He truly did hate guns. This was going to end badly unless somebody showed a modicum of common sense. "Has he shot anybody yet?"

Kincaid shook his head. "Two warning shots in the air. One hit the stoplight for the pedestrian crossing. Caused a bit of a stir."

"You think he hit it on purpose?"

"Better shot than I give him credit for if he did."

Grant craned his neck as if looking over the top of the building. "What's that around the back?"

A tree-lined embankment ran at an angle across the back of the parking lot. Several big, square metal arms stood out above the trees like robot siblings. More than several. Lots of arms with terra-cotta pots and heavy cables. Kincaid followed Grant's gaze. "Electricity substation, then the railroad track beyond that. Behind the trees on the left are half a dozen civilian homes. Traditional—wooden porches, big gardens."

"You got everybody out?"

Kincaid threw Grant a dirty look. "Yeah. BPD knows about stray rounds and crossfire. Cleared the other business premises too."

The other business premises shared the same parking lot. There was a low structure on the right near the entrance from VFW. Grant couldn't make out what it was. A longer two-story building nestled in the trees to the left. It stretched along the parkway and had an employee parking lot with a separate entrance. Behind the gas station was another building that looked like some kind of small factory. There were cars parked outside all three buildings. The side of the auto repair shop was scattered with rusting vehicles they hadn't been able to repair.

Kincaid nudged Grant and pointed at the workshop doors.

"Disgruntled customer wrote a review in the local paper. Said his girlfriend's car wouldn't start after the pump jockey filled it up. Mechanic tried to charge twenty-five dollars to fix the starter. Boyfriend turns up, hits the starter motor with a hammer. Two minutes. Girlfriend's in tears. Said they bullied her into paying."

"He get her money back?"

"Oh yeah. With a hammer."

"Nice place."

"Edge of town before you get into the country. Different rules."

"Keep expecting 'em to start playing 'Dueling Banjos.' Better watch out for the K-Y Jelly and the butt plug."

Grant didn't think his No Entry tattoo would stop the locals fucking him over a fallen tree. He looked over at the black-clad military types loading their weapons behind the mobile command center and the SWAT truck. The hairs prickled up the back of his neck. "These boys look eager."

Kincaid didn't look happy about it. "They do have a certain edge to them, don't they?"

Grant looked at the dormer window of the living quarters. "Sullivan got any hostages?"

"Didn't say."

"But these guys are gonna charge in anyway." It wasn't a question.

Kincaid shrugged. "I'm sure they'll do some tactical assessment first."

"Then they'll charge in." Again, not a question.

"Yes."

The helicopters hovered in the background, but the *thwup, thwup, thwup* of their blades made dramatic music. Cameras angled down on the scene. Waiting.

Grant looked up at them and then at the Parkway Auto Repair. "Have SWAT cut the TV feed and power yet?"

"No. I believe they want him to see what's ranged against him."

"On the news?"

"Twenty-four-hour coverage. They got to fill the airwaves with something."

Grant glanced up at the choppers one more time, then across the dusty parking lot with its automobile graveyard. Open ground. An unprotected killing field. Dust swirled in the gentle breeze. He wouldn't have been surprised if a tumbleweed came rolling across. "We're both police. You know I'll cover for you if needed, right? What I need to know is will you back me?"

"It's the code. Course I will. So long as you don't shoot the president."

"Then can I make a suggestion?"

Grant wasn't sure it was the best idea he'd ever had. The breeze was getting stronger. Dust swirled around his ankles. The trees behind the auto repair center whipped and danced as if warning him off. He was halfway across the parking lot before he saw the deadly Cyclops eye of the rifle through a gap in the curtains. Not the dormer window. Sullivan Junior had obviously moved down into the main living quarters.

Grant stopped in mid-stride. He held his arms out from his sides.

The faded orange windcheater was unzipped. It flapped open in the breeze. A sudden gust blew grit into his eyes, and he had to bring one hand over to protect his face. He coughed the dust out of his mouth and flapped the hand to waft the cloud away. The breeze died down for a moment. The air became still. Grant lowered his arms and stared into the muzzle of a thirty-odd-six rifle.

No, this wasn't the best idea he'd ever had.

The orange jacket made him an easy target. Nobody could miss seeing him coming a mile away wearing that jacket. There could be no sneaking up or trickery while he wore the orange signpost. That was the idea. Grant contended that crooks shot at cops because cops would shoot at them. The best way to avoid getting shot was to pose no threat. The orange windcheater posed no threat. It was so obvious he was coming, even the most trigger-happy gunman should take encouragement from Grant's open and nonthreatening approach.

He started walking again. Past the trio of petrol pumps with their delivery arms holstered like three wise men with one hand on hips. Past a rusty John Deere tractor with one wheel missing, propped up on a pile of bricks. It felt like walking down Ravenscliffe Avenue in Bradford. The only thing missing was a pair of sneakers dangling from the telephone wire by its laces. Judging by the run-down gas station, that was only because there weren't any telephone wires nearby.

As he approached the canopy, he moved to one side so that Sullivan could keep him in view. Grant didn't want to spark a stray shot because he looked like he was trying to sneak under cover. The orange jacket. Bright and in plain sight. He stopped ten feet from the front of the building. The single black eye pointed down at him. The window was partly open. The breeze picked up again, and the curtains twitched. The movement might have unnerved a lesser man, but Grant had slid down into that vortex of calm that prefaced enemy action.

He breathed in through his nose and out through his mouth. One breath. Two.

He looked up at the window. The rifle looked down at him. Nobody moved.

Somewhere among the houses, beyond the trees, a dog barked. Across the embankment and on the other side of the electricity substation, a train rattled along the track. No engine noise, just the gentle rhythm of wheels on iron. The helicopters sounded like they were miles away. Grant could feel their cameras on his back. He could hear the familiar cadence of a newsreader building the story up from a TV through the open window. The wind whipped at Grant's coat. More grit stung his eyes. The pain reminded him of why he was here.

"We stand here like this much longer, Sean, I'm gonna get sandblasted."

The curtain twitched, not with the wind this time. The rifle barrel didn't. It remained steady, pointing right at Grant's chest.

"I know you don't want me climbing through the window. Stray bullet might bust your TV."

Mention of bullets twitched the rifle barrel up towards the massed police vehicles across the road. Then it dipped back down to Grant. He kept his voice calm as he stared at the window. "I'm guessing you've got a personal entrance. For when the place is closed."

Still no words from behind the curtain. Just TV noise and the newsreader commentating on the deadly standoff. Grant played his trump card. "Freddy asked me to look out for you. Don't think this is what he had in mind."

There was a moment's silence at the mention of Sean's big brother. They'd been inseparable as kids and stuck together as adults. Wherever Freddy went, Sean was bound to follow. Even to America. The rifle barrel flicked towards the corner of the workshop. A familiar Yorkshire accent drifted down from the apartment. "Stairs 'round the back. Come alone."

As if Grant had anyone else with him. "Sean. You've been watching too many films. I *am* alone." Then he put his arms down and disappeared around the corner.

CALLING THE ROOM above the garage an apartment was like calling a Pekinese a dog. Strictly speaking it might be true, but in the end size was the difference. It was like all those women who couldn't judge distance because their husbands told them two inches was six. No man ever admitted to having less than a six-inch dick. The apartment was nowhere near six inches.

It wasn't carpeted either. The floorboards creaked as Grant came in through the back door. The room was small and square, but the lack of furniture made it look bigger. There was a two-seater settee and a portable TV on the floor in front of it. That was all. The far wall had a washbasin, an electric cooker, and a refrigerator, all of them small, like the ones sold for mobile homes or caravans. Grant couldn't see any sign of a bed. He reckoned that was upstairs in the dormer attic room. If this room was six inches, the bedroom must be two. Nothing to brag about.

Greasy food and oil smells hung like fog. They were almost a physical barrier holding Grant at the door. He glanced around the apartment and then at the skinny young man pointing a rifle at him loose from the hip.

"I love what you've done with the place. It kind of reminds you of home, doesn't it?"

Grant wasn't joking. He remembered the first time he'd arrested Freddy Sullivan, dragging him out of his mother's house by the scruff of his neck. The house was bigger but no less sparsely furnished. At least it had a carpet, even if your feet did stick to it on your way out.

"This ain't no better than your mum's place back at Ravenscliffe. Only without the home cooking. What the fuck you follow Freddy over here for?"

"You ever tasted Ma's cookin'?"

"Can't say as I have."

"Lucky you."

"Point taken. But why Freddy? You musta known he'd get you in trouble sooner or later."

"He's my brother. Looks out for me."

"Yeah, well. That's why I'm here."

Grant had been trying to talk without breathing, but the smell was getting to him now. He glanced at the window overlooking the parking lot. "Mind if we let some air in? Forgot my oxygen mask."

He walked to the window and paused with one hand under the sash.

Sullivan tensed. The rifle quivered. "Don't do nothin' stupid, constable."

Grant flicked his eyes towards the TV on the floor. The parking lot outside Parkway Auto Repair hovered on the screen, then the news crew replayed shots of Grant in his orange jacket, arms held out like Jesus on the cross. Then there were images of black-clad cops with rifles and shotguns lined up across the hoods of half a dozen police cars. "I think you got stupid covered, Sean."

He yanked the window all the way open and waved through the gap. Live footage suddenly snapped him back on TV. The man in the orange jacket waved out of the window. The scene intercut with shots of the SWAT officers training their weapons on the window. Grant gave a thumbs-up sign and waved them back. The rifles appeared to relax, sagging on flexed wrists across the vehicle hoods.

Grant stood with his back to the window. He didn't want some sniper lining up a shot if Sullivan came into view. This was a situation that could easily get out of hand. "Polite thing would be to offer me a drink."

He glanced at the grease-encrusted cooker. "Just nothing you need to make on that."

Sullivan let the rifle hang from his arms but still roughly in Grant's direction. Whatever fight he had displayed when the police arrived evaporated now. Having someone from back home to talk to appeared to help. That was good. He looked at the Yorkshire copper but didn't smile. This wasn't a smiling situation. "Polite thing ain't to disparage a man's home."

"I'm not disparaging it, Sean. I'm protecting my life."

Sullivan raised the rifle. "You think?"

"You're not going to shoot me over a greasy cooker, are you? Not with the marines outside waiting to storm the place."

"I didn't do nothin'."

"That's a double negative. Means you did something."

"No, I didn't."

"You shot a traffic light."

"Weren't aiming for it."

"You'd better keep that thing aimed at me then. Safest place for me to stand."

The helicopters throbbed in the distance. A strengthening breeze began to whistle through the window and gaps in the rear door. The floorboards creaked as Grant shifted the weight from his left leg to his right. Standing for a long time was an art. He'd learned it doing overnight guard duty in the army. Even typists had to pull their share of guard duty. He glanced around the room, noting the one thing that was missing. "You know, if you're gonna pull this armed siege shit, keep 'em at bay while you negotiate for a million dollars and a car to the airport. You really shouldn't forget the hostage."

"Hostage?"

"The only reason they didn't shoot your ass right at the beginning."

Sullivan's finger tightened on the trigger. "Got one now, though, don't I?"

"What you've got so far is damage to a traffic light. That'll get you more jail time than shooting me. This is Boston. Place is overrun with Micks. They'd be glad to shoot me themselves. BPD don't give a shit. They aren't going to negotiate with you to let me go."

"They're calling you the Resurrection Man."

Grant was confused. "The BPD?"

"The news."

They both looked at the TV. The news had gone back to the studio, where a woman with more makeup than Liberace smiled across the desk at a man so tanned he looked like he'd been creosoted. He grinned back at the woman. Insincerity dripped from the screen. In the background they replayed footage of Grant being wheeled to the ambulance at E-13, his orange jacket fizzing off the screen. Then they showed him walking across the parking lot towards the lone sniper, his arms held out like Jesus on the cross. The woman's voice was sickly sweet. The words *resurrection man* featured several times, driving home the point.

Sullivan's shoulders sagged. The strain finally showed on his face. He moved to put the rifle down on the settee, but Grant held a hand up to stop him. "Better keep hold of that for now."

He jerked a thumb at the TV. "Don't want them catching you with your pants down and the cavalry charging in before we get this sorted out."

Sullivan kept hold of the rifle, but there was no threat left. He indicated the refrigerator with his eyes. "Got cold beer if you'd like."

"Now you're talking. I'd love a cold beer."

Sullivan walked to the kitchen area. Grant stayed where he was, blocking the window with his back. The orange windcheater filled the TV screen. The Resurrection Man. Sullivan came back with two cans of light beer. He tugged the ring pull, and the friendly *pffft* noise punctured the tension. He handed one to the Yorkshire policeman.

Grant tilted his head and took a deep swig. He closed his eyes and let out a sigh. The beer was crap, but it was cold and wet. After the sandstorm outside, cold and wet was good enough. He held the can in one hand and rolled it gently across his forehead. Condensation cooled his brow. After a few seconds he took another drink, smaller this time, then he put added friendliness in his voice. "Now then. What was Freddy up to, got us into this mess?"

FOURTEEN

THEY WERE ON their third beer each by the time Grant decided that Sullivan had no idea what his big brother had been up to. It took that long because there were no straight answers in the Sullivan family. They had never answered a direct question back in Bradford, so why should Grant expect it to change just because they'd relocated to Boston, Massachusetts?

Sullivan took a sip from his can, making it last. The fridge was empty. "I'd be more worried about watching your back than what Freddy was up to."

Grant subconsciously glanced behind him out the window. His orange jacket still blocked the view from outside. He could almost feel the dozen or so rifles trained on his back. "Come on, Sean. You must have had some idea."

"Nope. He might have been a bad lad, but he kept his baby brother out of it." Moisture formed in Sullivan's eyes at the memory of the brother he would never see again. Family ties were strong in the criminal fraternity. If you were pond life, you stuck together to protect your lily pad. Bottom feeders understood the importance of family more acutely than those who were better off. It was often the only help they had. It appeared that Freddy Sullivan was looking out for his little brother right to the end.

Officer Grant. Promise you'll protect my brother. He's nowt to do with this.

"He said he was just the importer."

"Then I guess he was just the importer."

"But importing what? My first choice is drugs. It's what he's got form for."

Sullivan shook his head. "He ain't got no shame, I give you that. But he was clean from that business years ago. Anyway, they got more drugs than you can shake a stick at in America. Why'd they want to import some from England?"

"What then?"

"Beats me, officer."

"He said, 'This shit ain't my fault.'"

"Then it ain't."

"But what shit?"

"Don't know."

"Best guess—you've been around him long enough. What kind of stuff did he mess with?"

Sullivan took another sip. This last beer was going to last an eternity. "He liked guns and blowing shit up."

"Blowing shit up?"

"Yeah. Bang, bang, boom, boom."

Grant shifted the weight from one leg to the other. It had been a long time since he'd last done guard duty. Standing for a long time was beginning to make his back ache and his legs stiffen. The pain from the explosion settled in again. "He wasn't doing bank robberies?"

"No, more like target practice. He had some fancy putty stuff. He liked setting it off by shooting at it in the woods over by the pond."

"There's that Irish heritage for you. You can take the boy out of the IRA, but you can't take the IRA out of the boy."

"He weren't never in the IRA."

"Figure of speech."

Grant thought about the collection jar in Flanagan's. The continued fundraising even though the conflict was over. Maybe some of the arms they had supplied were coming back into the country. That would need somebody with Irish connections and a UK passport. Perhaps it didn't stop at exploding putty and firearms. Perhaps it extended to bar fights and hand grenades. "Who was he hanging with these days?"

"Oh, no. I'm not getting into that."

"What d'you mean?"

"I mean that who he was hanging with got him killed. I'm having nothing to do with 'em."

"Not your choice anymore."

They both sipped beer in unison, then stared at each other. A moment of clarity entered the room, and for the first time they appeared to be on the same page. It was Sean Sullivan who voiced what Grant had been thinking, though.

"Did you ever wonder how come you was in the front interview room?"

Grant played devil's advocate. "Busy night in the cells."

"It was a busy night in the cells because a bunch of Irishmen started a bar fight and torched a building."

"So?"

"So. You think that was a coincidence? These people can organize anything. They got men would cap their own mothers, given the word. So what's a few bruises and a torched building if it gets Freddy where they want him?"

Just what Grant had been wondering but couldn't quite believe. "Pity about Flanagan's. Served a nice pint."

"It wasn't Flanagan's. Fight started there. They aren't going to torch their own place. 'Twas the empty place across the street. Result was the same. Flood the police station with prisoners. Force you into the front room. Boom, boom."

Grant felt a shiver run down his spine. The thought of being manipulated made him angry. The thought that somebody was powerful enough to pull the strings gave him pause. This was bigger than the burglary at Patel's he'd come to interview Freddy Sullivan about. You didn't get killed because of some cigarettes and a few quid from the corner shop.

Sullivan watched the Yorkshire copper's face. "I'd be more worried about watching your back if I was you."

"That's the second time you've said that."

"Glad to see you can still count."

"To say Freddy kept you out of his shit, you're a cheeky little fuck."

"Watch your back. You see *The Departed*?"

"I prefer *Dirty Harry*."

"More clear-cut. I can understand that. But you've seen it, right?"

Grant knew what Sullivan was getting at. "You think I've got a rat in my crew?"

"Jack Nicholson channeling his inner Whitey Bulger. Yeah. But not a rat in his crew. The other rat."

"Matt Damon?" Grant didn't believe it. That sort of stuff only happened in movies and crime fiction. In real life nobody got bribed and most cops just wanted to catch bad guys. Some got lazy and some weren't as committed to fighting the good fight, but none of them were bent. Not in the real world. Not in Yorkshire.

But he wasn't in Yorkshire.

Sullivan watched realization dawn on Grant's face. "See?"

Grant asked the obvious question. "Who?"

"I have no fuckin' clue. I just know these people have fingers in everything."

Grant squared his shoulders. "Like the boy with his finger in the dyke."

"Not exactly."

"Yes, exactly. Lots of holes. Lots of fingers. Well, I'm going to cut one of them off. Then the dyke'll come tumbling down."

"You think?"

"I know."

"Well, know this. They killed Freddy 'cause of what he knew. They got to figure he told you. Like I said. Watch your back."

The TV news played in the background, but Grant tuned the commentary out. He saw his own back filling the screen as if to emphasize Sullivan's words. Across the parking lot a dozen rifles took aim. The news choppers hovered. The zoom lenses remained focused on the window above Parkway Auto Repair.

Grant finished the last of his beer and crushed the can in one hand. "Same goes for you. Get you in a cell—who watches your back?"

Sullivan drained his can and dropped it on the floor. Both hands tightened around the rifle. It wasn't sagging towards the floor any more; it was pointed square at Grant's chest. "No cell for me. The airport and outta the country. I got a hostage. Remember."

"The Resurrection Man. Remember?"

Grant dropped the crushed can. It bounced off his foot and scuttled across the floorboards. Sullivan couldn't help but watch it out of the corner of his eye. Grant took half a pace to his right. The orange jacket slid to one side on the TV screen. In the background was a shadowy figure pointing a rifle at the unarmed man. Grant raised his arms out to his sides, like Jesus on the cross. The TV caught that too.

"Sean. Don't do anything stupid now. I ain't no traffic light."

"I lied. I did aim for that damn blinker."

"Good shot, then. Congratulations. Still only criminal damage, though."

"Safest thing for you, officer, is to come on the plane with me."

"Don't think they want me back home just yet."

"Snake Pass. Right. You kicked some serious arse there, didn't you?"

"Wasn't my intention."

"Things don't always work out the way we hope, do they?"

The helicopters' throbbing rotors seemed a thousand miles away. The wind grew stronger. It whistled through the gap in the back door and ruffled the curtains behind Grant. He sidled another half step to his right. The TV cameras zoomed in. The orange-clad figure stood like the crucifixion. The man with the rifle tightened his grip. You could see it right there on TV. Across the nation. Live.

Grant kept any confrontation out of his voice. "Most crooks only shoot at cops because they know the cops are going to shoot at them. That's my theory anyway."

"Your point is?"

"I hate guns. Never carry one."

"Thought you was in the army?"

"I was a typist. Deadly with a four-letter word. Not a gun."

"Good for you."

"You know I'm not armed."

The silence and swishing curtains faded as the helicopter noise swelled. They weren't coming closer; it was just his senses becoming more finely tuned as action approached. It was always that way for Grant. He didn't know if it was working for Sullivan.

"I ain't going to shoot you."

Grant stood very still, his arms as solid as the electricity pylons out back. "That's not the way it looks on TV."

Sullivan glanced at the portable television on the floor. He appeared shocked to see himself on the breaking newsfeed. Grant watched him realize what a dangerous position he was in. That was the plan. Next stage was to talk him into putting the rifle down and taking a walk in the dust together outside. Somebody else had other plans.

Three shots rang out almost simultaneously.

Sullivan's chest exploded out of his back, taking six ribs and a section of spine with it. The look of surprise on his face would have been comical if it weren't so tragic. Two brothers down in less than twenty-four hours. The fourth shot was unnecessary and blasted him backwards over the settee. He was dead before he hit the floor.

Grant lowered his arms.

The ringing in his ears dulled the noise of the helicopters. There was no smell of cordite to accompany the destruction. No shot had been fired in the apartment that was really a Pekinese. No man ever admitted to having less than a six-inch dick. No man ever wanted to admit being stupid. Sullivan had paid the price for his vanity.

Grant wondered if he'd been stupid too.

I'd be more worried about watching your back if I was you.

He turned and looked out of the window. Twelve rifles pointed in through the opening. Twelve men in black knelt behind the patrol cars parked in the dusty turn-in across VFW Parkway. One man stood out from the crowd. A hulking figure looking straight at the man in the orange jacket.

Sam Kincaid locked eyes with Grant and nodded.

Grant didn't nod back.

PART TWO

Secret is, when it's raining shit, get a shit umbrella. Deflect the shit so you can get the job done.

—Jim Grant

FIFTEEN

THEY DEBRIEFED GRANT at Boston Police Headquarters at One Schroeder Plaza downtown. The third-floor conference room was blue and grey. It was bigger than the report-writing room at Ecclesfield Police Station back home and roomier than the entire custody suite at Jamaica Plain station. It said everything about the modern police service that Grant hated. Top-heavy with brass and admin facilities and narrow-based in the trenches.

The mahogany conference table took up half the room and could have landed jet fighters. Comfortable chairs were arranged all the way around it. The far side of the room had three rows of less comfortable chairs facing a podium and a drop-down screen on the wall. The left-hand side was all glass. A picture window replaced the wall and looked northeast towards Back Bay and Beacon Hill. The expensive part of town. It was no surprise that the bosses got that view while the frontline cops lived at ground level. In the valley. Shit view for the shit collectors.

Grant had driven down with Kincaid. He hadn't spoken much. Kincaid appeared to understand. That close to a shooting, most people needed time to adjust. Grant tried not to be too obvious about it. He'd made a big thing about at least not getting blood on his favorite jacket and spoke only when spoken to but other than that had kept tight-lipped. The SWAT officers had traveled en masse. Just like in the army, the infantry always stuck together. Uniform patrol officers made up the rest, and a lone secretary to take notes.

Now they were all in the same room, but even then they fell neatly into three groups. Patrol, SWAT, and plainclothes. If they could have split it down further, then Grant would have been in a group of his own. English visitor versus Irish Americans. He could feel the enmity oozing like sweat from everybody except Kincaid. That threw up its own problem. Kincaid was Grant's only ally in the room, but Grant wasn't sure about the big detective.

He thought about the interview.

He thought about the grenade.

He thought about who had argued strongest to let Grant use the insecure front interview room instead of waiting for the ones in the custody area.

And he thought about Sean Sullivan.

I'd be more worried about watching your back if I was you.

The district commander from E-13 called the room to order. He'd been in charge at the scene and was in charge of the debrief. The chief of police wouldn't get involved unless mistakes had been identified and only then if he needed to apportion blame and deflect the press. The press were already all over the story. It was big news. The second coming of the Resurrection Man. That didn't sit well with Anglo-Irish relations either. The chief made a cutthroat sign across his throat for the secretary not to record anything yet.

"Okay. Let's get one thing straight. This was a clean shoot."

There was a murmur of approval.

"They said so on TV, so it must be true."

A smattering of laughter.

"But let's not forget what got us into this mess. Some fuckwit with a gun shooting at cops in the street."

Grant felt his hackles rise. His patented calming technique worked in reverse when his bullshit detector kicked in. It always kicked in when the bosses started shit spreading. He waited all of three seconds before he abandoned restraint and spoke his mind. "He shot a traffic light."

"That's a traffic signal, me lad."

"Not a cop, though, is it?"

"I didn't say a marksman with a gun. Same general direction as cops in the street is close enough for me."

A murmur and a smattering of laughter. Somebody clapped briefly. The man with the gold braid on his cap leaned both elbows on the podium. "And let's not forget the other reason the shit hit the fan. The Resurrection Man walking in there like Jesus fucking Christ and forcing officers to take the shot."

"Sullivan was going to hand the rifle over."

"Didn't look like that on TV."

Grant couldn't argue. He'd said as much to Sullivan. The chief indicated the three shooters sitting apart from the rest of the SWAT.

"And it didn't look like that to the officers entrusted with protecting your life."

No murmur this time. The room fell silent apart from the chief. "A life that was only at risk once you went inside, since the subject didn't have a hostage up until that point. When a respected and decorated BPD detective made the suggestion."

Kincaid appeared to shrug off the criticism. You needed broad shoulders to bear the weight of service. Most of the weight came from above, not outside.

Despite Grant's reservations, he didn't like the bosses shifting the blame to the guys in the trenches. "You were mobile command at the scene."

The chief pushed off from the podium and stood erect. Grant continued. "So the decision was yours. You saw a way of ending the siege without any of your officers being at risk. Just some mad fuck Englishman, and what's to lose there, right?"

There were other things to be said, but this wasn't the place to say them. Things that Sullivan had suggested before he was shot. Grant didn't hold with conspiracy theories so he didn't see Sullivan being killed as a way of silencing whatever he knew about his brother. For the bad guys, you'd have to say it was very convenient, though. Life was rarely convenient; mostly, chaos reigned.

The chief regained his composure. "We're going to lose you anyway. With both Sullivans dead, there's nothing to detain you further. Be sure to say goodbye before you leave."

Grant felt the weight of opinion was on the chief's side. He glanced around the room and couldn't find a single friendly face. It surprised him because his view had always been different. If you were part of the emergency services, whether it be the police, ambulance, or fire department, you were brothers. Army, navy, or air force: same thing. He'd never understood the rivalry between army and navy. He'd never understood the antagonism between police and fire, especially in America. Didn't they all shed the same blood in the Twin Towers? There was no arguing against it in Boston, where the Anglo-Irish mix gave the debate added spice.

The chief waved down the smattering of applause and laughter and brought the room to order. He nodded to the secretary to begin recording the meeting.

"Informal proceedings over. Let's get down to business. Individual reports from each branch of the operation, starting with the first officers on the scene—over to you."

The debrief proceeded. Each part of the operation was discussed. There would be an IAD investigation into the shooting later, but this was simply to get the facts straight for the official report. Grant took a backseat to the sworn officers of the BPD. He went over to the water cooler and filled a paper cup. The view out of the window was breathtaking, but he wouldn't be sorry to leave it behind. The holiday assignment had proved to be anything but a vacation. He was sick to the back teeth of listening to bosses protecting their careers and Internal Affairs sticking the knife into the frontline cops. As he stood beside the water cooler, what he saw was the filing trays at Ecclesfield Police Station.

"I WANT TO lock crooks up."

Jamie Hope kept his voice low. He looked uncomfortable as Grant put his tie and epaulettes in the clerical tray and prepared to leave for the last time.

"You will. Got to keep your job long enough first, though. What did I tell you about stab vests?"

Hope smiled. "They cover both sides for the bosses stabbing you in the back."

"That's right." Grant pushed the tray closed and turned back to Hope.

"Don't stick your head above the parapet until you know it's safe."

Hope nodded. "I'll remember that. But you'll be back soon, won't you?"

Grant thought about lying but decided on being vague instead. "We'll see."

Out in the car park, smoke drifted in the cold night air. From the unofficial smokers' corner beside the dog kennels, Inspector Carr, the D&C bulldog, stubbed his cigarette out on the floor. His gold fillings caught the light again as he grinned. "Warrant card?"

Grant took a step towards the D&C inspector. "I've been suspended, not sacked. I keep my warrant card."

Carr took one step backwards to preserve his personal space. "For now."

Grant struggled to keep his anger in check. To remain calm on the outside despite being pissed off on the inside. He wasn't completely successful as he took another step towards Inspector Carr. "For always. And if I find out you've gone after PC Hope, they won't find your teeth with a metal detector."

"Still protecting the weak, eh, Grant?"

"Still backing my colleagues. You should try it sometime."

He turned away from the D&C inspector and got into his car. It was late and the realization was finally setting in that tonight he was no longer a policeman. There was only one place to mourn that, so he turned left out of the driveway and headed towards the Woodlands Truck Stop and Diner at Snake Pass.

"You want a lift back to the Seaverns?"

Grant shook his head. He needed some fresh air. The debriefing had finished twenty minutes ago, and it had taken that long for him to get the anger out of his system. Not at the way they'd painted Sean Sullivan as some kind of low-level crook—because that's pretty much what the Sullivan family was, a nest of petty crooks—but at the part he'd played in the younger brother's downfall. If he hadn't walked in there like Jesus walking on water, there'd have been no need to shoot him. Having said that, if Sullivan hadn't decided to hold off the police with a thirty-odd-six, they wouldn't have had to shoot him either.

The Resurrection Man. That name certainly hadn't applied to the Sullivan brothers. Just the man in the orange windcheater, arms held out like the crucifixion. The name was going to dog him for the rest of his stay, he could sense that. Coming out of the conference room had proved it. A faceless uniform shouting across the corridor: "They'll be checking your hands for stigmata next."

Grant hadn't risen to the bait. He'd simply stalked off down the stairs, ignoring the bank of elevators, and out the front door. Kincaid was lighting a cigarette around the corner from the main entrance. It was the first time he'd noticed the big detective smoking. It was surprising the things you learned about someone if you waited long enough.

"You sure about the lift? No problem."

"I'll take the T. Thanks."

He walked to Ruggles Station around the corner. Moving traffic on the main road became parked cars in the back street. Big cars. Gas guzzlers. The low price of petrol was one of the few benefits of visiting America, if he had a car, but the price of petrol wasn't

Grant's primary concern as he walked, head down, along the back streets to the T. It was the Sullivan brothers and some of their pearls of wisdom.

This long in the nick, they ain't gonna believe I said nowt. I'm dead.

That had been Freddy, five minutes before his squashed eyeball had been plastered on the ceiling. Said nowt about what? What could the ex-Ravenscliffe burglar know that was so important? And if whoever killed him thought he'd spoken about it, who did they think he'd spilled the beans to? The Resurrection Man.

I'd be more worried about watching your back if I was you.

Sean this time. A warning about the inside man who'd set Grant up with the insecure interview room. It could also be taken a different way. If the person pulling the strings thought Freddy had spoken out of turn, what would he do about the man he spoke out of turn to—the Resurrection Man?

He shook his head as he walked. That argument didn't hold water. If Freddy Sullivan had divulged incriminating evidence to the cop interviewing him, there'd be no point killing the cop. The information would already be in the system, on file with the BPD and any other agency with access to their records. It would make no sense.

Grant climbed the stairs into the darkness of the transport hall. It had been a long day, and he hadn't realized how late it was. Dusk settled over Boston. The lights were on inside, but there weren't many people milling around. It wasn't rush hour. There were just a handful of passengers, some traveling individually and some in groups. A smattering of conversation and laughter echoed around the hall. Grant checked the map on the wall. The orange line. He selected the southbound platform, then bought a token.

His mind was still playing with the possibilities as he descended to the platform. Nobody was going to start killing cops. It was the single biggest mistake anyone could make. Cop killers got hunted to extinction. It was a unifying factor that would draw together all the warring factions of the emergency services. No more army versus navy games. No more police versus fire rivalry. They would all pull together to get a cop killer. That was human nature. If someone was willing to kill a cop, then they'd be capable of killing anyone. Public enemy number one.

He dismissed the possible threat as not credible.

The crowd thinned once he reached the platform. Just a couple of women up at the far end. Three scruffy-looking guys talking near the stairs. Half a dozen individual males and females waiting patiently for the next train. Like any station on the London Underground. Like any platform on the Paris Metro. The evening sky outside was sliding from blue to dark blue. The track began to hum. The next train was coming.

He stepped towards the edge of the platform.

Nobody was going to start killing cops.

Unless the cop got killed in a fatal accident.

The humming grew louder, accompanied by an ever-growing rattle and shake of wheels on track. Sparks lanced into the gloom like fireflies in the distance. Then closer. The chatter stopped. The expectant crowd moved towards the edge of the platform and spread along its length. Grant sensed movement behind him. The train came into view around the distant curve in the track.

Dusk crawled down into night. It came early this time of year.

The rattle and shake became a solid noise. The train was a greyed-out silver tube hurtling towards him. Interior lights glowed yellow in the darkness. Grant looked down at the track. The wooden cross supports were splintered and worn. Oil and dirt stained the aggregate, turning the big grey stones into chunks of coal. His mind went back to a suicide he'd once dealt with in Bradford. A manic depressive who'd waited all night in the tunnel coming out from the station, smoking himself to death while he built up courage to step in front of the first train of the morning. They'd found his feet three hundred yards from his brains. The rest of him had been spread over the distance between the two. Just like Freddy Sullivan, with one hand on the floor and his eyeball on the ceiling.

The noise became deafening. The train was speeding into Ruggles Station. The squeal of brakes filled the night. Sparks exploded from the track and the wheel arches. He glanced around him at the waiting passengers.

Nobody met his eye. They were all looking at the arriving train.

The edge of the platform was twelve inches from his feet.

The brakes slowed the onrushing metal tube.

A metallic voice announced the arrival of the train to Forest Hills, calling at… The voice trotted out a list of stations, including Green Street. It was the right train. He never got on the wrong train. Warm air was displaced ahead of the lead carriage. A surge of forward passenger movement was barely contained. Just like the London Underground. Just like the Paris Metro. Impatience trumping common sense. There was plenty of room.

The train was still moving fast.

It was almost at the start of the platform.

Grant felt a sharp nudge in his back.

Sparks flew. The brakes squealed. Grant spun around fast. One hand formed into a fist and the other prepared to fend off the attack. Something clattered on the floor. A shadowy figure crouched sharply, fast but not fast enough. Grant's open hand flashed out just in time to—

He stopped as quickly as he'd started. The woman bent and picked up the cell phone she'd dropped on the platform. She apologized, and Grant swiftly picked the phone up for her. The train stopped. The doors opened. The crowd melted away as it separated into the several carriages that made up the length of the T.

Nobody was going to start killing cops.

Unless the cop got killed in a fatal accident.

Grant settled into a forward-facing seat and dismissed the speculation as the effects of a hard day that had seen two brothers killed and more questions raised than answers given.

The doors closed and the train moved off. Slow and even. The gentle swaying of the carriage was relaxing, the sparks outside less fierce. He settled in for the short journey. Four stops. It should be uneventful after the excitement of the day.

When he looked into the glaring eyes of the man in front of him, Grant realized he was wrong.

SIXTEEN

The man with the staring eyes was wearing a stained T-shirt and khaki combat pants. The stains looked like vomit and dribble down the front, wiped clean as best he could. The combat pants were crumpled and faded and looked like they'd covered a lot of miles. He wore scuffed black leather boots that might have come from an army surplus store a long, long time ago.

Grant breathed in through his mouth and out through his nose.

Gently.

Twice.

He didn't need to glance around the carriage to get his bearings; he'd already done that before he sat down. The layout was simple. Long silver tube with sliding doors on either side at both ends and in the middle. No connecting door between carriages. Seating was traditional tubular steel and preformed seats and backs. They were arranged in double rows facing forward, with matching double rows facing backwards behind them. There was a single seat on either side of the doors with its back to the wall, facing inwards.

The man with the wild eyes was sitting in the side seat in front of Grant.

The rest of the carriage was sparsely populated. A woman with a young girl sat farther down on the left, facing the front of the train. Another woman, on her own, was sitting on the other side facing Grant. She looked older and was fiddling with something in a shopping bag. She kept looking over at Grant, then back down into her bag. A teenage boy in an NFL shirt and a baseball cap sat with earphones behind Grant but on the other side. His eyes were dull and listless as he listened to whatever was pumping into his ears. The three scruffy guys were sitting at the very back of the carriage, facing front.

Nobody immediately behind Grant. There was a minimum buffer zone of two rows of seats or the center aisle in any direction apart from the front, but he wasn't facing any threat from that direction.

The threat was the man with the wild eyes.

Grant studied him. He didn't hide the fact. It was often the best way to discourage an attack, staring down the opposition and letting them know you weren't afraid. Any sign of weakness could trigger a predator. Grant never displayed a sign of weakness. His eyes flicked over the man, making mental notes in case he needed them later.

Under six feet tall. Slim but not skinny. Gaunt features and pale skin. Not been out in the fresh air and sunshine much lately. Unshaven but not a beard. Greasy black hair cut short but still long enough to be scruffy. The sleeves of the T-shirt were long and baggy but couldn't hide the large white patch stuck to the upper arm, like a quit-smoking patch, only bigger. His right forearm was bandaged from wrist to elbow. The other wrist wore a loose white plastic nametag. Grant subconsciously stroked his own wrist, but the hospital wristband wasn't there anymore. The combat pants were snug fitting. They didn't have a belt. The boots didn't have laces.

The eyes were alternately angry and staring, then dull and listless. When they were angry, he was glaring at Grant. When they became dull and listless, he was staring into space towards the back of the carriage. The patch on his upper arm said he was hiding something. The bandages and lack of belt and laces said that whatever he was hiding made him more of a risk to himself than to others. Suicidal types weren't usually aggressive. They were usually insular and depressed and unable to cope with life outside their own little bubble.

This guy looked like his bubble had burst. He was the exception that proved the rule. This guy was aggressive, and he was building up to doing something about it. The darting eyes became more pronounced. Staring first at Grant, then at the teenager with the earphones, and finally beyond Grant towards the rear of the carriage. It was a quick-fire staccato cycle that became faster the angrier he got. He was getting pretty angry.

Grant relaxed his hands and arms. He flexed his neck and continued to breathe evenly. He watched for the added twitch that would signal the man changing from passive aggression to enemy action. Everybody had one—a subconscious giveaway that was almost impossible to hide. You just had to know how to recognize it. Grant had plenty of practice. He watched everything. The guy's hands lay open in his lap. His feet tapped erratically on the floor. His eyes went through their staccato cycle. Grant. The teenager. The back of the carriage.

The feet stopped tapping.

Grant prepared for the parry.

The eyes locked on Grant for a second, then darted away. Then he lunged.

The head fake didn't fool Grant. He was on his feet almost before the angry man made his lunge. The legs inside the combat pants were strong. They propelled him up and forwards at incredible speed. The hands were relaxed as they flashed up.

Grant was faster. So fast that he had time to stop when he realized the man wasn't lunging at him. The triple click of three switchblades flicking out snapped Grant's attention behind him and he saw the reflections in the window before he saw the men themselves. The three scruffy guys from the back seat, knives in hand, coming for Grant's unprotected back.

Everything else happened in less than five seconds.

In the confined space of the center aisle, the three attackers had to separate. The first one came straight for Grant, while the other two were delayed slightly in the cramped space. Angry Eyes went for the leading knife, blocking upwards with his forearm, then whipping the other arm out with his palm heel open to the guy's chin. The knife arm was swept aside and up. The chin was jerked backwards with such force it broke three of his teeth and bit off a chunk of tongue.

Grant wheeled around on the other two. They couldn't come side by side, so one was slightly behind the other. They held their knives lower, hoping for a quick stab forwards or a slashing cut up from the waist. Grant stepped inside the fighting arc and jabbed down with his left forearm. He brought his right arm up, bent at the elbow. Forward momentum doubled the weight of the blow as he drove the elbow into the guy's throat. The momentum also carried the knifeman back into the guy behind him, becoming a human shield for Grant's next move.

The third guy had lost before he even started. There was nowhere for him to go. His knife was impotent. The second guy stumbled backwards and knocked his comrade into the second row of reversed seats. Grant stepped past him and stamped down hard on the back of his leg just below the knee. He went down hard, wedged between the seats. He tangled the third guy's legs, and all Grant had to do was launch a palm heel strike to the chest, and his balance went. He let out a scream as the weight of the fall snapped his right leg.

The scream coincided with the squeal of brakes. Sparks lit the night outside. The train was coming into the next station. It slowed down on the run up to Roxbury Crossing. The lights flickered. More sparks outside. Grant leaned down and picked up two of the switchblades. Angry Eyes did the same with the third. The woman with the shopping bag stared goggle-eyed at Grant. She couldn't keep the smile off her face.

The train slowed to a stop and the doors opened. The scruffy guys scrambled backwards through the middle door, two of them dragging the third with the broken leg. The mother and daughter got off at the far end. The teenager ignored the commotion and continued to listen to his own private world. The woman with the shopping bag came over before getting off. "I knew it was you. Saw you on TV. Will you sign this, please?"

She pulled a notepad from her bag. Grant scribbled a signature. An electronic voice warned that the doors were closing, and the woman dashed through just in time. She waved through the window as the train pulled out of the station. Grant didn't wave back.

He scanned the carriage. Nothing had changed apart from the passengers who had got off at Roxbury Crossing. Nobody else had got on. The teenager continued to listen, eyes half closed, oblivious to the commotion. Another thought struck him briefly. *Nobody was going to start killing cops. Unless the cop got killed in a fatal accident. Or a mugging.* Once Grant was satisfied that the danger was over, he concentrated on his unexpected helper.

The man looked more focused than at any time since Grant got on the train.

"Thanks."

Grant didn't hold out a hand to shake on it. This guy didn't look like the type for effusive handshakes. He looked like a guy with enough problems of his own, and that made his intervention all the more impressive. It was the kind of thing people of a certain nature did. Emergency service kind of people. Or military. He thought he knew what was hiding under the patch on the guy's upper arm.

Angry Eyes didn't reply. He simply nodded, then suddenly seemed to weaken. He slumped back into his seat. Grant noticed the bandaged forearm had begun weeping. Blood seeped through the clean white dressing. He sat but didn't try to examine the wound. Men capable of self-harming didn't like physical contact, especially with strangers.

"We'd better get that seen to."

The man jerked upright, cradling the bandaged arm like a baby in his lap. "No hospitals."

"Okay."

The man wouldn't meet Grant's eyes, a marked contrast to his behavior earlier. This guy was damaged goods, and Grant reckoned he knew what branch of the services had damaged him. It was an old story. This was a case for tact and diplomacy. Grant could occasionally come up with a bit of tact and diplomacy.

"Still needs seeing to, though. I think I know just the place."

The train rattled through the night. Two more stops before it was time to get off. He hoped the pharmacy would still be open.

SEVENTEEN

THE CVS PHARMACY ON Centre STREET was a haven of bright lights and friendly voices. The staff were pleasant and helpful. Grant found what he was looking for at the back of the shop, past displays of children's books and cuddly toys. He'd never understood the sell-everything mentality of modern shopping. There were no speciality stores anymore. Back in his youth, a chemist sold medicine and a toy shop sold kids' stuff. Nowadays you could buy everything from men's clothes to condoms all under one roof. He didn't need condoms, but the men's clothes were a bonus.

The shuffling figure Grant had met on the T had become more confident with each step as they'd walked along Green Street and cut through Seaverns Avenue onto Centre Street. By the time John Cornejo followed Grant into the pharmacy, they were more comfortable in each other's company.

Grant checked the medication display and selected crepe bandages, gauze pads, alcohol wipes, and antiseptic cream. He asked Cornejo about painkillers, but he'd been given some to take with him at the hospital. The T-shirt was a problem. Grant went to the clothing section and found a sale rack advertising two for five dollars. "D'you want Mickey Mouse or American Eagle?"

Cornejo looked blank. The question was rhetorical. Grant nodded. "Yeah. Gotcha."

Grant picked two dusky beige T-shirts that wouldn't look out of place with Cornejo's combat pants. Having just met the man, he didn't think having him take his trousers off was a good idea. He checked the T-shirt sizes. They ranged from M through L to XXXL. There were far more XXXLs than Ms. He held one up. It could cover the state of Texas. He couldn't imagine anyone being big enough to fill it, but then he remembered the fat family at the Purple Cactus. And they hadn't been eating a Santa Fe chicken salad you could graze your herd on, they'd been eating something bigger.

The L was a UK equivalent to XL. The M was more Cornejo's size. Grant used the T-shirts as a makeshift basket and wrapped the medication in them. Halfway to the checkout he passed a refrigerated food cabinet with cold drinks and vacuum-packed sandwiches. "You eaten?"

"This year? A couple of times."

Grant smiled. Military humor. That was a good sign. "You won't need anything just yet then?"

Cornejo looked sheepish. Accepting charity appeared to weigh heavy on him. "I could manage a bite."

"Take your pick."

"No. You."

The prices varied. He reckoned Cornejo didn't want to pick anything too expensive. Grant split the difference and picked a ham and cheese sandwich. That was everything. He nodded to the exit. "See you outside."

Cornejo went through the doors that Grant had last gone out of in a rush just the night before. Grant went to the checkout. A young girl stared at him as if Elvis had just walked in. She took his money and put everything into a plastic CVS Pharmacy bag. Grant was putting the change in his pocket when she stopped him.

"I just want to say I thought you were great. On TV. With that poor guy at the auto repair. You were, like, so cool."

Grant didn't know what to say. "Thanks."

"You were, like, Crocodile Dundee or something. Wow."

"Yeah, well. G'day, mate."

He followed Cornejo into the street. A faint hint of smoke still lingered in the cool night air, but the disruption of last night had left no lasting scars. Grant thought of looking in at Flanagan's, but now wasn't the time. In the aftermath of battle, field dressings were the first order of business. He turned towards the Seaverns Hotel, and they fell into step. Two old soldiers together.

GRANT DIDN'T OFFER to wash Cornejo's cuts or dress his wounds. He simply pointed him at the bathroom and gave him the medical supplies. No words were exchanged. This wasn't battlefield emergency treatment. Most soldiers could do the basics until they reached an aid station. Having a bathroom, plenty of time, and no bombs going off around you was a luxury. Grant was beginning to understand that the combat pants weren't army surplus bought from some corner shop. They looked worn out because they had put on the mileage in real life. "Go knock yourself out."

"I will."

That was all they said for half an hour. Cornejo went in the bathroom and closed the door. Grant turned on the TV to cover any noises the veteran might make. Local news was delivered with the same dripping insincerity he'd seen during the day. He wondered how they managed to keep the smile going without being medically altered. And they hadn't even got to the Lassie moment they always ended the news with—the smile, life's-not-really-that-bad story that was supposed send you away from the TV with hope for humanity.

The newsreader voice-overed a story about the price of petrol going up while images of queues at a gas station played on the TV. She then segued into a story about the forthcoming oil summit being held in downtown Boston over the next few days. Footage of a group of Arabs sweeping into Logan International was followed by a grinning politician waving at a crowd, then police setting up trestle barriers in front of an expensive glass and chrome building.

He could hear the faucets running in the bathroom but no cries of pain. If Cornejo had been in the regiment he thought he'd been in, cries of pain were the last thing Grant would hear.

The penultimate story on the news confirmed why the check-out girl thought Grant was Crocodile Dundee. He saw himself being stretchered out of the wreckage of the E-13 police station and into an ambulance. That switched to pictures of him walking towards Parkway Auto Repair. The orange windcheater bloused open in the wind. Dust swirled around his feet. It was a biblical moment, walking with his arms out like Jesus on the cross. What the fuck had he been thinking? No wonder the news was bigging him up.

The Resurrection Man strikes again.

He thought he even detected an Australian accent as the news-reader unraveled the story, but Americans often got that mixed up with a Yorkshire accent. The story played up the fact that the quaint visiting English cop patrolled the mean streets of Bradford unarmed and had walked into the face of a sniper's rifle without a gun. It played down the fact that the sniper was shot by Boston police, although they did link the tragedy to the death of his brother the same day. That brought the pictures full circle, right back at the scene of the explosion and the orange jacket being carried to the ambulance.

The Resurrection Man.

Grant turned the TV off before the Lassie story. Any more saccharine and he thought he'd be sick. The sudden silence highlighted the fact that the faucet had stopped running. The bathroom door was open.

"Sounds like you've been busy." Cornejo was standing in the doorway, holding the loose ends of a freshly wrapped bandage. He looked clean and fresh with his new T-shirt and washed face. He held the bandaged arm out to Grant. "I need a hand with this."

The dressing was tightly wrapped from elbow to wrist, but there was no elastic gripper to fasten the ends. Grant stood up and knotted the length of bandage about six inches from the end, then tore the crepe down the middle to form two ribbons. He wrapped the bandage all the way to the knot, then used the ribbon ends to tie it off. He waited a few seconds, then checked both sides of Cornejo's forearm. There was no blood. Good.

Grant indicated a plastic kettle on the bedside table. "You want tea or coffee with the sandwich?"

"Coffee. Black."

No please or thank you. There was still a hint of madness in Cornejo's eyes, but it was toned down from the stuttering flicker he'd displayed on the T. Grant thought there was more sadness than anger in them, but occasionally anger flared in the background.

Coffee. Black. For some reason American servicemen always seemed to like strong black coffee. Maybe that's why they always seemed so hyperactive. He filled the kettle from the bathroom and switched it on. "Caffeine overload. Is that wise?"

"You mean because I'm suicidal? Decaf won't slow that down."

"You're not suicidal. You're just misunderstood." Grant wasn't sure if that was true, but for sure if Cornejo really wanted to kill himself, he was more than capable of doing it. The kind of training he showed on the train proved one thing. He was military right down to his boots. "Marines, was it?"

Cornejo's eyes steadied. He stared at Grant without blinking. "Better put two sugars in that. Help sweeten me up."

"How long you been out?"

"How long *you* been out?"

"Too long."

"Asked and answered."

"It was the marine corps, wasn't it?"

"That's my business."

Grant thought he understood. Being in the forces was like being in a family with lots of brothers and sisters. Being in the United States Marine Corps was like being in the closest family imaginable. Mustering out, whatever the reason, would be like cutting your arm off. You could still feel the hand and fingers, but they weren't there any more. Grant had been in that situation. "Life goes on, you know?"

"That's what they told me at the VA. It goes on better for some than others."

The kettle boiled, then clicked off. Grant made the coffee and mashed himself a cup of tea. The Englishman's brew. He left the coffee for Cornejo. He wasn't a waiter. He went to the window and leaned his back against the sill. Cornejo sat in the bedside chair and unwrapped his sandwich. Conversation dried up while he ate and drank. Grant knew better than to probe but couldn't resist making one observation. He tapped his upper arm, then pointed at the large square plaster on Cornejo's. "Wear it with pride. You deserve it or they wouldn't have let you in."

"It's pride that covered it up."

"Don't be ashamed of it."

Anger flared behind the eyes, and Grant thought Cornejo was going to kick off, but he simply finished chewing before he spoke. "Ain't ashamed of it being seen. I just don't want it seeing me."

"If it could see you, it'd see someone who stepped in when he didn't need to."

"Don't patronize me."

"Not patronizing. Hard truth. Whatever you had with the corps, you've still got now. The family's still there. They leave no man behind. Keep in touch. Keep up to date. You've still got what it takes."

"Holy Christ. This is the most expensive sandwich I ever had."

"You paid on the train. That don't come cheap."

Cornejo ate the last of his sandwich. He looked hungry, but Grant reckoned it was to give him time to think. Coffee swilled it down. Grant had only drunk half of his tea, but it was cold now. He set the cup on the tray beside the kettle, then went back to the window. Didn't look out. Leaned against the sill again and looked at the man opposite. The ex-marine wiped his mouth and stared back. "You know why you joined the po-lice? So you could replace the family you lost when you mustered out."

Grant thought about that. It was true that lots of cops were ex-military. There was something about being in a disciplined service that appealed to old soldiers, even ones who were only typists. He often told himself it was just because he wanted to help people, but that wasn't true. He could have become a school-crossing warden and still helped people. No, it was more to do with righting wrongs and putting bad guys behind bars. That's what he really told himself, but talking to Cornejo made him realize that wasn't true either. He was a cop because frontline cops were the same as frontline troops. They were a band of brothers, and he couldn't imagine what it must be like to lose that. He couldn't imagine how bad Cornejo must feel. So maybe he had been patronizing. "You're right. I'm sorry."

He hadn't noticed the tension cranking up until he said that. Now the room felt calmer. Cornejo appeared to unwind, the madness in his eyes dialing down. He put his cup down and indicated the TV. "What was that all about? You can't trust the news."

"Ain't that the truth."

"No, it's not. That's why you can't trust the news."

Grant laughed. Cornejo smiled. This was the closest to barrack-room banter the ex-marine had probably had since being treated at the VA hospital. A closeness that was more intimate than marriage.

"Go fuck yourself."

"Been trying for years."

A siren sounded in the distance, some emergency across town being attended by the police or fire or ambulance. The emergency services. Grant looked over his shoulder at the traffic on Centre Street. There wasn't much. A few big American cars guzzling petrol. A couple of pedestrians walking to a restaurant or bar. Night owls spreading their wings across Boston.

"Well, it's like this." He told Cornejo about Freddy Sullivan and his brother Sean. Not everything but enough to give a flavor of why he was over here. He explained about the drugs in Freddy's past and the possible gun connections now. Illegal imports leading to two deaths and one media icon.

Cornejo smiled. "The Resurrection Man. Yeah. They're going to haunt you with that shit."

"Tell me about it." He offered Cornejo another coffee, but he turned it down.

"Better be going. Thanks for your help."

"You need a lift? Where you staying?"

Cornejo shook his head. "You ain't got a lift. Else why you using the T?"

"Call you a cab?"

"Don't call me a cab. Name's John."

"Very funny. Do you need one?"

"No. Only one stop to Forest Hills. Got a place round back of the cemetery. Keeps me grounded."

"As long as you're above ground and sucking air. That's grounded enough."

"So they say. Thanks again."

They shook hands, and Grant walked him to the elevator. The doors pinged open and Cornejo stepped inside. He pressed the button, then threw one last glance at Grant. "That Sullivan guy. The first one?"

"Freddy."

"Yeah. Him. Whatever he was importing, it wasn't guns. This is America, man. Place is full of guns. Don't need to import any more."

Before Grant could say anything, the doors closed, and Cornejo was gone.

How long you been out?

Grant didn't spend a lot of time dwelling on the past, but the past was always there, buried deep in his subconscious. Talking about the army with Cornejo simply brought it to the surface. Grant went back into his room and considered making a fresh cup of tea but opened his T-shirt drawer instead. His fingers reached under the clothes and brought out the long velvet case. The velvet was soft to the touch. It was dark blue. There were scars and creases that betrayed its age. It had a spring-mounted hinge like the flip-open jewelry boxes for necklaces, but it was much longer than that. He felt the satisfying weight in his hands, then put it on top of the dresser.

How long you been out?

That wasn't the most important question. *How long were you in* is what Cornejo should have been asking, a question with hidden subtext. *What did you do while you were in?* That's what always dredged up the memories.

Memories and dreams have one thing in common: they are no respecters of timing or sequence. This memory always began with the helicopter. Heavy thudding blades thumping through the night. A big military chopper with an expansive cargo bay and pneumatic ramp. Grant sat with his snatch squad on hard bench seats along one side of the cabin.

The army medic sat alone on the opposite bench, her short-cropped hair hidden beneath the camouflaged helmet. Her shapely figure was all but unrecognizable in the desert fatigues and combat jacket, but Grant remembered it as clearly as if she were sitting naked in front of him. Cruz was checking the supplies and repacking them into her canvas rucksack. The last thing she examined was a long blue velvet case. She flicked it open and took the stethoscope out, ensured that all the parts were connected, then put it away again.

The helicopter shuddered.

Next thing, there was no helicopter. No cargo bay ramp. Half the snatch squad were dead or missing. A few hours later? The following day? Grant and his team and the female medic were hiding in a dusty ruin that was no more than three walls and a section of bombed-out roof. Dusty and hot and dangerous. Because the natives were restless, and they'd already carved Mack up with their machetes. Cruz leaned against the wall that shaded her from the baking sun, blood soaking through the dressing she'd applied to her own injured leg. "Rescue team. They aren't coming for us, are they?"

Grant looked into her eyes and couldn't lie, even to make the end less painful. "They don't know we're here."

"It was so secret?"

Grant nodded, fatigue showing in the creases of his face. "Fella we were supposed to snatch. Very nasty man. His supporters out there."

He waved towards the sound of chanting and bloodlust in the plaza down the street, where the machete-wielding mob was still cutting pieces off Mack's corpse.

"They know that's who we came to get. Our command team. Need-to-know basis. Diverted the supply chopper to use as cover. The ones who know where we were heading can't admit it. Everybody else? We don't exist."

Cooper passed a canteen of water to Grant, who shook his head and waved it towards Cruz. She glanced at the life-giving liquid with thirsty eyes before shaking her own head. She was a medic. She knew more than most how important that water would become. Cooper screwed the lid back on without drinking.

"Well, that's just fine and dandy."

Fast rewind. Another bombed-out building the day before. Cruz examined Mack's broken leg and said there wasn't anything else she could do with it. She'd splinted and dressed the wound, but they all knew Mack wasn't going to walk out of there. In order to get close enough to make a run for the safe zone, they'd have to dart from cover to cover and hope they didn't draw attention to themselves. That was when Mack volunteered to be the decoy.

Fast forward. The final night. Only two of them left. Grant and Cruz. Out of water. Low on ammunition. One rifle between them, which was just as well because Cruz couldn't shoot for shit. She smiled when Grant told her that. He leaned forward and kissed her dry lips. She had already made her decision. Grant wanted to argue against it but knew it was the only choice. Her leg had gotten worse. She was less able to make the dash for freedom than Mack had been. She took the blue velvet case out of her haversack and held it in both hands. They sat in silence as the sky paled in the west. Dawn began to remove the cover that had been hiding the final stretch of road to the safe zone. Grant should have gone while it was still dark, but darkness would have also hidden the decoy.

She handed Grant the velvet case. "My father gave me this. Make sure he gets it back."

At first Grant couldn't take it because that would be accepting what was to come next. She held it out to him. After a few short moments he reached out and took it. His hand brushed her fingers. Her eyes became serious.

"Can you take the shot?"

"Before they lay a finger on you."

"It's not their fingers I'm worried about."

Joking to the end. Cruz sidled up against the half-demolished wall and peered towards the fires that signaled the final battlefield. She took the flare out of her pocket and didn't look back. Dragging her ruined leg behind her, she clambered over the debris and yanked the fuse. When the flare went up, Grant was already halfway across open ground towards the last piece of cover. Easy range to take the shot before the machetes did their work.

Grant took one more look at the faded American flag stitched inside the silk lining, then shut the past away. He didn't read her name scrawled beneath the stars and stripes. He didn't need to. One of these days he'd have to fulfill his promise, but he still couldn't face the grieving father. Still couldn't forgive himself for taking that shot. Being in the military was like being in the police. You always back your comrades. You always trust who's covering your back. Grant needed to know who to trust now. He could only think of one way to find out, and that would entail another visit to the police station. He put the velvet case back in the drawer. Maybe he would have another cup of tea after all.

EIGHTEEN

GRANT WAS BACK AT E-13 by half past nine the following morning. He got stopped for his autograph twice and was stared at most of the way. If this was what celebrity did for you, then he'd give it a miss. The media frenzy had died down at the police station, and the exterior was quiet. The damaged patrol cars had been taken away. The window cavity had been boarded up. The fingerprint powder had been cleaned off the front doors, and the reception was empty.

His orange windcheater got more stares from the front office as he was buzzed through the inner door. The metal stairs echoed as he climbed to the second floor, but the corridor to the detectives' office was muffled and quiet. He could hear raised voices coming through the closed door.

He paused with his fingers touching the handle. Following the debriefing yesterday it had been made clear he was no longer welcome, and the reason for him being here wasn't applicable. That meant he had no excuse for asking what he was about to ask. Also, the man he needed to speak to was the man who'd steered him to the insecure interview room. He wasn't expecting any cooperation.

He grabbed the handle, opened the door, and walked straight in. Whatever he was expecting, it wasn't what he got. Miller was backing off in shock. The other detectives sat at their desks open-mouthed, and Kincaid was standing on his desk with a cardboard folder in one hand. His face was red with anger.

KINCAID SAW GRANT come through the door and paused for a second. That was all. Then he screamed his rage at the ceiling and dumped the folder in the waste bin at his feet. "Goddamn limp-dicked motherfuckers."

He jumped down from the desk, and the floor shook. He kicked the waste bin across the room. Grant watched with a mixture of surprise and amusement. The bin ended up against the wall near the door, its contents scattered across the floor. One pace and Grant was standing next to the bin. He nudged it upright with one foot, then picked up the battered folder. He left the rest of the rubbish on the carpet. "Strictly speaking, anyone with a limp dick can't be a motherfucker."

Kincaid growled a response. "Strictly speaking, pencil pushers don't make good cops."

"I was a typist. Didn't push pencils."

"I wasn't talking about you. It's them pencil-pushing bastards downtown."

Grant tapped the folder in his hands. He glanced at the creased flap. A name was printed neatly across the top in black.

FREDERICK SULLIVAN

Below that was Sullivan's date of birth and home address. In the bottom left was the date of arrest and a note stating "hold for foreign force inquiry." He tapped the folder some more while he weighed his options. They'd told him at headquarters that the foreign force inquiry case was closed. The homicide and bombing of the police station would be a BPD investigation—nothing to do with the foreign force inquiry officer, which was Grant. Basically, go home and don't come back. The detective in charge was Sam Kincaid. It looked as if Sam Kincaid wasn't happy about something. Grant wondered what it was. "Jobsworths rise to the top. That's why they run the po-lice."

Kincaid sat heavily at his desk. "Cream rises to the top. Not assholes who don't know their asses from their elbows."

Grant dropped the file on Kincaid's desk. "Cream rises, but shit floats. Shits usually know how to play the system, so they end up running the system. Secret is, when it's raining shit, get a shit umbrella. Deflect the shit so you can get the job done."

"You volunteering?"

"Depends what kind of shit you've got."

"The kind of shit is, I've been pulled off the case for three days."

"Not more pizza robberies?"

"Oil robbery."

Grant looked blank and leaned against Kincaid's desk. "Oil?"

Kincaid swiveled in his chair and looked up at the man in the orange jacket. "Oil. Petrol. Gas. Whatever you want to call it. Bunch of Ay-rabs coming over to steal the franchises."

Grant remembered the news story. Arabs at the airport. A smiling politician. Police erecting trestle barriers outside an expensive-looking building. "The delegation."

It wasn't a question. Grant knew how this worked. It had been the same in the army whenever a royal visit demanded extra security at the barracks. It was the same in the West Yorkshire Police whenever politicians decided to hold an important meeting with world leaders. "Let me guess. All police leave cancelled. Emergency personnel only to work the streets; everyone else drafted in for security and crowd control."

"Everyone except the pencil-pushing bastards that run this department."

"They pulling all the detectives?"

"All but two. Emergency cover only. One working nights and one working days. Investigations suspended—for three days."

"Don't they know the forty-eight-hour rule?"

"They don't know there's more than one twelve o'clock in a day."

"Yeah, but. Evidence gathered in the first forty-eight hours nearly always has the answer. Forensics. Witnesses. House searches."

"I know what we're missing. We'll just have to play catch-up is all."

Grant folded his arms across his chest. "So who've you got left?"

A gentle voice spoke from behind him. "Me."

Miller was grinning from ear to ear. This was his chance to shine. Taking primary on anything that came in during the day for seventy-two hours. Youthful enthusiasm went a long way, but Grant knew it couldn't replace experience. At least the young detective did have enthusiasm on his side. Grant glanced at Miller, then back at Kincaid. "Emergency cover?"

"Yep."

"But not the Sullivan investigation?"

"Nope. Not until I get back."

The doubt returned. If Kincaid had indeed steered Grant to the insecure interview room, what better way to stall the investigation then by taking the lead detective off the case for a while? Grant just didn't see this going right to the top, though. That sort of thing only happened in the movies. Corruption only lived at the grassroots. Conspiracies didn't exist, especially in the police service. For a conspiracy to work, dozens of people had to keep the secret. The police force couldn't hide toilet paper.

That put a different slant on things. Whoever had been paid to ensure Grant interviewed Sullivan out front had also arranged the riot that filled the cells. That was grassroots level. Surely the best way to shit-can the investigation was to keep your inside man on the case. Kincaid. Then again, maybe that was why Kincaid was so upset about being removed. Because the bosses weren't involved.

There were too many possibilities. There was insufficient evidence. One thing Kincaid wouldn't want, if he was the inside man, would be having Grant snooping around. So here was an opportunity to sound the big guy out.

"You still got Sullivan's property?"

"Freddy's? Yes. Down in custody."

"Can I have a look at it?"

"Sergeant Rooney won't be happy about that."

"That's why I need you to organize it."

Kincaid laid a hand on the Sullivan file and drummed his fingers on the flap. He flicked it open, then smoothed it shut. Open and shut. Open and shut. He closed his eyes for a moment. Drummed some more. Then stopped. "Okay. I've got half an hour before they ship me downtown."

Grant felt a weight lift from his shoulders. He was beginning to like the big man all over again. Kincaid pushed away from the desk and stretched his back. Bones cracked like gunshots. He stood up.

"You need anything else, see Miller." He gave Miller a nod. "Give him a hand with anything that doesn't involve going to jail."

"You bet."

Miller looked even happier than usual, and Miller's usual was pretty happy. Kincaid held a hand out for Grant to lead the way. "Let's go take a look."

KINCAID WAS RIGHT: Sergeant Rooney wasn't happy. In marked contrast to Miller's youthful enthusiasm, Rooney was the epitome of old-timer obstructiveness. The custody sergeant stood ramrod straight behind the counter. "His property is sealed until the inquiry concludes otherwise."

Grant kept quiet. Kincaid knew how to play the game. "The inquiry can't conclude anything until we check his property."

"You got written authority from the investigating officer?"

"I am the investigating officer."

"Got to have it in writing. For the custody record."

"He's not in custody. He's in the morgue."

"His custody record isn't. His property neither."

Grant kept quiet. Kincaid gritted his teeth. "So let's see it."

"Can't see it without written authority."

Grant couldn't keep quiet any longer. Jobsworths were the bane of a working cop's life. Jobsworths in uniform were even worse. "Is that like, 'Prisoners can't go out to an insecure interview room'?"

Rooney stared at Grant and lowered his voice. "And we all know how that worked out, don't we?"

Grant felt a shiver run down his spine. "You get in trouble? Allowing that?"

"Not yet, but I will. Once the inquiry is complete. There are procedures for a reason."

Kincaid took the lead again. Grant was even quieter than before. "I am the inquiry. And I need to see Sullivan's personal property."

"Not without written—"

"I'll give you written authorization. Get me some paper."

Rooney looked at Kincaid, then at Grant, and back to Kincaid. "He's not the investigating officer."

"He was the interviewing officer. Fresh eyes. Now get me the fucking paper before your stripes are the last part of your career you see."

Rooney slapped a sheet of paper on the counter. "Snuggling up with the English, now, are you? Your mother must be proud."

Kincaid wrote in silence, his knuckles going white around the pen. He scrawled a signature, reversed the paper, then slid it across the counter. He slammed the pen down so hard Grant thought ink would shoot out like blood from a squashed bug.

"Bag."

"Coming right up."

Rooney turned his back and went to the property lockers. Each locker had a number that corresponded to a cell number. There were two unmarked lockers at the bottom. Sullivan wasn't in a cell anymore. The sergeant unlocked the right-hand locker and took out a ziplocked plastic bag with a numbered seal protecting the zip. He placed it on the counter, then busied himself attaching the authorization letter to Sullivan's custody record.

THEY OPENED THE BAG in a secure vacant interview room in the custody area. It had the same layout as the one out front except the table and chairs were bolted to the floor and the tape deck was fastened to the wall. It was one of the rooms that Grant should have interviewed Freddy Sullivan in if events hadn't conspired against him—events that had been orchestrated by someone with incredible power over the locals and a modicum of control over the custody sergeant. There was insufficient evidence to prove anything just yet, but Grant felt relieved that he could at least strike Kincaid off his list of suspects.

The big fella broke the plastic seal and unzipped the bag. He sat back in his chair and held his hands out. "It's all yours."

Grant interlocked the fingers of both hands, reversed them palms outwards, and flexed. The knuckles cracked. He released the fingers and wiggled them like a safecracker preparing to work the combination dial. He looked at the bag on the table for a few moments, then leaned forward and tipped the contents out onto the black vinyl surface.

There wasn't much.

He wished he'd brought the official record of the contents. It was sometimes helpful to know where each item was found—left-hand trouser pocket, back pocket, jacket pocket, etc. More importantly if any had been hidden down the back of Sullivan's trousers or down his socks. That would give added weight to certain items. Having said that, his experience of custody searches was that the property location wasn't noted. It was simply a record of items taken into protective possession and a search for weapons or other methods of self-harm, hence the belt and shoelaces in the bag. A street search was different. In a street search every detail was recorded, as much for relevance as to rebut any claims about civil liberties being violated. Strip searches had to be authorized and carried out in a controlled environment. Find a bag of drugs up his arse and you'd better have followed procedures. And washed your hands.

First things first. List the property. Grant took a notebook and pen out of his inside pocket. The orange windcheater held many secrets. Then he sifted through the items on the table and arranged them in a short line. Working from left to right, he noted each item in the book.

- $25.75 cash
- brown leather wallet, containing…
- Walmart store card in the name of F. Sullivan
- Blockbuster video card in same name
- photo of a naked woman dancing

Grant looked at the dog-eared photograph. The woman was slim and athletic and appeared to be dancing around a silver pole in the middle of a stage. Pole-dancing clubs were known in England but not widespread. There was an illuminated Budweiser sign in the background. He turned the photo over, but there was nothing written on the back. He put it down and continued.

- brown leather belt
- 1 pair of black shoelaces
- 1 yellow metal ring
- 1 yellow metal heavy linked chain

He fingered the chain, shifting the links into different shapes. It was obviously gold, probably 24 karat. Standard procedure was to describe chains and jewelry as yellow metal or white metal simply because cops weren't metallurgists. Saved being sued later when the property was returned. This property wasn't getting returned. The ring was gold too. A wedding band. Too small for a man, so probably handed down from Sullivan's mother. Grant couldn't remember if the Sullivan matriarch was still alive, and he felt a little guilty at not knowing. The ring had no doubt been worn on the chain and only removed during the cataloguing process. He moved on.

- matchbook containing sealed condom
- multiblade pocket knife with tools
- 2 keys on a Ford key fob

He picked up the keys and examined the leather fob. The Ford symbol was a bright metal disc hinged at one end. He lifted it, then checked the fob for hidden compartments. Nothing. He held them up for Kincaid to see. "The car he was stopped in?"

"Yes. It's a clunker. Routine traffic stop. Name check flagged him up."

"Impounded?"

"Impounded and searched. Nothing of interest."

Grant nodded and put the keys down. Standard procedure again. If a traffic stop results in an arrest, the police have the right to search any vehicle the prisoner was using or had control over at the time of his arrest. At least that's what they did back in the UK. He had no doubt the same applied here. Also, if the police impounded a vehicle, they had to list anything in it to rebut any claims of missing property when it was returned. Sullivan's Ford wasn't getting returned. Next item.

- 3 keys and an imitation four-leaf clover
  on a rabbit's foot key ring

Grant examined the rabbit's foot. It was a standard key ring type, furry pad enclosed at one end by a metal band attached to the short chain and key ring. He tried unscrewing the band. It was solid. He held it up to his ear and shook it. There was nothing loose inside. The four-leaf clover was green-painted metal. The keys were traditional Yale types, two large and one small, maybe a padlock. He held these up for Kincaid. "House?"

"Yes. Front and back doors. Don't know about the small one."

"Searched?"

"Did you ever miss a chance to search a crook's house?"

Same procedure applied. Police had the right to search any premises where the prisoner lived and any premises the prisoner had control over at the time of his arrest back in the UK. Same over here. Kincaid qualified that. "Cursory search. Since he was being held for you, we didn't have probable cause to go fishing for other cases. Now he's dead, we'll do a thorough search. Just have to wait until I'm back."

Grant dangled the rabbit's foot. "Not exactly lucky, was it?"

"Not for the rabbit either."

Grant put the keys down. That was the last of the property. He left it lined up on the desk and ran his eyes over it a couple of times. He checked the list to make sure he hadn't missed anything. He randomly touched various items as if the contact would kick-start a new chain of thought. It didn't.

He leaned back in his chair. The movement would have normally translated into pushing the chair away from the table, but it was fastened to the floor. He laid both hands flat on the table. What had he learned? Not much. Sullivan loved his mother, had a beautiful girlfriend, and practiced safe sex. He drove a clunky old Ford and lived alone. Not much to go on.

"You managed to make any inquiries yet?"

Kincaid leaned back too. "Checked the local Irish bars, but nobody talks to cops in an Irish bar."

Grant snorted a laugh. "Tell me about it. You want to try being English in an Irish bar."

"Or being English in the BPD."

"The debrief. Yeah. I felt real welcome."

"Like a fart in a space suit."

Grant started to put the property back into the bag. "Well, thanks for this anyway."

Kincaid looked to be considering something. He watched Grant repack the bag and zip it shut. It would need a fresh seal and the number recording on the custody record. "You've got one thing over on other Englishmen."

"What's that?"

"You're a celebrity. The Resurrection Man. You've noticed it already."

Grant remembered the stares he'd got on the way to the station. The requests for autographs and the Crocodile Dundee references. Being on TV was a gift and a curse. "So?"

"So, maybe they'll talk to you where they wouldn't talk to us."

"You asking for my help?"

"I'm saying, I've got three days of fucking about with crowd control. You've got three days before I'm back and you're out. Why not make the most of it?"

They stood up in unison. Grant hefted the bag in one hand.

Keep out of trouble. Don't get involved.

Too late. He was already involved. Keeping out of trouble was the only thing to do now. With unofficial backing from Kincaid and a little help from Miller, he thought that should be easy enough to do.

He was wrong.

NINETEEN

IT WAS THE THIRD BAR, after Flanagan's and Costello's, before Grant started to make some headway. O'Neill's Traditional was hidden away off South Street at the junction of Child and Lee. It was small but perfectly formed, an independent among giants. The surrounding streets were mainly residential, with clapboard structures and wooden porches. American flags hung from every porch. Stickers in the windows proclaimed support for the troops overseas. It was surprising to find a bar in the middle of all this domesticity, but somebody must have got planning permission. It reminded Grant of home. Every housing estate had a parade of shops and a local pub. The only thing missing here was a fish and chip shop.

From the moment Grant stepped through the door, he had a good feeling about the place. The red brick two-story building had the solid feel of somewhere that had been there for decades. The green-painted window frames and shutters echoed the rest of Jamaica Plain, but the lighting inside was brighter. The walls had been plastered and painted a neutral cream, adorned with photos of JP in its youth. Faded sepia prints of old Boston reminded Grant of Frank Meadow Sutcliffe's aged photos of Whitby and its fishing port. Green-shaded wall lamps lit the booths along one side. Chain-hung globe lights brightened the rest of the room. A mahogany bar ran the length of the room opposite the booths. O'Neill's was traditional by name and traditional by nature.

It also seemed to be family friendly, with a children's area at the rear that looked out of place in an Irish bar. No doubt part of the reason it survived in the middle of the residential area. The old man polishing the brasses behind the bar looked a touch less friendly. He stopped what he was doing when Grant came through the door. The two other people in the room, two customers sitting at the bar, stopped drinking and looked at the intruder. The good feeling Grant had when he opened the door evaporated. This had that Anglo-Irish vibe already, and he hadn't even spoken yet.

The door flapped shut behind him. He stood for a moment, soaking up the silence. There was no music. Probably another side effect of being in the middle of a bunch of family houses. Grant thought about the scene in *An American Werewolf in London* where the travelers went into the Slaughtered Lamb for a drink. A darts player thunked an arrow into the wall, then turned to the intruders. "You made me miss." Grant felt like an English werewolf in Boston.

Nobody was playing darts.

Nobody was doing anything.

Except watching the stranger from across the pond.

Grant walked across the stripped and polished floorboards towards the bar. His footsteps sounded loud in the silence. The floor creaked. All it needed was a pair of spurs jingling with each step and you'd have the clichéd Western entrance of *The Man with No Name*. The bartender slapped the towel he'd been using over his shoulder and waited until Grant stopped in front of him. Nobody spoke. An old grandfather clock ticked on the far wall. One of the customers put his glass down with a sharp clink.

The bartender's tone was neutral. "Well, now. Look at this. I never thought I'd see the likes of you in here."

Grant sensed trouble. He just hadn't expected it to start so soon. "Is that the likes of me being English or the likes of me being a cop?"

"Oh, we don't mind the po-lice. And I can just about stomach the English."

"What then?"

The bartender just looked at him. The two customers didn't hide their stares. Grant thought he must have grown two heads, but he was becoming immune to the Boston hospitality, even among the BPD. The bartender's frown lines deepened. Then he jerked his head towards a wall-mounted TV behind the bar. The news channel was replaying Grant's walk across the dusty parking lot of Parkway Auto Repair. The bartender broke into a smile, and his entire face lit up. The frown lines transformed themselves into laugh lines. "The Resurrection Man. In my bar."

He held out a hand. "Gerry O'Neill. At your service."

Grant shook the hand. "Jim Grant. Pint of Tetley's, please."

"Oh my gosh, I'm sorry. I'm just a small business here. Imported beers I can't afford. But I'll give you the nearest we've got."

O'Neill pulled a pint of something that was nowhere near Tetley's. Grant didn't complain. The good feeling returned. If there was one place in JP he was going to get answers, he reckoned this was it. The two drinkers began talking again, and the clink of glasses sounded like music to Grant's ears. He settled onto a barstool and started slowly. He didn't want to scare O'Neill off.

"THEY GIVE US MICKS a bad name, those Sullivan boys."

An hour later they'd got past the preliminaries, and O'Neill was moving into the territory Grant was steering him towards. He was on his second pint of piss, a poor excuse for beer, but he wasn't complaining. The conversation was more than making up for the lack of quality. He reckoned if he opened a Yorkshire bar with a fish and chip restaurant he'd be minted.

The TV on the wall had cycled through all today's news and was back at the beginning again. The Resurrection Man's solitary walk into the jaws of death. Twenty-four-hour news was just as bad in the UK, filling space with tripe and reruns. The orange jacket stood out on the badly tuned set. The color needed turning down to match the volume.

"Both of them? I thought Sean was the good brother."

"Only compared to Freddy. Next to him, Whitey Bulger would look like the good brother."

"As bad as that?"

"Maybe not. I'm Irish. And prone to exaggeration."

"I'm a cop. I need you to dial down the exaggeration, if you don't mind."

"Not at all. Not at all."

"So, what was Freddy up to?"

"What wasn't he up to? That boy had a bad case of the couldn't-give-a-shit-and-fuck-everyone-else-itis."

"Pretty much like he was back home."

"Turds don't change. They just get more flies around them."

"What kind of flies was he hanging with lately?"

O'Neill cleaned the bar even though it was already clean. "A bad crew. Got a liking for guns and explosives. Was always disturbing the neighbors around the back of Delaney's place on Jamaica Pond. Shoot a gun in the woods and you'll upset the wildlife. Shoot at a wedge of plastic explosive and you'll wake the dead. Destructive for no good reason."

"That only works in the movies. Shooting at sticks of dynamite. Plastic needs a detonator."

"Whatever. He used to make a lot of noise—that much I know. He surely liked blowing things up."

"Touch of poetic justice there, then."

"Poetic?"

Grant mimicked an explosion with his arms. "Kaboom."

O'Neill moved onto polishing the brasses. He laughed at the pantomime. "Somebody should have told him you play with fire, you might get burned. That boy had no fear."

"He was pretty scared when I spoke to him. Something got him spooked. He reckoned he was dead meat for talking out of school."

"Did he talk out of school?"

"Doesn't matter. Whoever it was couldn't take that risk."

Grant took a sip of beer. The clock ticked quietly. Glasses clinked further along the bar. The place was almost empty. He wondered briefly how it managed to stay open. Maybe O'Neill did family barbecues at the weekend. He pressed on. "You think he could have been smuggling guns and stuff?"

"Gunrunning? That went out with ponchos and prohibition."

"Drugs?"

"No. Last I heard, he'd moved into people trafficking."

"Smuggling? Like across the border?"

"Mexico? No. He was supplying the escort agencies with foreign pussy—East European, Russian, and the like—for the niche market."

"He was pimping?"

"No. Just importing."

Grant put his glass down with a bang. A shiver ran down his spine. The clock continued ticking, but he didn't hear it. He hadn't been able to get his mind away from smuggling guns or drugs. He'd never considered prostitution. Sullivan had whined about only being the importer. That this shit wasn't his fault. What kind of shit could smuggling prostitutes get you into?

"Importing for where?"

"Here and there. Check the Internet. There's dozens of websites for Boston escorts. They cater for all tastes. Eastern Europeans are very popular. Some pretty exclusive places."

Grant looked at the elderly bar owner and gave him a quizzical smile. "I wouldn't have put you down as a silver surfer."

"The Internet? It's the future. I'm not dead from the neck down, you know."

"No wonder you can't afford to import Tetley's."

"Window shopping doesn't cost. The wife holds the purse strings. If you want to check out the quality, nip over to the Gentlemen's Club off the Arborway at Jamaica Pond."

"What's that?"

"Strip club. Pole dancers. Lap dancers, if you like. It's not one of the more exclusive clubs. Residential association was up in arms about him getting a permit. Delaney must have greased some palms down at city hall. Had to keep the exterior plain so it blends."

Grant stared into his beer. For the second time in five minutes, he felt a shiver run down his spine. Since he'd arrived in Boston, sex and violence had mingled with his daily routine. It had been varied and destructive. The sex had been great. The violence conclusive. Some of it connected. Most of it not. Voices replayed snatches of conversation in his mind.

Don't let Mr. Delaney hear you say that. Concrete shoes aren't out of fashion just yet.

The bartender whom Grant had mistaken for the owner at Flanagan's Bar.

He stamps car number plates.

In prison? That's what they do over here, isn't it? Like sewing mailbags.

Naw. At Delaney's over in West Roxbury. He don't do prison. He's the good brother.

Freddy Sullivan talking about his brother, Sean, just before the interview turned nasty. Grant hadn't put the name together when he'd walked the dusty parking lot at Parkway Auto Repair, apparently owned by someone called Delaney. And now it turned out Sullivan had been importing women for the Gentlemen's Club, owned by the one and only Mr. Delaney.

"They have a dress code?"

O'Neill stopped polishing. He appeared to sense a change in his famous customer. The frown lines returned. The twinkle in his eye was subdued.

"You don't need a suit and tie or anything. Clean and tidy will do it. No swastika tattoos or bones through your nose. They do frisk you for guns."

"I hate guns."

"Then you should be okay as long as you've got the entrance fee."

"Do I need to start saving?"

"No. They want customers inside. That's when they start ripping you off."

Grant downed the last of his beer and let out a satisfied sigh. He slid off the barstool and stood up. His legs ached, and he suddenly felt the strain on his body after two days of sex and fighting. O'Neill gave him the check.

"You going in undercover?"

Grant paid and nodded to the news reruns on TV. "I don't think that's an option. Do you?"

"Maybe you'll get a discount."

They shook hands like old friends. Grant thanked him for his help. O'Neill held onto Grant's hand. "Don't go getting into trouble now, will you?"

Grant patted the bartender's hand and let go. "I'm not looking for trouble. I just want to check out the show."

He nodded, then walked out the door, leaving Gerry O'Neill with the same two customers who'd been there when Grant arrived. The clock ticked. The bar fell silent.

TWENTY

The Gentlemen's Club wasn't exactly Stringfellows of London, but it was a long way short of being a low-rent dive. On the south shore, the exterior looked like a rundown country club, a tastefully designed frontage that incorporated New England charm and Old West ruggedness. The two-story wooden structure was the size of a large barn but with a flat roof and full-length porch out front. The obligatory stars and stripes hung limp from a flagpole beside the steps. The window frames were painted dull green. Surprise, surprise: they needed repainting. The entire outside looked faded and worn. Even the parking lot was in need of fresh tarmac.

The inside of the club was anything but faded. Color hit Grant in the face as soon as he walked through the door from the foyer. It was like walking into a cinema. The reception sold tickets and popcorn. The double doors led into a world of darkness and sensuality.

He went inside. Grant felt right at home.

The doors closed behind him, and he stood with his back to the wall for a moment while his eyes adjusted to the dark. It didn't take long. That was another piece of baggage Grant carried around with him, the ability to adjust quickly. It was another thing that made him so dangerous. His eyes scanned the room. His ears waited for the inevitable musical assault that all nightclubs seemed to feel was necessary.

The aural assault didn't come. Instead, the soft thumping intro of Ennio Morricone's theme for *The Good, the Bad and the Ugly* pulsed from hidden speakers. The darkness was lifted by blue neon lights surrounding a raised stage in the middle of the room. A silver pole stood out from the middle of the stage. Three rows of seats with individual tables circled the arena. The seating was about half full, but there were no empty seats in the front row. Several ceiling-mounted spotlights blinked red with each beat of the introduction. They pulsed brightly, then faded. The effect was stunning, but not as stunning as the vision of loveliness wrapping her arms and one leg around the silver pole.

She moved like a snake. Her arms slithered up the pole. Her entwined leg slowly crawled right around it. Her hips pulsated in a soft gyration that replicated gentle penetration if she'd been riding her man. The pulsing beat grew louder. The red lights grew brighter before each fade to black. Then the main theme kicked in and a brilliant white spotlight skewered the woman and she began to dance.

She was naked.

She was toned.

There wasn't an ounce of spare flesh on her, and everything on display screamed muscle and strength. She had very short bleached blond hair and piercing eyes. Her lips were savage red. Perfectly formed buttocks alternately pinched then jiggled as she rode the pole, using the strength in her legs to lower her ass to the ground, then raise it back up again. What every man watching was thinking was, "That could be my pole she's sinking down onto."

Grant thought the same.

He kept his back to the wall and watched the show. A quick glance on either side of him for protection. The easiest time to attack would be when he'd just entered the room and before he got his bearings. Distraction technique. The woman dancing on stage was very distracting. Grant checked his flanks for enemy action. There was nobody near him. He focused on the dancer's lithe moves.

She hugged the pole and slid her hands up and down its silver length. No prizes for guessing what she was suggesting with that move. Then she locked one leg around the pole and suddenly leaned backwards with her upper body. Her torso folded in half until her head almost touched the floor. Her face was upside down. She held her arms out wide, then shook her chest. Medium-sized breasts jiggled. Even upside down there was no mistaking the truth in those breasts. They promised softness but weight. They changed shape as her body inverted, from the slight downward sag of all the weight being in the bottom to the sensual shift in weight that forced the nipples to point at her mouth. The gentle sway as she jiggled them proved they were all natural, with no artificial additives. There was no football-shaped bag of silicon or surgical scarring beneath each breast. These were real.

She snapped her body upright again, and Grant felt dizzy just watching her. She turned her back to the pole, raised her hands above her head and grabbed it higher up, then lifted her legs off the ground. They stuck straight out in front, and her stomach muscles became taught as cables on a suspension bridge. Bands of muscle stood out. Her thighs looked solid. Slowly, ever so slowly, she opened her legs.

The music was building to a crescendo of screaming and whistling. The pulsing beat in the background grew louder. The dancer's love mound was completely shaved. The softness of it pulsed in time with the background beat. Her stomach tightened, then relaxed, pulling her hips away from the pole then settling back against it. Using just the strength in her arms, she slowly twirled around the silver rod, giving everyone a view of what they could never have. It was cruel. It was sensual. It was what the punters paid for when they came through the double doors. It was what some of them might pay more for after the show.

The music stopped, and a thunderous round of applause broke out. There were a couple of wolf whistles. The dancer strode around the edge of the stage, doing a lap of honor, then she sank to her knees, folding her feet under her, and let the grateful audience tuck twenty-dollar bills into an elastic belt Grant hadn't noticed around her waist. There were cries of encore, encore, but she ignored them. A few minutes later she stood up and bowed to her viewers, both towards them and away from them, giving one last glimpse of her gleaming sex before she strode off like a tiger in the jungle. Like a predator.

Grant watched the house lights turn up a couple of notches but not enough to banish the dark completely. He scanned the rest of the room. An outer circle of dining tables surrounded the stage area. There was a brightly lit bar to one side. There were several pedestal tables with three barstools each dotted around the bar. There were no barstools at the bar itself. Waitresses who were almost as beautiful as the dancer ferried drinks to the tables, mostly the ones around the stage. Anyone dining at the outer circle was served separately.

Grant went to the bar.

There were two bartenders, both male, both young. They were a nonthreatening presence that wouldn't scare the punters. The heavyweights stood in the shadows against the walls around the room. Grant had pinpointed them when he'd come in, and that was why he'd chosen his spot at the wall. Nowhere near any of them. In the bright pool of light at the bar there was no danger, only drinks, nibble trays, and something else.

Grant ordered a Coke with ice, no lemon. He took a handful of peanuts from one of the nibble trays. Then he looked at the neatly stacked tray of matchbook condoms that he had seen several times before.

A CRASH OF CYMBALS and the haunting strings of Lalo Schifrin's opening theme from *Bullitt* came over the speakers. The house lights dimmed as another dancer took to the stage. This one had long dark hair tied back in a single ponytail. Her head was lowered so that the ponytail hung forward between her ample breasts. The red lights pulsed as the intro shifted gears, adding elements of jazz. A sharp note sounded. The dancer flicked her head, turning the ponytail into a whip that encircled the pole. She gyrated her shaved pussy against the silver shaft and tightened her buttocks until they looked as solid as rock.

The single white spot highlighted her performance.

In the shadows around the walls, classic movie posters Grant hadn't noticed when he came in explained the choice of music. He'd never been in a movie-themed strip club before. The music was more relaxing than the usual thumping pop songs that drilled into your brain and precluded any kind of conversation. The gentle rhythm added a sensual tone to the dancing. Slow and eager.

Grant concentrated on the condoms on the bar.

He picked a pack up from the tray. It was black, with a swirl of flame forming a symbol in the middle. The flame held a silhouette of a naked woman at its heart. It reminded Grant of one of the James Bond teaser posters back when Pierce Brosnan had been playing Bond. The name on the bottom wasn't the Gentlemen's Club. It didn't say CVS Pharmacy. It said nothing. Three times.

TRIPLE ZERO
Gentlemen's Services

Not as catchy as Double-Oh-Seven but catchy enough that Grant remembered the name. He'd seen it in Sullivan's property bag at District E-13. He'd seen some at Flanagan's Bar, even though he hadn't paid any attention. He'd worn one twice. More than twice actually. A couple of times at the Airport Hilton and once at the Seaverns Hotel. Terri Avellone had provided them. Judging by the packaging, they weren't available at the pharmacy. Judging by the address on the back, they didn't come from Jamaica Plain either. He didn't recognize it. Somewhere in downtown Boston, he presumed.

He wondered how widely available they were. He hadn't noticed any at O'Neill's. None at Costello's either. If they were a promotional tool, they were probably only dispensed at point of sale, like the peanuts. Designed to get you eating for free so you needed a drink to quench your thirst. Between the condoms and the lap dancers, there would be plenty of thirst to quench. Paying for the drink was what ended up costing you.

They want customers inside. That's when they start ripping you off.

Gerry O'Neill had been right, only he wasn't talking about peanuts to drive your thirst. What they were selling here cost more than a pint of Tetley's. That didn't bother Grant. If the urge became too great and there was no woman in his life, he had no qualms about engaging professional help. It cleared his head, didn't involve commitment, and you weren't stuck with saying goodbye in the morning. What did bother him was how this related to Freddy Sullivan getting blown apart and his brother getting shot.

Grant flicked open the lid. In all those private investigator movies, the clue was always inside the flap or in the name of the premises giving away free matches. He wondered how PIs ever solved a case without the aid of a fortuitously placed book of matches. There was nothing on the inside of this one. The matchbook produced more questions than answers. He closed the flap. *Bullitt* continued to play. The dancer continued to dance. The fine structure and prominent cheekbones suggested Eastern European, but that could just be Grant clutching at straws. She certainly had the tight body and perfect breasts of a professional. Whether she was an imported professional remained to be seen.

No point asking the bar staff. The waitresses either. They were just window dressing for a service industry that gave good service. Too many questions in the wrong place could get his ass kicked. If anyone wanted to try. He turned his back to the bar and scanned the pedestal tables. An overweight guy was sitting alone, leaning on the table as he concentrated on the dancer. He was wearing a crumpled business suit with the tie undone and collar open. He looked like a regular. Grant took a dish of peanuts and his drink and sat at the next table.

Bullitt finished, and the dancer did her lap of honor for tips. The house lights came up. The front-row patrons waited eagerly for the next act. Grant dropped a handful of peanuts in his mouth. They were dry and salty. He swilled them down with ice-cold Coke. The man stretched his back without standing up. No wonder he was overweight. Grant raised his voice but kept it conversational. "They sure know how to throw a party, don't they?"

The man looked startled at being spoken to. Grant supposed a lot of men came here for solitude and female entertainment, not conversation. Guilty husbands getting a look at what their wives wouldn't provide. Lonely men watching what they could only dream of having. Grant didn't fall into either category. He liked sex and wasn't ashamed of it. It's what red-blooded males were all about. Anyone who said they didn't think about sex when they saw a beautiful woman was a liar.

"Corking norks."

"Pardon me?"

Grant held his hands curled and upturned in front of his chest as if cupping a pair of heavy breasts. "Sorry. Arthritis."

The man still didn't understand.

"Nice tits. Nice rack. That's what you call 'em over here, isn't it?"

The man looked embarrassed but no longer scared. He relaxed slightly. "They most certainly are."

Grant ignored the peanuts and took another drink. "You know what they say. Save a mouse, eat a pussy."

The man laughed. The blush left his cheeks. "Good one. Never heard that. Save a mouse. Funny."

The man didn't introduce himself, and Grant didn't push it. This wasn't the sort of place most customers wanted to be exchanging names and addresses. He didn't look intimidated anymore, though. That was a good sign. Grant kept his tone light. "You ever hear them talk? The girls—they look foreign."

The man gave Grant a look, his confidence rising. "Compared to you, do you mean? You're not from around these parts."

"Very astute of you. No. Across the pond."

"North shore?"

Grant feigned a laugh. "Not Jamaica Pond. *The* pond. The Atlantic."

"English. Well, not being Irish makes you foreign around here."

"So I've discovered. You can be an unforgiving bunch."

"Not me. I'm third-generation Canadian. In Boston on business."

So, not a regular. Shit. "Then we're all foreign, then. What about the girls, though?"

"No clue."

The lights dimmed, and the blue neon took over. The red spots pulsed twice, then a familiar voice boomed across the room. *"Ah, ah, I know what you're thinking. Did he fire six shots or only five?"*

A tall, leggy blond walked confidently up to the pole and spun her back to it, folding her arms around the shaft behind her. She tilted her head backwards and stuck her breasts out. Grant was right. Corking norks. Some wag in the audience shouted above the speakers. "I'd like to fire six shots."

Somebody laughed. One of the heavies around the walls stepped forward but didn't intervene. This hadn't turned into trouble yet. Just overexuberance. Clint Eastwood continued. *"Well, to tell you the truth, I forgot myself in all this excitement."*

The dancer prepared herself. Grant saw a businessman slide into one of the booths beyond the bar. The staff were all but bowing and scraping. This was a very important person.

"But being as this is a .44 Magnum, the most powerful handgun in the world, and would blow your head clean off, you've got to ask yourself one question: Do I feel lucky?"

Grant did feel lucky. Whoever it was over there obviously carried a lot of clout. If anyone could answer his questions, that was the man. He doubted he'd answer them in here, though, so he watched and waited. Clint Eastwood finished. *"Well, do ya, punk?"*

Drums rolled and a gentle refrain mingled with the beat, then the main theme from *Dirty Harry* filled the room. The dancer strutted her stuff, firm breasts and shaved pussy looking to save a mouse. Grant watched the businessman and bided his time.

Three dancers later, Grant wasn't interested in saving any mice. He'd seen shaved pussy, Brazilian pussy, and bikini-waxed pussy. The only pussy he hadn't seen was Garfield. The movie themes veered from British gangster flick *Get Carter* back to spaghetti Westerns with *For a Few Dollars More*. Grant was whistling the less-famous Morricone theme when he followed the businessman out the back door.

The man was heavyset and greying, but Grant couldn't get a good look at his face in the darkness. Even when the rheostat raised the house lights, the club was still gloomy. When the show was on, all he could see was blue neon, red flashes, and the spill from the dancer's spot. Grant couldn't go over for a closer look without being obvious. The man had an aura about him that kept the heavies on their toes and the waitresses busy. They served him finger snacks and soft drinks. It looked like the boss was watching his alcohol intake. Maybe he didn't drink on duty.

Then business was concluded, and he slid out of the booth and walked behind the bar. Nobody moved. The bouncers kept station against the walls. The waitresses stood to attention until he'd gone. He wasn't going out the front. Grant stood quickly and went around the other side of the bar.

The back door had a sign stating Staff Only. It was swinging shut as Grant came around the corner. He could just make out the reflected light from a dozen cars in the parking lot and the glitter of moonlight on the lake. Calling it a pond was like calling your bathtub a washbasin. Grant reached the door before it clicked shut and wedged his foot in the gap. He opened it slowly and peeked outside.

The man was disappearing around the side of the building. Grant stepped outside and followed him. At best he'd get a shot at asking a few questions. At worst he'd get the plates of the car he drove away in. It was a win-win situation.

Wrong.

Gravel crunched underfoot as Grant rounded the corner. The parking lot didn't need a fresh coat of tarmac, it needed the gravel tarmacking altogether. The dull grey he'd seen coming in was just fine pebbles and aggregate. It was noisy. He couldn't follow the departing businessman without signaling his approach. The noise was also a distraction.

Grant didn't hear the men coming up behind him until it was too late. Not bouncers from the club. The two big guys from Flanagan's the other night. A car door slammed as Grant came around the front of the building. An expensive black car built like a tank. Grant stopped to read the plates. That's when he heard the footsteps in the gravel, and he spun around.

The big guy from the alley beside CVS Pharmacy stood facing him. The other guy took up position to one side. Two bouncers came around from the front. Grant glanced both ways, and the big guy saw it. He smiled. "Ah, ah, I know what you're thinking."

Grant nodded and smiled.

TWENTY-ONE

THE GREAT THING about being relaxed is that you think clearly and act fast. The dumb thing about witty one-liners is delivering them before you've beaten your opponent. Grant wasn't thinking witty.

The black car spat gravel as it sped out of the parking lot. That kind of noise was hard to ignore. The four heavies couldn't ignore it. They all threw a split-second glance towards their departing boss. A split second was all Grant needed.

The great thing about being relaxed is that you think clearly and act fast. Grant acted fast. He stepped inside the big guy's fighting arc and stamped down hard on the outside of his leg at knee height. The leg collapsed. Before the witty one-liner guy had hit the floor, Grant spun on his heel, jerked his arm out straight, and hit the other guy in the windpipe while he was still watching his friend go down. He grabbed his throat and turned red in the face. Grant kept the forward momentum and drove his knee up into the guy's balls. The guy dropped to his knees, confusion on his face over what to clutch, his throat or his wedding tackle.

Two down.

Two to go.

The other two were barroom brawlers, thickset with short necks and slow movements. Ideal for enclosed spaces. Not so good for out in the open. Lots of room to maneuver. Grant stepped over the fallen windpipe guy and skipped to one side, away from the ugly twins. The nearest one made a lunge for the orange windcheater but missed, opening a gap between the two bouncers. Grant swiveled on one leg and darted into the gap.

The first bouncer was confused and tried to correct his aim. That meant trying to turn faster than he was capable of turning, leaving him off-balance. As Grant moved between them, he tucked his arm in and whipped the elbow in a short arc at the guy's face. Punching was for boxers and pub fights. There are too many bones in the hand that can break if you thump somebody in the face and hit the forehead. The elbow is all bone and muscle weight. It smashed the nose and shut one eye before the bouncer knew what hit him. He didn't go down, but he was blinded with pain.

Three down.

One left.

Except it wasn't one anymore. It was four. Three more heavies came pouring around the corner and split to cover all angles. Grant was back where he started but without the element of surprise. He stepped back, keeping the wall close behind him. The four were all in front and to either side, but nobody could get to his back. A siren sounded in the distance. Somebody had called it in. Time for delaying tactics until the cavalry arrived. "You four want to share a cell, or you okay being separated?"

Nobody spoke. One grunted as he lunged and retreated. When he stepped backwards, the one on the other side lunged forward and swung a haymaker fist. Grant slapped the arm down on the follow-through, grabbed the wrist, and twisted it full circle. Downwards and back the way it came. Balance was shot. The guy's full weight followed his arm or the wrist would break. He flipped over like a gymnast and crashed to the floor on his back. The sirens grew louder. "You hear that? That's room service. One cell each."

No matter how loose Grant stayed, the three remaining heavies outweighed him. It had taken them a while, but they'd finally realized that the Musketeers tactic was the way to go. All for one. At the same time. They surged forward from all sides and caught Grant in the middle. A fist the size of a Yorkshire ham smashed into his stomach, driving the breath out of him. A knee came up as Grant doubled over, and he managed to turn his head just in time to avoid a broken nose. The blow sent him reeling. A two-handed hammer blow came down on the back of his neck and he hit the gravel face first. The sharp grey stones drew blood.

The distinctive snap of a switchblade focused Grant's attention. A flash of silver caught his eye and pain flared down the side of his face. Warm blood flushed his right eye. Somebody laughed. Even the laughter had an Irish accent. A shadow fell over him, and he looked up at the big guy from Flanagan's. He was smiling through the pain in his balls. He leaned forward and tucked a five-dollar bill down Grant's T-shirt. "Get something for the swelling. There's a pharmacy just up the street."

The five-dollar guy reached down and snatched the money back. "Nah, you won't need a doctor. You'll need an embalmer."

He pulled a small black gun from the back of his trousers and wracked the slide. The noise was sharper than the switchblade. It focused Grant's attention and forced a deep breath out of his lungs. Out through his nose. To relax. The big guy was all talk. He leaned close to give Grant a good look at the end of his life. The gun swung into view. Closer still.

Big mistake.

Grant moved like a rattlesnake. He flashed one arm up and over in a short arc, meeting the gun hand forearm to forearm. The gun swung up and over in the same arc. Grant spun on his hip, stamping his foot upwards into the big guy's knee. From the front. The knee buckled in the wrong direction, breaking the joint with a vicious snap. The howl of pain forced the other three back a pace.

The gun dropped to the floor. Grant grabbed it and spun onto his back, keeping his legs facing the attackers. The switchblade magically disappeared. Red and blue lights were flashing into the junction of Pond Street and Arborway. The sirens were deafening. The last three ran around the back of the club. Grant's hand moved in a blur. Within seconds the gun was in pieces on the parking lot. Magazine. Slide. Barrel. Pistol grip. Assorted springs and bullets. Nobody saw him do it. Grant stared at the pieces for a second, then kicked them away. He tried to stand up but felt dizzy and collapsed against the wall.

He couldn't think of a witty one-liner. He was bleeding too much. Three squad cars skidded into the lot, spitting gravel as they braked. Officers dashed around the back of the club. Somebody came over to Grant. There was no gallows humor from him either, just an urgent request for an ambulance into his radio.

CAMERAS FLASHED as they wheeled Grant into the hospital. The MGH was awash with them. A bright light shone out of the darkness, and Grant could just make out the earnest tones of a newsreader mentioning the Resurrection Man. He felt like kicking the camera, but he was strapped tight to the gurney. A helicopter hovered overhead but too high to see inside the city limits.

Then everything was cut off as the gurney went through the sliding doors. One hardy photographer tried to follow but was held back by the police. Everything was hazy and indistinct. Grant's head was spinning from the pain medication and the constant movement of the gurney. He felt sick. He was sick. Down the front of his T-shirt. He thought about John Cornejo and his vomit-stained clothing. His lack of shoelaces and a belt. He tried to check his jeans but couldn't move his arms. He could see his K-Swiss tennis shoes, though, laces intact, and felt at least he wasn't on suicide watch.

The hospital corridor kept turning on its axis. The overhead lights swam in and out of focus. He was sick again. Nauseous through loss of blood. Then he was being unstrapped and transferred to an examination table. The world tilted. It didn't right itself until he woke up in a curtained cubicle smelling of vomit and antiseptic. The two people at the foot of the bed didn't seem glad to see him.

"Don't think this is what Kincaid meant when he said you should ask around." Miller had lost the smile but not his enthusiasm. "Good job that Canadian called when he saw the bouncers follow you out."

Grant was awake, but his mouth wasn't working yet. He flexed his lips, but his tongue was stuck to the roof of his mouth. He tried to salivate, but no moisture would form. Miller passed him a paper cup of water. Grant drank it in one swallow. Miller went out to the water cooler and refilled it. Grant drank half and nodded his thanks. The nod felt like it unleashed a ton of rocks inside his head. He made a mental note not to nod or shake his head again. "You get 'em all?"

"Only the ones who couldn't run. Variety of injuries. Some are down here."

"Good for them."

Grant noticed the grey plastic MGH bag and suddenly realized he wasn't wearing his clothes. The hospital gown was clean but rough against his skin. His eyes widened when he saw the foot-tapping nurse standing in the doorway. He mimed a pair of scissors with two fingers of one hand. "You didn't—?"

"Your favorite jacket? No. Your jeans neither. Not sure you want to keep the T-shirt. It's in a separate bag."

The third-generation nurse from York folded her arms across her chest and began tapping her foot. The look on her face said more than her words. She was pissed at him. "Usually, somebody signs themselves out, they don't get a second chance. But the Mass General's PR consultant didn't want us turning the Resurrection Man away on national TV."

Grant looked sheepish. "I didn't come up with that."

"I know. You'd have probably called yourself the Shit-Deflector Man."

Grant looked from the nurse to Miller. Miller shrugged and smiled. "I had some time to kill. What else was there to talk about?"

The nurse almost smiled, but all it did was lessen her frown slightly. "Don't worry. You're covered by the doctor/patient privilege."

Grant snorted a laugh and nodded. He'd forgotten the mental note. His head felt like a ton of loose rocks was banging around inside. The headache was massive. He grimaced and felt fresh pain up the side of his face. The nurse gave her professional opinion. "Don't smile."

"I'm not smiling."

The nurse unfolded her arms. "Medical matters: you've got three bruised ribs and a grazed cheekbone where they kicked you in the head. X-rays show no other broken bones. Wounds have been cleaned. You're going to need stitches in the knife wound. Don't smile until they're done."

"Don't think I'll smile much after."

"Your choice. Probably a good decision."

She turned on her heel and went out to get a suture kit. Miller stepped closer. "There was no sign of the knife. Do you remember which one cut you?"

"No."

"Doesn't matter. Joint venture. They all cop a charge for it."

"You want another statement?"

"Later. The witness gave enough for now."

Miller glanced over his shoulder to make sure the nurse wasn't back yet. "This your idea of deflecting shit?"

"More like learning shit. I was going to ask the owner about some stuff. Seems that Sullivan was importing foreign girls. I guess his boys didn't want me talking to him. I thought you were day shift."

"I'm dedicated. We got 'em for assault. Can't tune it up to officer on duty."

Grant couldn't argue with that since he was most definitely off-duty. His body ached. His face was sore. The bruising hadn't gone down from the explosion yet, never mind the new bumps from tonight.

He felt tired.

Miller fixed him with a firm stare. "Funny thing is, we found a gun at the scene. Dismantled and scattered across the parking lot. Every moving part. In bits."

There was no reason not to tell Miller about the gun. Grant wasn't sure why he didn't. Some memories were best kept hidden. He'd been a typist. That was all anyone needed to know. He shrugged but didn't shake his head. He was learning. The curtain swished open and the nurse came in holding a tray.

"*A Stitch in Time.*" Grant looked at the suture kit on the tray. "Norman Wisdom. Pinewood Studios. 1963."

"*Nurse Jackie.* Now."

Miller stepped back. "Well, boys and girls, I'll leave you to it." He nodded to Grant. "Call in to the station tomorrow. I'll take your statement."

The nurse waved him away with her free hand. "Assuming he's been released by then. He's staying until we say otherwise tonight. Even if I have to call security."

Grant interjected. "You won't need security."

"Good."

She set the tray down beside the bed and opened the suture kit. Miller left and closed the curtain behind him. The nurse, whose name Grant still hadn't learned, held a curved needle up for inspection. "This is going to hurt you a lot more than it will me, I'm happy to say."

"*Zulu.* Diamond Films. 1964. Surgeon Reynolds to Private Hook."

"You watch too many movies. See what this reminds you of."

She put the curved needle down and picked up a syringe for the local anaesthetic. Grant watched it approach the open wound in the side of his face, eyes wide. His breathing was coming in rapid, shallow breaths. The relaxation technique wasn't working. He didn't like needles. He felt faint. Then pain skewered the side of his face before blessed numbness took over.

IT WAS AFTER TWO in the morning before they agreed to let him go. Nurse Jackie gave him the good news and helped him into his clothes. She was right about the T-shirt. He threw it in the bin and zipped the orange windcheater up to his neck. There were a couple of nicks in the left sleeve and a tear in one knee. The K-Swiss were scuffed across the toes. Another plastic nametag hung loose from his wrist.

The smell of evacuated bowels and disinfectant gave way to the scent of Nurse Jackie's perfume. Grant wondered if she chose it for strength or beauty. Like most cops, he used to carry a pack of mints for evacuated bowel moments like sudden deaths and postmortems. Nestle Polos. Working in an environment like the ER, it made sense to deflect the shitty smells with a little perfume. A kind of shit deflector for the nasal passages.

Grant looked up from the nametag and smiled. His face didn't hurt so much anymore. It was probably the tablets she'd given him before he got dressed. He kept the smile brief. The dumb thing about witty one-liners was delivering them before you'd beaten your opponent. The good thing about them was they made good parting shots. "Well. Don't forget to write."

Nurse Jackie almost smiled back. "Sean Connery in *Goldfinger*. Pinewood. 1964."

"Now who watches too many movies?"

She pointed to the reception desk. "You're signed out. Please don't call again."

Then she was gone with a swish of the curtain, leaving Grant to walk slowly through reception and into the night. He stood for a moment on the sidewalk and took a deep breath. The fresh air was bliss after the contaminated atmosphere inside. Two ambulances were parked across the road. A patrol car drove past the end of the hospital, cruising not blue lighting. The night was peaceful.

Headlights came on and an engine started to his left. A Hertz rental car pulled up to the entrance, and the passenger window slid down. A throaty voice told him to get in. Grant ducked to look through the window but didn't need to see the driver. He never forgot a voice. She raised an eyebrow. "Next of kin?"

"So you can get my body."

"Well, they got the right number then."

Grant got in and slammed the door, then Terri Avellone drove him away.

TWENTY-TWO

Soft hands and a CVS Pharmacy natural sponge soaped his body down in the shower. The showerhead was fastened to a sliding bar up the tiled wall for height adjustment, but it only adjusted to the full height of a midget. Grant stood head and shoulders above the hot spray. That was good. His face was sore. The stitches holding his cheek together were dressed with medicated gauze and sticking plaster. It needed to be kept dry.

Terri Avellone stood naked in the shower with him and washed everything else. As they'd discussed before, cleanliness was next to godliness. Avellone was having a religious experience cleaning Grant's man parts. As before, at the Airport Hilton, she was employing the full body-washing technique. Her hands and the sponge soaped and rinsed his stomach while her breasts and love mound slithered up and down his back and buttocks. She was gentle with him, shocked by the vicious bruising that was already purple down one side of his chest and blackening one eye. The grazing was restricted to his face. The torn jeans and orange jacket had protected the rest of him, leaving red marks but not breaking the skin.

The tattooed No Entry sign was the only constant. Everything else about him had changed since their last encounter. Almost everything. She soaped that with the sponge, then slid her hand up and down it to make sure it was clean. It sprang to life. Grant didn't need much encouragement. "This is getting to be a habit."

She continued the gentle rhythmic action. "You know it can't go anywhere. Don't you?"

"That's the best kind."

She suddenly squeezed her fist tight. He almost came in her hand. Her other hand spanked his backside. Twice. "Naughty boy. Don't you know a woman likes to think she's the only one?"

"If I knew what women liked, I'd be awesome."

She relaxed her fist. "You are awesome."

He turned to face her. The soap on his stomach lathered her breasts as they pressed against him. His hardness prodded her stomach, high up just beneath her ribs. The benefits of having a shorter woman. She flexed her knees and her breasts slid down either side of him. They felt even nicer than her fingers. He moaned. A deep and contented sound that vibrated his chest against her face. She straightened her legs, and her breasts released his manhood.

Grant smiled at a private thought.

Avellone saw the look and raised one eyebrow. "What?"

His smile broadened. "You know what they say. Save a mouse, eat a pussy."

She laughed a dirty laugh that was deep and throaty. "You're an animal lover. Right?"

"RSPCA."

"That's English?"

"Royal Society for Prevention of Cruelty to Animals."

"I'm impressed."

She reached behind him and turned the shower off. "So, go ahead and save a mouse."

He crouched slightly, squeezed her in a bear hug, and picked her up standing upright. The cubicle was too narrow to sweep her up into his arms. He walked like that, with her body crushed against his, into the main room and laid her on the bed. He stroked her stomach, gently opened her legs, then proceeded to save a mouse. More than one.

THERE WAS SOMETHING very freeing about sex without actually having sex. It relieved the pressure of having to perform and allowed you to simply have fun. Like playing with your favorite toy. It also meant you didn't have to mess about unrolling a condom, even if Terri Avellone's condom-unrolling technique was better than most. Grant's mouse rescue left her completely satisfied.

The condom stayed in its cardboard matchbook on the bedside cabinet.

Until after.

Grant listened to Avellone washing herself in the bathroom and picked up the distinctive black matchbook with the flame and nude silhouette. He flicked it open. There was nothing written inside the flap. Not like those PI movies. He read the name on the front.

TRIPLE ZERO
Gentlemen's Services

He read the address on the back. Somewhere downtown. He wondered if it was another club or simply a business address—like a dead-letter drop. Burst in to search the place and find a bunch of old ladies knitting socks for the troops. He also wondered where Terri Avellone got so good at what she did. She didn't learn the putting-a-condom-on-with-her-mouth technique at pharmaceutical training.

Time to tread carefully. Because she was so good at what she did. He didn't want to look a gift horse in the mouth. Or kill the goose that laid the golden egg. She was fantastic at laying his golden egg.

The water stopped. A few seconds later Avellone came out of the bathroom wearing a towel and a smile. She took one look at Grant twirling the condom matchbook and the smile faded. "You look like you lost a fiver and found a penny."

"Shouldn't that be lost a dollar and found a nickel?"

"I'm trying to make you feel at home. What's the problem?"

"No problem." He held the matchbook up. "Just wondering where you get these from?"

"I'm in pharmaceuticals."

"Pharmaceuticals. Not prophylactics."

He watched her face. Her eyes specifically. It was standard technique when questioning someone. Being a cop, it often slipped into his normal life, and some people found it disturbing to be having a conversation with him while he stared them in the eye. Her usually confident look slipped a touch, but she soldiered on. "Pharmacies stock rubbers."

"Not these rubbers. Triple Zero only supplies sex clubs and bars."

"That what they told you at the Gentlemen's Club?"

"That's a fact."

"Well, here's a fact for you."

She took the matchbook out of his hand, opened the flap, and ripped the sealed condom out. She turned it over. The lettering was too small for him to see.

"Condoms supplied by Blue Rhino, third largest prophylactics manufacturer in the United States." She flicked the cardboard flap. "Packaging supplied by Lindley Print, a rather smaller business in Boston."

She tossed the matchbook and the condom onto the bed. "Pricks supplied free of charge by anyone with too much sap needs milking."

Grant got off the bed and held his hands up in surrender. "Now I've gone and pissed you off. Sorry. It's the copper in me."

Her expression softened. "So long as it's the cop that's inside me."

He sat on the bed and dragged her down beside him. He kissed her gently on the forehead. "Not tonight. I'm stiff as a board."

"All the better."

"And sore as a limp-dicked motherfucker."

She kissed his nose. "Someone with a limp dick can't be a motherfucker."

He laughed and laid her down across the bed. He leaned over and stroked the side of her face, then kissed her forehead again. He kissed her left eye and then the right, forcing her to close them. He kissed her nose then laid one finger across her lips. She opened her eyes. He leaned forward and kissed her lips, gently at first, then with more force. She kissed him back, avoiding touching his damaged face. He was glad they'd made friends again.

It was just a pity she was lying.

TWENTY-THREE

THEY WERE FRIENDS AGAIN, but something had changed. Grant felt sad about that but knew it was inevitable. Sooner or later they were going to move on; it was just the natural law. No recriminations. It was good while it lasted. What he needed now was answers. The best way to get answers was to avoid confrontation and slide in from the blind side.

The blind side was the Internet. "You got a laptop with you?"

"I've got a Mac."

"I don't want a burger."

She slapped him on the shoulder, careful not to hit the bruises, then went over to the case she'd brought up from the car. She never left anything of value in the car. The case was too small for clothes and too big for makeup. She unzipped it and took out a heavy white laptop with a silhouette of an apple with a bite missing on the top. She opened the lid and the MacBook automatically switched on.

Check the Internet. There's dozens of websites for Boston escorts. They cater for all tastes. Eastern Europeans are very popular.

Gerry O'Neill had been way ahead of Grant on that score. The Resurrection Man was good at many things, but being computer literate wasn't one of them. The secret of good policing though wasn't knowing everything but knowing who to ask.

"Can you check for Boston escort services?"

She gave him a funny look, then typed the request into Google. A list of advertisers came up almost straightaway, with a small map in the corner. The map of Boston had red pins dotted around, marked with A and B all the way to K. Sponsored links next to the map had corresponding As and Bs and Ks, giving more details for the locations shown. An indicator at the bottom showed this was page one of ten and there was an arrow next to number ten saying *More…*

O'Neill had been right. There were lots of escort services on the Internet. Grant scanned the list on page one. They had colorful names.

After Dark Escorts.

J'Adore Escorts.

Boston Pussycats.

Eros Guide.

The Twilight Club.

Triple Zero Gentlemen's Services.

Avellone appeared uncomfortable. Grant wasn't sure if it was a specific name on the list or her knowing that he suspected she was lying. Once distrust entered a relationship, it was curtains. The fact that Grant considered this to be a relationship was a bit of a surprise too. Discomfort filled the room.

He concentrated on the list. Triple Zero came up on the first page alongside a similarly named Triple X Escorts. That name seemed more fitting, echoing the XXX rating on hardcore porn videos and DVDs. It reminded Grant of the Northern X massage parlor chain back in Yorkshire. A rogue ex–West Yorkshire police officer, Vince McNulty, had finally brought that chain to its knees. Grant wasn't sure yet if bringing down Triple Zero was his mission, but zero tolerance had always been his credo. His shift inspector would no doubt label him a rogue cop.

He indicated the computer screen. "Triple Zero."

Avellone clicked on the link. A very professional homepage came up with a colorful image of the Boston cityscape viewed from the river, all glass and chrome skyscrapers set against a blue cloudless sky. There were various headers across the top of the screen linking to different pages on the site.

Introduction.

Rates.

Triple Zero Beauties.

Gallery.

Bookings.

Employment.

Grant was curious. He pointed at the screen again. "Let's check employment."

"You thinking of changing jobs?"

"My inspector wouldn't argue to keep me."

She clicked the link, and a separate page opened. There were various sections promoting the benefits of becoming a Triple Zero escort. Grant thought it looked like any regular recruitment page. He read the special invitation.

"If you are a lady of exceptional beauty and you possess poise, personality, and that something special, we would like to extend an invitation to join our team."

He smiled in disbelief. "Sounds like being headhunted by Microsoft instead of giving head."

He wondered if the ones being imported by Freddy Sullivan had been given the same incentive? He doubted it when he read the qualifications.

- You must be 18–42.
- You must have a cell phone.
- You must be completely reliable, ambitious, and purposeful in life.
- You must be articulate and well spoken.
- You must have a remarkably pretty face.
- You must have immaculate and well-cared-for skin.

Whoever Freddy Sullivan was importing must have been for the lower end of Triple Zero's market, because he doubted Freddy had ever met anyone that filled this criteria. He wouldn't know how to speak to an articulate woman if his life depended on it. Grant felt a pang at that last thought. He brushed it aside and read the benefits section.

- Unlimited income.
- Brand-new car.
- Company-paid gym membership.
- $2,000 Christmas and New Year bonus.
- Company-paid vacations.
- Private in-call locations.
- On-site security.

Grant sat back in his chair and puffed out his cheeks. He let out a long, low breath and rubbed his eyes. Computers did that to him.

"Jesus. No wonder they give away free condoms. I bet they don't pay that in pharmaceuticals."

"Well, I don't get the unlimited income and on-site security."

Grant asked her to click on the gallery. A selection of studio portraits came up that made the dancers at the Gentlemen's Club look like back-street strippers. They were stunning. Playboy centerfold standard. There were blonds and brunettes and raven-haired beauties. The only thing they all had in common was their obvious Eastern European bone structure. The Russians were coming, or women from that general direction. There was a banner across the bottom of the page with the same headings as the top but with two additions.

Links.

Contact.

He pointed at the links heading. Avellone clicked on it. A new page opened with a collection of advertising banners for separate clubs, including the Gentlemen's Club. These were obviously for lower-income customers. Grant didn't bother noting the addresses. He'd already visited one location. The others would simply be more of the same. He did get her to click on the contact heading, though. There was an e-mail address and a telephone number. He wrote the number in his notebook and picked up the condom matchbook. He wrote down the address on the back.

One Post Office Square

"Do you know where that is?"

"Downtown somewhere. In the business district. Exclusive."

"Head office then, d'you think?"

"It certainly won't be a strip club."

"Escorts neither?"

"I doubt it. Not down there."

Grant turned the matchbook over in his fingers, looking at the front and then the back. He lifted the flap. This was where being in one of those old PI movies would come in handy. The vital clue written inside the flap. The flap was empty. The clue was there, though. He just needed the right person to interpret it. It was time to push a little harder.

"D'you think your friend could get me some info on Triple Zero?"

Avellone's face turned to stone. "My friend?"

Grant was watching her eyes again. He held up the matchbook.

"The one you were protecting. Over the condoms."

Her face remained impassive, but her eyes couldn't hide the lie. "I don't know what you're talking about."

"Terri. I'm not judging anybody. But this is serious. Two men are dead." He indicated the cut on the side of his face. "Somebody did this. I need help. Your friend might be able to help."

Avellone lowered her eyes, unable to meet his stare. She took a deep breath. Her usual self-confidence seemed to evaporate. When she looked up, she had made a decision. Then she told him what he wanted to know.

TWENTY-FOUR

GRANT DIDN'T EVEN MAKE IT across the police station reception the following morning before being accosted. At least the attractive blond with the stitched-on grin wasn't pointing a camera in his face. Not unless she was filming from a helicopter with a zoom lens like last time. It put him in mind of that scene in *Die Hard 2* where the news reporter stuck a camera in Bruce Willis's face and he told her to fuck off or something. Bruce Willis was always telling somebody to fuck off, or to shut the fuck up, or calling them a motherfucker.

Grant didn't tell the reporter to fuck off. She was being too polite.

"Excuse me. Mr. Grant. Can I speak to you for a minute?"

"So long as you don't expect me to speak back."

The cameraman stood up from the waiting-room chair where he'd been nursing the shoulder-rigged camera in his lap. Grant gave him his pissed-off-Yorkshire-copper glare, and the cameraman sat down again. Grant turned his attention to the reporter. She was even more attractive up close, with a remarkably pretty face and immaculate, well-cared-for skin.

Items five and six on the Triple Zero qualifications page.

She turned off the stitched-on smile and began to resemble a normal human being, albeit an incredibly attractive and well-dressed one. She waved the cameraman to stay where he was and moved closer to Grant. Her perfume was subtle but addictive. One smell of it and he wanted to take a deep breath. It smelled clean and fruity and erotic all at the same time, like she'd bathed in apples with a hint of mint. He wondered if her skin felt as silky as it looked. He'd bet it did. Her voice, now that she'd toned down her news-reader twang, was low and sexy. "How are you feeling this morning?"

"Compared to what?"

"Compared to before you got beaten up and stabbed last night."

"About the same. I'm not a morning person."

"You seem to be having a hectic visit to Boston."

Grant lowered his head and tilted it to one side. He looked her in the eyes. "Do I need to search you for a wire?"

She didn't blush, just stared right back. "No. I always ask permission before recording someone."

"Good to know."

He glanced at the cameraman. The camera on his lap was pointing in Grant's general direction. There didn't appear to be any lights blinking or parts moving, but Grant wasn't sure how these things worked nowadays. They didn't use film any more, he knew that, so maybe there were no moving parts to indicate it was recording. He did know about directional microphones. If the camera had one, it was aimed at the couple talking off the record. When it came to reporters, Grant didn't believe anything was off the record.

"Step into my office."

He opened the interview-room door and ushered the reporter in. He followed and closed the door behind him. The room had been cleared but not repaired. The table had gone. The glass and debris had been removed. The walls had been cleaned of blood and grime but not repainted. The reporter's perfume overpowered the last vestiges of cordite, that bonfire night smell that always lingered for days after. That was good. The other smell you got when someone was blown inside out was soggy shit and burned flesh. The cleaners had sprayed enough air freshener to get rid of most of that too. Almost.

There were two chairs against the wall. Slightly torn and scarred but clean.

"Have a seat, Miss—?"

"Kimberley Clark. Call me Kim, Mr. Grant."

"Jim."

"Like Captain Kirk?"

"Nothing like Captain Kirk. What can I do for you?"

They both sat, Grant pulling his chair to face Clark's.

"I want to tell your story."

"I don't have a story."

"That's not how it looks on TV."

That familiar phrase again. Grant was beginning to find it irritating. "Nothing's like it looks on TV."

"Maybe not. But you've hit the triple so far. The explosion. The shooting. The stabbing. You're getting more reruns than *Friends*."

"They should can *Friends*."

"They won't can you. You're good coverage."

"D'you cover crime scenes much, Kim?"

"Some."

"D'you know that bit where they say, 'A police spokesman said'?"

Clark looked resigned. She knew where this was going. Grant continued.

"Well, a police spokesman said we are conducting a vigorous investigation. All avenues are being explored, but there is no further information at this time."

"About the investigation?"

"Yes."

"Yes, there is? Or yes, the investigation?"

"Yes, I'm not going to say anything about the investigation."

Her look of resignation vanished. Grant reckoned she was a woman who didn't like to take no for an answer. A woman who brushed off disappointment and focused on the positives. An admirable trait to have. She looked him in the eye, and he saw what it must be like for people who talked to him. The eye contact was very important. She smiled. "What about Snake Pass? You got anything to say about that?"

Grant smiled back. "It's a winding road in Yorkshire between Manchester and Sheffield."

He had to admit she was good. The curve ball was supposed to unsettle him, but he'd been interrogated by the best. The same technique he employed for everything applied. Relax. Breathe easy. Don't panic.

Keep out of trouble. Don't get involved. You're off-duty.

His shift inspector's parting words. Snake Pass was history. Another story for another day. The fallout from it was Grant being sent to Boston. The fallout from that was two men dead and a police station being bombed. Just like old times, in older countries. No matter how many times he told himself he was only a typist.

She didn't give up. "The incident at Snake Pass."

His smile didn't waver. "A police spokesman said."

"Same answer, eh?"

"Open investigation. What did you expect?"

"I don't want the investigation. I told you. I want your story. An Englishman in a strange land."

"You got that bit right."

"Like Crocodile Dundee in New York."

"This is Boston."

"But you're Crocodile Dundee."

"No, I'm not. I know what a bidet is, and I don't sleep on the floor."

"Figuratively speaking. You're the Resurrection Man."

"You come up with that?"

"No. That was Fox News. But once you've got a name, it sticks."

He knew that was true. He'd been called plenty of names back in Yorkshire. Quite a few of them stuck. None of them were printable. There would be no getting away from the Resurrection Man as long as he was in Boston. Getting away from Boston depended on what he found out about Triple Zero Gentlemen's Services. He thought about that for a moment. "What's your view on oral sex?"

That caught Clark by surprise, but she recovered quickly. "Depends if you mean talking dirty or the act itself."

He waved the thought aside. "Doesn't matter. Forget it."

She stared at him, clearly not forgetting it. Grant stood up. This interview was over. The answers he needed were upstairs, not on WCVB News. All they'd have would be hearsay and misinformation. That's what the news was all about. And don't forget the Lassie moment at the end to leave your viewers with hope and a smile.

"A police spokesman said."

"'A source close to the investigation said'—that's another tagline."

"Well, this source said goodbye. Nice meeting you."

She slipped a business card in his hand before he even realized she had a bag. He was impressed. This girl should be working the con. Working for WCVB News, maybe she already was.

"If you change your mind, give me a call. You're going to be on the news if you like it or not. Might as well get your side of the story out there."

"That's what I usually say. Just before dropping a vital clue in an interview."

"Drop away."

"Not today. Take care."

He opened the door and crossed reception, waving at the desk sergeant to let him in. Clark called after him from the doorway of the bombed-out interview room. "It's you who needs to take care. The triple can easily become the quad."

"You'll have your story then, won't you?"

Sergeant O'Rourke pressed the button, and the internal door lock buzzed. Grant pushed the door into the stairwell, then watched the news crew going out the front. The tight trousers of Kimberley Clark's business suit hugged her backside, each buttock moving separately in a tight little cycle. He thought of Terri Avellone and what she'd told him last night.

It was time to put some meat on the bones. He closed the door and went up the clock tower stairs, his feet echoing all the way up.

THE DETECTIVES' OFFICE WAS empty. Grant walked straight in without knocking. He felt like part of the furniture now. It was funny how that always happened. When you started at a new station, you felt like an outsider, not knowing anybody and having to find your way around. Some old-timer would show you the ropes, point out the stationary cupboard and where the coffee machine was. A couple of days later you knew where the basics were. Not long after that, once the sarcasm and van culture kicked in, you felt right at home. He felt right at home here.

Except there was nobody to be sarcastic with. The detectives' office was empty.

Grant stood in the doorway for a moment while he absorbed a sight so strange it didn't immediately compute. They say that Times Square in New York is never empty, apart from when they found that car bomb recently. That may well be true, but Jim Grant had never been in a CID office that didn't have at least have one detective scrutinizing a file or making coffee or bollocking somebody over the phone. The E-13 detectives' office was empty, and there wasn't even a car bomb to explain why.

He took a step into the room and glanced around the desks. The desktops were in various stages of disarray, the sign of a hardworking cop. A neat and tidy desk indicated somebody more concerned with keeping a neat and tidy desk than a detective deep into someone else's shit. There should be notes about possible suspects, crime scene photos or forensic reports, and messages to call informants back as soon as possible. All of that was the case here. Every desk had its own selection of work-related debris. There just wasn't anybody to action the many tasks required. It was a ghost town.

Then the door pushed open behind him, and Miller came in rubbing his hands dry. If he'd come in pulling the zip on his fly up, he couldn't have signaled a return from the restroom any clearer. He stopped when he saw Grant. "Christ. You scared me to death."

"I could say the same. Thought I'd wandered onto the *Mary Celeste*."

Miller resumed drying his hands. "Bermuda Triangle is what it is around here at the moment."

"Glad to see you wash your hands after pointing Percy at the porcelain."

"Pardon me?"

Grant pointed at Miller's crotch. "Don't forget. More than three shakes is a wank."

Miller blushed. It seemed out of place in the world of hardened detectives, but along with Miller's boundless enthusiasm it was one of the things Grant liked about him. He was still in touch with his former self, before he entered the real world of police work. Miller went to his desk and held up a cup for Grant. The true sign of acceptance in a new station. "You're a funny guy, Jim. If I knew what you were talking about."

He wiggled the cup. "Coffee?"

"No thanks. Had my caffeine fix out of a can."

"Okay. How you feeling this morning?"

Grant felt a touch of déjà vu but didn't use the same retort. Miller was on the side of the angels. He worked the streets, didn't report about them.

"Stiff and sore. Like most mornings."

"Saw you on the news again. You're a regular media star."

"Maybe next time I can make it without ending up in hospital."

Miller waved at Grant's orange windcheater. "Change jackets and they wouldn't recognize you."

"Undercover isn't my thing. I want people to recognize me so they know I'm not armed and dangerous. Diffuse the situation."

"Hasn't worked so far."

"They haven't got to know me yet." He indicated the empty office. "I take it you've not got any staff for a bit of door knocking?"

Miller held his arms out. "What you see is what you get."

"The oil conference?"

"Everybody. In uniform. Kincaid looks kinda strange. Only ever see him in uniform at funerals, and we haven't had one of those since I transferred."

Grant leaned over and laid his fingers on a wooden cabinet. "Touch wood it stays that way."

Miller did the same. "Yeah. Be glad when this oil bunch go home."

"So you can go back to dealing with regular shitbags and lying scummers?"

"Regular liars instead of corporate liars. Yeah. All this foreign rights and politics makes my skin crawl."

Grant walked to Miller's desk and leaned against it, crossing his legs. He laid both hands on the desktop behind him for balance. He looked right at home, as if he'd been working at the BPD all his service. "Well, here's some regular shitbag stuff. What do you know about the Gentlemen's Club?"

"Junction of Pond and Arborway? From last night?"

"Yes. And Triple Zero Gentlemen's Services?"

"Ah, yeah. Both the same but different. Prostitution."

"Escorting."

"Same thing."

"So, what do you know?"

Miller wheeled his chair out and sat down. It meant he was looking up at Grant instead of down at him, but that didn't seem to bother him. Miller was keen and eager no matter where he sat. Pecking order wasn't a problem. One-upmanship wasn't in his nature. He leaned back in his chair.

"I know it's not a district priority. Sex crimes don't even register on city hall targets for JP. City hall wants to keep the figures down for volume crime. Rapes and attempts are around ten or eleven the last four months. Burglary and attempts about seventy. Larcenies almost three hundred. Robberies, fifty-eight. Vehicle theft, sixty-nine. Drugs don't even feature on the reported crime stats. Separate issue."

He swiveled in his chair, rocking gently from left to right. "Prostitution? So long as it's off the street. Not a problem. There are still offenses there, but it generally gets the BPD blind eye. Resources like they are, we can only do so much in a day."

Grant nodded. "You can't fit a quart in a pint pot."

"Thought you'd gone metric?"

"Same principal applies."

"Basically, if it doesn't trouble city hall or the stats, it doesn't trouble us."

"Must be a thriving business then."

"It is. There are lap-dancing clubs all over the place, but the escort business is booming. Mostly online. Big money in that. Main man around here is a guy called Frank Delaney."

The name bristled Grant's neck again. Mr. Delaney. This was the first time he'd got a first name, though. The owner of Flanagan's Bar and the Gentlemen's Club and employer of Freddy and Sean Sullivan. The kingpin in charge of Triple Zero Gentlemen's Services, with headquarters at One Post Office Square in the business district. "Delaney?"

"Yeah. Real nasty piece of work. Goes back a long way. You ever shake his hand, count your fingers. That was his speciality, cutting fingers off his rivals. Said it helped him recognize the opposition. Get this. He once had a run-in with a local butcher. Proper meat man—steak, lamb, best in the business. Come Thanksgiving, he used to donate pies to all the JP charities. Anyway. Delaney falls out with him. Has him cut down to a torso and hangs him in his own shop window on a meat hook. Gives a message to anyone thinking of standing against him."

Grant whistled softly. Miller continued.

"Fingers in a lot of pies, most of them legitimate now. It's not like the Whitey Bulger days. There are more crooks at city hall than running the streets. We just deal with the dregs."

"In shit valley. I remember."

"He doesn't rob pizza deliveries or steal McDonald's cash registers."

"So he gets a pass?"

Miller nodded and stopped swaying his chair. "On prostitution. Yes. The man's a philanthropist. You know what he does? Get this. He not only donates to the VA Hospital"—he leaned forward and rested his elbows on the desk, fingers interlocked—"he helps the war effort by supplying returning veterans with free sex and condoms. Help them get over the trauma. Do you believe that?"

Grant believed it. Her Majesty's government didn't supply anything like that when he mustered out of the forces. He doubted she'd be amused. But this was America, man. Entrepreneurs ruled.

What he was thinking, though, was that it wasn't what you knew but who you knew to ask.

Grant reckoned he knew just the guy to ask.

TWENTY-FIVE

John Cornejo's house was a traditional green-painted clapboard on Woodlawn Street. It had a porch, a yard, and the inevitable stars and stripes hanging above the steps. It was the smallest house on a tree-lined street that ran up the hill towards a dead end backing onto Forest Hills Cemetery, a more permanent dead end. The other houses were painted in shades of pale blue or pink, and all displayed Support Our Troops stickers in the windows. Most had a stars and stripes hanging somewhere out front, the brilliant red and white glowing in the afternoon sunshine.

The only house painted green was Cornejo's.

It was the condition of it that Grant hadn't expected.

The doorbell rang somewhere inside the house. Grant stepped back from the door and held his hand up against the American flag. Its folds moved gently in the breeze and caressed his fingers. There was something deeply moving about a country's national flag during times of war. Just looking at it brought home the pain and sacrifice being offered by men barely out of their teens. Feeling it brush against his fingers brought goose bumps out on the back of his neck.

Nobody answered the door.

Grant examined the front of the house. Considering the state Cornejo had been in when they'd first met and the obvious depression that had settled over the marine vet, Grant had expected a run-down shack on the edge of the cemetery. What stood before him was a beautifully appointed family home on a street that was filled with color and cleanliness.

Cornejo's house was no exception.

Grant pressed the doorbell again. He heard it deep inside the hallway. He could see through the lace-curtained window next to the front door but could only detect shadows and light. There was a staircase to the right. A telephone table at the bottom of the stairs. A closed door on the left. An open door at the end of the hall leading into a bright room. Probably the kitchen.

There was no movement.

If there was one thing Grant had learned during his military service, it was that men suffering from stress and depression seldom looked after themselves. An air of torpor hung over them that affected their general demeanor and cleanliness. It showed in their clothing, like the soiled T-shirt and scuffed boots Cornejo had been wearing on the T. It was also reflected in the places they lived. If you felt lethargic and unwanted, then keeping your house clean and tidy was not a priority. So Grant was surprised to find Cornejo's home looking pristine and shipshape.

He ignored the doorbell and knocked on the door. His copper's knock. The knock that let whoever was inside know that the police were calling. In Cornejo's case, Grant hoped it let him know the

Resurrection Man was calling. That should diffuse the "Halt, who goes there" response. "Friend or foe?" Grant wanted Cornejo to know he was a friend.

He knocked again, louder this time. He was about to shout through the letterbox, but the clapboard house didn't have a letterbox. Letters were left in a mailbox on a stick beside the sidewalk. He leaned close to the door and raised his voice.

"Come on, John. Stick the kettle on. It's your shout."

There was still no movement in the house. Grant tried the door handle. That usually worked in the movies. He half expected the door to creak open, leading him to find a dark secret inside. Just like the message written on the matchbook flap, that didn't work in real life either. The door was locked.

"John."

No response. He wished he'd checked before coming out here whether the ex-marine lived with his parents or alone. A wife perhaps? Although he didn't think that was the case. He hadn't got a married vibe from him the other night on the T, nor at the CVS Pharmacy after. The fact that Cornejo used the T meant there would be no car parked outside, so there was nothing to indicate if he was home or not. He glanced up at the windows. They were all closed. He was about to go around the side of the house when the door unlatched and swung inwards. Grant hadn't even seen Cornejo come along the hallway, but there he stood.

"What's shouting got to do with anything?"

"Sorry. Didn't mean to shout."

"No. 'It's your shout.' What's that?"

"Your turn. I made the last coffee."

"Thought you'd prefer tea. That's what the allies drink, isn't it?"

"So long as it's hot and wet. The British Army motto."

Cornejo stood in the doorway but didn't invite Grant in. There was an awkward silence. Cold calling on a witness canvas often produced that. People who weren't expecting the police having to rapidly adjust to the invasion of privacy. That went double for ex-military trying to put their pasts behind them and being reminded of it by visiting forces. Grant understood. Tact and diplomacy were needed. They weren't Grant's strengths as a copper.

"Forgotten how to extend the hand of friendship to a fellow soldier?"

"Thought you were a typist?"

"An army typist. Trained to kill with a cutting phrase."

Cornejo still didn't move aside.

Grant held up a black matchbook with the flame and silhouette logo. "You need any more of these?"

Cornejo glanced at the condom packet, then back at Grant. He didn't speak. After a few moments he stepped aside and waved Grant inside.

THEY SAT in the living room nursing a mug of coffee each. Grant's was milky with two sugars, evidence that he didn't really like coffee but suffered it as the easiest drink to make. Americans didn't know how to make a decent cup of tea anyway. Cornejo's coffee was black, no sugar, evidence of the dark place he found himself in with nothing to sweeten his life outside the brotherhood of the corps.

The living room screamed "family home." There was a sensible three-piece suite. There was a glass trophy display cabinet with assorted ornaments and miniature Lilliput Lane cottages from the UK. A standard TV stood in one corner with a VHS recorder underneath. A pendulum clock hung on the wall beside the door. The room smelled of air freshener. All very clean and tidy. There was no clutter. Nothing to suggest this was a bachelor pad. This had mother and father written all over it.

That made the omissions all the more pointed.

There were no framed photographs on the fireplace or trophy cabinet. There were none hanging on the walls. Proud parents always had photos of their children in uniform. There were always family group shots and father and son shots and pictures of grandma and granddad. Nieces and nephews. Cousins. Grant noticed the patches of wallpaper that were less faded than the rest. Square patches and rectangular patches. Three oval patches. Photographs that were missing, and not recently either. The nails had been removed long ago, leaving no sign of where the pictures had hung apart from the ghostly shapes on the wall.

There were no trophies in the trophy cabinet—something else that parents with a military background would have proudly displayed. Their son's first baseball. His high-school football trophies. Any other proof of his success growing up. Grant was certain Cornejo had been successful. You didn't end up in the US Marine Corps if you were a failure.

There was no evidence of Cornejo's family life at all. And yet the house was a shrine to his parents. Everything about the living room was as it had been when they were here. It was a living reminder of better times. Because Grant knew they had passed on. That was obvious too. The parents who had raised him and the corps that had nurtured him. All evidence of them removed. Cornejo was more depressed than Grant had thought.

Grant didn't ask about them. He decided on a different tack. He put the condom matchbook on the coffee table and flicked it across to Cornejo. The marine corps veteran looked at it, then took a sip of his coffee. "Am I supposed to feel embarrassed?"

"Hell no. Wish the army had given me a leg up when I came out."

"It isn't a leg up they're providing."

"Leg over then. Whatever. Forward thinking is what it is."

"It helps."

"I bet it does. Make love, not war. My mind's never clearer than at the point of *pffft, pffft, bing*."

Cornejo almost smiled. "There is a theory that if all men were satisfied in bed, they'd be too happy to go making war on their neighbors."

Grant nodded but added a caveat. "Providing the neighbors didn't have more oil or water or food than them."

"There is that too, yes." Cornejo flicked the matchbook back across the table. "So, what's the problem?"

"At this level. No problem. What bothers me is this."

Grant gave Cornejo the edited version of his adventures in Boston so far. The reason he was here to interview Freddy Sullivan. What Sullivan said just before he died. The brother's suggestion that Grant watch his back. Then the revelation that Sullivan was importing women for Triple Zero's sex services and the fact that Frank Delaney's name kept cropping up wherever Grant turned. Including providing relief for returning servicemen. "An admirable quality. But you don't get owt for nowt."

"Translation?"

"Anything for nothing."

"You're gonna really struggle if you don't learn proper English."

Grant indicated the empty walls. "Struggling seems to be what you're doing."

"Surviving is what I'm doing."

"Surviving isn't all it's cracked up to be. Living's what you should be doing."

"Listen to Sigmund fuckin' Freud over there."

Grant put his cup on the table. "Let's cut the crap, John. Delaney's up to no good. I just want to know what was so important he'd have Freddy whacked and risk setting the entire BPD on his tail."

"How the fuck should I know? Go ask him."

The burst of anger evaporated as quickly as it materialized. Cornejo seemed to realize he was in his mother's living room and his cheeks colored slightly. Swearing in front of your mother was unforgivable.

"I just know this was arranged through medical services. At the VA."

"You've heard of Delaney, though?"

Cornejo leaned back in his chair. "This is JP. Everyone knows about Delaney. It's like Whitey Bulger in the Southie Projects. He's a legend. Just not like Robin Hood."

"He's a crook, you're saying?"

"He hasn't invaded as many countries as our crooks."

"Scale isn't the issue. Legality is."

"Then yes. He's a crook. Nothing they've been able to pin on him, though."

Grant leaned back too, crossing one leg lazily over the other. He let out a sigh and let his eyes wander over the walls again. Then he focused on Cornejo's upper arm, where the patch was just visible below the T-shirt sleeve. Tact and diplomacy. Or simply sliding in from the blindside. The blindside, in this case, was Cornejo's love of his family and the corps.

"Covering the tattoo." Grant indicated the empty walls. "And removing your family. You can't hide from what you've done."

Cornejo didn't speak.

Grant uncrossed his legs and leaned forward in his chair. "You want to talk about it?"

"Sigmund Grant?"

"Somebody who's been there."

Cornejo sat completely still. Even his head didn't move as he spoke. "You want to talk about what you've done?"

"No."

"Or where you've served?"

"No."

"There's your answer, then."

"I've moved on. You haven't."

"Because you're a cop? Doing something useful again?"

"Because I've learned to live with what I've done."

"Good for you."

"And I'm not hiding what I used to be."

"I told you. I'm not hiding from it. Just protecting them from having to see what I've become."

"Now who's Sigmund Freud?"

They sat in silence for a few moments. The pause stretched into an awkward stalemate. Grant could see it working on Cornejo and waited just long enough to let him think. Then he played his ace. "I need your help."

Cornejo held his breath, his face impassive. Grant lowered his voice.

"How about we go stir the pot a bit?"

TWENTY-SIX

Grant and Cornejo stood outside One Post Office Square in the late afternoon sunshine, most of Post Office Square Park in shade but the eastern corner still painted gold by the sun's dying embers. Grant marveled not at the size of the glass and concrete tower but at its sheer opulence. The lobby windows were high and wide and gold trimmed. The interior looked like a palace from their position out on the street. Even the sidewalk seemed more expensive than the rest of the square. Pretentious six-feet-tall polished steel nameplates were fastened to the pillars on either side of the main doors, acid etched with the address.

One
Post
Office
Square

Even the sign looked expensive. The building reeked of money. The doorman wore a uniform that probably cost more than the BPD clothing budget for a year. Grant disliked the place immediately. He pushed the door and crossed the lobby.

"Triple Zero, please."

"I'm sorry, sir. There is no business listed by that name."

Grant's first judgement from the sidewalk had been right. The lobby was like a palace. Royalty could live here and not feel out of place. Everything metal was gold plated. Everything wood was highly polished or hand carved. The floor was marble tiled and shiny as an ice rink. The concierge was as rigid as the Coldstream Guardsmen outside Buckingham Palace. If he didn't bend, a strong wind would snap him like a twig. He didn't look in a ledger or check the building index; he simply stood erect and answered in the negative.

Grant wasn't surprised.

The building looked too exclusive to be the headquarters of a sex trafficker. Whatever name Delaney's business was registered under, it would have nothing to do with condoms, lap dancers, or prostitutes. There would be no free matchbooks with a nude silhouette against the flames. Grant glanced up at the back wall for a business listings plaque. The acid-etched steel nameplate fastened to the wall was the same as outside.

One
Post
Office
Square

There was no list of businesses. There was no index of residents. This wasn't *The Towering Inferno's* glass tower or the Nakatomi Plaza building from *Die Hard*, where John McLane could tap a name into the search screen and come up with the correct floor. This was far more exclusive. Far more secretive.

Back in Yorkshire, Grant would have simply flashed his warrant card and asked to see Frank Delaney. Being out of his jurisdiction, the warrant card wouldn't help. Not officially anyway. He flicked his wallet open and shut, allowing just enough time for the West Yorkshire Police badge to register and the checkered band to suggest police authority. "Police. Here to see Frank Delaney."

Cornejo had changed out of his desert fatigues into cleaner combat trousers and a khaki T-shirt, but he still exuded military presence. He stood behind and slightly to one side of Grant, with his arms folded across his chest. The concierge looked from Grant to the soldier and back again. He didn't unbend in the slightest. "That ID card is for the West Yorkshire Police. This is not West Yorkshire."

"Tell that to Delaney when I tell him you turned the police away."

"Mr. Delaney is perfectly entitled to turn you away. You have no jurisdiction in Boston."

Grant was beginning to think jobsworths were trained to be obstructive. This was as bad as talking to Sergeant Rooney in the JP custody suite.

"But Mr. Delaney would need to know I'm here to turn me away."

"If you do not have an appointment, Mr. Delaney does not need to know anything about you."

"No, but he wants to. Trust me."

The concierge was about to formulate another argument when the desk phone rang with a polite little buzz. Twice. He picked up the receiver, identified himself as front desk, and listened for a few seconds. Grant noticed the CCTV camera on the wall behind the desk and smiled at it. He resisted waving. The receiver clicked back into its holder. The concierge didn't even blink when he spoke.

"Delaney Enterprises is on the twenty-fifth floor. Elevators are over there."

Over there was half a mile away at the rear of the lobby. Felt like it anyway. In *Die Hard*, McLane's shoes echoed on the marble floor. In One Post Office Square, Grant's K-Swiss rubber soles squeaked with every step. The sound mocked the stiff guardsman demeanor of the man behind the desk.

The bank of elevators was four wide and gold trimmed, just in case you forgot you were entering one of the most exclusive premises in Boston. Grant pressed the call button, and the right-hand doors opened immediately. The interior throbbed with golden promise. Auric Goldfinger wouldn't have felt out of place here.

They stepped inside, and Grant pressed floor twenty-five.

The doors sighed closed, and the elevator took them up.

THE DEEP PILE CARPET of the twenty-fifth floor made the Airport Hilton feel like the Seaverns Hotel. Grant was impressed with just how much difference expensive carpet and wallpaper could make. Growing up, it had been woodchip and vinyl silk emulsion. The floor had been linoleum and throw rugs. This was like stepping into the lair of a Bond villain, and it was only the hallway and elevator station.

Whereas the lobby gave no indication of what businesses had offices in the building, the twenty-fifth floor landing had fingerposts on the wall opposite the elevators. Delaney Enterprises was on the right. Grant and Cornejo fell into step as they passed inset lighting and small wooden tables with displays of dried grasses. The displays were scented like potpourri and were no doubt attended daily by a servicing contractor. They came to a tall, wide door of pale wood with gold fittings. The door was taller than necessary and wide enough for two adults to fit through side by side. American excess at its most discreet. A pissing contest in all but name. Designed to make visitors feel small before they even entered. The polished brass plaque next to the door gleamed.

Delaney Enterprises

Even the nameplate reminded Grant of Enterprises Auric. He didn't knock. The door opened easily considering its size, probably using assisted hinges. If he was expecting some kind of overweight Goldfinger clone or a typical Boston gangster, he was mistaken. There was no reception lobby and there was no receptionist. The office was a corner suite on the southeast corner, and the man who stood to greet them was tall, well dressed, and polite. In the darkness of the Gentlemen's Club he'd looked older and rougher. He didn't bother hiding the CCTV screen he'd been watching.

"You're that guy off TV. From England. Thought I recognized you."

"Still on TV by the looks of it."

"Yes. I like to keep my eye on things. Welcome to my world."

Frank Delaney didn't hold his arms wide for them to examine the office, but the invitation was implicit in the greeting. Cornejo kept a pace behind Grant. Grant accepted the invitation at face value and took a moment to acclimatize. The first thing he did when entering any room.

Exits. The main door behind them. A normal-sized door behind the leather-topped desk. Another door in the far left corner. No doubt where the muscle waited. The furnishings were in keeping with the rest of the building: heavy, minimalist, and expensive. Deep-cushioned leather chairs. A solid hand-carved wooden desk. A low, wide, smoked-glass coffee table in the angle of the windows with a three-seat settee and two easy chairs. Plush cream leather. Matching beige carpet and floor-to-ceiling vertical blinds.

It was the windows that provided the wow factor.

The entire outer walls weren't glass like the conference room at BPD Headquarters, but the view east through the large rectangular windows was breathtaking. There were several equally impressive skyscrapers, but they didn't block the view across Boston Harbor. In the foreground, just across I-93 and Atlantic Avenue, the northern finger of Rowe Wharf stuck out into the harbor. Beyond that it was boats and water. In the distance Logan International twinkled in the sunlight. The place where Grant's Boston adventure had begun.

Grant turned his attention to the interior walls. They were neutral beige but expensively papered. Large framed posters from classic movies were evenly spaced around the room, indicating why Delaney had chosen that theme for the Gentlemen's Club. There was Steve McQueen in *Bullitt*. Clint Eastwood as Dirty Harry. There were a couple of early Leone westerns, *A Fistful of Dollars* and *For a Few Dollars More* but not *The Good, the Bad and the Ugly*. Jack Nicholson was part of the ensemble on *The Departed* poster. There was a Re-Elect Senator Clayton campaign poster and an original UK quad for *Goldfinger*. Grant wondered if Delaney modeled himself on the Jack Nicholson character, who was in turn modeled on Whitey Bulger? Or maybe the golden-themed office building gave him delusions of *Goldfinger*-style grandeur. Whichever it was, the lack of personnel in the office was surprising.

Grant decided to massage Delaney's ego. "You could live in an office like this."

"You could, but regulations don't allow it. I keep rooms at Le Meridien."

"The hotel downstairs. Linked by a secret passage?"

"Hardly secret. But a private corridor for tenants, yes."

Grant filed the information away but didn't stand on ceremony. "We almost met the other night."

"Oh, really? Where?"

"At the Gentlemen's Club. In Jamaica Plain."

"Ah, JP. My old stomping ground."

"I wouldn't put you down as the titty-bar type."

"Depends on the titties. I think you'll agree they were top quality."

"They were. But not local titties."

"Indeed not. I don't remember you there, though."

"I got distracted before I could talk to you."

"I saw that on TV too. Sorry about that. I won't tolerate violence at my establishments. That's why we employ security staff."

"It was your security staff."

"Not anymore." Delaney turned to Cornejo. "And who is your friend?"

Delaney looked cool, calm, and collected. This was his domain. Visiting cops didn't appear to worry him. Visiting cops with no jurisdiction shouldn't be a problem anyway. The man in army combat pants was a different matter. Delaney clearly used the "identify the threat" module of personal security. Grant stepped aside.

"John Cornejo. One of your customers. Or do you prefer clients?"

"One of our brave boys, by the looks of it." He extended his hand. "Glad to meet you."

Cornejo shook it. Grant wasn't offered a handshake. He was glad. At least he wouldn't have to count his fingers. Delaney continued. "Beneficiary of our Returning Veterans Program, I trust."

Cornejo nodded but didn't speak. That was what they'd decided before getting out of the elevator. Let Grant do the talking. Delaney had the floor at the moment, though. "We don't have a returns policy. Faulty goods aren't an issue, I hope."

Cornejo stood mute. Grant took something out of his pocket. "You remember that scene in *Bowling for Columbine* where Michael Moore takes a bullet used in the shooting back to the shop where they'd bought it—only the bullet was still inside one of the victims?"

Delaney waited with hooded eyes, then looked at Cornejo. "You haven't been shot, have you?"

Cornejo remained mute. Grant answered for him. "Not lately. But here's the return."

Grant tossed a condom matchbook across the room. Delaney didn't attempt to catch it, letting it bounce off his chest and drop to the floor. He looked down at the familiar flame and silhouette logo. "That's not a used one, is it?"

The answer was smooth, but Grant detected a flicker behind the eyes, more than a corporate condom pack warranted. He didn't know what it meant but filed the reaction away for future use. "Guy who owned that one won't be using it. His dick got plastered over the police station ceiling a couple of days ago."

"I saw that on TV too. Your point is?"

Grant lied. "That belonged to Freddy Sullivan. Worked for you."

"A lot of people work for me."

"Not doing what Freddy did."

"And what was that?"

"All those pretty foreign girls you've got at the club—the Eastern European ones? Freddy imported them for you."

"Immigration is not one of my businesses."

"People trafficking for the purposes of sexual activity is."

"That's illegal."

"Yes, it is."

"I don't do illegal. I make enough money with legitimate businesses."

"Gas stations and campaign contributions, is it?"

"Many things. Like you're a cop, a soldier, and a media star."

"You saw that, huh?"

"Of course. Very dramatic footage. Two hospital visits and a shootout at high noon. The dusty street. The lone gunfighter."

"I hate guns."

"Can't have been easy in the army, then."

"I was a typist."

"And I was a paperboy. But we both grew up, didn't we? Now I've become a respected businessman, and you're the Resurrection Man. You have made me a lot of money."

"I have?"

"On the news. I own 15 percent of WCVB."

"And you employ a lot of people."

"I do."

"But you never met Freddy Sullivan?"

"No."

"That's not what Freddy said. Just before he died."

Bluffs are designed to do two things. Give the impression you know more than you do and/or flush out an adversary by tricking them into revealing something you don't know. Sometimes both. Always at least one. The next few seconds would reveal which one applied today.

The room fell silent. There was no sound from outside. No traffic noise. No airplanes landing across the harbor. The windows must have been triple-glazed to keep so much noise out. The plush carpet and heavy door did the same for the corridor. The three of them stood in a cocoon of silence. By the same token, Grant reckoned nobody outside could hear what was happening inside Delaney Enterprises' office.

That was a sobering thought.

"I can see you, Muscles."

Grant never stood with his back to the door unless he had to. Cornejo had his back covered as far as the corridor was concerned. The door behind the desk was in front of him. The door in the far left corner should have been out of his sight line, but his peripheral vision was as acute as his foresight. He was right. It was where the heavies waited in case their boss needed help. One of them had slid quietly into the room and closed the door.

"Why don't you come and join us?"

The man was built like a brick shithouse. Tall and wide and with a neck that was thicker than the head it supported. He was Oddjob without the bowler hat. Grant smiled at the analogy. Grant loved the early Bond movies. Oddjob glanced at Delaney, who gave a barely perceptible nod. The big guy came over and stood to one side of his boss, mirroring Cornejo's position behind Grant. Mexican standoff.

Delaney remained calm. This was his office.

"When you arrived at Logan, at the luggage carousel, were you alone?"

"Yes."

"No. You were in a roomful of others collecting their baggage. Did you know any of them?"

"No."

"Ever meet any of them?"

"No."

"Not strictly true, though, is it? You probably rubbed shoulders with half of them. Spent, what—eight hours in a confined space with all of them? So you did meet them. You just don't know them."

"That's a really clever argument. They teach you that in gangster school?"

"You think I'm a gangster?"

Grant felt his body relax. Preparing. One eye on Delaney. One on Oddjob.

"I think you're a low-rent toad who climbed out of the pond and made it big. So big you had your employee whacked in case he blew the whistle on your latest venture. Well, guess what? He blew."

Oddjob flexed his muscles but didn't move. Delaney smiled. "Blew up. Yes. The only thing we didn't get on WCVB."

Grant breathed in through his nose and out through his mouth. Twice. His arms hung limp at his sides. He flexed his knees so they could move quickly. Half turned to face the threat without actually moving at all. "Maybe you should have tipped them off it was going to happen. Got the cameras there early."

Delaney ignored the comment. He let out a sigh, and his face took on a nostalgic, thinking-of-the-past look. His smile developed a sinister twist. It danced across his lips, but his eyes remained hard as flint. Dangerous.

"I always wanted to be a carpenter. Do something with my hands. Or maybe a butcher. Carving meat and hanging it to drain. You know? It must be very relaxing doing something like that. So long as you're not the meat."

The flint eyes focused on Grant.

"How is Terri Avellone these days? She still compensating for the loss of her little sister by befriending prostitutes?"

The mention of Terri shook Grant. He felt a shiver of unease run down his spine. He was beginning to like her more than just as a one-night stand. Delaney's smile became a smirk.

"You really don't know what's going on, do you?"

"More than you think."

"But less than you think. Which adds up to nothing at all."

Grant could sense something big coming. The bluff had worked. He was about to learn something he hadn't known before. He waited. Oddjob waited. Grant remained alert. The best time for the bodyguard to attack was just after the big reveal. He took half a step to his left, giving Cornejo a direct line to Delaney if Grant had to defend against Oddjob. Delaney's eyes noted the move but didn't look worried. "You think I bombed the police station to silence Sullivan?"

Grant waited.

"You think that. The BPD thinks that. Maybe that's because somebody else wants you to think that."

Grant waited.

Delaney was savoring the moment. He was practically licking his lips.

"But I've got local knowledge on my side. JP is my—what do you call it? Patch?—lived there man and boy. I hear things."

Grant looked straight at Delaney but was really watching Oddjob. Out of the corner of his eyes he saw Cornejo move into the open space to his right. Delaney was on a roll.

"What I've heard lately is this."

Delaney paused for effect. Grant kept his knees loose. Delaney smiled.

"What if Sullivan wasn't the target?"

A smokescreen. A distraction. Grant hoped that was the case.

"Is that a question or a statement?"

"The statement is, you pissed a lot of people off at Snake Pass. And the Dominguez cartel don't forgive and forget."

Grant felt the small hairs on the back of his neck bristle. "They're not Boston-based."

"They weren't Snake Pass–based either. Boston's closer than Yorkshire. You need to watch your back."

I'd be more worried about watching your back. That phrase kept coming back to haunt him. For the first time since he'd entered the room, Grant was unsure of himself. A half-glance towards Oddjob confirmed he wasn't going to attack. The no-necked bruiser had relaxed his stance. Delaney bent down and picked up the matchbook. "Not easy to keep a low profile when you're national news, is it? Maybe you should change the color of your jacket."

"It's my favorite."

"Maybe go for one of those Quadrophenia coats—you know, the ones with the bullseye on the back."

"And ride around on a Vesper?"

"Optional but not recommended."

Oddjob took a step backwards. Confrontation over. Cornejo looked confused but kept quiet. Delaney was milking the situation for all it was worth. He looked like the cat who had swallowed the cream.

"But thanks for dropping by. It's always nice to meet a celebrity."

The office on the southeast corner of One Post Office Square had slipped into darkness as the sun set in the west. Logan International was in shade. The sky turned a darker blue in preparation for night. The room lights came on automatically as dusk settled over Boston.

Delaney tossed the matchbook to Grant, who caught it one-handed.

"We don't keep those here. I'll send you some if you like."

There were no farewell handshakes. Grant nodded and walked to the door. He let Cornejo out first, then threw one last glance at the head of Delaney Enterprises. Frank Delaney looked like a man in total control.

Round one to the bad guys. Back to the drawing board for the good guys.

TWENTY-SEVEN

Back to the drawing board for Grant meant reviewing the evidence. The only evidence was the CCTV footage at E-13. There was also a forensics report and the bag of Sullivan's property, but it was the recording of the incident that might shake things loose.

It was dark by the time Grant arrived at the reception counter. Dusk had come and gone. Night had taken over JP. What little light was left in the sky was dark blue and fading fast. The streetlamps had come on automatically, just like in Delaney's office. The parallel was amusing. The streets of Jamaica Plain were where Delaney had grown up. The plush office suite at One Post Office Square was alien territory that the big man had assimilated, but the streets were where he belonged. The gutter if Grant had his way.

Grant left Cornejo on the train, with a promise to contact him tomorrow. The combat vet had seemed more upbeat than Grant had seen him before. Perhaps being part of a police operation, even off the books, made him feel useful again. But he was still only a well-meaning amateur. Grant was a cop.

Miller was finishing his shift, doing what all cops did at the end of the day: trying to catch up on paperwork that the bosses insisted be completed before going off-duty. There was no clocking on and off time in the police. Hours were flexible. Overtime unlikely. The night detective was out on a burglary call at Arborway and Custer, just below Centre Street.

"Not been stealing pizzas again, have they?"

"That would be robbery. He's at a domestic burglary."

"I don't want to keep you. Could you let me at the CCTV stuff?"

"You know how to work it?"

"I'm a quick learner. Your kit's just better than ours, is all."

Miller let him into the viewing room and quickly explained the controls for the Multiplex console. He signed out the recording, then left Grant to play. Grant thanked him and waited for the door to close. He didn't know what he was looking for, but whenever he was stuck on a case, it relaxed him to simply go over old ground. Check for anything he might have missed.

He found the point on the recording just before the bombing, then rewound it to half an hour earlier and pressed Play. The front office played its time-lapse jerky day. Grant zoomed in to remove the main office and only show the front desk and glass doors. He saw himself go into the interview room with Freddy Sullivan. He watched the front doors, looking for any sign of the man mountain who'd slapped his hand against the window. There was only a brief glimpse of him passing the front doors. Grant paused the picture. The frame was grainy and indistinct at three times zoom. Just a big guy, almost as tall as the doors, maybe six feet six or more.

The smaller guy in the baseball cap and hooded sweatshirt came in. Grant froze the picture again. Sat with his chin on clenched fists and focused on the man who'd tried to kill him, according to Frank Delaney.

The guy's own mother wouldn't have recognized him. The bill of the cap hid the face. You couldn't tell if he was black, white, or sky-green purple, let alone if he was one of the Dominguez cartel. They didn't advertise themselves like in the movies, wearing flowered shirts and *Miami Vice* sandals. This was just some guy wearing a grey sweatshirt with a logo on the left breast.

Grant focused on the logo. He tried zooming two more notches, but it only became more indistinct. He squinted and deliberately blurred his focus. That worked sometimes if you were looking at faces, taking away the fine detail and concentrating on shape and color. It didn't work for sweatshirt logos. He thought it might have been the Triple Zero logo, but that might have been wishful thinking. If you take the inkblot test, you can see all sorts of things, mostly how fucked in the head you were as a kid.

Half an hour later he gave up. He hadn't expected to find anything, but the act of sitting in a police station helped make him feel like part of the investigation. Part of the team. Being part of the team was what Cornejo was missing. Mustering out of the corps was like having one arm cut off for an ex-marine. Losing your family and the brotherhood of combat. It was something you couldn't explain to anyone who had never served. It was something Grant never thought about. Part of the process of convincing himself he hadn't done some of the things he knew he had done.

He put the tape back in the drawer and signed it back in. Noted the time for continuity of evidence. Locked the room and handed the key in downstairs. The front office was quiet. At night all police stations were the same. They were only populated by cops, not administrators and typists. Typists did shit-all except type. That was something else he kept telling himself. *All I did was type.*

He thanked the desk officer and went out the front door.

Washington Street was dark.

The streetlights were sparse and dull. This wasn't downtown with all its glitzy lighting and reflective skyscrapers. This was a dirty back street on the outskirts of town, even if that back street was the longest road Grant had ever seen. Washington Street ran from downtown to the back of beyond. God only knew how the postman ever found an address.

There were several cars parked outside the police station. The parking lot of Ruggiero's Market was full, the restaurant apparently doing a roaring trade this evening. In contrast, Yessenia's Market looked sad and empty. The lights were on, but nobody was shopping. Grant began to cross the road, intending to buy a Coke just to give the Greek at least one customer.

He was halfway across when an engine started farther down the street, six car lengths below the intersection. Headlights came on and flicked to high beam. Grant smiled and turned to face the oncoming car. Terri Avellone. He was wrong.

THE SQUEAL OF TIRES alerted him that things weren't right. That and the roar of the engine. Low gear. High speed. Somebody setting off in a hurry or somebody building to ramming speed. A big American car pulled out from the sidewalk and settled on its rear axle as it surged forward.

There was no time for deep-breathing exercises.

There was no time to think himself relaxed.

Grant assessed the situation in a flash. Limbs loose. Mind sharp.

The sidewalks on both sides of Washington Street south of the intersection were choked with parked cars. Small foreign jobs. Large

American gas guzzlers. Three SUVs the size of small tanks. There was no escape from the road. El Ambajador Restaurant was the reason for so many parked cars. Four illuminated signs jutted from the wall advertising the restaurant, the beer it sold, and the credit cards it accepted. The car headlights tried to blind him as it pulled into the road just beyond the vacant lot.

The engine gunned.

Tires screeched.

Grant moved fast.

Towards the onrushing car.

Logical thinking said run away from the threat. If someone was trying to charge you down in a stolen car, go in the opposite direction. False assumption. Like all those guys in cartoons trying to outrun a falling tree. Can't be done. The tree will always win. The car is faster than the feet. In cartoons they never thought to just step aside. They always tried to outdistance the tree. They always lost. Grant couldn't simply step aside. The sidewalks were full. By the time he got around the corner into Green Street, he'd be just so much roadkill on the tarmac. Plan A was a washout. It was time for Plan B. Use the adversities. Don't try to outrun what you couldn't outdistance.

He darted towards the car, diagonally across the street. Use the adversities. The parked cars blocking his escape. He was up on the hood of a small Japanese model before the big American car could change direction. Closing the gap gave the driver less time to think. At speed, the car swerved towards Grant, but he was already up on the roof of a black SUV before it collided with the parked cars. Glass shattered. Sparks flew. Metal crumpled as the big car tried to crush Grant between the SUV and the El Ambajador's front wall. It hit the first car with a glancing blow. Then the second. Slammed the parked cars into the wall amid noise and mayhem.

The front fender came off and got caught under its wheels, but it charged on. Three cars. Four. Leaving a trail of destruction and smoke. Grant felt the SUV shift under his feet, but he was already aiming for what he'd seen in that flash assessment. The four illuminated signs jutting from the wall, separated by six-inch gaps. Like a ladder. He climbed in three easy movements and vaulted onto the flat roof. The car trailed sparks up Washington, hindered by the trapped fender.

Decision time. Grant saw the car and knew where it would go next. Not straight up Washington past the police station. Not right into Glen Road with its ribbon of narrow back streets. Left into Green Street and a free run towards Armory or Centre. Grant was up and running before the car even made the intersection. Over the roof onto the next building. The corner premises were flat roofed with one peaked roof at the end but not too steep to negotiate. He cut the corner, coming down onto the single-story extension of Peak Performance on Green Street. A delivery truck provided a quick way down, like giant steps from the roof to the truck to the Chevrolet parked next to the sidewalk.

He was fast but not fast enough.

The fender crumpled and twisted beneath the big American car, coming out from under the back wheels in a shower of sparks and dust. Freed from its anchor, the car sped off. Burning oil from a cracked seal created a smokescreen that James Bond's Aston Martin would have been proud of. Grant didn't even try to read the plates. It would be stolen. It would be found abandoned somewhere in JP or Roxbury or in any of the side roads in between.

Grant stood in the middle of the road with his hands on his hips, catching his breath. He turned back towards the intersection and began the slow walk back. He'd have to report this but knew it would only go down as dangerous driving. Arguing that it was a drug cartel's hit team wouldn't cut it. Or that it seemed a bit of a coincidence, fronting Delaney in his office that afternoon and someone trying to run him down tonight. Best keep it simple. Report a hit-and-run driver and give a description of the car. Another hitch in the drunk-driving statistics.

Making the report took less time than Grant had expected. At the front counter with the desk officer he'd spoken to earlier, he gave a written statement, and the officer called for a unit to come and check the damage to the parked vehicles. Grant dropped the twisted fender on the counter. It wouldn't be difficult to match once they found the car. He doubted they'd do a full forensic examination on it. Not for drunk driving. Just a lot of insurance claims in the morning.

It was after ten when he entered the Seaverns lobby and climbed the stairs to his room. He was ready for a shower and an early night. His body ached. The bruises were sore. It seemed like a day didn't go by when he could simply relax and recover. He took the room key out of his pocket and grabbed the door handle. It turned easily in his hand. It wasn't locked.

TWENTY-EIGHT

GRANT LET GO of the handle and stepped back from the door, exploring his options. He'd locked the door, so it hadn't been left open by mistake. That was option one. The other options assumed that whoever was in there wished him harm. Possibly the same guy who'd tried to run him down.

He considered that and dismissed it. Running him down was supposed to look like an accident. What were they going to do in his room? Drown him in the bath and say he slipped? If they thought that, they were even dumber than the driver, because nobody was going to drown Grant in the bath. Room 305 didn't even have a bath, just a shower.

So? What else? Shoot him as he came through the door? That wouldn't look like an accident. Even the knife attack on the T had been set up as a gang-related thing. No way this would look like anything other than an officer-involved shooting. Do that and the shit would really hit the fan. Kill a cop and every agency would draw together, throwing their combined weight against the killers. Delaney wouldn't want that. The Dominguez cartel wouldn't either.

He glanced at the foot of the door. There was no telltale strip of light from inside. The lights were off. Either the killer was waiting in the dark or whoever had entered his room had left already. That presented another option. Someone had tossed his room to see what he knew. That one made sense. Burglars in Bradford didn't usually turn the lights off afterwards, though. Maybe Boston crooks were more environmentally friendly, saving electricity and therefore the planet.

Grant closed his eyes and examined the virtual room in his head. Bed opposite the door and to the right. Chair next to the bed. Dressing cabinet on the left. Windows with a view of Centre Street on the far wall. Door opened inwards, hinged on the right. Light switch on the left. Anybody lying in wait would be in the chair facing the door, slightly to the right. Grant would be partially blocked by the door until he stepped into the room.

He listened. No movement inside.

He moved half a step to his left and opened the door six inches. Reached through the gap and turned the lights on. As soon as the room lit up, he opened the door fully and walked in. Instead of Grant having to adjust to the dark, whoever was in there would be momentarily blinded by the light. Grant sidestepped to his left without closing the door. Any snap shot would be high and wide to his right, following the only movement the assassin could detect, the door swinging open.

There was no assassin sitting in the chair. The room was empty. That changed the scenario. Not an attack, a burglary. His first concern was for the T-shirt drawer. He went straight there and opened it. The T-shirts were still neatly folded and squared off like they'd taught him in the army. He remembered the CSM doing weekly room checks. Not the regimental sergeant major, just the company version, making sure the clothes in the open wardrobes were exactly the same width.

Grant slid his hand beneath the T-shirts and took out the scratched velvet box. He felt a weight lift from his heart. The blue velvet was soft to the touch. He hefted it in his hand and nodded. Good. He glanced around the room. There was no sign of disturbance. Either they were the neatest burglars he'd ever encountered or ransacking wasn't the reason the door was unlocked. He considered tripwires and IEDs, but that wouldn't look like an accident either. Improvised explosive devices. Roadside bombs didn't have to be at the roadside, but one thing they most definitely couldn't masquerade as was an accident. See options two and three above.

He opened the box just for comfort. He knew it was still inside but sometimes just liked to touch it. His fingers ran along the sleek black tubes and dallied over the silver disc at one end. He touched the earpieces that had been the last things to touch her flesh. He folded the stethoscope back into the box and closed it. Slid it back under the T-shirts and closed the drawer.

Then he saw the strip of light beneath the bathroom door.

Back to square one. Only with a different room. The master switch didn't control the bathroom light and he knew he'd turned it off before leaving. He didn't go through the various options this time. He doubted anyone lying in wait would do it in the bathroom. He went straight to the door and looked inside, then froze in the doorway.

THE ONLY SCENARIO HE hadn't considered was the frame-up. He should have. It happened in so many of those PI movies, almost right up there with the address inside the matchbook flap as a staple of private detective fiction. He looked into the eyes staring back at him and held his breath.

The eyes blinked. Terri Avellone sitting on the toilet with the lid down as a seat. The second pair of eyes belonged to an attractive dark-eyed beauty from south of the border, or looked like it. About Avellone's age and standing beside the shower cubicle as if she could hide behind the frosted glass and the opaque curtain. Grant was going to make a joke about all his birthdays coming at once but saw the fear in the woman's eyes. He wondered if she looked like Avellone's sister but knew it wasn't something he could ask. Instead, he held his arms wide to include both women. "Don't forget to wash your hands. Like a coffee?"

Avellone stood up with such force Grant thought she'd take off. For a second it looked like she was going to slap him. "Jeepers creepers. You scared the shit out of me."

"Then you're in the right place, aren't you?" He pulled a disgusted face and sucked in air. "Sorry. That wouldn't even be funny with a bloke."

He offered the visitor his hand. "Jim Grant."

She shook it. "The Resurrection Man."

"You too? Small world. I took you for more of a Mary Magdalene."

She smiled and the fear receded. Grant nodded towards the main room. "Tea or coffee?"

"They have hot chocolate?"

"Let's have a look."

He went over to Avellone, held her face in both hands, and kissed her gently on the forehead. She was shaking. He gave her a comforting hug before stepping back. "Then you can tell me why you're hiding in my bathroom."

There was no hot chocolate, so they all had to make do with coffee. Milky with two sugars for Grant. Black with Equal for the others. Grant sat in the bedside chair facing the door. The girls sat on the bed facing him. Their fear of the door had evaporated with Grant sitting there. Terri Avellone's anger had not. "What on earth were you thinking, sneaking in like that?"

"I wasn't thinking there were two beautiful women waiting inside."

"Flattery will not work. I heard the handle turn, door opened a crack—almost had a heart attack. Fastest I've ever moved. Into the bathroom. The two of us."

"Why the lights off?"

"So nobody'd know we were here."

"Well, it worked. I didn't know you were here."

"Not you. The other nobodies."

Grant was going to ask who, but after the black guys on the T, the grenade at E-13, and the hit-and-run driver, he knew there were nobodies out there who didn't like him. It stood to reason they might not like his friends either. He leaned back in the chair and crossed one ankle over his knee. Relaxed. Aimed at relaxing his visitors. "Now you've got that out of your system, how about introductions?"

Avellone took a deep breath and let it out slowly. She was learning. The frown lines eased and her eyes softened. She put a protective arm around the woman next to her. "This is the friend you were asking about—the one who gives me her spare matchbooks. The condom queen."

Grant smiled into the dark eyes. "You got any of those ribbed ones with that sticking-out thing at the bottom like a finger puppet?"

The woman stared back. "What flavor?"

"Hardly affects me, does it? Not being double-jointed."

"You're not? I am."

She held a hand out, then realized they'd already shaken in the bathroom. There was just a slight accent. "Melissa Quintana."

"Not Mary, then?"

"Not Resurrection either."

"And you're an escort?"

Without even a hint of a blush. Confident. "Yes."

"That your stage name?"

"I don't work on the stage. It's my real name."

"Okay, Melissa. Thanks for coming." He shifted in his seat but kept his legs crossed. "What can you tell me about Triple Zero?"

"They're good employers."

"I know. I read their recruitment page. I should be so lucky. Pay like that."

"You're not double-jointed."

"That count against me?"

"That and the whiskers."

Grant rubbed his chin. It was dark with growth, the bristles harsh against his hand. Between that and the ugly plaster down the side of his face, it would probably rule him out under the "immaculate and well-cared-for skin" clause.

She shook her head. "That's the top end of the wage structure. I'm more like lower middle. The girls at the club are towards the bottom but still earning good money."

She didn't appear shy. He supposed that was a job requirement too.

"Go on."

Melissa explained how Triple Zero Gentlemen's Services worked. Pretty much how Grant understood the escort business to work after checking the Internet. Girls were listed on the website with a photo portfolio to rival any top models' glamour shots. They could be booked for incalls at specific locations, with on-site security in case of trouble, or for outcall visits to any hotel in the Boston area. Exclusive apartments. Stuff like that. Very expensive. Not the kind of clients who were going to cause trouble. They were mainly businessmen or politicians or corporations giving incentives to valued customers. Melissa's accent was soft and enticing. "Triple Zero has a range of ethnicities."

"The girls?"

"Yes. I'm on the South American list."

"I'd never have guessed." He said it with a smile. She was getting over her initial shock, but there was still something lurking behind her eyes. He suspected that Triple Zero wasn't all she was painting it to be. She hesitated before speaking.

"Some clients have…exotic tastes."

"Like snakes and whips exotic?"

"Like overseas exotic."

"Foreigners?"

"This is America. We're all foreigners."

"More foreign than you?"

"Yes. There's one client—a businessman who deals in South African diamonds. He likes proper deep-black South Africans."

"African American?"

"No, from South Africa. Non-English speaking. Traditional but perfect."

"Immaculate and well-cared-for skin. Yes, I read that."

"There's another. He likes Iranians, Armenians, Iraqis. He'd sleep with the Taliban if they didn't blow up whenever you got close to them."

"That's very funny. I'll have to remember that one."

"Then there's this politician. He likes Eastern Europeans. Triple Zero bends over backwards to get what he wants. A Bostonian. I even voted for him at the last election."

Grant felt a whisper of disquiet tickle his spine. Posters in Frank Delaney's office sprang to mind. *Goldfinger. For a Few Dollars More.* The campaign poster.

"Oh yeah? Did he win?"

"Yes. Senator Clayton's been in office for three terms now."

TWENTY-NINE

Grant uncrossed his legs but didn't stand up. He was suddenly more focused than he had been the last three days. Invisible threads were beginning to connect, but Grant couldn't untangle the web they were forming. Freddy Sullivan accounted for several of the threads. He connected to Frank Delaney, who in turn was connected to half of Jamaica Plain. He owned Flanagan's. He owned Parkway Auto Repair and the gas station where Sean Sullivan had worked. Both Sullivans were obviously connected. Delaney ran Triple Zero and its related clubs for which Freddy supplied imported girls. Some of the girls were diverted to Senator Clayton, a politician that Delaney had supported on his reelection campaign.

"His wife must have something to say about that."

"He's a widower. Doesn't hide the fact he's got a pretty girl on his arm."

"Fairly open about it, then."

"Not where the girls are from. This is Boston—very conservative. It's not Happy Hooker territory. But it gives him a certain glamour. He doesn't advertise Triple Zero, though. Not like sponsoring Nike or anything."

"Charismatic? Leadership qualities?"

"Extremely charismatic. Ex-army. War veteran—don't know which war—got a few medals, wounded, all that stuff."

"And he likes the ladies."

"Lady. He doesn't play the field. Got a favorite."

"East European?"

"Yes. Her sister's with Triple Zero too. A friend of mine."

Avellone became very still, her face pale and expressionless. Grant couldn't worry about that now. "He's doing sisters?"

"One sister. My friend works in JP at the Gentlemen's Club."

"Pole dancer?"

"Yes."

"I might have seen her. I was there the other night."

Terri Avellone spoke up. "That the night you got the shit kicked out of you in the parking lot?"

"Not all the shit. I kicked some back."

Melissa's eyes widened. The fear was back. "See? They're very bad people."

"First you've mentioned of it."

"Triple Zero pays well. But there are…consequences."

"I thought you had on-site security?"

Avellone interrupted again. "So does the Gentlemen's Club. You've met some of them, haven't you?"

"Point taken. So that's why you were waiting in the dark."

It wasn't a question. He leaned back in his chair. No wonder Melissa had been reluctant to come see him. Grant had already proved to be a target. It must be true; it had been on TV. Associating with him could be bad for her health. "You want to stay here for a while?"

Melissa gave the room a disdainful look and shook her head. "Hell, no. I've seen the bathroom."

So much for helping the damsel in distress. The bathroom was a step up from what he was used to. Overseas, and even back home, when he'd been serving his country, he'd used bathrooms that were just holes in the ground. He didn't think telling her that would improve his stock. "I'll give it a spray next time the bad guys are after you."

"They're not after me."

Not yet, he thought but didn't say. He changed the subject. "How'd they bring the girls in?"

Melissa leaned forward, resting her elbows on her knees. "Did you see *The Wire*?"

"The TV series?"

"Just like that. For the lower-level girls."

"Container ships at the docks."

"Yes. I don't know which docks."

"Must play havoc with the immaculate and well-cared-for skin."

"Oh, no. The expensive girls, the ones that apply via the website, they're homegrown, very exclusive. That's why the perks are so good. The exotic varieties from overseas are brought in through normal channels. Having a senator on your side helps cut a lot of red tape."

"Seems a bit out of Sullivan's league."

Melissa tilted her head. "The Irish guy from the police station?"

"Freddy. Yes."

"He was always hanging around—maybe was a gopher. But he didn't have anything to do with bringing the girls into the country."

Grant dropped his hands onto the chair arms and drummed his fingers. "You sure about that?"

"Would you trust him with a million dollars' worth of merchandise?"

"Merchandise? That's a bit callous."

"It's realistic. It's good business. I've got it. I sell it. I've still got it."

"And you enjoy it?"

"I'm double-jointed. Wouldn't you?"

Grant smiled. It was good he'd met Terri Avellone first. Melissa might have put his back out. He supposed there was little difference doing what you loved and getting paid for it, but he was glad Terri Avellone had another line of work. For her, sex was purely recreational. She didn't need to lie about it or dodge the IRS.

The only lies seemed to have been coming from someone else, and that someone wasn't around to answer any more questions. He should have known the lying little turd wasn't telling the truth. The Sullivan family was so bent they couldn't lay straight in bed. "What *did* he do, then?"

"I don't know. It made him sweat, though, whatever it was. He was one nervous motherfucker."

Terri sat upright. "Melissa."

"Sorry."

Avellone laughed. Melissa giggled like a schoolgirl caught smoking by the teacher. Grant got up to make a fresh round of coffees. He filled the kettle in the bathroom and sprayed the shower cubicle with air freshener, just in case. It was all a diversionary tactic to give him time to think. He would let the girls out the back door after they finished their drinks, then hope Miller wasn't busy tomorrow. Grant had a few more questions for Freddy Sullivan, and the only place with the answers was locked and sealed by the BPD.

THIRTY

"Bureaucratic, pencil-pushing bastards."

Miller was being uncharacteristically vocal. Grant walked through the door to the detectives' office and walked straight back out again. He checked the name on the door, gave Miller a comedy double-take, then went back in. "That's not like you. Where's the universally upbeat Miller gone?"

"Drowned in a shower of shit."

"I can't deflect it all."

"Neither can I when they strip us down to skeleton staff."

"Welcome to the trenches, kiddo."

"Welcome to the valley."

"Got it in one. What's going on?"

Miller's desk was cluttered with papers, evidence labels, and photographs. The normally methodical detective had a fit of pique and shuffled the papers up with both hands. His anger spent, he stood up and jiggled his coffee mug. "Milky. Two sugars, right?"

"Right."

While Miller made the coffees, he told Grant the story. Two Hispanics had been arrested overnight breaking into a car in Brookline.

The B&E Motor Vehicle led to Pena and Ortega admitting twenty-six MV breaks across Brookline, Norwood, South Boston, West Roxbury, and Jamaica Plain. House searches uncovered a stash of stolen property ranging from car radios to shock absorbers and credit cards to driving licences. The entire mashup required cross-border cooperation that involved the night detective being tied up until three hours after he should have gone off-duty and Miller catching the fallout of the JP searches.

The coffee was good. Grant let Miller blow himself out. Once the storm had subsided, he leaned on a desk and waved at the mountain of paperwork Miller had mixed up in the shuffle. "Just give me the keys and I'll go do it myself then."

Miller almost agreed without thinking, distracted by trying to arrange the papers into some kind of order. Almost but not quite. His hands paused among the desktop muddle. Steam spiraled up from his mug. He stepped back and turned to face the overseas cop. "What keys?"

Grant put on his innocent face. He took a sip of his coffee and blew steam off the top of his cup as a distraction, not because it was too hot. He nodded toward the door, as if that explained everything. "Freddy's place. I want to have a look."

GRANT SAT AT A computer in the corner of the room, his fingers dancing across the keyboard. He had foregone the search warrant request template and was using a blank document page. Single-spaced. Aligned left. He double-tapped for a new paragraph, then glanced over his shoulder. "I don't know why you need a request completing. This isn't going to court. Sullivan's dead."

Miller spun away from the tidy stacks of papers and photographs on his desk. "Even more important to cover all the bases then."

"What bases? I just want to have a look where he lived."

"The bases of probable cause that allow us to legally search the premises and seize any evidence found therein."

"I'm not looking for evidence. I'm looking for answers."

"Answers that might lead to a court case against others further down the line. Therefore we need to show probable cause."

"Jesus. You sound like Sergeant Rooney."

"Sergeant Rooney's on sick leave. And I sound nothing like him."

Grant absorbed that latest piece of information. He doubted Rooney would be back on duty anytime soon. Without any evidence to make it permanent, at least the fly in the ointment was removed for now. "Probable cause is what Freddy told me in the interview room."

"He said he was an importer."

"The other stuff he said—about what's at his house."

"What is at his house?"

"We'll find out when I take a look."

"That's fishing. And there's nothing in your statement about him talking about his house."

"There will be in the second draft."

"That's illegal."

"That's practical. Kincaid told you to help."

"Kincaid said to give you anything that doesn't end up with me in jail."

"You won't end up in jail. Trust me. Something's wrong here."

"What's wrong here is you have no jurisdiction in Boston and we have no authority to search a dead man's house."

Grant leaned back in his chair. "Think laterally. You do have authority. In fact, you have a legal obligation. Sullivan was in custody at the time of his death. His keys are among his personal possessions downstairs."

He tapped the side of his nose and winked. "Think. What did you do with his car?"

"Took it to the impound lot."

"To search it?"

"Well, sort of."

"But officially?"

"To list all property and protect it while in police possession."

"And if we've got his house keys?"

"Then the keys and anything related to them are the responsibility of the police."

"So we need to look in his house to see what needs protecting. Right?"

The voice from the doorway was loud and friendly. "Now there's a man thinking on his feet."

Kincaid shut the door behind him and walked to the coffee machine. His dress uniform jacket was open and his collar unbuttoned, but he was still an imposing figure as he strode across the office. Tall, wide, and handsome. Like men in uniform were supposed to look.

Miller stood up and went to Grant's computer. He leaned over and tapped a couple of buttons. The office printer started up in the corner. Two pages slid out of the tray and he picked them up. "I still want something on paper."

He glanced at the neatly spaced writing, then began to read. After a few moments he stopped and looked at Grant. "What the fuck?"

KINCAID SAT BESIDE MILLER with a mug of coffee in one hand and the search warrant request in the other. He read the page and a half Grant had already typed and then dropped the sheets of paper on the desk. He barked a laugh and took another sip of coffee. "I thought you were a typist?"

Grant shrugged. "I never said I was a good one."

Kincaid slid the pages toward Miller. "There's more spelling mistakes and missed words than a dyslexic's first novel."

"I didn't engage spell-check."

"You didn't engage your fingers either."

Grant shrugged again. "Doesn't matter. Protect and serve. Life and property. We need to protect Sullivan's property. That means letting me have a look in his house."

Kincaid put his feet up on his desk and held the mug of coffee in both hands. He leaned back but didn't take a drink. He glanced at the paperwork on Miller's desk, then up at the young detective. "When you've finished that lot, Tyson, grab the keys from custody."

Miller bowed to experience. "Be this afternoon at the earliest."

Kincaid looked at Grant. "That okay?"

"Fine by me. You fancy tagging along?"

Kincaid stared back at Grant. "Nothing I'd like better, but I can't. This detail's shit. Should be over tomorrow, though, once Senator Clayton gives his speech and the Ay-rabs go home."

Grant had a minor flashback. News footage of the foreign delegation arriving at the airport. A smiling politician greeting them. The same smile that adorned a campaign poster in Frank Delaney's office. Senator Trevor Clayton.

PART THREE

Point I'm making is, if one small prick can fuck over ten big pricks, then one big prick like you's got no chance.

—Jim Grant

THIRTY-ONE

Freddy Sullivan had lived as he had died, in a rundown shithole with his ass hanging out. At least that was the impression Grant got as Miller pulled into Terrace Street. Not that the E-13 interview room was a rundown shithole before the grenade had exploded, but it certainly was afterwards. Terrace Street was rundown no matter which way you looked at it.

"People actually live here?"

"According to his custody record."

Miller stopped the unmarked Crown Vic. Terrace Street ran along the west bank of the railroad tracks between Jackson Square station and Roxbury Crossing and was mostly industrial and borderline derelict. A telegraph pole had a Tow Zone sign ten feet up. Somebody had shot it full of holes. Grant couldn't imagine parking being a problem.

Miller looked at the address in his notebook. "134A."

Grant looked along the street. "Numbered from which end?"

"The Mississippi's Restaurant is 103 at the junction with Cedar. I guess that puts the even numbers alongside the tracks."

"You think we're going to find any numbers along there? Place is a fucking bombsite."

"Let's just try anything looks like a house."

Miller put the car in gear and set off along Terrace Street. Cruising speed just in case a building number leapt out at them from the sprawl of urban decay and graffiti. The engine purred. Grant consulted the map in his head, now pretty much ingrained since he'd scoured it the first couple of days of his visit. He overlaid the district boundaries.

"Bet it makes you glad you don't work B-2 if the rest of West Roxbury's anything like this."

"Every district has its open sores. JP's just a bit more scenic."

They found 134A halfway along on the right. It was one of four wooden houses between a stretch of overgrown scrubland and a parking lot for the factory opposite. The four houses backing onto the railroad tracks looked old and jaded. Green paint flaked off the woodwork. The ground-floor windows of one were cracked and taped. The front door of another was nailed shut. There were two houses alongside the road and two more smaller ones around back. 134A was around the back, accessed through a dusty yard behind a stand of stunted pine trees and an industrial dumpster. The only thing missing was the traditional rusting car on bricks instead of wheels. A sign on the telegraph pole at the entrance to the yard read

Parking 2-Hour Limit

—as if anyone would want to park here for more than two hours. It was almost as funny as the Tow Zone sign down the street. At least nobody'd shot this one full of holes. Miller pulled up alongside the yard but didn't drive in. He parked on the street. Grant doubted they'd exceed the two-hour limit.

They got out the car and stood for a moment, Miller checking for rusty nails that might flatten his tires, Grant taking stock as he always did when he approached an uncertain future. His eyes scanned the yard and the pine trees to the right. The unkempt bushes alongside them. The trees were too sparse for anyone to hide behind. The bushes too thin and straggly. The industrial dumpster sat like a squat toad in the far right corner. It didn't look as if it had been used for months, the rubbish sticking out of the top dusty and rotting. It backed onto the trees. No room behind it.

If this had been a hot zone, that corner could have been a possible threat. It wasn't a hot zone. It was a house search. Still, Grant went through the motions out of habit. The yard was clear. No movement. No enemy activity. He concentrated on the nearest house, 134 alongside the road, and the crumbling wreck behind it, 134A. He didn't think the point could be overstated. "People actually live here?"

Miller looked at the glorified wooden shack. "Did. Before his ass hit the ceiling."

Grant glanced at his companion. "I thought you were more sensitive than that."

"Don't get youthful enthusiasm mixed up with soft."

Grant checked the windows facing the yard. 134 first. The curtains were all closed. They looked like they'd been closed for years. The side door had a notice taped across it. Weeds were growing out of the welcome mat. Nobody home. Not for a long time. 134A next. It only had one window and the front door faced the yard. The rest of the house was hidden behind 134. Any views that Sullivan used to have would be around the back, facing the railroad tracks. Ideal for trainspotters. Not bad for criminals wanting to keep their activities private.

None of the windows showed movement. Hot zone cleared. They crossed the yard, raising little clouds of dust with each footfall. Grant half expected the cliché dog to bark or cat to hiss and knock a dustbin lid over, but their approach was silent. Miller held up the keys. Grant waved him forward. "Be my guest."

Miller nodded and unlocked the door. Grant opened it and stepped inside.

THE SMELL HIT THEM like a smack in the face. Freddy Sullivan had been in custody a good few days before Grant arrived from England to interview him. It was three days on top of that since he'd been killed. Something in the house hadn't stood the test of time well. Rotting food. Or something dead.

The ground floor was almost as basic as Sean Sullivan's apartment above Parkway Auto Repair but not quite. There were at least more rooms than the single bedsit and kitchenette at the gas station, but the rooms were just as sparsely furnished. The front door opened into the lounge. There was a door to the left for the kitchen, small and functional with a dropdown flap table, and a door next to that for the downstairs bathroom. The living room was large and square and empty apart from a two-seat settee, an ever-present TV, and a throw rug that covered the floorboards in the middle of the room.

Two windows overlooked the railroad tracks out back. First thing Grant did was dash over and open them to let the stench out. Neither of them spoke. To open your mouth was to invite all sorts of shitty possibilities in. Grant breathed through his nose but kept one hand clamped firmly over it as a filter. He wished he'd brought the postmortem Polos but hadn't expected anything like this during his holiday assignment.

Keep out of trouble. Don't get involved. You're off-duty.

This felt like anything but off-duty. This was a house search in a cesspool. It didn't get much more on-duty than that. Opening the second window helped. A gentle breeze wafted some of the smell out into the open, bringing much-needed fresh air into the room. He went to the front door and wedged it open, setting up a three-way action that allowed him to remove the filter. "Thought they'd searched this place already?"

"Cursory search only. Anything out in the open. Guess it didn't smell as bad back then."

Grant knew how that went. If Sullivan had been arrested for burglary or theft, the BPD could have searched the house for any items related to those offenses and any property stolen during their commission. Back in the UK they'd have to state what items they were looking for—TVs, car radios, DVD players, etc. Good practice was to list a few items that were small enough to fit in cupboards and drawers, then at least you could turn the place inside out looking for them. If it was just TVs, you'd find it difficult arguing in court later how you found the stolen checkbook taped to the back of the cutlery drawer. Sullivan wasn't arrested for burglary or theft—at least not in America. He'd been detained for a foreign-force inquiry and therefore, as Kincaid had said, it was basically an address check rather than a full search.

Grant surveyed the room. An open staircase next to the front door led to the first floor. Grant corrected himself. In the US it was the second floor. He glanced at Miller, then nodded towards the stairs. "Start at the top and work down?"

"Sounds good to me. What are we looking for exactly?"

"Nothing specific. Anything looks out of place."

"What's out of place in a shithole like this?"

Grant raised one leg. His foot stuck to the floor, only coming up with an effort. Looking through the kitchen door, he couldn't imagine eating anything cooked on the grease-splattered gas rings. "Anything clean."

It was only partly a joke. Everything belonging to Sullivan was grimy and careworn. Anything cleaner than that was probably someone else's. "Anything to do with Triple Zero or Frank Delaney."

"Gotcha."

Miller led the way. Grant followed, wondering what mysterious life forms they were going to find in the bedrooms. At least the smell grew fainter as they reached the landing.

THEY FOUND NOTHING IN the bedrooms—there were only two—just clothes and bedding. A few skin mags and a supply of Triple Zero condoms in a bedside cabinet. Grant looked out of the master bedroom window. The railroad embankment was steep and began right at the building line. In common with most railway networks, the banking was weedy and overgrown. It discouraged kids from playing on the tracks. Trees and bushes dotted the long grass. Occasional clear spots allowed a view of the nearest set of tracks. As he watched, a six-carriage commuter train rattled by. He noticed for the first time that the T had different tracks than the traditional railroad, and that the north and southbound T ran nearest the house. Beyond that were three more sets of tracks for heavier trains.

He turned his attention back to the bedroom. He'd been ruthless during the search, and everything was either overturned or askew. Police searches tended not to stand on ceremony. Villains and their relatives could tidy up later. Sullivan hadn't been much on keeping the house tidy anyway. He went onto the landing and looked in the next room. Miller was almost finished too.

"Anything?"

"No."

Grant looked at the only other door off the landing and smiled.

The bathroom and toilet. Sullivan's favorite hiding place.

He nodded at Miller and pointed to the bathroom door. It was partly open but not enough to see inside. The landing and stairs were bare wooden floorboards. They creaked as he crossed from the bedroom. The stench from downstairs had pretty much gone, but up here musty bedroom odor and piss-stained toilet smells made Grant breathe slowly and evenly. He walked with economical movements to avoid breathing heavy.

He stood three feet from the door and inserted the toe of one K-Swiss tennis shoe into the gap, then nudged the door open a few more inches. The door was heavier than he'd expected. It moved slowly. A slice of curled linoleum came into view. A stained bathroom rug. The pedestal base of an ivory washbasin. A few more inches and he could see the mirrored bathroom cabinet on the wall. That gave him line of sight behind the door.

Something was hanging from a hook in the ceiling.

It swayed gently, the rope groaning under the weight as the door tried to push it aside. Grant held up a hand. Miller wasn't moving, but the signal spelled danger. He drew his sidearm and stepped to one side so that Grant wasn't between him and the bathroom door.

The smell. It had almost gone, but Grant wondered again where it came from. He nudged the door. The thing in the mirror swayed again. The smell didn't start up again. That gave him confidence. Rotting corpses tended to release more gasses when they were disturbed. Dead people farted worse after a few days. That kid in *The Sixth Sense*—he should be thankful he only *saw* dead people.

Grant stepped forward and moved his head to get a better view in the mirror. Up. Down. Left. Right. Whichever way his head went gave him the opposite angle in the mirror. There were no other hidden surprises in the bathroom.

He shoved the door with his shoulder and stepped through the gap.

Freddy Sullivan's dirty washing swung in the laundry bag. Being a complete imbecile, he'd fixed the hook in the ceiling directly behind the door instead of in open space. Grant unhooked the bag and kicked it aside. Discolored jeans and sweatshirts spilled onto the floor. He opened the door and smiled at Miller. "Attack of the killer laundry."

"Is that what the smell was?"

"No. That's not from up here."

Grant quickly searched the bathroom cabinet and the shelves above the washbasin. As expected, there was nothing of note. Now he stepped back and looked at the bathtub. He kicked the bath panel. A dull echo indicated what everyone knew. It was hollow. Boxed-in bathtubs hid more storage space than your average chest of drawers. It was just never used. Unless you were Freddy Sullivan. Grant remembered doing a drug raid on the family home in Bradford. The house was clear. It was only when Grant had ripped off the bath panel that he had founds stacks of rolled up banknotes and boxes of dealer bags loaded and ready for distribution.

He dropped to his knees and prised open one end of the panel. It was stiff, and the effort hurt his fingers. He banged the panel with one elbow and shook it loose. He banged again, and a gap opened up. His fingers hooked inside and pulled. The panel creaked. It wouldn't move. It creaked some more. Then it came away with a loud crack.

Grant set the panel aside and looked into the hollow beneath the bathtub. It was empty. Just dirt and dead spiders.

"Shit."

Miller nodded at the toilet. "Be my guest."

Grant threw him a dirty look. He stood up and shifted the dirty laundry with one foot. That was the upstairs done. So far they'd drawn a blank. He wasn't ready to give up yet, though. Grant came out of the bathroom. "Start at the top and work down?"

Miller holstered his weapon.

"Time for downstairs."

This time Grant led the way as they went back down to the living room.

Half an hour later they were down to one last room. The living room had been easier than the bedrooms since there was hardly any furniture and no cupboard space at all. Grant ripped open the lining of the settee, and Miller took the back off the TV. New flatscreen televisions had no hiding places, but the good old cathode ray tube sets had big cabinets and lots of room. Nothing. The open staircase meant there was no storage cupboard under the stairs.

The kitchen was the worst. The floor was stickier than the lounge and the surfaces as greasy as a Turkish wrestler's jockstrap. Grant had to explain that one to Miller. British humor. The cupboards held only limited amounts of food, but they searched the packaging anyway. Nothing.

That left the ground floor bathroom. Grant corrected himself again. The first floor. He wasn't sure what Americans called the lower ground floor, like in hotels that had underground parking. He opened the door and a hint of the bad smell from before came back. He went in and opened the window and stepped back out again. Gave it time to clear. While he waited, he glanced at Sullivan's handywork.

The corner bath was big enough for three people. "Who'd have put Freddy down as a Jacuzzi kind of guy?"

Miller glanced through the door. "I didn't have him down as a washing at all kind of guy."

The bathroom was a work in progress. The corner bath was lime green and ugly as a roadkill toad. Stripped pine paneling boxed in the tub, and off-cuts leaned against the wall. The plumbing hadn't been connected. The mixer faucet hung loose out of the top of the toad's head. There were no cabinets. There was no toilet. The frosted-glass window had been badly puttied, great big thumbprints squashing the sealant around the frame. Grant went over and noticed it had set. The work had been done a while ago. "You think he got discount at Home Depot for all this stuff?"

"I'm not sure Home Depot would admit to selling a unit this color."

Grant leaned against the doorframe. "How many houses you visited have the Jacuzzi downstairs?"

Miller shrugged. Grant pressed on. "I mean, you put in something like this, it's always upstairs. Downstairs toilet is usually a smaller affair. Guest toilet type of setup."

"I guess."

Grant stuck his head through the door and took a sniff. The smell was still there. Not as strong as when they came in, but whatever it was, it was coming from this room.

"You know why convicts smear themselves with shit in a prison riot?"

"Deter the guards from grabbing hold of 'em?"

"That's right. Gives you pause, having to wrestle a man to the ground covered in squashed turds and piss dribbles."

Miller was catching Grant's drift. "Bad smell puts them off."

"Bad smells tend to do that."

Grant looked at the stripped pine paneling. Freddy Sullivan's favorite hiding place. The Jacuzzi was tall and wide. Plenty of room underneath. He took two steps into the room and kicked the panel. It sprang off easily. What he found behind it surprised them both.

THIRTY-TWO

THE DEAD RAT on a stick wasn't the surprise. It was the hatch in the floorboards under the Jacuzzi. The flip-up entrance was two feet square and hinged at one end, with a handle to lift it up with. Not directly under the Jacuzzi section of the bathtub but the plumbing end where the hatch wasn't compromised by the sunken tub. The lip of the Jacuzzi stood two feet above the ground. The hatch could open upwards and still not snag on the framework or the preformed tub. It explained why the plumbing hadn't been fitted. Grant reassessed Sullivan's DIY skills. The hatch was a lot sturdier than the wood paneling.

Grant knelt beside the handle and rested one arm on the lip of the bathtub. "Smeared shit."

Miller agreed. "Bad smell."

Grant picked up the rotting corpse by the stick shoved up its ass like an unsavory lollipop. He held it away from his body and expertly flicked it up through the open window. A train rattled past. He hoped he hadn't hit it. He drummed his fingers on the edge of the bath while he considered his next move. With the dead rat gone, the air gradually became more breathable. The question was, what other surprises lay in store beneath the hatch?

Grant's fingers stopped drumming. He leaned forward and slid his fingers into the handle. The hatch was solid. It was heavy. The muscles in Grant's forearm tensed as he opened it, expecting a black hole smelling of damp soil and rat shit. What he got was a room flooded with daylight from a window in the back wall. It was the smell that gave him pause. The sickly sweet smell of marzipan.

"Watch your head."

Grant called up as he stepped away from the ladder, only having to bow his head slightly. He watched Miller come down backwards until his feet touched the floor. The reason the hatch was sturdier than Sullivan's paneling was because the hatch had obviously been here a lot longer than Freddy's makeshift camouflage. The Jacuzzi hid the entrance, but the cellar had been part of the house for years. It had a solid floor, plasterboard walls, and a decent-sized window facing the railroad tracks. The only thing it didn't have was a door.

"And don't touch anything."

Miller turned to face the room. "At least it smells better down here. What's he got? A confectionery store?"

"It might smell better, but I'd rather have the dead rat."

"How come?"

"Because rat corpses don't explode."

"Exploding marzipan?"

"Certain explosives give off a smell. Whatever he's got down here smells of almonds, and he's not been making almond slices."

Miller stepped back and banged his head on the ladder. "Shit."

"Toilet's upstairs. Down here—much more serious. The rat wasn't to stop us looking. It was to stop us smelling the other smell."

Grant stood still. He dropped into a crouch and surveyed the room from a lower angle. Light from the window showed a film of dust on the floor. The only footprints were his, gathered in a cluster around the base of the ladder. Having recognized the smell, he'd been very careful where he'd put his feet. Before moving deeper into the room, he wanted to check if anyone else had been in here recently. Indication was, nobody had. Miller stood beside the ladder and looked down at Grant as if he'd gone crazy. "What you doing?"

Grant glanced up at him, then continued his scan. "You ever see *Where Eagles Dare*? They've just been disturbed in the luggage office and climbed out the window. The weaselly little Nazi walks along the aisle. Tripwire comes into focus. Twang. Kaboom."

"You watch too many movies."

"Not if the tripwire comes into focus."

"You really think Freddy Sullivan could think of tripwires and booby traps on his own?"

"He wasn't on his own. Whatever he was up to, somebody else was pulling the strings. That's why he was so frightened in the interview room. He knew the deep shit he was in."

"But tripwires? Guy's a fuckup."

"*Where Eagles Dare*. Every kid in England's seen it on TV. Guarantee every one of them remembers the booby traps."

Grant stood up, satisfied. He went to the workbench against the far wall. It too was covered in a film of dust. A week, maybe two. There were tools hanging from a board on the wall, each within its own outline. Hammers. Saws. Pliers. A soldering iron. Just the basic DIY expert's tools. There were several outlines with tools missing.

Couple of screwdrivers. A pair of long-nosed pliers. Some others Grant couldn't figure from the shapes. Not all of them missing. A few of them were scattered across the work surface.

"Freddy, Freddy, Freddy. What were you up to?"

Sullivan might have been a more accomplished handyman than he was a drug dealer, but he was just as untidy down here as he had been upstairs. A good workman always looked after his tools. An efficient builder always cleaned up after himself, because that way he was ready for the next project without having to clear up after the last one. Grant tried to channel his inner psychic. Divine from the evidence before him just what project Freddy had been working on.

He liked guns and blowing shit up.

That was Sean Sullivan, in conversation during the hostage siege that wasn't.

He had some fancy putty stuff. He liked setting it off by shooting at it in the woods over by the pond.

The putty stuff could have been the almond smell. Not marzipan but close. It was a deadly game to play, shooting at explosives, but it wasn't the way to go if you were planning on blowing shit up. Grant hoped the Bradford scummer was more careful about storing explosives in the cellar. He checked the cupboards underneath the workbench. Nothing, just more tools and sandpaper. He wondered again just who the fuck Freddy was mixed up with.

A bad crew. Got a liking for guns and explosives. Was always disturbing the neighbors around the back of Delaney's place on Jamaica Pond.

That was Gerry O'Neill, in conversation at O'Neill's Traditional pub. The ancient bartender had his finger on the pulse of JP. Grant stepped back from the workbench and tried the soft-eyes technique. Not focusing on one thing specifically but taking in the entire picture. Dust and tools and pieces of scrap. There were bits of stripped wire. Short lengths of pealed insulation. Droplets of dried solder. Scraps of cloth and stretch webbing. Half a dozen condom matchbooks without the condoms. That boy was ruled by his cock. Grant was surprised there weren't any skin mags down here too, although he doubted he brought any women down here for sex. That must surely have been a bedroom activity.

Something else flashed across his mind. Not Gerry O'Neill or Sean Sullivan but something he himself had said in response to Sean's observations.

There's that Irish heritage for you. You can take the boy out of the IRA, but you can't take the IRA out of the boy.

Sean had responded. *He weren't never in the IRA.*

And following on from that Grant remembered the widows and orphans jar at Flanagan's. The troubles in Northern Ireland might be over as far as most people were concerned, but there were still plenty of splinter groups prepared to carry on the fight. Sean might not have been lying about the IRA, but that didn't rule out any of the other groups.

The underground room grew darker as the sun descended towards dusk. It suddenly felt like a very scary place. Shadows crept across the floor and turned the shapes on the wall into deadly weapons. The marzipan smell became cloying and sickly. This place had seen very bad things done—not down here but prepared down here. The problem was, where had the very bad things been done? More importantly, where were the ones in the future going to be done?

Grant spoke in a quiet voice, more to himself than anyone else. "Freddy, you sick fuck. Grenade up the arse was too good for you."

Miller kept his distance, sensing a change in Grant's mood. Then the young detective's cell began to ring. Grant jumped. Mobile phones around an explosive device were a disastrous combination. Radio signals could trigger whatever was set to be triggered. Thank God there were no explosive devices left in 134A's cellar.

Miller saw the look on Grant's face and his eyes opened wide. Grant waved a hand. It's okay. Miller answered the phone. Nodded. Then handed it to Grant.

"Someone called Terri Avellone. Says it's urgent."

THIRTY-THREE

They met Terri Avellone on a park bench at Mission Hill playground on Tremont Street, not far from Terrace Street. That is, Grant met Terri Avellone. Miller waited in the car. Grant felt a wave of affection as he crossed the road.

Our Lady of Perpetual Help Mission Hill Church overlooked the playground, an imposing structure that Grant seemed to remember was the place where Teddy Kennedy was buried, or where his funeral was held. Something like that. The view across Boston from the playground was stunning, benefiting from its raised position at Mission Hill. It looked even more spectacular in the dying light of sunset. The brightly colored play areas, variations on a theme of circles and flowers, were empty. It was getting late for kids to be playing on climbing frames and merry-go-rounds. Grant didn't even notice if there was a merry-go-round. He was concentrating on the woman sitting next to Terri on the bench. Melissa Quintana.

Melissa looked a shadow of her former self, sitting huddled like a refugee on the deportation train. Her eyes were sunken and frightened. Terri had a comforting arm around her shoulder. Terri looked up when she saw Grant approaching. "You should get a cell."

"Mobile phone. Got one. It's in my bag."

"That's okay if I wanted to talk to your bag. You should have it with you."

"I know. Sorry."

Avellone hadn't finished venting her anger. "I had to call the station house. Got the runaround. Took an hour for someone to realize you were with Detective Miller. Another twenty minutes before they agreed to ring him."

Tears of frustration showed in her eyes. She stamped a foot. The act seemed comical, like a petulant child, but the circumstances robbed it of humor. That and a family history that they would have to talk about when all this was over. Grant let her blow herself out. "Feel better?"

"Not really."

He sat on a large decorative stone opposite the bench, facing them. "You said it was urgent."

Now that she'd gotten him in front of her, Terri seemed to have trouble getting the words out. Melissa shivered beneath Avellone's protective arm. The church behind them may have offered perpetual help, but the help wasn't reaching the two women sitting on a park bench overlooking downtown Boston. Terri finally managed to get the words out. "I think this is bigger trouble than the orphans at the airport."

Grant shifted his position on the stone to stop his backside going numb. It was at times like this he thought the fat family at Purple Cactus had one over on him. More padding instead of his own bony ass. The stone was cold, but he didn't want to sit next to the girls. It was hard to get answers if you had to lean around one to talk to the other. Best interview position was facing the person being questioned. In the dying rays of sunlight he prepared to listen. Somewhere in the distance a dog barked. He almost laughed at the delayed cliché.

THE BASEBALL DIAMOND below the playground was in shadow by the time she'd finished. It wasn't so much that she took a long time explaining as it was the night's drawing in. Sunset, dusk, night. Like dominos tumbling, there was no stopping it once it began. They were at the dusk stage now. Shadows in the park.

Interview technique kicked in. PACE module. Back in West Yorkshire, the police and criminal evidence module dictated procedures and rhythm. Rhythm was more important to Grant. First thing was to let your witnesses tell it in their own words. Just leave them to it, without interruptions. Now it was time to put meat on the bones by asking specific questions. "Simonovich?"

Melissa nodded. "Yes. But they changed it to Simone."

"Anna is the one works with Senator Clayton."

"Yes."

"Her sister's Kristina."

"Yes."

"The one who's gone missing?"

Melissa sobbed an answer that should have been yes but was just a sound.

Grant wasn't making notes. For one thing, it sometimes intimidated the subject. For another, this wasn't going to court. This wasn't evidence that needed gathering in keeping with the rules; it was information required to find a missing girl, possibly held against her will in order to pressure her sister. "When was she last seen?"

"About a week ago. Five or six days—around that. Now I find her door forced and room empty."

A week ago? Roughly. That put it a couple of days before Grant arrived to interview a Bradford burglar about Patel's Grocery Store on Ravenscliffe Avenue. A couple of days before Freddy Sullivan pleaded it was nothing to do with him, he was only the importer. The lying piece of shit. Grant wasn't sure how it all fit together, but he was certain it was all connected.

"Who was last to see her?"

Stress robbed Melissa of her fluent English. She reverted to the frightened child from the old country. "Some of the other girls. Ones she was also very close to. They noticed she was, how you put it? Chilled. Cold. Frightened. She not want to talk about it. But they were friends. They notice things."

"What things?"

"She talk about her sister a lot before. They were so close. Like twins." Melissa's eyes glazed over, her mind's eye turned inwards, remembering. "Her sister was private property. Not on the books. Because she was with the big man."

"Senator Clayton?"

"Yes. So she was not often with the other girls. Kristina was proud that Anna had found"—she struggled to find the words—"found security. This is not a very secure occupation. Like acting. Regular client is good. Anna had regular. Kristina more like rest of us."

Terri kept her arm around Melissa's shoulder but kept quiet. She had done her part, bringing the escort and the cop together. Melissa seemed to take comfort from the contact. She was beginning to open up.

"Then Kristina stopped talking about her sister. Became jumpy if Anna was mentioned. Something was not right. We thought the senator might be badly treating her. Kristina was too frightened to say."

She shivered, and Terri squeezed her shoulder. "It's okay. Don't worry."

The most redundant advice ever in times of trouble but well meant. Despite the fact that everything was far from okay and Melissa had plenty to worry about, the kind words appeared to calm her. She took a deep breath, then carried on. "Then the big man took her away."

"Took Anna away?"

"Kristina."

"Why would Clayton take Kristina?"

"Not Senator Clayton. Triple Zero big man."

Grant felt a shiver run down his spine. "Frank Delaney?"

"Yes. The girls, they talk. They say Anna would do anything for her sister. That Kristina was being held to make Anna do something, against her…I not sure the words. Something Anna not want to do. Against her free will."

The playground was almost completely dark now. The lights of the city sparkled beyond the baseball diamond. Our Lady of Perpetual Help Church loomed over them like a protective mother, offering help but providing no protection whatsoever. If it had, then one girl wouldn't be missing and her sister being coerced into doing something she didn't want to do.

The question was, what something?

The other question was, where would Delaney hold her?

He smiled at Terri and Melissa even though they probably couldn't see his face in the gloom. He nodded and stood up. The girls stood up too. He leaned forward and kissed Terri on the forehead. "Thanks."

He turned to Melissa. "Thank you very much. Is there anything I can do for you?"

"No. I think I need a change of business."

"That couldn't hurt. You got relatives you can stay with?"

"South of the border. I be all right. Have friends. Savings."

There was nothing else to say. He looked at Terri and could only just make out her face. He didn't like goodbyes, but this felt like goodbye. Things were going to get bloody. When that happened he needed his mind to be clear. You can't carry internal baggage into combat.

He nodded and walked away towards the Crown Vic parked opposite the playground. It was time for the local police to get involved.

THIRTY-FOUR

MILLER'S YOUTHFUL ENTHUSIASM evaporated in a split second.

"So we've got a missing hooker nobody reported. Suspected of being held against her will on the info of another bunch of hookers, with a third hooker who hangs with a United States senator possibly being coerced into a criminal act by the biggest crook in Boston. We've got no witnesses that saw anyone being abducted. We've also got no evidence to link said abduction to either Frank Delaney or Senator Clayton. And we've no idea what criminal act hooker number three is being coerced into committing. Have I missed anything?"

That was fifteen minutes after Grant got in the Crown Vic opposite the playground on Tremont Street. Ten minutes after Grant began to explain what Melissa Quintana had to say. Thirty seconds after Grant stopped talking. Miller sat and stared at his passenger. "That about right?"

The engine purred. Grant put added friendliness into his voice. "You ever have one of those robberies where they kidnap the bank manager's family, then make him go to the bank and open the vault?"

"That's a rhetorical question. Isn't it?"

"The bank manager does it because he's in fear for his family. Wife. Kids. Whoever. Somebody goes with him. Steals the money. Accomplice back at the house threatens to kill 'em all if he doesn't do it. You ever have one of them?"

"Can't say as I have."

"But you've heard of it happening, haven't you? Must happen in Los Angeles all the time."

"In LA they just rob banks the traditional way."

"Somewhere, though, in the great big US of A. Broadcast on CNN or Fox News or WCVB. You've heard of it. Right?"

"Yes."

"Well, that's what we've got here."

"A bank robbery?"

"A criminal act being forced on an innocent by having her sister threatened."

"Except we don't know about the criminal act or the threats."

"We don't, but we have reasonable grounds to suspect all of the above."

"That won't wash for a search warrant or an arrest warrant or a fully fledged SWAT and helicopter assault. You imagine running that by a judge?"

"I thought this was the land of the free and home of the brave. Where's all that go-getter spirit?"

"You were a real cop once, weren't you?"

"Still am."

"In the real world, where you needed evidence and stuff?"

"In the real world, not the pen pushers' world."

"Legality is still important on either side of the pond. You can't go kicking in doors, even in Yorkshire, without some kind of evidence."

"Actually, I often kicked in doors without evidence. I damn well found plenty by the time it went to court, though."

"That won't wash either. Kincaid said to do anything that won't end with me in jail. Go charging in on a United States senator to rescue his girlfriend and I'll be shot for treason."

"I'm not talking about charging in on Clayton. I want to charge in on Delaney."

"D'you know how long I've had my detective's shield?"

"Not long."

"D'you know how long I'll keep it if you talk me into this shit?"

"Not much longer."

"That's right. That's why I'm not doing a damn thing until we've looked at it all angles up. Now fasten your seatbelt. I don't want a citation on the way back to the station."

Grant fastened his seatbelt. "You're a moody little bastard, aren't you?"

"I wasn't until today."

Miller checked that the road was clear, then did a U-turn back towards Columbus Avenue. Serious tactical discussions needed coffee. That meant the detectives' office at E-13. Grant was already beginning to feel like part of the furniture there.

GRANT STOOD WITH HIS COFFEE in front of the E-13 District wall map. The district boundaries were marked in blue. A black shield with a white P in it showed their location: 3345 Washington Street, Boston, Massachusetts. A white circle with a black T inside it showed the MBTA stations. Green Street station was just round the corner. Centre Street junction with Seaverns Avenue was a bit farther away. Grant's hotel, his mode of transport, and his police station all in front of him in cartographer's ink.

It was after eleven o'clock. The final domino had fallen, and dusk had become night. The Yorkshire detective was trying to work out how to tumble a bigger domino, because when it came to criminals, domino theory ruled. You just had to know which domino to push. Grant reckoned he knew which one but had to persuade the BPD to help push it.

That was Grant's dilemma as he sipped his milky coffee, two sugars. "No search warrant request, then?"

Miller swiveled his chair to face the map, office phone to his ear. "We'd never get one. I've seen your typing."

"What about exigent circumstances? Protect life. Girl in danger."

"If somebody'd seen her snatched off the street, that might fly. She's been missing a week and nobody's bothered to report it. How urgent do you think we can make that sound?"

"She's tight with a US senator."

"Monica Lewinsky was sucking cock with the president. You didn't see them storming her house, did you?"

"Her sister wasn't abducted to coerce her."

"From what I remember, she didn't need coercing. And we can't prove Kristina Simonovich has been abducted anyway."

Grant turned away from the map. "Hey, give me a break here. Abductions you prove later. If you suspect someone's been abducted, you'd better be damn sure she hasn't before you call off the dogs. Find her body in a ditch tomorrow, you'll be in more shit than disturbing some bigwig scumbag."

Miller hung up the phone. “No reply. Kincaid must be on early detail tomorrow.”

“What about the night detective?”

“Dealing with a double shooting. Couple of kids over on Parker Street.”

“Kids?”

“Teenagers.”

“That age. They’re not kids anymore.”

“Still, he’s got one critical and one stable. Forget the night detective. Uniforms are doing crowd control and traffic. Forget them too.”

Grant sipped his coffee, looking at the map again. Farther west than his hotel. Farther north than E-13. He looked at the sweeping curve of the road and the network of back streets. “We only need blue lights for effect. A bit of weight behind the threat.”

“What threat? There isn’t going to be any threat. Aren’t you receiving this transmission? We have no probable cause.”

“Oh, yes, we have. We just haven’t formulated it yet.”

“You want to go kicking in doors on Frank Delaney based on something we haven’t formulated yet?”

“One thing you’ll learn as you go on—it’s not what you do as a cop, it’s how you write it up. Hindsight is always 20/20. Cover your ass. Dot the i’s and cross the t’s.”

“That’s not very comforting.”

“You get sat in a room with some DA flunky about any case, what’s the first rule of evidence?”

Miller looked like he felt he should know this one but didn’t want to sound like the rookie he was. It was another rhetorical question anyway. Grant was going to answer, no matter what Miller said. He did.

"First rule is, it's not what you know, it's what you can prove. Same applies to us. Whatever happens, we'll fix it in the edit."

"Go charging in without a warrant and there'll be no fixing that."

"We won't need to charge in."

"You think the doorman at One Post Office Square is just going to let us in?"

"Not Post Office Square."

"That hotel next door, then."

"Le Meridien's in the middle of the business district. He's not going to keep her prisoner down there."

Miller threw up his hands in an "I give up" gesture. Grant was staring at the map again, but his mind was replaying past conversations. *Got a liking for guns and explosives. Was always disturbing the neighbors around the back of Delaney's place on Jamaica Pond.* Gerry O'Neill hadn't realized how important that little snippet of information was proving to be. Then there was Frank Delaney himself. *Ah, JP. My old stomping ground.* If he was holding the girl against her will, he'd want to keep her close to his base of power. Not the glass and concrete tower that was only a high-class façade. Where his roots were. His old stomping ground.

"The Gentlemen's Club at Jamaica Pond."

"You think his bruisers are going to let us in without a warrant?"

"You don't need a warrant if you get invited in."

"What's this? A vampire movie now? Tap on the window and they let you in? Just make sure it's before dawn."

"It'll be dawn soon enough if we don't get a move on."

"Not gonna happen."

Grant finished his coffee and put the mug on the nearest desk. He filtered all the confrontation out of his voice and smiled. It was amazing what you could achieve with a smile. If that didn't work, there was always brute force and ignorance. "Wasn't it one of your presidents who said, 'Talk quietly but carry a big stick'?"

Miller nodded but didn't say which president. Grant didn't think he knew. It didn't matter. He'd have put his money on Teddy Roosevelt. Maybe not word-for-word correct. Grant could sense the young detective's resolve crumbling.

"Get me some blue lights and a couple of uniforms, I know where to get hold of a big stick."

Miller didn't look convinced. "The marine?"

"He's very imposing."

"No trouble?"

Grant's smile turned icy. "I'm just going to talk quietly. Honest."

THIRTY-FIVE

Miller called in some favors to get them a uniform backup. Two officers on the four to midnight shift who were late off because of the shooting. One of the kids had died at the hospital, so it was now a homicide investigation. There was nobody coming on duty to take over their patrol car, so Miller had his blue lights and the big stick. Cornejo they picked up on the way to the Gentlemen's Club.

It was quarter to one when they finally pulled into the parking lot. Red and blue lights washed the front of the building. The marked unit parked across the entrance. The unmarked Crown Vic blocked the exit at Arborway and Pond Street. Miller deployed the portable blue light on the dash. Disco fever had come to visit.

Grant got out of the car and adjusted his orange windcheater. Cornejo got out of the back and flexed his shoulders. Miller simply got out and closed the door. The stars and stripes hung limp from the flagpole on the porch. The night was still and airless. A chill threatened frost but not yet. For now it was just cold. The night sky twinkled with stardust.

A club like this at this time of night, you'd normally hear music thumping into the night. But this was JP. Delaney might have swung planning permission with help from his pet politician, but polluting the night silence would have caused too many waves. The place was soundproofed and tasteful. Grant made a mental note to tell Delaney that when he met him again. He crossed the gravel lot that he'd mistaken for rundown tarmac the last time. He remembered how he'd learned it was not. Floored by a sucker punch and a knee in the face.

That wasn't going to happen twice. He breathed in through his nose and out through his mouth. Twice. His muscles relaxed. His mind cleared. He nodded for Cornejo to come with him and walked towards the front steps. Miller checked his sidearm and flicked his jacket over the holster on his belt. He hung back. This was Grant's show. About as far off being legal as it could get without landing them all in jail. Miller hoped.

Grant paused for a moment. A thought was stillborn and wouldn't take shape. Something he'd seen as he got out of the car. It wouldn't come. He brushed the unease aside and climbed the steps onto the porch. Cornejo followed. Miller next. With barely a pause for thought, Grant pushed the doors open and entered the foyer.

He hadn't realized before just how prevalent the theme was in Delaney's business. Grant noticed the movie posters around the lobby that he'd not seen on his first visit. There had been the posters surrounding the stage inside and the dancers cavorting to the themes from *Dirty Harry* and *The Good, the Bad and the Ugly,* but he hadn't paid attention to the foyer. Then there was Delaney's office at One Post Office Square. More posters. Delaney was obviously a movie fan. Grant would bet money Delaney's favorites were *Goodfellas* and *The Godfather*. Maybe *The Departed* because of the Boston connection. Grant's would have to be *Dirty Harry* and *Bullitt*. Vengeful cop dramas or men on a mission films like *The Dirty Dozen*. Except they were the dirty three. Dirty five if you included the two uniforms outside.

The girl behind the ticket desk was stirring popcorn in the display cabinet when they came in. She stopped and glanced up at the clock above the door. Her face was blank, no expression. She was chewing gum. Grant expected her to blow a bubble and fuss with her hair. She did neither.

"Sorry, gentlemen. We close at one. Can't let anybody else in. It's the law."

Grant couldn't resist. "We are the law."

The girl showed more salt than Grant gave her credit for. "Not around here, you're not."

"Tell Mr. Delaney the Resurrection Man's here to see him."

"Mr. Delaney isn't in tonight."

Grant stood in front of the counter. "Are you a local recruit? Or you one of his overseas imports?"

The girl looked flustered, not knowing what to say.

"Because if you were imported, you'd really want to tell me where he is. Because the girl he's got with him has one chance of going home again. And I'm that chance."

A door opened in the far corner. Grant sensed it more than heard it. His battle instincts had kicked in the minute he walked across the porch. The man that came out of the door had no neck and shoulders like Arnold Schwarzenegger.

"You returning condoms again?"

Grant remembered him from Delaney's office. Oddjob. That was a good sign, Delaney's personal heavy being at the club. His disquiet in the parking lot dissolved into a feeling of confidence. This was going to work out. There'd be no gunfight at the OK Corral. He turned to Oddjob.

"Funny thing about condoms. Johnnies, we call 'em in England. Or rubbers."

Oddjob remained impassive. Like a rock. Grant kept his tone light.

"Well, funny thing about them is this. As a kid I never dared trust 'em. 'Cause adults used to say the fellas working the condom factory—you know, on the conveyer belt or whatever they used—they said these fellas would prick one in ten with a pin. So having sex was like Russian roulette. One chance in ten of getting some girl pregnant."

Oddjob sighed. Grant wasn't deterred. "One small prick for ten big pricks. Not that I'm bragging."

Cornejo moved away from Grant to widen the gap. Miller stayed back.

Grant smiled.

"Point I'm making is, if one small prick can fuck over ten big pricks, then one big prick like you's got no chance."

Oddjob proved he was listening by smiling back. "According to what you just said, one little prick only fucks up one big prick. The other nine're okay."

"True. But that stacks the odds even more. And you're that one big prick."

The foyer fell silent. The girl behind the popcorn display stopped chewing. The second hand on the clock above the front doors swept silently around the face. Miller kept his gun hand loose. Cornejo braced himself for the onslaught. Grant waited. Ready.

Then Oddjob threw a spanner in the works. "If you want to have a look around, why didn't you just say so?" He stepped aside and waved them forward. "Anywhere you like. I'd check the stage first, though. The girls are doing their finale. Not quite Busby Berkeley, but close as you can get without water."

Grant could just make out the faint strains of *Once Upon a Time in the West* through the double doors in the auditorium. A single popcorn popped in the display like a knot of wood on a fire. It made the girl jump. If Oddjob had the bowler hat from the movie, he'd have taken it off and bowed. "I'll be sure to let Mr. Delaney know you was here."

Grant nodded. "Depends which one of us sees him first."

"True. But you won't be seeing him here. He isn't in tonight."

The girl blew a bubble and it burst over her lips. "I told him that."

The unease returned, but Grant didn't show it. Instead he waved Cornejo and Miller forward. It was time to search the premises. Without a warrant. Like vampires in a Hammer Horror film, they'd been invited in.

A THOROUGH HOUSE SEARCH takes hours, using a three-bedroom house as the base standard. Once that house becomes a business premises—with storerooms, wine cellars, public areas, and changing rooms—then the hours multiply. Admin facilities and offices take even longer. That's with dozens of police securing the perimeter and doing several rooms at a time.

Grant had three cops and two outside.

Here's how he did it. Grant did the searching while Cornejo and Miller waited in the corridor, one either side of the door, in case somebody sneaked out. As they cleared each room, it became sanitized. The trailing watchman, Miller, always kept one room behind Grant just in case.

Grant knew he wasn't going to find anyone.

He just needed time to think.

They did the stage and bar area first. Watched the dancers perform their erotic finale, as much to give Miller a glimpse at what he'd been missing as anything else. A cursory search of the dressing room, cellar, and security room. Then it was upstairs to check the storage rooms and offices. Admin and managerial. Ninety minutes later Grant was in the last office, and he still hadn't come up with a suitable plan B. He was running out of time before they'd have to admit defeat and leave with their tails between their legs.

Grant didn't do tail between the legs.

The final office was the largest. It wasn't as grand as the office at One Post Office Square, but it was obviously Delaney's. There was a selection of classic movie posters on the walls. A couple of framed photos on the desk. Delaney with a group of topless beauties that made him look like Hugh Hefner at the Playboy mansion. Delaney at a political rally with a smiling Senator Clayton. There was no desktop diary. Grant doubted the invitation would cover searching the drawers.

Oddjob took two paces into the room and stood in the middle of the floor. Optimal positioning, like Andre Agassi controlling the middle of the tennis court. A couple more minutes and Grant's time would be up. He glanced around the office. There was a narrow door behind the desk. There was a broad window with a door onto the balcony on the far wall. He glanced through the window and the thing that troubled him when they'd arrived came back full force. *He liked setting it off by shooting at it in the woods over by the pond.* Quickly followed by: *Was always disturbing the neighbors around the back of Delaney's place on Jamaica Pond.* This was Delaney's place on Jamaica Pond, but there were no woods behind it, just the waterfront.

The answer came with equal force. He ignored the view and turned to the small door behind the desk. Opened the door and went inside. It was an individual restroom. Toilet and washbasin. No bath or shower. Oddjob crowded the door just inside, as Grant expected. Good.

Grant didn't need to relax. He'd been relaxed ever since he stepped into Delaney's office. The view across the lake had relaxed him even more. The twinkle of lights from the house in the woods on the northern shore. Now it was time for some Q&A.

There was no room to maneuver in the tiny room. Nowhere for Oddjob to go. Grant turned to face him and brought his knee up in one swift movement. Oddjob's balls squashed like popped grapes, and he doubled over. Grant used the forward motion, grabbed the back of Oddjob's head, and slammed his face down on the edge of the washbasin. His nose spread across his face. Teeth fell into the washbasin. A squirt of blood splashed the mirror on the wall. Oddjob collapsed on the floor in an ugly heap.

Grant dropped to one knee, pressing all his weight on Oddjob's chest. "I'm going to ask you a couple of questions."

Oddjob gurgled blood down his shirtfront.

"And before you ask for your lawyer, think of this: I'm not legal in the state of Massachusetts. This isn't going to court. I'm just a guy who's been blown up, beaten up, stabbed, and run over. I'm under a lot of stress. I am unhinged. That'll be my defense if you ever complain about this interview. If you survive this interview. You understand all that?"

Oddjob gurgled more blood down his shirt front. It might have been an answer.

"Nod if you understand."

Oddjob nodded.

Grant eased the pressure of his knee and reached up with one hand. He turned the cold faucet on, took a glass from the wash-basin, and filled it. Stood it on the edge while he turned the faucet off. Then lifted Oddjob's head gently with his other hand while he tipped the glass to his lips. "Sorry about the teeth. I hear Triple Zero has excellent medical."

Oddjob looked pale. His eyes were glazed. He swilled his mouth out and spat it down his shirt. Next mouthful he drank. His eyes came into focus again. Grant leaned back against the wall, taking his knee off the big guy's chest. It was such a small room that he was still inside Oddjob's fighting arc, but the no-necked bruiser had no fight left in him. Grant kept his tone friendly.

"After you've answered my questions, you're going to make a phone call for me. That all right with you?"

Oddjob nodded.

"Good."

Grant smiled and patted the big guy's shoulder.

Then he asked the first question.

THIRTY-SIX

PRE-DAWN LIGHT lifted the gloom of Jamaica Pond's northern shore and painted the dusty turnaround outside the lodge an unearthly grey. Lights from the windows threw yellow squares across the porch, but they began to fade as dawn brightened the early morning sky.

Jim Grant stood in the middle of the parking lot and waited.

He sensed movement to his left but didn't take his eyes off the front door of the frontier cabin structure that felt completely out of place so close to the thriving community of Jamaica Plain. Like somebody playing cowboys and Indians in a built-up area. The woodland promontory jutted out from the northern edge of the lake. The trees were sparse around the front of the lodge, giving a view of the water and the Jamaica Pond boathouse halfway down the eastern shore. The jetty had a smattering of boats and small yachts moored on either side. There was also a clear line of sight to the rear of the Gentlemen's Club on the south shore. Trees around the back and sides of the lodge were thicker, providing cover and privacy. An ideal place for blowing shit up and playing with guns.

Grant sensed movement to his right. Good. They were almost ready. Dawn grew brighter. It muted the yellow squares from the windows and the red and blue flashing lights behind him. Somebody racked a shell into the chamber. A heavy sound. A shotgun. Several sharper noises followed as automatic side arms were deployed.

Grant waited, his orange windcheater hanging loose and open.

He glanced at the three cars parked at the side of the lodge. Big American cars. One bigger than the rest. Big and black. He remembered it spitting gravel as it sped out of the parking lot at the Gentlemen's Club. The cars were caked in dust. Grant reckoned Delaney should invest in having the parking lots tarmacked.

Still he waited for a sound coming from the west. For the cavalry. While he waited, he smiled at the memory of Miller's reaction half an hour ago when he'd opened the trunk of the Crown Vic and prepared for action.

"YOU THINK THEY'LL GIVE ME a job in Yorkshire when I get out of jail?"

The trunk lid sprang open like a steel trap in reverse. The lock box was the full width of the trunk and fastened against the back of the seats. Warning stencils were painted across the grey metal lid. Miller unlocked the box and flipped the lid. The shotgun rested loosely in its cradle. There was enough firearms and sundry assault team equipment to start a war. Miller held up a blue nylon overjacket with POLICE written on the back. Grant shook his head and tugged at the orange windcheater that was his calling card. Cornejo accepted the coat, and Miller took another out.

Grant looked at the array of equipment and clothing in the trunk. "When you get out of jail, you could start a hunting store."

The marked unit from the Gentlemen's Club was parked behind the Crown Vic at the beginning of the drive opposite Jamaicaway and Moraine. Grant realized he'd slipped into the American way of dropping words from street addresses. Moraine was Moraine Street. It used to annoy him that Americans could never complete a sentence without missing words out. In England you'd say "three hundred and sixteen," but in the US it became "three hundred sixteen." Or "he went out of the door" became "he went out the door." Now he was doing it himself, even in his thoughts.

Miller had called in more favors and got them an extra marked unit. They were now deploying like that scene from *Terminator 2*, outside Cyberdine, just with fewer cops. Oddjob's answers had provided enough probable cause, but without going through higher channels Miller couldn't get SWAT. Time was of the essence. They needed to go in now.

Grant reviewed the information in his head. Three men plus Delaney. Armed and dangerous. Kristina Simonovich held against her will but not chained up or anything. Not locked away. The trio of heavies would be watching TV and eating sandwiches. Coffee to keep them awake. Delaney would be doing whatever he wanted. He was the king of Jamaica Plain.

Grant bristled at the thought. "You know why bullies bully?"

Miller paused as he slipped the POLICE jacket on. "Rhetorical, right?"

"Because they can. They get away with it because nobody dares stand up to them. Happens at school all the time. Same thing here. JP is too scared to put this ugly mug in his place."

Miller finished putting the jacket on but didn't zip it up. He needed free access to the holster on his belt. This was still rhetorical. He let Grant continue.

"And you know when bullies stop bullying?" Grant leaned into the lock box and selected a dull black .45 automatic. "When somebody bullies 'em back."

Cornejo slipped a POLICE jacket over his T-shirt. "He gets all philosophical like this just before going into action."

Miller looked from the ex-marine to the Yorkshire cop and back again. He held a hand out for Cornejo to take his pick from the lock box. If he was going to jail, might as well be in for a pound as in for a penny. That was an English thought. Grant was beginning to rub off on the young detective. Cornejo nodded his thanks and picked up the shotgun. He cradled it across his stomach, barrel towards the ground. His body language told the story. It was good to be back on the side of the angels.

Miller glanced at Oddjob sitting in the back of the Crown Vic, then at Grant. "You think she'll come?"

Grant fingered the business card in his pocket. As if prompted by the contact, a caravan of mobile news vans pulled up across the street. Kimberley Clark got out of the WCVB camera van and came over to Grant. She was smiling but serious. Grant wondered how she did that. She raised an eyebrow. "Remind me again why all the other news crews are here?"

"Same as I told you. While I'm sure everyone in Boston watches WCVB, how can I be certain them buggers in there aren't watching Fox News?"

"Buggers?"

"Buggers. Bastards. Fuckwits. Whichever you want."

"I like fuckwits."

"Well, I need them fuckwits in there to see this on TV. Same as before."

"Yeah. And look how that worked out."

"This time? Works out like that? Fine by me."

"So where's my exclusive out of this? Every channel's here."

"Kim. I've only got eyes for you. My story's yours alone. After."

Vans were unloading. Equipment was being set up. Cameras, microphones, satellite links. Some of the vans even had extendable platforms coming out of their roofs. Grant looked at the sky. It was brightening from dark blue to lighter blue. Soon it would be dawn proper.

"Helicopter coming?"

Kimberley Clark followed his gaze. "Scrambled ten minutes ago."

"Good."

Grant went to the side of the Crown Vic and spoke through the open window. "How's the nose?"

Oddjob shrugged and nodded.

"Sorry about that. It goes with the rest of you."

Oddjob found his voice. "It's been broke before."

Grant nodded, glad the bruiser could talk. He needed him to be able to talk.

"When everyone's set—when I walk into the open—make the call."

Oddjob nodded.

"What you gonna say?"

"Turn the news on. Now."

"That's right. I don't want 'em watching the funnies."

Grant went back to the trunk and held the .45 over a clear space. His hands moved with practiced ease. Fast and smooth. He stripped the gun down to its component parts, checked them, and reassembled it in record time. Worked the slide action twice before inserting the magazine and working it once more. One round in the chamber. He reset the safety and jammed it down the back of his belt. The orange windcheater hid the bulge.

Miller's jaw dropped open. "I thought you hated guns."

"I do. Didn't say I couldn't use 'em, though."

"Typist, huh?"

"QWERTY."

"You lying motherfucker."

"But not limp-dicked."

The cameras were in place. News reporters began doing their intros. It was time to get started. They got back in the Crown Vic and the marked units started up. The three cars drove along the driveway at speed and skidded to a halt, the plain car in the middle, the marked ones either side. Red and blue lights flashing for effect. This wasn't a silent approach. Grant wanted the people in the lodge to know they were here. The uniforms deployed across the hoods of their units, guns raised. Miller and Cornejo separated, one right and one left.

Grant waited a couple of seconds, then walked out into the dusty turnaround, his orange windcheater hanging loose and open. Tiny puffs of dust exploded with each footstep. When he reached the middle, he stopped. He stood still and raised his arms out straight at shoulder height. Nonverbal communication. He hoped the verbal communication was happening in the Crown Vic behind him.

Still he waited for a sound coming from the west. For the cavalry. Then he heard it. The dull, heavy thunder of approaching helicopter blades.

THE RESURRECTION MAN. Arms held out like Jesus on the cross. Orange jacket hanging open, revealing an unarmed man in a baggy T-shirt and faded jeans. Black K-Swiss tennis shoes that were grey with dust. Grant heard the telephone ring inside the lodge. The helicopter was approaching fast but was still distant enough that he could hear the annoying ringtone. Even back in England the traditional ring of the phone had been replaced by dozens of electronic variations. They didn't sound like telephones anymore. He reckoned they'd got that idea from the Americans too. Some of them even played songs from *Jungle Book,* for crissakes.

Grant held his arms out straight and scoured the front of the lodge. There were three dormer windows set into the sloping roof facing him. None were open. No curtains twitched. There was no Sean Sullivan clone pointing a thirty-odd-six rifle at his chest. Despite the seriousness of the situation, this felt more controlled than his walk across the parking lot at Parkway Auto Repair. The downstairs windows were the threat. He saw urgent movement through the glazed yellow squares. The blue light of a TV flickered below the left-hand window. A slim female shape was hustled away to the back of the room. Nobody came to the window to look out. Everybody had apparently seen what happened to Sean Sullivan.

Good. Grant wanted them to know how that had ended. He also wanted them to remember he'd been unarmed when he'd approached the window above the gas station. There was still hope for a peaceful outcome this time. Keeping his arms held out, he began to walk towards the porch steps.

The curtain moved in the window beside the TV.

The same in the window to the right of the front door.

Grant kept walking, slow and easy. He breathed in through his nose and out through his mouth. Twice.

He was ready.

The helicopter grew louder but held its position over the lake beyond the trees and shoreline. The sparse trees that allowed a perfect view of the Jamaica Pond boathouse and the Gentlemen's Club. The ideal place for a telephoto lens to pick up the man in the orange jacket with his arms held out. TV pictures that would be fed live to the breaking news story. No back holster dangling below the windcheater. Nothing hidden behind his neck like in *Die Hard*, the first one. He wanted the heavies inside to know he came in peace.

He stopped at the foot of the porch steps. He suddenly noticed that it was the only building he'd been to without a stars and stripes hanging outside. He checked the windows—no Support Our Troops stickers on the glass. It wasn't as bad as having swastikas or KKK badges outside, but he thought it was a bad move politically. Could be Delaney's first misstep in his grasp for power. If he was up for office, that would definitely lose him votes.

Votes? Ever since Senator Clayton entered the equation, with his beautiful East European escort provided by Triple Zero, Grant had struggled to understand just what Delaney hoped to gain by kidnapping the girl's sister. What pressure could Anna Simonovich exert on Clayton and to what purpose? Then it came to him. Votes. Whatever this oil delegation was all about, he'd bet there'd be voting required for it to go through. Anything to do with oil affected everyone with interests in the industry. Especially gas station chains and their investors. Having a senator in your pocket must help. Having that senator coerced by his blue-eyed girl was insurance that the senator voted the right way.

Grant looked at the downstairs windows. They were closed.

He raised his voice. "Mornin', Frank. Sorry to come around so early, but we need to talk."

A gust of wind swirled dust around his feet. The trees on either side of the lodge swayed, their leaves whispering lazily. Wind chimes jingled at the end of the porch. A stray crisp packet somebody had dropped on the jogging path around the lake blew across the open space like a tumbleweed. Grant corrected himself. Not crisps over here, potato chips. Chips were French fries. Even though they weren't in France.

"Been meaning to tell you, though. These car parks—they really need tarmac. Keeps your shoes clean. The cars over there, they're a mess. Think what it would save on cleaning bills."

There was no reply.

"I'm just coming up the steps. Take it easy in there. All right?"

He put a foot on the first step.

Nothing happened.

He climbed to the second.

Nothing happened.

The third step and then he was on the porch. The front door opened a couple of inches.

Grant stopped. He could hear the feigned serious tones of a news reporter coming from the TV in the lounge and wondered if it was Kimberley Clark. He tried to picture the images being broadcast across Boston over breakfast. News channels liked to use strategic planning. Every news story they showed had a script as surely as any Hollywood production. They had the wide shot to set the scene. The shaky camera to denote urgency. Shots of the massed forces of the cops and the very atmospheric red and blue flashing lights. That always looked good.

Whenever they had an aerial unit, you could guarantee there'd be a zoom shot of the cops on the ground. Or in this case, the negotiator walking up to the door where armed gunmen were holding their hostage. They'd be sure to let the public know it was an innocent female hostage to promote sympathy. Quivering females were almost as important in news stories as in Hollywood thrillers for painting the villains as dastardly bad men. Right alongside kicking the dog. Didn't sound like there was a dog at Delaney's lodge.

The zoom shot of Grant's back was what he was hoping they'd be showing now. The close-up of the Resurrection Man trying to calm the situation down. As if to confirm he was right, he heard the name *Resurrection Man* used several times on the TV. He kept his eyes on the gap in the door and ignored his peripheral vision. Left and right. Miller and Cornejo would be in position now, or they wouldn't. There was no point worrying about it. In his experience you should concentrate on what you had control over and let the rest take care of itself.

Another gust of wind blew up. There was a cloud of swirling dust, more violent this time. The breeze was getting stronger. The trees weren't whispering anymore, they were shouting. Chimes that had been gentle became warning bells.

A voice sounded through the gap in the door. Could have been Delaney. "Not returning condoms again, are you?"

The door opened another couple of inches. Grant tried to see through the gap, but it was just darkness inside. The lights had been turned off. Daylight had brought dawn fully awake but had thrown the interior into shadow. It made the orange windcheater stand out even more.

"Funny, that. Your mate—the big guy from your office—he said the same thing over at the club earlier. That place is very tastefully soundproofed, by the way. I meant to tell you that."

Grant stepped toward the opening. He lowered his arms halfway down and relaxed the elbows for quick movement. He still couldn't see inside.

"We had this discussion about how they used to prick one in ten on the production line." He squinted into the gloom. "You know. About how one little prick could fuck up one big prick."

There was movement through the gap.

"Well, the big prick. That'd be you."

A chrome-plated gun barrel came up in one swift movement. It poked through the gap in the door and pointed straight at Grant's chest. There was no pause for negotiations. The gun fired three shots at point-blank range, blasting Grant backwards down the steps. He landed, a deadweight in a cloud of dust. The last thought to go through his mind was, "Who's the prick now?"

THIRTY-SEVEN

PAIN FOCUSES THE MIND. Shock fragments it. Pain and shock together can be too much for some people to handle. Grant was shocked at how painful being shot in the chest could be, even wearing the Kevlar vest from Miller's trunk. It felt like being hit with a sledgehammer three times, all at once. The force of landing on his back from three steps up knocked the wind out of him. Everything seemed to be coming in threes. He heard three gunshots inside the lodge.

The other thing that pain does is prompt an angry response. He'd seen it many times before. Even a simple thing like missing the nail and hitting your thumb with a hammer. First thing you felt like doing was smashing something with the hammer. His father had been a middling boxer in the navy but without the killer instinct—until he got punched in the nose and suddenly technique went out the window and a raging bull came out swinging. Grant had been trying all his life not to be his father. He failed. Being shot three times in the chest brought out the raging bull.

Now he was really pissed off.

There was another gunshot. A girl screamed.

Grant ignored the pain in his chest and thrust himself onto his feet. The forward motion carried him up the three steps and across the porch. His shoulder hit the door going full-tilt, and it flew open. He immediately dodged left, the .45 already in his hand.

There was nobody behind the door. The hallway was empty. There were three doors—that trifecta link again—and he quickly assessed what led where. Door on the right would be a reception room. Door on the left would be the living room with the TV. The door at the end of the hall would be either the kitchen or the rear lounge. A dogleg staircase on his right climbed to the upstairs bedrooms—three, he'd guess, judging by the dormer windows he'd seen outside. Trifecta.

He tried the right-hand door first. Quick turn of the handle and kick it open. Nod the head through, then back out again. A heavy-set man with a gun was lying on his back in a pool of blood. Massive chest wound. Cornejo stood over him, kicking the handgun out of the big guy's fingers. He jerked the shotgun up as the door flew open. Saw it was Grant and nodded. "Clear."

Grant didn't wait. He crossed the hall and did the same with the other door. The TV played to an empty room. Fast cuts of the armed police sighting across their patrol car hoods, the red and blue flashing lights, and repeat shots of Grant being blasted out of the doorway. He scanned the living room. Comfortable furniture. A dining table with four chairs beside a door through to the back room. One of the chairs was overturned. There was blood smattering against the wall behind the chair. A bullet hole amid the blood. On the opposite side of the room, next to the side door from the wraparound porch, there was another bullet hole. No blood this time. Good. Miller had made it through without getting shot.

A strangled scream came from the back room.

Grant ran the floor plan through his mind. Based on what he'd seen so far—hallway and stairs, reception room to the right, living room to the left with dining table, door from the side porch, door through to the back, door from the hallway through to the back and into the same room, kitchen extension, three bedrooms upstairs. Judging by the office at the Gentlemen's Club, Delaney seemed to like balconies. He'd put money on there being a balcony along the rear of the bedrooms, away from the lake for privacy.

He heard movement overhead. Something was knocked over in the kitchen. There was a muffled whimper. Grant tried to picture the scene. The hostage being dragged backwards with a strong arm across her mouth and a gun poking out from behind her. One man. Maybe two. Another upstairs. Doing what Grant would have done in his place. Outflanking the lone cop. Ignoring the cop from England they'd just shot three times in the chest.

Decision time. Grant didn't need to relax. Didn't need to breath in through his nose and out through his mouth. He was in dynamic action mode. Everything would flow from whatever came his way. He contemplated warning Miller that there were three bad guys left but dismissed the thought. Miller had the same information Grant did. He could count. He'd heard the shotgun blast. One down, three to go.

Grant kept quiet. He was dead already, as far as the bad guys knew.

He went back into the hallway just as Cornejo stepped out of the other room. Grant pointed forked fingers at his own eyes, then up the stairs. He held one finger up, wavered the hand, then two fingers. One man or two. He pointed at Cornejo, then up the stairs. He pointed at himself then made walking fingers towards the front door and around the back. Cornejo nodded. The ex-marine began to climb the stairs. Grant stepped back outside into the strengthening wind.

He was right about the balcony. He was right about the flanking maneuver. It was the numbers he'd got wrong. Not because he couldn't count but because he'd placed so much faith in Oddjob's math. The big lug couldn't count worth shit. There were five left, not three, ruining Grant's run at the trifecta. Ruining his plan at sneaking up and ending this thing without losses for the good guys.

At least he was out of sight of the cameras now. Whatever went down from here on in would be private. Anybody wanting to argue about it would have to prove what happened. The first rule of evidence: it's not what you know, it's what you can prove. Given enough time, you could make the evidence support any version of events. The version Grant wanted now was the bad guys down and the good guys uninjured. That wasn't going to happen. They were outnumbered, but not by much. Time to even the odds.

As he came around the back corner of the lodge, he saw what he was up against. One man creeping around the outside of the kitchen to draw a bead on Miller. Two men through the kitchen window, with Miller moving his gun between them both. The girl held in a neck lock by one of them. Upstairs, two men edging out onto the balcony overlooking the kitchen windows. Five against three. One of the three more vulnerable than the rest: Miller. Grant liked the young detective. Had liked him from the moment they met. The responsibility of seeing him through this weighed heavy.

Time to even the odds.

Without giving a shouted warning, Grant stepped into the open, .45 raised. This wasn't the time for any of that "Stop, police" bullshit. There was none of that "aim to wound" rubbish either. He shot the man on the porch in the back twice, then immediately swung upwards and shot the first man on the balcony.

Three on three. Trifecta.

The second man on the balcony spun round and fired a snap shot at Grant. Wood splintered off the porch railing two feet away. The heavy blast of the shotgun shattered the dawn air. Cornejo wracked the slide and fired again. The gunman was blasted over the balcony and somersaulted to the ground.

Grant didn't wait. He darted to the kitchen door and kicked it open. Confusion reigned. That was good. Delaney had gone from six men standing to two against three. The big guy kept hold of the girl but didn't look committed anymore. Frank Delaney lowered the silver automatic.

There was no witty response. There was no gallows humor. Grant had just killed two men and watched a third shot to death. Gallows humor might come later, when he needed to cope with what he'd done, but not now. Now he was all business and dangerous to know.

It looked like they might have just about got away with it. The magnificent three. The big guy lowered his gun. Delaney looked deflated. Miller breathed a sigh of relief. Then the porch door opened behind the young detective and Oddjob's math came back to haunt them. A final heavy came through the door, gun arm raised, and sprayed the room with bullets.

He was the worst shot Grant had ever seen, but even a blind squirrel would find a nut every now and then. The electric toaster beside the breadboard exploded. The cupboard door above it took two hits. Panic flared the heavy's nostrils and fixed his eyes wide open. A stack of dinner plates standing in the washbasin drainer shattered. Glass in the kitchen door behind Grant smashed. Delaney dropped to the floor with both hands covering his head.

Miller took one in the neck above the protective Kevlar vest.

Grant roared his anger. "Nnnoooo."

He stepped into the room and shot the seventh man in the throat. He didn't aim there. Perceived wisdom was to always aim for the body mass, giving less chance of missing. The perceived wisdom was right. He loosed off three shots at the man's chest, but in his rage his gun hand aimed high. He didn't miss, just killed the guy with two neck shots and one in the shoulder.

Grant rushed to the fallen detective.

Cornejo rushed through from the hallway.

Grant jerked Miller's radio out of his pocket and yelled into the mouthpiece. "Officer down. Officer down. Get an ambulance. Scene clear."

Blood oozed down Miller's neck. At least it wasn't pulsing; that was good. Grant snatched a tea towel from the rail and folded it into a thick pad. He shifted Miller onto his side and pressed the pad against the wound. Miller's eyes were flickering. He was going into shock. Delaney started to get up, but Cornejo racked the shotgun's slide. Grant glared at the small-time gangster with ambitions of an empire. The suave businessman had disappeared. His face was pale.

Cornejo came over and took over from Grant. "Field dressing. I'm good with this."

Grant didn't speak but nodded his thanks. He stood up, the .45 hanging loose at his side. The big guy holding the girl had dropped his gun on the floor. Grant kicked it aside. The kitchen smelled of cordite and burned toast. A hint of coffee but the gunpowder overpowered the smell.

"Sit."

The big guy sat on a stool at the breakfast bar Grant hadn't noticed when he came in. Kristina Simonovich gasped for breath and clutched her throat. Tears welled in her eyes. She sat next to the heavy and coughed the tears away.

Sirens sounded outside, coming from a distance. The uniform officers from the barricade charged through the front door. The big stick Grant had hoped they wouldn't need. His chest felt like he'd been kicked by a horse, but he indicated the heavy to be arrested and explained the others were dead. The uniforms handcuffed the big guy, and one made a move towards Delaney. Grant blocked the way. "I've got this one."

One of the extra uniforms crouched beside Miller and helped Cornejo stem the flow of blood from his neck. The girl stopped coughing and took several deep breaths. She turned to Grant with anguish in her eyes.

"Pliss. Save my sister. She iss bombed. With bomb. Don't let her blow up."

Grant didn't understand at first, then it hit him. He saw Freddy Sullivan's workbench with the solder and the tools and the pieces of cotton webbing. He saw the empty matchbooks and the missing condoms. He suddenly realized it wasn't webbing but pieces of bra strap. Delaney wasn't hoping to influence the vote by coercing

Senator Clayton. He'd imported his very own suicide bomber, and Clayton was her ticket to the party.

THIRTY-EIGHT

THERE COMES A TIME in every cop's life when he has to make a choice between doing what's right and doing what's lawful. You'd think both were the same, but the way things have become, the law is often stacked in favor of the breakers over the protectors. Grant had made that choice before and had no qualms about cutting legal corners to get a result, but the price had never been as expensive as right now. He made the same choice he always made: right over lawful.

He shot Delaney in the leg, then dragged him into the restroom under the stairs. "Q and A. No wrong answers."

The door clicked shut behind them, and Grant locked it with the twist lock in the middle of the handle. He took a hand towel off the drying rail and wrapped it around Delaney's leg. Blood soaked through immediately. Grant took the gangster's hand and pressed it against the wound. He didn't explain. It was up to Delaney if he bled to death.

Delaney had plenty to say. "You fuck—you shot me!"

Grant sat on the toilet with the lid down for a seat. He said nothing, just stared at the man crouched on the floor. Delaney stared back, tears of pain welling in his eyes. "Holy Christ bleedin' on the cross—you fuckin' shot me."

"You said that already. Want to try for the other leg?"

Pain was etched all over Delaney's face. Grant had aimed for the fleshy part of the thigh. There were no broken bones, and he'd missed the vital artery. A .45 at close range made a helluva mess, though, and he knew that shock would rob Delaney of rational thought soon enough. "Where's the girl?"

"In the kitchen."

"The other girl. Her sister."

Delaney pressed the towel into his leg. It was almost completely red now. He shook his head in disbelief. His face turned ashen grey. Sweat broke out on his brow. His hands began to shake. He shook his head again. Grant fired one shot into the tiled wall beside Delaney's head. Shards of glazed tile cut the gangster's cheek. His head snapped up and his eyes focused on the man sitting on the toilet seat. Grant held the .45 against Delaney's good leg. On the knee. "Last chance."

Delaney told him everything.

GRANT LISTENED with increasing amazement that someone who had achieved so much in the field of crime could be so completely stupid. The man had climbed out of the sewer that had formed him and had crafted a criminal empire that spread far beyond Jamaica Plain and the rest of Boston. He'd reached the stage where he didn't need the criminal side of things anymore; his money was invested in so many legitimate businesses that he could go straight. Instead, he'd begun to believe his own publicity and was going for the championship. It wasn't a case of power corrupting and absolute power corrupting absolutely; it was just that Delaney believed he was beyond the law.

Grant leaned forward. "And you actually thought that would work?"

For Delaney, talking appeared to bring him around. He looked more focused than when he'd been dragged in there bleeding fifteen minutes ago. "Why not?"

"Because you're not Goldfinger, and this isn't Fort Knox. You blow up the oil delegation, you think the deal's going to go away? Hell, no. You've got interests in gas stations and stuff. Big money. You think America gives a shit where the oil comes from? Christ. You've invaded more countries than the Nazis, and it's nearly always about oil instead of national security. Ask them in Louisiana what they think about American oil."

"That's British Petroleum."

"It's off the coast of America. Ain't from Abu-fuckin'-Dhabi."

Delaney shrugged. He didn't even seem to grasp what a monster he'd become. Grant reminded him. "Let's get to the point. You've got the girl wired. Liquid explosives in the condoms hanging from a harness in the bra. How you going to detonate it?"

Delaney held a fist up with the thumb sticking up. He bent the thumb a couple of times as if pressing a button. "Wireless remote. Guy in the food court."

Grant stood up and pressed his foot against Delaney's injured leg. Delaney writhed in agony. Grant pointed the .45 at the gangster's head, then took it away. He took a deep breath, then blew out his cheeks. "You fuckin' arse. Anybody on their cell phone matches the frequency and they could all go up in flames."

He unlocked the door and was about to go out but changed his mind. He stepped back inside and kicked Delaney in the side of the leg. Then he went into the kitchen. A paramedic was attending to Miller. The young detective looked pale and frightened. Cornejo was leaning against the breakfast bar. The uniform cops had taken the last prisoner away.

Grant dropped to a squat beside Miller and rested a hand on his arm. "We have to shut down the convention center."

Miller found it hard to talk. He couldn't shake his head. "Can't."

The paramedic held up a hand to stop Grant. "This officer needs to be at MGH. Right now."

A second paramedic prepared the gurney. The pair of them lifted the backboard Miller was strapped to. A telephone began to ring. Not the house phone—the "James Bond Theme." In Miller's pocket. Grant took the cell out and gave Miller a quizzical look. "You've got to be kidding me."

Miller managed a weak smile and pointed at himself. "Double-oh-seven."

Grant tapped his own chest. "QWERTY."

Grant flipped the phone open and answered. It was Kincaid. "Where's Miller?"

"Paramedics are taking him out now."

"He gonna be okay?"

"I think so."

Grant didn't think Miller would be okay, but there was no need to tell Kincaid that. There were more important issues to be sorted. He cut through Kincaid's protestations about getting his protégé shot. "You need to get Clayton and his girl out of there."

"Hey. There's bigger shit to slop today."

"You bet your ass there is. Listen—"

Kincaid cut Grant off. His voice could be heard throughout the kitchen. He was angry, and when he was angry he shouted. Loud. "I've just hit the shit valley jackpot. Surprise late attendee. Security just got cranked up to red alert."

"Sam, listen: there's a—"

"*Fuck* listening. The crown prince of Saudi-fuckin'-somewhere-or-other arrives in twenty minutes."

Grant tried to tell Kincaid to shut down all communications, but he was talking to dead air. Kincaid had hung up.

THIRTY-NINE

THERE WAS NO TIME to go through official channels. Grant had to improvise. It was what he did best. He searched Miller's pockets and took out his handcuffs, keys, and detectives' shield. The cuff key was on the bunch. Grant pocketed them all. He patted Miller on the shoulder, avoided the clichéd "Hang in there, kid," and nodded Cornejo towards the hallway restroom. "Field dressing. Get Delaney ready for transport."

Then he stuck the .45 down the back of his belt and went out the front door.

The first thing he noticed was that the wind was now strong enough to bend the trees. The second was that the media cordon had disintegrated. TV cameras and news reporters were swarming over the parking lot out front of the lodge. There were no uniforms to hold the line; they were all engaged securing the crime scene or guarding prisoners. Dust swirled like mini tornadoes, the noise almost drowning the sound of the WCVB helicopter that was still hovering over the lake. He was glad it was still there. Improvise.

What he needed next was Kimberley Clark. He spotted her among a huddle of reporters talking directly to cameras.

He walked straight up to her, slapped a hand over the lens, and dragged her away by the arm. He nodded at the cameraman, the same one he'd first seen sitting in the reception of E-13 with the camera across his lap. "She'll call you back."

She was about to protest when she saw the look on his face and the three bullet holes in his T-shirt. He led her towards the porch steps and shouted above the noise of the wind and the helicopter. "You're affiliated, aren't you?"

"Channel 5 with ABC, yes."

"Satellite links. Hi-tech shit and stuff?"

"Yes. What—"

He held a hand up. "This is bad. I need fast, with no questions. Later, I'm all yours."

She shut up and listened.

"Don't know how, but you can block mobile phone signals, can't you?"

"Not personally."

Grant pointed at the sky. "Up there. Your connections. They can, yes? Radios too?"

"Yes."

"There's a bomb at the convention center. I need every signal blocking."

"Oh my God. The Hynes? Can't you give them a warning call?"

"That would use a signal. I want them blocking. Can you do it?"

"I think so."

"Good. And I need your helicopter."

They both looked out across Jamaica Pond. The WCVB helicopter was bobbing and weaving over the choppy waters. Tree branches were whipping into a frenzy.

Not good.

Kimberley Clark looked doubtful. She took a radio handset out of her pocket.

"Carl, come in. It's Kim."

The radio squawked static, then a voice that sounded like it was in a spin-dryer shouted a reply. "Go, Kim."

Grant left her talking to the pilot and went inside. Miller was being wheeled out the side door as he entered. There was no emotional farewell. There was no time. He strode across the room. Cornejo had taken his POLICE overjacket off and was finishing a field dressing that consisted of sanitary towels, whiskey for anaesthetic, and wadded dishcloths. Grant didn't ask where he'd got the sanitary towels. Cornejo secured the dressing with strips of kitchen towel from under the washbasin. Delaney had more color in his cheeks but still looked wide-eyed and panic-stricken. Grant ignored him and stood facing Cornejo. "Okay, John. Time to 'fess up."

He pointed at the square of sticking plaster showing beneath the sleeve of the ex-marine's T-shirt. "What theatre were you in?"

Cornejo tensed. "Don't matter which war I fought in. So long as you know I fought."

Grant waved Cornejo's reluctance away. "Your theatre of operations determines your specialist training."

Cornejo nodded his understanding. Grant reached forward and took hold of the bottom of the plaster. Cornejo didn't resist. This was important. He looked Grant in the eye without blinking, then nodded once. Grant ripped the plaster off in one swift movement leaving hairless flesh, an inflamed rash, and two tattoos.

The first one was the traditional US Marine Corps insignia in faded blue ink. It was the second one Grant was interested in. A narrow strip of ink running the width of the main tattoo but separated from it. The curled wire and dynamite clock of the improvised bomb disposal team. IEDs. The biggest killer of troops abroad in the last two major conflicts.

Grant smiled, but his face was deadly serious. "Glad I was right. We're gonna need your expertise."

He took the POLICE jacket from the back of the breakfast barstool and tossed it to Cornejo. "Don't want you getting shot by mistake."

Cornejo put the jacket back on. "What about you?"

Grant took out Miller's handcuffs and pointed at Delaney. "I'll have him."

He was about to snap one cuff on Delaney's wrist when Kimberley Clark came into the kitchen. She looked windswept and dusty. Her makeup needed retouching. A quick glance at Delaney's bloodstained bandage was enough to convince her she shouldn't ask. Instead she turned to Grant. "I've got good news and bad news."

GRANT KICKED THE STOOL across the kitchen and thumped a clenched fist on the breakfast bar. Salt and pepper shakers bounced. A neat pile of folded napkins fell to the floor. "Limp-dicked motherfuckers get everywhere."

Kimberley Clark pursed her lips but didn't explain about motherfuckers and limp dicks not being compatible. She held a hand up for Grant to calm down.

"It's blowing a gale out there. No way it's safe to fly. They've called him in."

Grant paused to reconsider his options. He thought back to his police driver training in West Yorkshire. Emergency response driving. The aim was to get where you were going fast, but the important thing was to get there safely. Going full speed to an emergency was fine, but if you crashed on the way you couldn't help the people you were supposed save. Helicopter in high winds was a recipe for disaster. Crash on the way and he'd be no use to anyone at the John B. Hynes Veterans Memorial Convention Center. "Plan B."

He took Miller's keys out and quickly checked them. Car keys for the Crown Vic were on the ring. He handed them to Cornejo. "Dump Oddjob. Bring the car around back."

Cornejo was down the hallway and out the front door before Grant turned to the WCVB anchorwoman. "What's the good news?"

"Head office has shut down the airwaves. They can only give you half an hour before every media authority and watchdog makes them reconnect."

"Great. Thanks."

He grabbed a shaky Delaney by the arm and forced him towards the back door. The Crown Vic came around at speed and skidded to a halt out of sight from prying cameras. Grant paused in the doorway and looked back towards the reporter. "I don't need to tell you that this bomb thing is not for broadcast yet. Panic in a closed space. The triggerman's going to see it. I want that bastard waiting for the signal to push the button."

"I understand. But later—you're mine."

"Gotcha."

He dragged Delaney across the rear porch and slapped the trunk of the car. Cornejo popped it open, and Grant bundled the wounded gangster inside. He slammed the lid shut and went to the driver's door. "Slide over."

Cornejo slid across to the passenger seat. Grant leaned an arm on the back of the seat and looked over his shoulder. Reversed along the secondary drive until there was room to spin the Crown Vic around. When he was facing front, he glanced at Cornejo. "You do know the way?"

Cornejo nodded.

"Fastest route."

Grant flicked the warning lights on in the front grille and gunned the engine. The wheels spat gravel and dust as it sped along the drive towards Jamaicaway. "You hum it, son, I'll play it."

"What?"

The PG Tips chimpanzee advert went right over Cornejo's head, but Grant was in no mood to explain. It was time for some aggressive emergency response driving. This was one time where getting there late would be just as bad as not getting there at all.

FORTY

The Crown Vic blasted through the JP traffic, horn blaring and warning lights flashing. The Saudi prince would be arriving about now. The signal blackout would last maybe another fifteen, twenty minutes. It was going to be tight. The unknown factor was Kincaid's reaction to the radios and cell phones going down. The Saudi security team's reaction. His experience with the Hot and Duskies was they could get very hot very quick. Restraint wasn't in their nature.

Grant dodged lanes on the narrow roads until they hit Columbus and headed north. The wide, straight road allowed them more speed. Cornejo kept the directions coming fast but found time on the straight for a question. He jerked a thumb over his shoulder towards the trunk. "You really think he's going to ID the triggerman?"

"Won't need to. Haven't seen a Delaney thug yet won't stand out like a sore thumb in McDonald's."

"You think?"

"Doesn't matter. When I walk Delaney through the food court after, he's gonna avoid looking at his man like the plague—

guarantee you. The look his guy is going to give Delaney? Won't be able to hide that."

"How'd they get the bomb through security?"

"Security's for everyone attending out front. Clayton's girl is with the dignitaries. When the president shows up for a speech, they don't strip search the first lady."

Grant concentrated on the timeframe. Maybe ten minutes left before the communication signals were unblocked. The Hynes was on the right, just along Boylston Street. Two minutes, tops.

Cornejo tensed.

Grant relaxed.

They flew towards the long scenic walkway and sidewalk in front of the John B. Hynes Veterans Memorial Convention Center. The longest name in Christendom. No wonder everyone called it the Hynes. The Crown Vic screeched to a halt in the parking lane outside the Boylston Street entrance. Grant popped the trunk and was dragging Delaney out before the engine stopped. Cornejo dumped the shotgun in the luggage space, grabbed the tool bag, and slammed the lid.

Eight minutes to go.

DELANEY WAS GROGGY AND SLUGGISH, but Grant was big and strong. Delaney did whatever Grant wanted. To make sure, Grant slapped one cuff on Delaney's wrist and the other on his own. He took out Miller's shield and held it above his head as he charged through the main doors towards the bank of escalators. "Police. Police. Emergency. Coming through."

Cornejo was right behind him, the POLICE sign on the back of his jacket flapping with the speed of their entrance. It was a good job. The cops on the door looked edgy and trigger-happy. The radio blackout had obviously had an undesirable side effect. The temporary metal detectors beeped.

The lobby was enormous.

The escalators looked like something out of *Star Trek*.

The floor names were all to pot. Neither the English nor American way. Why the fuck couldn't they make their minds up? The street entrance was the lower level, even though it was on the ground floor. The next one up was the plaza level, not the first or second floor. Then it was the second level and third level. The ballroom was on the third level. The oil delegation was using the ballroom.

Grant reached the up escalator going full-tilt. He took the steps two at a time, dragging Delaney with him. His and the escalator's forward movement doubled his speed, but it was still a long way up to the top floor. Faces looked over the balcony surrounding the enormous circular vestibule that reached all the way to the roof. Each level had its own balcony. The escalators climbed to each floor, then there was another escalator to the next floor. Everything was bright and clean. Potted plants and creeping ivy adorned the lobby of each level.

Grant kept the detectives' shield held up. SWAT officers leaned over the rail on level two and level three. Deadly black snipers' rifles pointed down at the trio of gatecrashers. Grant shouted at the faceless cops. "Police. Emergency. Coming up."

The shouted warning, the shield, and the POLICE jacket kept them from getting shot out of hand. The threat level was high. Radio and phone communication cut off. Everyone was jumpy. The trio reached level two before anyone tried to stop them. Two BPD cops, guns raised, blocked the top of the escalator. "Halt."

Grant kept taking two steps at a time. Delaney was flagging but was dragged along. Cornejo kept an easy motion flowing. This was second nature to the ex-marine. He could do this in his sleep. One of the cops kept touching his ear, as if that would magically bring the radios back. Delaney gave him a confused look. Grant waved the shield. "Police. Urgent. Where's Detective Kincaid?"

"Stop or I'll shoot."

Grant didn't stop. He was almost at the top of the second escalator. "Then shoot or get the fuck out of my way. Radios are down 'cause I shut 'em down. You've got a bomb in the ballroom."

The BPD cops wavered. One lowered his gun; the other tapped his ear again.

"And they aren't coming back no matter how much you tap your ear. Where's Kincaid?"

The ear-tapper jerked a thumb up the final escalator. "Ballroom lobby, sir."

Grant flew past the cops and hit the last stretch of moving staircase. He was beginning to think that dragging Delaney with him had been a mistake. Grant was fit but flagging with Delaney's weight. Cornejo looked like he could climb another three floors. Grant called back to the BPD cops. "Where's the food court?"

"Plaza level, sir."

"Secure it. Nobody in or out. You've got a remote triggerman in there. Could be armed."

"Doubt it, sir. Detectors and x-rays on all entrances today."

"Get SWAT down there anyway. And stop calling me sir."

"Yes, sir."

Delaney was out of breath. Grant could see his leg had stopped bleeding, but he'd already lost a lot of blood. He was pale and shocked and worn out. Grant didn't care. He reached the top of the last escalator and held the badge up for everyone to see. Everyone included several more BPD cops, guns raised, in a semicircle around the mouth of the moving staircase.

Grant kept his voice calm and lowered the shield. "The ballroom. Kincaid?"

The semicircle didn't move. Nobody lowered their guns. "Identify yourselves."

Grant was getting annoyed at all the delays, even though he understood the officer's caution. There was a US senator, assorted foreign dignitaries, and the crown prince of somewhere-or-other inside a security cordon that had lost all communications. No wonder he was jumpy. Grant cut him some slack and didn't bite his head off. "I'm the Resurrection Man."

He pointed at Delaney. "He's the guy set a bomb to go off in there."

Then at Cornejo. "And he's the guy going to diffuse it. Now, where's Kincaid?"

Grant checked his watch. Five minutes to go.

THE SEMICIRCLE FELL BACK half a pace and opened a gap in the middle. The lead officer nodded over his shoulder towards a wide corridor. The ballroom foyer and the prefunction area. The ballroom doors were closed and recessed, with two more cops on either side of them. A giant figure stepped out of the recess, looking strange in his dress blues. Sam Kincaid.

"Hold up over there. Let them through."

Grant didn't waste any time. He went straight over to Kincaid and gave him the short version. Bomb strapped to Senator Clayton's mistress. Remote trigger in the food court downstairs. Radio blackout. Speed racer. That was all he needed to say. Kincaid didn't even blink. He thought on his feet and didn't waver. A half-turn towards the doors as he spoke over his shoulder. "Let's get it done, then. Natives are restless, so be careful. The Saudi team are armed with itchy trigger fingers since the radios went down."

Delaney got his breath back and tugged on the handcuff chain. "You can't go charging in."

Everyone looked at the JP gangster. "She's got a trigger too. Told if anyone tries to stop her"—he made the fist again and flexed his thumb—"or her sister's toast."

Grant yanked the cuff. "You slimy bastard."

Delaney looked more worried than shamefaced. "That's not all. When you cut the signal, you started the secondary protocol."

Kincaid's shoulders sagged. "This can't be good."

Grant glared at Delaney. "And what's that?"

"Delayed activation countdown."

"How long?"

Delaney shrugged. "I don't know. That was Sullivan's job."

Cornejo stepped forward, the tool bag hanging from one hand. He tapped his watch with one finger. "Doesn't matter how long. Anybody makes a call once the signal's back—"

He didn't need to continue. Grant checked his watch again. Three minutes to go. He hoped Kimberly had been right and the network might be able to give them more time. Hope for the best, prepare for the worst. Preparing for the worst meant bursting through the door and disarming the bomb before the girl set it off or the Saudis started a fire fight.

Grant dragged Delaney towards the door. "Fuck it. Whatever happens, *you're* getting a front-row seat."

He opened the door and entered the ballroom.

FORTY-ONE

THE RECESSED DOORS were the first of a set of three opening into the left-hand wall of the ballroom. Double doors along the prefunction area, then triple doors halfway down and another set of double doors at the far end. The nearest doors got in towards the back of the room, and the first thing Grant noticed was, like everything else he'd encountered in America, how bloody big the room was. It was huge. A curved ceiling ran the length of the roof, designed to look like skylights, with hidden lighting giving an outdoors look even though they weren't real windows. There were hidden wall dividers that could be deployed to turn the enormous function room into three separate areas. None were deployed. This was one big motherfucking room filled with more people than Bradford.

That was going to be a problem.

It wasn't the main problem.

The main problem was he should have come in the bottom doors because they were nearest the stage and presentation area. Grant had forced Delaney through at the back of the room, leaving a long way to go to charge down the suicide bomber.

The suicide bomber looked pale and frightened, even from this distance. She was also the spitting image of her sister. Anna Simonovich was beautiful. Her pale complexion, immaculate and well-cared-for skin, and high cheekbones set her apart from the other women in the audience. It would make it all the more difficult for Grant to shoot her, but if her hands made any sudden movements, that's exactly what he'd have to do.

Kincaid and Cornejo came in behind him. Kincaid went left, Cornejo right. Grant went straight to the aisle that ran down the middle of the room between row upon row of chairs facing the stage. The rows towards the back were empty; the organizers must have overestimated the appeal of a bunch of oil barons and the local politician, but the seats from halfway down all the way to the front were full, interspersed with tables for the wealthier guests. Clayton certainly had sex appeal on his side, the widower coming over somewhere between Kevin Costner and that guy from *Sex and the City* and *The Good Wife*—Chris Noth, if Grant was up to date.

Nobody noticed the intruders for a good ten seconds. That gave Grant time to make it down twenty-five rows. The podium speaker was the first to realize they weren't just a bunch of latecomers. The podium speaker was Senator Clayton. His smile faded. Concern furrowed his brow. The look on his face prompted half the audience to look round. Somebody gasped.

Kincaid raised his voice. "Police officers. Please stay in your seats."

Cornejo picked up speed, the POLICE jacket flowing like a cape.

Grant kept Delaney moving and put the detective's shield away. He'd need the hand free. He slid it round his back and drew the .45 out of his belt but kept it behind him. His eyes never left the girl's, while at the same time taking in everything about the podium guests.

Senator Clayton was standing at the lectern, both hands resting on the sloping top. Anna Simonovich, the dutiful wife substitute, was standing to his left and slightly behind him. Further to the left was a long, heavy table draped to the floor with an expensive white cloth. Five oil company delegates, two Americans and three Middle East–types, sat behind the table. The Saudi prince sat slightly apart, between the table and the lectern, in a bigger chair. Not quite a throne, but Grant reckoned that was the intended image. Half a dozen foreign security guards stood behind the prince, hands cupped loosely in front. They were the danger element. Unpredictable.

Kincaid's security team were covering the doors, with a token presence at either end of the stage. Two men. This hadn't been a high-threat level until the crown prince showed up. Even then, it wasn't a case of national security. The place wasn't swarming with Secret Service or FBI in their black sunglasses and earpieces.

Anna Simonovich saw the intruders and took half a pace away from Clayton. Grant watched the movement and relaxed his grip on the .45.

He glanced up at the clock on the back wall.

Two minutes left.

The two cops and the ex-marine surged forward. They were passing the posh seats now, the front three rows interspersed with tables and flower displays. The Saudi bodyguards recognized the threat and reacted accordingly. Three closed in around the prince. The other three separated for a better field of fire. All six drew their weapons.

The girl locked eyes with Grant. She stared unblinking until her eyes watered. Her face was pale with fear. Grant saw indecision flicker behind her eyes. Noticed her hands twitch. The flowing gown hung limp around her body. One hand moved slowly towards a gap in the folds. She looked resigned. Her shoulders sagged. The hand was six inches from disappearing into the opening.

Grant reached the foot of the stage and whipped the .45 forward and up.

Six assorted weapons snapped into the firing position. All aimed at Grant.

Somebody screamed in the audience, and there was a sudden gush of sound as chairs toppled and people ran for the exits. Panic filled the room. Bad news. Panic was infectious. The oil company delegates shifted their seats away from the crown prince. Senator Clayton stared in horror but stood tall. Maybe he wasn't such a jerk after all. The girl continued moving her hand towards the gown.

Grant aimed front and center.

Kincaid saw what was going to happen and held his arms wide. "Police emergency. Lower your weapons."

Six pairs of eyes focused on Grant. Six dusky faces with furrowed brows and beads of sweat. For a second Grant was in another place, with a different set of sweat-soaked dark faces. Dusty and noisy and dangerous. He saw machine guns and pistols and machetes. Dusty streets and a swinging stethoscope. The vision disappeared as quickly as it had come. He gulped down the moisture forming in his mouth.

The girl's eyes remained locked on him.

Grant stared at her.

The world slowed down. He felt like he was running through treacle. His heart thumped loud in his ears. Perceived wisdom was to always aim for the center mass. Body shot. Except when you were dealing with somebody strapped with enough explosives to level the third floor. He didn't translate that into the American system. He was English. Fuck the American system. His finger tightened on the trigger. He raised his aim. The throat. Empty the magazine at the throat to sever the spinal cord and stop any motor response of the fingers. Stop the girl pushing the button.

He stared into her eyes and saw someone else's.

A swinging stethoscope.

Anna Simonovich blinked.

Grant did not.

Cornejo took everything in. A split second—that was all it took in combat. You only had a split second to recognize the threat, make your decision, and act upon it. He began to move immediately, but everything happened slowly.

Kincaid yelled with his arms held wide.

Cornejo moved forward and in front of Grant.

The girl blinked, twice.

Grant picked his spot and made his decision.

His finger relaxed but remained in place. The .45 didn't waver. Grant stared into Anna Simonovich's eyes and shouted above the commotion. "We've got your sister. She's safe."

Hope flooded the girl's eyes. Grant kept moving forward. "Keep your hands up where I can see them."

She held her arms out wide, like Jesus on the cross, and the irony of the pose was not lost on the Resurrection Man. Grant began to lower the .45 to the ready stance, but it was too late. Panic is infectious. Six guns pointed at the Yorkshire detective. It only took one to overreact.

The gunshot sounded loud beneath the vaulted ceiling. Grant was halfway up the three steps to the stage. Cornejo got there before him. He threw himself in front of Grant and took the bullet full in the chest. He wasn't wearing the Kevlar vest. It was still hanging over the barstool in Delaney's kitchen. The impact dropped him to the floor and tripped Grant, who stumbled forward onto the stage, Delaney in tow.

Kincaid stepped in front of the security guards, yelling.

Six firearms were lowered, one still smoking.

The crown prince turned and slapped the shooter across the face.

Grant had no time to mourn his fallen comrade or find another bomb disposal expert. He rolled back onto his feet, dragging Delaney up the steps with him. The clock was ticking. He jammed the .45 down the back of his jeans and grasped the gown. "Sorry."

He ripped it open. There was no gasp of amazement. Everyone was too shocked at the shooting and the mass exodus. Senator Clayton was the only one to show surprise. He stepped forward to put his arms around the woman who was his lover, but Grant pushed him back. The harness was complicated and heavy. The bra straps had been reinforced and the condoms securely fastened. Wires circled her body and the firing mechanism was small but deadly. A pushbutton trigger hung at her waist. Including the stockings and suspenders, she looked like the most dangerous dominatrix in the world. She also looked like the most frightened bondage freak he'd ever met.

Her eyes pleaded with him.

Grant looked for the timer but couldn't see it. He wasn't sure if it was best to know. He glanced up at the clock on the wall. Time was up anyway; unless WCVB had managed a miracle, the signal blockage had been lifted. The first phone call to match the device's frequency and they were all goners. Fast and decisive action was needed to disarm the bomb. The only person who could have done that was gurgling blood onto the stage.

Grant looked at Kincaid. "Get everybody out. Now."

Kincaid surveyed the complex network of wires and explosives, then looked back at Grant. He didn't nod or smile or say anything. He just acted. That was always the way with the best. Cornejo hadn't hesitated. Neither did Kincaid. Grant felt proud to have known both of them.

The oil company delegates didn't need any persuading. They were out the door as soon as Kincaid clapped his hands and yelled for everyone to leave. The prince was practically carried out as his security team swarmed towards the door. Senator Clayton was the only one reluctant to go. He had tears in his eyes as he reached out for the girl who'd become so close to him. Kincaid yanked the senator's arm away and frogmarched him out of the ballroom.

The vaulted ceiling echoed with their footsteps. The doors slammed shut. The room fell silent. Grant looked at the half-naked woman and for the first time felt his pulse racing. No amount of relaxation technique was going to work this time. He stood frozen to the spot. His mind went blank. He simply didn't know what to do. The wires were too complicated. The timer undiscovered. And he had absolutely zero idea where to start.

A hand grabbed his leg.

The tool bag slid across the floor in front of him.

John Cornejo dragged himself around the podium and pointed two fingers at his eyes, then jabbed them towards the walking IED. He was coughing up blood. He tapped his waist, then nodded towards the girl. Grant followed his gaze. The button dangling at her waist. Grant reached out for the detonator and turned it over. A red numerical display shone from the reverse side. It was counting down fast. Seconds. Minutes. Hours. There weren't any hours. The seconds were changing too fast to read. The minutes had just clicked down to four. Delaney whimpered when he saw it.

None of that mattered if anyone started getting phone calls out in the hallway.

Cornejo forced himself to speak. "No tamper devices."

Grant opened the tool bag and shuffled around inside it. It was a standard car emergency toolkit, not bomb disposal tools. All he came up with that might be useful was a pair of pliers with wire-cutting blades and a sharp knife. He held up the pliers hopefully. "You mean I can just cut the wires?"

"No. That'll set it off."

"What then?"

Cornejo mimed undressing. "Just take it off her."

Of course. Grant had given Freddy Sullivan too much credit. He might have enjoyed blowing shit up in the woods of Jamaica Pond, but the Bradford burglar hadn't grasped the first rule of suicide bombing: don't let the bomber take the device off. She might change her mind. The only reason she hadn't done that was the threat to her sister. Or maybe she was so frightened she hadn't realized she could have simply undressed from her deadly wardrobe.

Grant reached forward, but being handcuffed to Delaney hampered one hand. He whipped out the keys and unlocked the cuff on his wrist. He paused for a second, not wanting to let Delaney go, then snapped the cuff on the girl's wrist. The bastard responsible wasn't going anywhere without the bomb he'd set in motion. Delaney let out a strangled cry. "No, please."

With both hands free, he set about unfastening the harness. There was the webbing belt around her waist and reinforced straps of her bra. He undid the belt and it fell open, suspended by the bra and myriad wires tangled around her body. Next he spun her around and unfastened the bra. The weight of her breasts pulled it forward, and he turned her forwards again. Her breasts swayed. He'd never felt so detached from such a spectacle. The bra hung loose but didn't come off.

The girl's eyes burned into him. "Pliss."

He had to force himself to concentrate.

He picked up the knife from where it had dropped on the floor and cut the shoulder straps. The device still didn't come away. There were too many wires holding it in place. Maybe Sullivan hadn't been so stupid after all. The wires formed their own anti-tamper device. They had become knotted and tangled like the random knotting of an extension cable when you weren't careful about unraveling it. Ropes and cables had a mind of their own and could tie the most intricate knots when you least intended. The girl was completely tied up. He couldn't cut the wires to free her. He couldn't rip the condoms from the harness.

The red numbers counted down.

The girl's eyes leaked panic. Tears formed. She closed her eyes.

A mobile phone rang in the hallway.

Her eyes flew open.

Another phone began to ring.

Then another. And another.

No time left.

Grant stared an apology into the girl's eyes. The girl returned it with a pleading glare. She let out a sigh that deflated her like a pricked balloon. Grant remembered blowing condoms into balloons as a kid, but the entire one-small-prick-fucking-one-big-prick scenario seemed foolish, macho nonsense now. Their eyes locked. Neither of them blinked. This was the end. When she spoke, her voice was calm and polite. "I do not want to die like this. Pliss."

She made a gun shape out of her fingers and thumb and held it to her head. "Pliss."

Grant stared into her eyes and saw someone else's. A swinging stethoscope. Dusty streets in a hot country. Another plea. Another gunshot. The reason why he hated guns. *I'm a typist*, he told himself, but that lie wouldn't wash today.

Cell phones were going off all over the place outside. Police radios squawked static. Grant dropped the knife and drew the .45 in one movement. In life-or-death situations, indecision kills. Grant's decision was no decision at all. Either way, the girl dies. He nodded once, placed one hand over her face to cover her eyes, and placed the barrel of the gun against her temple. He didn't say sorry, but he thought it. The dashing rescue had turned into a murderous debacle.

He pulled the trigger and shot her in the head.

WITH ALL MOTOR FUNCTIONS gone, she flopped to the ground, but that wasn't the end of it. Frank Delaney was dragged to the floor by the handcuff shackling him to the corpse. The JP gangster shouted to be released, but Grant ignored him. He stepped quickly around the end of the table. Cornejo was lying in a pool of blood behind him. The ex-marine was actually smiling.

Grant grasped the edge of the table and yanked it upwards. The table was heavier than the one in the interview room. It was bigger too. Jugs of water and flower displays tipped off the tablecloth as the surface upended. It flipped over, and Grant dropped to his knees behind it.

One last cell phone rang outside the door.

There was a hiss and a strange electronic wail beyond the table.

Then the ballroom was concussed with a deafening blast, and a ball of flame leveled the stage. The fake skylights in the vaulted ceiling shattered and rained shards of glass. The lectern disintegrated. The upended table blasted forwards, pushing Grant and Cornejo like snow before a plough traveling sixty miles an hour. They were swept from the stage like confetti.

Grant was slammed against the sidewall. Cornejo disappeared altogether. The ballroom was one huge echo chamber, the thumping explosion replaying in roles of diminishing thunder. It would replay in Grant's mind for days. He was lying on his back, arm broken and one leg twisted the wrong way, staring at the ceiling. There was no severed ear or squashed eyeball staring back at him this time. If Sullivan was looking down from above, Grant's message to him would be unprintable.

All he could think of to say was sorry, but his mouth wouldn't work. He wasn't sure if the message was for the girl, the woman from his past, or for himself. In the end it didn't matter. Cops live in a valley. Shit rolls downhill. Then you die. With that jolly thought, Grant faded into unconsciousness, unaware of the hands lifting the battered table off him or the sirens coming from all across the city.

FORTY-TWO

The private room in Massachusetts General Hospital was quiet. There was no steady beep of the heart rate monitor and no constant rustle of nurse's uniforms as they fussed around the recovering hero. That's because Grant wasn't hooked up to a heart rate monitor, and the room was empty except for the man in the bed and the bigger man standing near the window.

"Nice view they've given you."

Kincaid was looking out across Charlesbank Park to the Charles River Basin. Grant had already noted that when Americans called something a park, what they really meant was sports fields. Charlesbank was basically a grassy area protruding into the river with three baseball diamonds and a swimming pool. There were a few park benches and picnic tables, so he supposed you could just about get away with calling it a park.

Grant was sitting up on top of the bed sheets, one arm in a sling across his chest and one leg in plaster from ankle to thigh. It was the only thing giving the room a hospital feel. This was first class. It didn't even smell like a hospital room. Flowers and perfume fragranced the private ward so much he thought he'd gag. Kincaid was craning his neck to look left. Grant knew he wasn't looking at the Longfellow Bridge, as spectacular as that was, but beyond it. Farther south. The Hynes was just visible past the bend in the river. It was still there. The smoke that had been hanging over it the last few days was not.

Grant jerked the thumb of his good hand towards the door. "They do know I don't need protection anymore, right?"

He was referring to the big guy in a black suit standing outside the private room. He had the sunglasses, earpiece, and square jaw of the archetypal G-man. Grant smiled at the protective overkill. You'd think he'd saved the president or something. Kincaid followed Grant's gaze. "The Dominguez cartel?"

"Yeah—that was just smoke and mirrors. Delaney trying to deflect suspicion away from Triple Zero. Guy must have a real God complex."

"Had a real God complex."

"Exactly. He can take it up with the man himself now, can't he?"

"It's the other fella he'll be visiting. Hot and sticky down south."

"They can call off the Men in Black, then."

"Who said they were here to protect you? Don't want you signing yourself out again before the big guy comes for a chat."

"The president?"

"Now who's got the God complex? No. But close. The head of something way above my pay grade."

"I'm quaking in my boots."

"Well, quake no more. You coming tonight?"

"If they'll let me out."

"They'll let you out. Squad car'll pick you up at six."

Neither of them had spoken about their losses. In a different theatre of war, the media might have reported them as "Heavy casualties—the relatives have been informed." In frontline policing, the survivors never talked about it. Gallows humor was put on hold for that kind of thing. Kincaid pointed to the TV fastened to a wall bracket above the foot of the bed. "I see WCVB has a new media star."

Grant glanced at the blank screen. He hated daytime TV. America was even worse than the UK. Daytime soaps and quiz shows that would insult the intelligence of a germ. "You saw that, huh?"

"Hard to miss. I hear she's offered you a job."

"Seriously. Can you see me on *Live at Five* on Channel 5?"

"You were on *Live at Five*."

"Yeah. And what phoney bastards they were too."

"That's the news for you."

"Not for me, it's not."

"Kimberly Clark must be some compensation."

Grant held his hand out flat and quivered the palm. "The jury's out on that one. You know they cut my clothes off?"

"Normal procedure with blast injuries."

"Bet it was that short-arsed little minx from day one. She was pissed off I didn't let her the first time."

"Angels of mercy. And fashion police. Ruined your jeans, did she?"

"And more."

"Not the famous orange jacket?"

"In pieces. Can't even stitch it up."

"How will the bad guys see who to shoot now?"

Kincaid fell silent. He looked as if he were mulling something over before mentioning it. He made a decision and leaned his back against the window facing the bed. He lowered his voice so the guy outside the door couldn't hear. "Something I do know."

Grant sensed a change in mood. He kept quiet.

"I finally got some answers about your record."

"Criminal? Don't have one."

"Military."

Grant waited. Kincaid tried to be tactful. "She was American, wasn't she?"

Grant said nothing.

"The stethoscope. Army Medical Corps."

Grant didn't ask how Kincaid found out about the stethoscope. He already knew. The night Terri Avellone and Melissa Quintana waited in his room, Grant had thought somebody had searched it. When he discovered the women in the bathroom, he'd pushed that thought aside, but somebody *had* searched the drawers. It was an understandable precaution before working with the loose cannon from Snake Pass.

"The Ministry of Defence records've got you as a typist. US Joint Operations records have you as something else."

Grant shrugged. "Best way to keep a secret is to convince yourself it never happened."

"The governor knows it happened. State Department too. You've been put up for a Medal of Honor."

"We both know it's those who don't come back who deserve the medals."

"We do. But the media loves a hero, and governments love the media."

The door opened without anybody knocking. The G-man stepped aside and Senator Clayton came in, flanked by two men who looked even more imposing. Kincaid went to the door. "Time to go. Don't sign anything."

He winked, then left. The door closed behind him with a pneumatic hiss.

Senator Clayton smiled his million-dollar smile and shook Grant's hand. The smile was tarnished by a hint of sadness. Grant's hand was grazed and cut, but at least it was the right hand for shaking. His left arm was the one plastered and supported by the sling. Clayton's face morphed from that of a smiling politician into a grateful citizen.

"I cannot thank you enough. Never be able to. I am so sorry."

Grant saw the honesty in the senator's eyes and thought once again that Clayton might not be such a jerk after all. "Wasn't your fault. Guy like Delaney"—Grant shrugged—"wasn't your fault. I'm sorry for your loss. Wasn't her fault either."

"Thank you. That means a lot."

The other two men seemed anxious for the mutual backslapping to be over. The older one, with greying temples and an air of natural authority, was obviously the governor. Clayton introduced him, and there was another round of handshaking and congratulations.

"I'm sure your colleague has told you, even though he was not supposed to, that you have been cited for the highest award this country can give."

Grant nodded. One thing he'd learned in his combined police and army career was never to interrupt a politician when he was speechifying. The governor went on to explain how grateful the state of Massachusetts and the US of A were for the service Grant had performed, above and beyond the call of duty. Thanks to his actions, the ties between the Gulf and America had been strengthened and a terrible financial disaster averted. A terrible financial disaster. Oil and money. Grant wasn't surprised it all came down to that. Saving a few lives helped make it more palatable, but the bottom line was hard cash and the continued flow of crude into the gas guzzlers of America.

Grant thanked him but kept a wary eye on the third man. Despite keeping quiet and standing behind the politicians, the slim man in the dark suit exuded more power than the other two put together. He didn't step forward or shake Grant's hand. He simply waited for a pause in proceedings, then spoke in a quiet voice. "What are your plans, Mr. Grant?"

"Right now? Get some clothes on and go for a pint."

Hard eyes stared at Grant, but the voice remained calm. "For the future. What plans?"

Grant smiled. This man was so powerful he didn't need to be forceful. He decided to tread carefully. But he was still a cop. Cops are more grounded than the usual minions of government. And this man was the government, even more than the public faces standing with him.

"Extra leg room on the flight home. Then face the D and C tribunal."

"Discipline and Complaints?"

"Yes."

"About Snake Pass?"

"Yes. My inspector told me to keep a low profile."

A heavy thudding beat in the distance began to vibrate the windows. A helicopter coming in for the helipad on the hospital roof. More casualties from some other disaster, just a smaller one than avoiding the terrible financial disaster to the United States. Grant doubted the governor of Massachusetts would be greeting that flight.

"I've checked your records."

Grant bristled. "Seems like nothing's private anymore."

The man didn't bite. "I don't think the West Yorkshire Police would be sorry to see you go."

"Go where?"

"Go here."

"I'm already here."

"Stay here."

Grant leaned back against his pillows. The thudding of the helicopter grew louder, but the double glazing kept the noise to a minimum. The windows vibrated. The glass of water on the bedside cabinet trembled, forming concentric circles like a pebble thrown in a pond. The flowers and the perfume assaulted his nostrils. Normal hospital noises waited outside the door. "Immigration might have something to say about that."

"Immigration will have nothing to say about that."

"Joining the police in America. Application states it can only be positions you can't fill locally. By Americans."

"You have talents that can't be found locally."

"I do?"

The helicopter throbbed overhead. The pad must have only been a few floors above them. Grant thought he felt the thud as it touched down, but that could have been his imagination. He picked up the glass of water and took a drink. He suddenly felt very dry. The third man glanced at the ceiling, then back at Grant. "My lift has arrived. We will talk again."

He still didn't offer to shake hands.

"Enjoy yourself this evening. He was a good man."

Then all three swept out of the room, and Grant was alone. Where was Terri Avellone when he needed her? Even the big guy at the door had left. Grant swung his bad leg off the bed and struggled to the window. The view was indeed a beauty, but the park and the river weren't what he was looking at. He craned his neck to the left and focused on the distance. Somewhere beyond the Charles River Basin and the John B. Hynes Veterans Memorial Convention Center was a cop bar in Jamaica Plain, no doubt painted green.

It would soon be time to pay his respects. He doubted he'd enjoy himself.

FORTY-THREE

Doyle's Café was full when Grant arrived. Irish music came out into the street. Dusk was settling over JP, befitting the occasion. Even more fitting was the fact that Doyle's was on Washington Street, at 3484, only two blocks down from the E-13 police station. It seemed to Grant that he'd spent his entire visit crossing Washington Street at some point or other.

The patrol car dropped Grant at the intersection of Washington and Williams, opposite an athletics track, an American football field, and the ever-present baseball diamond. The low-slung, flat-roofed building was right on the junction, its green-painted window frames and redbrick structure aping the traditional pub without the need for an upper floor or gabled roof. Calling it a café was inaccurate. It served food, yes, but it was predominantly a place for drinking. An imitation gas lamp stood outside the door like a throwback to the old country.

Grant walked with the aid of a stick; he had refused to come out on crutches. He only had one good arm anyway. The music was loud and Irish and full of joy and laughter. A typical Irish American wake.

Kincaid greeted him when he came through the door. A roar of applause and whistles that bordered on jeers overpowered the music. Briefly. Any residue of the Anglo-Irish friction had disappeared. Even Sergeant O'Rourke was getting into the spirit of things with the aid of plenty of spirits, by the looks of him.

The coffin was on a table in the middle of the room. An open casket.

Grant avoided going near it, not wanting to look inside at the face he'd first seen only a week ago but now felt like he'd known all his life. Kincaid took him to the bar and ordered Grant's drink. A pint of Tetley's bitter, bottled, imported especially for the English copper who had somehow become accepted in the Irish neighborhood. He held his glass up for a silent cheers, and everyone else did the same. A salute to the fallen.

Kincaid had to shout over the noise. "You been offered a new job, then?"

"Got choices, it seems like."

"TV front man or get-down-and-dirty cop? That's no choice."

"You got that right. Somebody pick him up?"

"He's around here somewhere."

Grant nodded and took another drink. He was avoiding what he knew he'd have to do eventually, going to the casket to pay his last respects. He scanned the crowd. The bar was standing-room only. Mainly cops. Some women. Cops' wives and female officers. Some women who cops wouldn't want their wives to meet. This was a celebration. Always was in cop circles. Not the life that was lost but the life that had been lived.

The song changed, but the tone remained the same. Loud and friendly. Irish American.

Grant looked at the framed photos around the walls to distract himself. Senator Ted Kennedy. Bill Clinton when he was a presidential candidate. Former governor Michael Dukakis. The place went back to prohibition and beyond. Now it was the chosen place for seeing off a colleague, either by retirement, resignation, or death. Each celebration the same. Noisy and happy, with plenty of drink.

Grant pushed off from the bar and made his way slowly for the viewing. His eyes circled the room. There were some faces he recognized. Most had given him a hard time. All had accepted him now. But not the face he was looking for. The open casket loomed ahead of him. With each step, more of the silk lining became visible. A shoulder in full dress uniform.

He paused before moving closer.

The silk lining shone bright in the overhead lights.

The uniform looked clean and pressed, as Grant had expected.

The crowd continued to talk loudly.

The music continued to play.

There was laughter and the clinking of glasses.

Grant took a deep breath, then moved forward. The angle of his view into the coffin deepened. The shoulder grew broader. He was two paces from the edge when the crowd parted and a pair of khaki uniform trousers stepped forward. Grant looked up. John Cornejo smiled with difficulty, the bandages around his wounds making movement awkward. The tattoo he'd spent so much time hiding was no longer hidden, showing beneath the short sleeve of his T-shirt. There was no need to hide from his past anymore. The ex-marine had acquitted himself with honor. Because there was no such thing as an ex-marine. They shook hands and approached the casket together.

Tyson Miller was lying amid a drift of flowers.

Grant raised his glass, and the room fell silent apart from the music. No words were necessary. He simply nodded, took a deep swig of Tetley's, then put an arm around Cornejo's shoulder. A smattering of applause and more whistles. No jeers. If Grant had decisions to make, there'd be no pressure here.

For the second time in as many minutes, the crowd parted. A pair of shapelier legs stepped forward, and Grant looked up. Terri Avellone grinned at the Yorkshire policeman who was now regarded as a cop. Grant smiled back. He hated goodbyes but maybe this goodbye would be an exception, a fond and energetic farewell. Handing his pint to Cornejo, Grant put his arm around Terri and kissed her. This time the whistles were crude and there was more than a smattering of jeers.

Grant laughed, retrieved his beer, and turned away from the coffin. His eye caught a shapely blond smiling at him from across the room. The smile he threw back was mischievous, with a dark hint of promise. He was a man. What could he say? It was in his blood. His body focused on tonight. His mind began to speculate about the future. The music played on.

ACKNOWLEDGMENTS

As many authors will tell you, writing a book is not a solitary process. Getting the words on paper might be done alone, but after that there's a whole list of people who make it possible for that book to reach the shelves. *Jamaica Plain* is no exception. It has been a long road, and I owe thanks to many people for their assistance. Here are just a few of them: Rebecca Zins for doing such a sterling job editing the book and making me look good. Terri Bischoff for bringing me to Midnight Ink and remembering the strange Englishman she met in Los Angeles. And my agent, Donna Bagdasarian, for having faith in the man from Yorkshire despite all the setbacks and pitfalls, of which there have been many. Without any one of you, and more besides, this book would still be one of the great unread. Thank you.

ABOUT THE AUTHOR

Ex army, retired cop, and former scenes-of-crime officer, Colin Campbell is the author of British crime novels *Blue Knight, White Cross* and *Northern eX*. His Jim Grant thrillers bring a rogue Yorkshire cop to America, where culture clash and violence ensue. For more information, visit www.campbellfiction.com.

The following excerpt is from

MONTECITO HEIGHTS

The forthcoming book from Colin Campbell.
Available April 2014 from Midnight Ink.

THE SUN WAS HOT as Grant cut right off West Seventh up Alvarado. MacArthur Park was baked dry on his left, the grass practically scorched out of existence except for around the lake where residual moisture and spray from the fountains gave the grass at least a semblance of life. Most of the businesses he passed were Hispanic or Asian. The park was busy despite the time on a working day. Half past eleven. Maybe the locals took lunch early. The smell of hotdogs and onions mingled with candyfloss and diesel fumes.

Grant crossed Wilshire and continued up the hill. The bank was at the intersection with Alvarado and West Sixth, the next junction up. Traffic was light on the roads. The sidewalks were busy. Grant reckoned the pedestrian population increased in direct proportion to the wealth of the area. He hadn't seen a single walker on his way down through Beverly Hills.

The bright red decal of the Bank of America stood out on the single-story building across the intersection. Grant waited for the walking man sign to show, then crossed the road. The cash machines were to the left of the main doors, covered with a clear plastic shelter for privacy. There wasn't a queue. If there had been, things might have turned out different.

HE INSERTED HIS CARD and typed the password. It felt strange getting paid this way. When he'd been in the army, for the first couple of years anyway, soldiers had to attend pay parade once a week. The officer of the day sat at his desk at one end of the room while the squaddies stood in line at the other. Parade rest. At ease. A grizzled sergeant called the roll. Once your name was called, you had to stand to attention, shout "Yes, sir," and march to the desk. Halt. Salute.

Repeat your name and service number. The officer ticked you off the list and handed over your salary in a square brown envelope.

That soon changed when the Armed Forces moved to monthly payments, each soldier's wage being deposited in a bank account with Lloyds, the army's preferred bank. West Yorkshire Police used the same system but a bank of your own choice. You'd get a pay slip every month detailing the amount, your hourly rate, overtime worked, and total deductions. Tax, national insurance, pension, etc.

This new position was better paid but a lot more slapdash. He'd had a brief discussion about the salary and career prospects with the man who'd recruited him when he'd been released from Massachusetts General in Boston. Bottom line was Grant was still in law enforcement. His deployment and the nature of that law enforcement was more flexible than in Bradford. Grant reckoned it was the fact that he was off the books that made employing him desirable. He could be attached to various departments or police forces or asked to work alone, but if the shit hit the fan, then Uncle Sam could deny he worked for them. That and the fact that Grant didn't always work strictly between the lines seemed to be the attraction for the man with the dark suit and quiet voice. Grant had no problems putting bad guys away with scant regard for the rules of evidence.

He waited for the machine to verify his account and glanced over his shoulder at the passing traffic. Not many cars. A single-decker bus like the one out of *Speed* but without the bomb and the fifty-miles-an-hour minimum speed. A blue and yellow taxi, the ugliest color scheme Grant had ever seen. There was no sign of the big black car or the two heavies who'd been watching him yesterday. If they weren't following him today, he wondered why he felt the itch up the back of his neck—Grant's early warning system for trouble.

He looked around again, scrutinizing passing pedestrians, any cars that appeared to be going too slow, and tourists sitting in the park opposite. Nothing seemed out of place. He looked to his left along West Sixth, checking out the front of the Moxa Medical Group building and the mini market next door. Then he looked to his right across the intersection towards downtown. Glass and chrome towers fringed the skyline. There was constant movement but nothing that appeared threatening.

He rubbed his neck, but the itch wouldn't go away. It was one of the instincts that had helped him survive desert skirmishes and criminal confrontations. Something was wrong, but he couldn't put his finger on what it was. The ATM beeped impatiently. He selected Cash With Receipt from the display menu, then typed in the amount he wanted. The machine whirred as it counted $500.

He looked around again. Still nothing.

The machine pushed his card out of the slot and beeped again. He took it. Crisp new fifty-dollar bills came out of a different slot, followed by a printed receipt. He took them all and put them in his wallet but didn't step out from the ATM shelter. When he got this feeling, it was best not to move until he'd identified the source.

Two and a half minutes later, he did.

The bank alarm went off.

"Aw, shit." He looked at the door and waited.

THE ALARM WAS HARSH and annoying. That was the idea—make them hard to ignore. Grant didn't ignore it, but he didn't make any rash decisions either. He was unarmed and unprotected. No body armor. No gun. He hated guns but knew how to handle one. There were times when you had to embrace the thing you hated. Having a gun right now would have been helpful.

The ATM shelter was next to the front doors. Grant stayed inside it but shifted to the end nearest the door. Smoked glass made it difficult to see inside the bank, but he could just about make out violent movement. Two men. Fast and jerky. Not the smooth moves of veteran bank robbers. That was good and bad. Veterans were more ruthless. Amateurs were more difficult to predict. Grant didn't plan on giving them much choice.

The alarm was loud, but there had been no gunshots. Nothing bad about that. It suggested a modicum of self-control. Nobody wanted to go down for murder if they could help it. Armed robbery was practically an entry-level crime in LA nowadays. Killing people still took a lot of effort.

Grant judged speed and distance. The smoky figures through the glass door were coming this way but not fast. Not together either. They were separating. One holding back to cover the customers and staff, the other coming towards the door. Grant quickly scanned the curb. No getaway vehicle. Being right on the intersection, it would be hard to park for any length of time without drawing attention. A car would be coming, though. You could count on that. Even amateurs knew you needed a getaway car.

Traffic noises faded into the background.

Pedestrian chatter disappeared into silence.

The constant movement of the busy street slowed to a snail's pace.

Grant breathed easy, his heartbeat pulsing in his ears. Somewhere up above, the soft *thwup, thwup, thwup* of a distant helicopter droned across the sky. This was LA. He doubted if he'd seen the clear blue sky at any point without at least one chopper darting about like a dragonfly.

The smoked glass door began to open.

Six inches.

Grant stepped out from the shelter. Arms raised slightly but relaxed. Waist level. Hands open. Knees flexed ready to move quickly.

The door opened outwards.

Good. It formed a barrier between Grant and the gunman.

Twelve inches and moving.

Half open.

The sawn-off barrel of a pump-action shotgun poked through the gap as the smoky figure came forward. Grant kept his eyes on the dangerous end. The end that could kill you. As more of the barrel became visible, it seemed less rigid, not pointing at anything now but lowering as if the shooter felt safe now he was out of the bank.

Big mistake.

The door was wide open.

A car skidded to a stop at the curb.

The first armed robber came out of the bank. Medium height. Scruffy clothing. Dirty blond hair and three days' growth of beard. His hands were grubby, fingernails caked in black, and his teeth needed brushing. This wasn't a top of the range bank robber; this was a knobhead with a gun. Grant waited until he'd cleared the door. It began to close behind the gunman. Then Grant made his move.

He stepped forward and slapped the shotgun barrel down towards the ground with his right hand. His left came up swiftly under the trigger guard, grabbed the smooth black metal and jerked it upwards out of the guy's hands. He continued the sweeping movement until the shotgun did a complete circle, ending up the right way round in Grant's hands. His momentum carried him forward and he jabbed his left knee into the guy's leading leg behind the joint. The leg collapsed and the robber went down like a felled tree. Grant stamped on his balls.

One robber down. One to go.

The door opened again. All in one movement. The second gunman came out backwards. He held an ugly black handgun in one hand and a holdall leaking money in the other. He looked as dirty as the first robber, but at least he'd had a shave this morning. Grant heard a car door open behind him but couldn't worry about that now. First rule of engagement: face the most dangerous threat. The most dangerous threat here was the man with the semiautomatic.

The robber backed out of the door and it began to close. His shoulders braced and he puffed his chest out. He gave a short little fist pump with his gun hand and blurted a victorious expletive: "Fuckin' *yes*."

The door closed. The guy stood facing the bank as the reflections in the smoked glass stopped moving. What he saw was a big guy in an orange windcheater pointing a shotgun at the back of his head. Grant kept his voice hard.

"Fuckin' *no*."